James Alexander Kenneth Mackay

The Yellow Wave

A Romance of the Asiatic Invasion of Australia

James Alexander Kenneth Mackay

The Yellow Wave
A Romance of the Asiatic Invasion of Australia

ISBN/EAN: 9783337315757

Printed in Europe, USA, Canada, Australia, Japan

Cover: Foto ©Andreas Hilbeck / pixelio.de

More available books at **www.hansebooks.com**

THE CHARGE OF THE RINGERS.

Frontispiece.

THE YELLOW WAVE

A ROMANCE OF THE ASIATIC INVASION
OF AUSTRALIA

BY

KENNETH MACKAY

Member of the Legislative Assembly of New South Wales

AUTHOR OF

'OUT BACK,' 'STIRRUP JINGLES,' ETC.

LONDON
RICHARD BENTLEY AND SON
Publishers in Ordinary to Her Majesty the Queen
1895

NOTE

For my facts with regard to the Russian advance on India I have drawn on the writings of Mr. Charles Marvin and Professor Vambéry. To a pamphlet by the late Mr. George Ranken ('Capricornus') I am indebted for the scheme of Fort Mallarraway, and I have also received from him much generous help in all that appertains to our land system where touched on throughout the book. Mr. Ernest Favenc has kindly afforded me much valuable information as to the geographical features of the country traversed by the invaders. The illustrations employed to explain the subject of elective affinity were suggested to me by a work of Max Nordau's; and I have made use of an article by Mr. Hardacre, of Queensland, in describing the probable directions and effects on coast-trade of the proposed land-grant railways.

KENNETH MACKAY.

Wallendbeen,
April, 1895.

CONTENTS

BOOK I.

A CLOUD NO BIGGER THAN A MAN'S HAND.

BOOK II.

THE GATHERING OF THE STORM.

BOOK III.

THE LULL BEFORE THE HURRICANE.

BOOK IV.

THE WAVE BREAKS.

MAP OF

QUEENSLAND.

Zaroffi's Land Grant Railways
Other Land Grant Railways
Other Railways
Scale about 80 miles to 1 inch

TORRES STRAIT

Great

GULF OF

CARPENTARIA

THE YELLOW WAVE

BOOK 1.

A CLOUD NO BIGGER THAN A MAN'S HAND.

CHAPTER I.

PHILIP ORLOFF.

GIRDLED with flame, and leaving a phosphorescent gleam to mark her pathway, the S.S. *Genoa* moved swiftly on through the slumbrous Arabian Sea. Night had fallen, and the stars looked down on the silent waters—some fixed and cold, as though weary of their endless vigil over sin and shame, others twinkling and bright, as if for ever winking at man's impurities. From the argus-eyed Leviathan voices and laughter rose fitfully, as the music of Blumann's latest waltz died away. On her deck, hidden from the sea by a cunning drapery of bunting, the passengers were now filling in the interval before the next dance after the manner of comrades who have chanced on a good ship and congenial company.

1

He would have been a sour-souled stoic indeed who
could have stood apart with folded arms and pulseless heart unmoved by such a scene of *camaraderie*:
for to-night bright eyes caught from the soft glow of
the electric lamps a more alluring radiance, and
shapely forms borrowed new and quaint graces alike
from the dresses of long-dead queens and from peach-
cheeked peasant girls.   Though the majority wore
fancy costumes, here and there a plain dress-suit gave
its wearer a certain conspicuousness from its very
simplicity.

Among those thus rendered noticeable was a man
who stood speaking to an ideal Marguerite. As he
paused the girl looked up at him, half in interest,
half in wonder, and Philip Orloff's swarthy cheek
flushed, and, bending lower, he again spoke on in
a voice full of anxious questioning. As she listened, a
wave of painful unrest fled over the girl's face, but,
heeding it not, he still pleaded on, while, unnoticed,
a man garbed as Mephistopheles stood a little apart
watching them. Why he had chosen to personate so
malignant a spirit was certainly not explained by his
figure, nor did the somewhat receding chin and
features of almost woman-like delicacy present a
better *raison d'être*.   In the bright, restless gray eyes,
however, shone a flame, now tender and alluring, and
now, as he let them rest on Orloff, almost devilish in
its scornful malignity; but beyond an occasional
glance, he apparently paid little interest to the two,
devoting the most of his attention to the couples who
kept passing him in their promenade. As these moved
by, his glance fell with a certain triumph of power on

each woman's face, and in nearly every instance, sometimes certainly more tardily than in others, their eyes turned with a strange, fascinated look to meet his gaze. Disturbed in his strange occupation by the band, Mephistopheles turned his eyes towards Marguerite.

'This is our dance, I think,' said Orloff, as the girl rose.

'Yes,' she replied, laying her hand on his arm; then, with a little shiver, she withdrew it, saying, with painful hesitancy: 'I'm so sorry; you have made a mistake.'

Following her glance, Orloff saw Mephistopheles looking straight at her.

'Nonsense, Miss Cameron!' he retorted sharply, and pointing to his programme. 'I am quite right, I can assure you.'

Advancing, and keeping his eyes fixed on hers, Mephistopheles coolly remarked:

'This is our dance, Miss Cameron: am I not right?'

'Yes, Mr. Harden,' the girl answered, moving towards him, and totally ignoring her companion.

With a look of malicious triumph Harden led her away, leaving Orloff gazing after them in speechless and puzzled anger.

Unallured by the music, and totally regardless of the delightful companionship to be found on deck, Count Zenski sat alone in the smoking-room, a large and fragrant cigar between his lips.

'*Ma foi*,' he mused, as he watched a particularly large and perfect ring of smoke float gracefully upwards, 'what fortune to have half an hour with

no worse company than myself! It would go hard
with me to find better in this ship. How incompre-
hensibly dull these English are! If in trade, they
exude shops; if of the Church, what a wonderful
personage is their God, so merciless to the small
remnants who are foreign, so prone, at all things
English, to, as they have it, "wink the other eye."
Peste, they are *bourgeois* at heart, every one, utterly
ignorant of everything save their own particular shop.
And yet I do wrong them; they adore the horse,
and let the Jew *canaille* make fortunes out of their
worship.'

It must not be supposed that the Count ever gave
these opinions to the outer world. Being a Russian,
this would be unlikely; being in some sort a diplomatist, it was impossible. Who or what he had
originally been, he and the Czar alone knew. To the
English world he was a semi-military-looking man of
about fifty, and the managing director of a Russian
firm of contractors, with offices in London. According
to his own statement, he was travelling to Australia
with the twofold object of regaining his health and
seeking new outlets for his firm's capital; but with
all his delightful frankness, he omitted to add that
the prospect of securing from the Queensland Government the right to construct important land-grant
railway lines was the real motive for his voyage.

As a matter of fact, he was now on his way to
Brisbane, armed with full authority to undertake this
work if able to come to terms with the Government,
and posed as a devoted admirer of British liberty as
opposed to the slavery of his tyrant-ridden native land.

As he admired with a smoker's lazy interest the white and gradually-lengthening ash of his cigar, the door opened. With a weary shrug he looked round, then exclaimed cordially :

' Ah, *mon ami*, welcome ! What ! tired of *les beaux yeux* so soon ?'

For a moment Orloff hesitated ; then, seeing that the Count was alone, he walked in and took a seat at his table. Accepting a cigar, he sat moodily pulling at it. Meanwhile the Count observed him with a certain friendly interest.

Several things had helped to draw these two together ; for, apart from a common tie of blood, Zenski and Philip's father were old friends. A year ago, when dying, the elder Orloff had given certain last messages to Zenski, then in Sydney, to deliver to his son. This charge the Count had carried out on his return to England, and while doing so, and in after meetings, he formed as true a friendship for the young Australian as his cynical nature was capable of. Utterly bored by his fellow-passengers, who, with perhaps the exception of Harden, held out no possibilities above the commonplace, Zenski turned from their endless apotheosis of brawn, muscle, and horse-flesh to Orloff's fresh enthusiasm with positive relief. Gradually it struck the Russian that this man, with the form of a Hercules and the instincts of a leader, would be absolutely wasted among the Cabinet-moved dummies of Australian military life. On the other hand, the knowledge Orloff possessed of this very life might, under different conditions, be made the stepping-stone to a post which he could never

attain as a captain of the Queensland Mounted
Rifles. To that position Orloff was now returning,
having qualified himself during the last two years
in India and in England for a staff appointment in
Brisbane. Rather pleased at Orloff's silence, for the
Count looked on conversation during the best half of
a good cigar as barbarous, Zenski watched the firm,
dark face, noting with some satisfaction that the
heavy moustache pressed over the cigar as though the
teeth were set close.

'I am indebted to a woman for this companionship
and this silence,' he mused. 'Poor devil! women
have done much for Russia; who knows but that
this silly miss may save this man from himself and
for us, after all?' Dropping the butt of his cigar into
the tray, Zenski said quietly: 'What will *la belle*
Heather think of this desertion?'

'What she may think is no affair of mine,' his
companion replied shortly.

'Ah, you surprise me!'

'I fail to see why it should.' .

'My friend, you are not yourself. You grow
English. Believe me, no woman is worth losing
one's temper for,' murmured the Count.

'Zenski,' replied Orloff, rising and seating himself
beside the Russian, 'I needn't fence with you; you
know that I love this girl.'

'Then why, my friend, do you run away and leave
her?'

For a little while Orloff smoked on in silence. Then
he asked: 'Do you believe in hypnotism?'

'I think it possible; do you mean to practise it?'

' No ; but I begin to think it is being practised.'

' Doubtless ; but, my friend, what matter if it is ? One way of making a living is as honest as another.'

' You misunderstand me,' replied Orloff impatiently. ' Do you think a man by it might influence a woman against her will ?'

' Ah, the woman is in it, then ?' grinned the Count.

' Put your confounded cynicism on one side,' retorted Orloff, ' and answer me.'

' I might reply, "I'll see you d——d first;" but, thanks to my being foreign, and rendered affable by nicotine, I am at your service.'

' You remember that night when Harden tried his will-power on a lot of the passengers ?'

' Perfectly ; and, now that you recall it, his greatest success was scored with Miss Cameron. Am I not right ?' asked Zenski maliciously.

' Ever since then the fellow has seemed to exert a strange fascination over her,' Orloff replied bitterly.

' So this is your trouble,' laughed Zenski. ' She seems a willing subject, Philip.'

' I admit it,' replied Orloff, throwing away his cigar.

' Then, my friend, what is there left ? Call it hypnotism, if it will break your fall; fight on, if you think the game worth the candle ; but, for heaven's sake, don't spoil a good cigar for a woman's whim !'

' You don't understand,' replied the other ; ' I would save her for her own sake, not for mine.'

As he finished, Zenski looked at him in pitying astonishment.

' My poor boy, you are deplorably ignorant. When

a woman wants to go to the devil, never interfere unless you want to let her drag you after her.'   Then, seeing an angry gleam in Orloff's eyes, he added: ' But from what do you want to save her ?   After all, is it not a matter of choice; if she prefers Harden, why not ?'

Struck by the force of Zenski's question, Orloff made no reply, for though filled with doubts as to Harden, he yet had to admit that they might, after all, be the creations of his own jealousy. Still, Heather's manner, so unlike the frankness of a few weeks ago, so full of earnest and wistful tenderness when with him, and yet so wholly subservient to Harden, filled him with dark, intangible foreboding.

Before they had sailed he had asked her to be his wife, and though she had given no definite reply, her admission that she at least loved no one else, and her manner, until that night when Harden put her under the power of his eyes, had made him deem she loved him.   Devoted to his profession, Orloff had taken little heed of women before Heather came into his life ; but now she had absorbed all the love of his strong, self-contained nature, and to see her thus drifting away from him, not of her own will, but through the volition of another, stirred his soul into madness.   Still, he held her bound by no promise, and, as Zenski had put it, it might be, after all, a matter of choice, and if such were the case, what right had he to interfere, or, indeed, to impute any other than honourable motives to Harden?

For his part, Zenski, utterly sceptical on the subject of women, was content to suppose that Heather had tired of his friend, and this being so, he now decided to make capital out of her fickleness. Aware, however, that to continue the subject at once would be both wanting in tact and likely to further anger Orloff, he led him to speak of his profession. Anxious to escape from his own thoughts, and full of military enthusiasm, Orloff eagerly launched into the subject of arms. Knowing that his companion had made a study of Australian defences, and was keen enough to note their utter ineffectiveness, Zenski now began to point out how little honour was to be reaped in a field where active service was unlikely and where Parliamentary influence reigned supreme.

'My dear Philip,' said he, 'you will find yourself as surely bound as Napoleon to his rock. It is improbable that there will be any more goats to capture. And even if there should be, are you sure that you will get a chance? I doubt it. To give you a little illustration: When I was last in Australia, a colonel was asked to resign and again devote himself to making boots. As it happened, he had many votes in the electorate of a Cabinet Minister, so he called on him, and said, "You have taken away my living; you must find me another." "How?" "Dismiss the lieutenant who is adjutant of my battalion, and appoint me."'

'What! did he accept the adjutantcy of the regiment he had commanded?' exclaimed Orloff.

'*Pardieu*, yes! and the cream of the joke is that, when they appointed him, he was totally unfit to perform the duties.'

'But I have made my profession the study of my

life,' said Orloff; 'they could never displace me to
make room for one incompetent.'

'So had the man the colonel displaced, my friend,'
laughed Zenski. 'Now, if you had entered the service
of the Czar, how different !'

'What chances would I have had there?' retorted
Orloff; 'a stranger, the son of a merchant, how could
I have ever hoped to break my way through the aristo-
cratic ranks that encircle the Czar ?'

'Softly, my friend. You speak our language, you
are of our blood, and, if you are the son of a dealer,
you are the friend of Zenski, also a dealer, if you will,
but, for all that, possessed of a voice that reaches as
far as most men's. Then you have learned much
that a servant of the Czar should know in these days.
No need for such as you to dangle on the outskirts of
a palace undermined by plots. Asia lies as a rich and
boundless field for the feet of the servants of the Czar,
who have strength to tread them, courage to win them,
and no weakling scruples as to how they hold them.'

As the Count spoke in quick, low tones, one or two
men entered ; others, their smokes over, walked out,
while, mingling with his words, the music came
floating from above.

As one in a dream, Orloff listened. Then, as the
Count stopped, he roused himself, saying with a
certain air of surprise :

'I didn't know you had any influence at St. Petersburg.'

'Two years ago I had just enough to escape
Siberia,' replied the Russian coolly. 'To-day, as you
suppose, I have, personally, none.'

'Then, what did you mean just now?' asked Orloff impatiently.

'Just what I said,' retorted the Count coldly. 'For me the life is impracticable; with you it is different. You are young, strong, and a soldier; I, as your friend, but point out to you a career where you will find unlimited scope for your ambition. Further, I offer to interest myself in your behalf. For, though I am powerless with the Czar, I still have friends who, to oblige the man who acted as a scapegoat for their sins, would be glad to help on his protégé.'

'It is a splendid future for a Russian, Zenski,' said Orloff almost regretfully, 'but I am an Australian.'

Satisfied that he had interested him, and well aware that his one hope of eventual success lay in Heather Cameron's utter perfidy, the Count left his bread to the waters of chance.

'Pardon,' he replied; 'for the moment I forgot that little fact, my dear Philip.'

CHAPTER II.

IN THE TOILS.

On the night after the ball, Heather Cameron sat in a deck-chair looking out on the starlit water. Scattered about the deck or lounging against the railings, groups of passengers discussed the dance with animation born of narrow surroundings and poverty of incident; but the girl took no part nor any seeming interest in their chatter.

Flanked on either side by the wife and daughter of an Australian potentate who had made a fortune and bought a title by aid of his celebrated £5 cases, Count Zenski sat listening with polite resignation to the Knight himself.

Thus surrounded, the unhappy Russian was hearing for about the hundredth time how the Baggs family had been presented at Court, and on what singularly familiar terms the male Bagg chanced to be with a bewildering company of Dukes and such-like.

Just when Zenski had decided to escape, even, if need be, over the body of his tormentor, aid arrived in the persons of Orloff and Heather's father.

'They are waiting for us, Count,' said Cameron, stopping in front of the group.

'Ah, our rubber!' exclaimed the Russian. 'Sir John and ladies, this is most annoying, but these whist-players are inexorable. Can I say more than that the loss is mine?'

Bowing, he walked away with Cameron, while Orloff moved on and dropped into a seat from which unnoticed he could observe Heather.

Where she sat, a lamp cast a soft radiance on the coils of yellow hair that rested upon her shapely head like a woven coronal. Her hazel eyes, looking out from the dead whiteness of her face, scintillated with the brilliance of cunningly-set stones; but her hands lay listless and inert on the long arms of her chair. Not yet eighteen, she had spent the last five years of her life at school in England, and was now returning with her father to keep house on the station where she was born, and to which she was the only heir. During the five months she had spent in London before returning to the Bush, Philip Orloff, also engaged in a short holiday, had met her. To both love was then an unknown quantity, but while in her case it still in some sort remained one, with the strong man of twenty-six it was not so. His heart, till then asleep, woke in the presence of this tall, sun-crowned child, and out of her hazel eyes read a message writ by God, all unknown to herself. And so he loved her, not for her character, for it had yet to grow; not for her graces, for they had yet to bloom; not because she loved him, for as yet love was to her a sealed book, of whose contents she had but faint imaginations; and not, again, for any of those cunning fantasies with which men strive to render love logical, but simply because she was his kindred soul, set apart for all time as his alone. Gradually in the weeks that followed his hand broke the seal of the book she carried fearfully, and page by page, little by little, he read to her its message. And as he read she caught it, at first dimly as a flute played on distant hills, then sonorous as the notes of a time-mellowed organ, Love's grand, immortal anthem. So her soul awoke, but, as befitted a child, full of wonder and mantled with a tender fear.

On shipboard, cut off from the multifarious distractions of the great city, Heather turned more and more towards Orloff, the strong, but as yet latent, forces within her instinctively attracted by the man's potent individuality.

Nothing had interfered to check the growth of an admiration which promised later to develop into a passion worthy of his own, until the night spoken of by Orloff to Zenski.

From the first Harden had certainly paid her considerable attention, but as in this regard he appeared thoroughly cosmopolitan, Orloff, too generous to harbour the petty jealousy of a weaker man, felt no uneasiness.

On a particular evening earlier in the voyage the conversation had turned on will-power, and after several had attempted with more or less success to perform the stock-feats common to such gatherings, Harden took the subjects in hand. In his case success attended nearly every effort, Heather

Cameron in particular appearing, at least to Orloff, a singularly pliant hypnotic. Accounting for his success by the fact that he had the good fortune to practise on minds rendered peculiarly susceptible by the former experiments, Harden laughingly admitted his inability to perform any save the most elementary tests of the science. None the less, Orloff felt that the man believed more in his power than he wished others to do. Since then, though Harden had given no further exhibitions of his art, Orloff began to regard him with an aversion almost amounting to fear; for while unable to in any way prove it, he felt that the man was gradually exerting a strange, unaccountable influence over the woman he loved.

Harden, whatever he might have thought, affected not to notice the change.

To Orloff, Heather's manner grew daily more incomprehensible. Gradually the strong vitality of youth began to give place to slow and lingering movements. Her eyes, once filled with a questioning light of the newly-awakened, now wore the puzzled, fearful expression of a being haunted by an unseen yet ever-present mystery. To him she in one sense seemed to cling more than ever, and yet between their lives he was conscious of the rise of an impalpable while impassable barrier.

Not that all this happened at once. In point of fact, its growth was so gradual, that he had never properly realized it until the night of the ball. Now, sitting watching Heather, he felt that he had not guarded as he should this soul given into his hands to guide and cherish; that while he stood by with idle hands, its splendid possibilities were perhaps being rendered inoperative for all time.

He half rose, but again sank back. After all, what grounds had he for such a surmise? Then, as the memory of Harden's exhibition of power over her at the ball rose before him, he threw all doubts aside, and walked over to where the girl sat gazing out upon the sea.

'A penny for your thoughts, Heather,' he said.

As the girl turned towards him, he was conscious that her eyes filled with a look of relief. Getting no reply, he went on :

'Where have you been hidden all day?'

'I have been lying down,' she answered wearily.

'Why, you look half asleep now!'

'Do I? I seem always tired here. I wish we were in Sydney.'

Then, appearing to rouse herself with an effort, she said :

'I hope you enjoyed yourself last night?'

Astonished by the coolness of the remark, in face of her treatment of him, Orloff stared at her in silence. Had she been an ordinary acquaintance, such a calm shelving of the question would have been irritating enough ; to be so ignored by Heather was simply inexplicable.

'Why do you stare at me like that?' she asked peevishly, as he made no reply.

'Considering what happened, I wonder you ask.'

'What do you mean?'

'Heather, this is unworthy of you. Treat me as a dog if you will, but not like a fool!'

Glancing at him in utter astonishment, the girl faltered :

'Don't look like that, Philip. How was I to know my question would annoy you?' Then, as he looked moodily into her eyes, she added, with childish anger : 'I won't be treated like a schoolgirl. Go away; I did not ask you to come.'

Nonplussed by a manner so utterly unlike her own, and shocked at the littleness displayed by her affectation of ignorance, Orloff determined to end the matter one way or the other.

'Why did you give Harden my dance,' he asked, 'and leave me standing like a fool, without even a word of explanation?'

Watching her keenly as he spoke, he noticed with a certain feeling of dread a look of utter wonder in her eyes.

'Whatever are you talking about?' she asked.

'Do you mean to tell me you don't remember?'

'How can you expect me to remember what never happened?' she answered in a puzzled voice.

'Heather, for God's sake, think!' exclaimed Orloff, bending towards her. 'You were sitting in that chair. I was standing beside you. As the music began you rose, and put your hand on my arm—so. Then you withdrew it. Harden stepped up and claimed you; and then, although my name was on your programme, as I explained, you walked away with that man, and left me without a word, without a look!'

As he spoke, the girl listened with parted lips. Once or twice some faint glimmer of remembrance seemed to shoot across her brain. Then only surprise remained.

2

'You are dreaming,' she said absently. 'Do you think I would treat you like that for Mr. Harden, or any other man?'

Like a flash it struck him she was either mad or under some potent spell.

'Heather,' he asked with deep intensity, 'what power has this man Harden gained over you? For my sake, for your own, tell me.'

At the mention of the name, she again appeared struck by some faint remembrance, but it passed as before.

'Why do you ask me such a stupid question? Surely you are not jealous?' she exclaimed.

Comforted by the strain of reproach in her voice, but still unable to account for her strange loss of memory as to what had happened the night before, he asked:

'Has this man ever put you under the same influence he used that night when he hypnotized you in the saloon? Think well, child, for God's sake!'

Again the puzzled look came into her eyes, but at last she replied:

'No, Philip.'

'Promise me that you will never allow him,' he pleaded, taking the white, listless fingers in his.

'Of course I won't, Philip, if you don't wish it,' she answered softly.

Then, carried away by a passionate desire to guard her as only a husband could, he poured anew into her ears the story of his deep, strong devotion.

Powerless to resist an appeal backed up by the wakening desires of her own heart, the girl listened to his pleading. At last, in rugged, manly fashion, he asked her to marry him when they reached Colombo. But even as her lips moved to reply, she lifted her eyes, and the word died away in a low, inarticulate murmur.

' Darling, your answer !' murmured Orloff passionately. ' You love me; why hesitate ?'

Still no reply came through her white lips.

' For God's sake, don't say I've deceived myself! Heather, you love me ?'

Rising, she shook her head, and, waving him aside, moved quickly past him. As he turned to follow, he saw they were not alone. Facing him stood Henry Harden, with Heather at his side.

With clenched fist Orloff stepped towards them.

' You love me, Heather ?' said Harden.

' I love you,' she answered, in a strange, expressionless voice.

' Heather, this is madness !' began Orloff, stretching out his hand towards the girl.

' Kindly remember we are not the only people on deck,' remarked Harden with a mocking smile.

CHAPTER III.

A GLANCE THAT MARRED A LIFE.

DURING Orloff's conversation with Heather, the other occupants of the deck had gradually disappeared, driven to the shelter of the music-room and saloon by the mist which now drifted like a shroud over the sea. As Harden spoke, Zenski and Cameron came towards the group.

'I've been looking everywhere for you, Heather,' said her father irritably. 'Orloff, you should know better than to keep her up on such a night.'

'I fear I am partly to blame,' interposed Harden, picking up her cloak and throwing it over her shoulders. 'However, if Miss Cameron will help me, I will sing you "Scots wha hae" as a peace-offering, sir.'

'All right,' laughed the easy-going squatter; 'I don't suppose any harm's done, so come on, Philip.'

Declining the invitation, Orloff stood watching them till they disappeared.

'*Mon ami*, you look irritated—try a cigar.'

'Thanks,' replied Philip shortly. 'Why don't you go with them ?'

'Ah, you are both ungrateful and brutal !' exclaimed Zenski.

'Pardon me, I thought you came with Cameron.'

'And if I did, is that any reason why I should go with him to listen to the barbarous war-song of the Scotch ?'

Just then a gust of wind swept the mist in a fine shower in their faces.

'Come into the smoking-room,' gasped the Count. 'To smoke in such an atmosphere is a sacrilege.'

'You are right. Don't wait for me, Count.'

'Not so, my friend; if you will stop, so will I,' retorted Zenski, fearful into whose hands he might fall if without Philip. 'But in heaven's name let me get out of this wind.' He moved off.

Following him, Orloff threw himself into a seat.

'You are bad company to-night, Philip,' murmured the Russian, as the other smoked on in silence. 'Is it an affair of the liver or the heart ? If of the former, hesitate not to make me your confidant.'

'I am all right, thank you.'

'Then why, my poor friend, do you look all wrong ? You English are so topsy-turvy.'

'I am not English,' retorted Orloff savagely. 'Curse them !'

'And why ?. Because one from "perfide Albion" has, as my oppressive comrade Baggs would say, "put your nose out of joint " ?' grinned the Count.

'Don't play the fool, Zenski !' said Orloff; 'what right have you to pry into my affairs ?'

'Pardon,' retorted the Russian coolly; 'you forget that you have already made me in some sort your confidant.'

'You are right,' replied Orloff bitterly; 'and the doubts I then spoke to you of have become certainties. To-night I have seen this man exert his cursed power.'

For a little the older man remained silent, then said:

'If I may ask, in what manner?'

'Zenski,' exclaimed Philip, moved by that impulse to speak of his trouble which comes at some time or other to all men, 'for all your cynicism, I believe you are my friend. To-night I asked this woman to marry me.'

'*Mon Dieu!*' murmured his listener.

'By the light in her eyes, by the tender inflection of her voice, I knew she was mine; then, as her lips moved, they became cold, and without a word she left me. Turning to follow, I saw her standing beside Harden. "You love me," the devil said; and she replied in a voice expressionless as that of one repeating a lesson, "I love you." I swear she was no free agent, yet what can I do? She has no remembrance of the spells this man casts over her.'

'That is a defect common under certain conditions to all her charming sex, as you will discover later, my friend,' interposed Zenski sententiously.

Unheeding the interruption, Orloff went on:

'Distrusting Harden as I do, I feel that her father should be warned; and yet the subject, situated as I am, is so delicate that I fear he may misunderstand.'

'He would most certainly misunderstand. A man who trumps his partner's tricks four times in one night, and then excuses his perfidy by saying he is thinking about the rise in wool, is too wanting in every sense of right to grasp your most interesting theory.'

'Theory! Man, it is a terrible reality!'

'Even so, what then? Your rival says to the woman you have just asked to be your wife, "You love me?" "I love you," she makes answer. You say it is a spell. What more is all love? My friend, I myself was once so diseased. One day she mistook another man for me, and married him. *Mon Dieu*, I am glad of it!'

'Zenski, I can't let this girl go out of my life with your cold, damnable philosophy. Her love has grown into my being until it has become part of me.'

'The science of surgery lays down that all growths foreign to the body must be removed before the patient regains perfect health,' retorted Zenski slowly. 'Philip, what folly is all this, and for a girl un-formed, a child as likely to become commonplace as not; why render yourself absurd, striving after the improbable? Believe one who has known many women, seen the sordidness of their passions, the vastness of their betrayals; they are not worth it.'

'You speak of the outcasts of humanity, the wretched spies whose existence Russian tyranny has rendered possible,' retorted Orloff hotly. 'Surely to God you don't compare this pure, fresh girl with such as they?'

'I speak about what I know,' replied Zenski calmly.
'As toys, they are admirable; as stepping-stones,
often swift, but generally treacherous; taken *au
sérieux*, they are impracticable. Good-night, Philip.
Remember, the successful soldier saves all his worship
for the shrine of ambition.'

Left to himself, Philip Orloff sat looking out into
the dark, wind-swept space that stretched beyond the
narrow rays of the electric lamps.

Much as he hated Zenski's cold-blooded summing-
up, he still had to admit that in one respect the
cynical Russian had put his finger on his own position. Love with him was serious and impracticable.
More convinced than ever of Harden's power, he yet
failed to see how he could provide an antidote. To
denounce the man could only end in ridicule, if
nothing worse, while to warn Heather appeared even
more hopeless, looked at in the light of her inability
to remember what occurred during her hypnotic sleep.
Maddened by the consciousness of his utter helpless-
ness, he experienced the sensation of a man who,
bound and gagged, watches the approach of the
engine that must inevitably crush him. In his case,
however, the agony was even more intense, for he had
to stand idly by and gaze, not only on the ruin of his
own life, but on the possible wreck of Heather's as
well. For, judged by his standard of honour, the
man who would stoop to win a woman by the practice
of a power such as that possessed by Harden, was of
all men the most unlikely to satisfy when once the
awakening took place.

Weary at length with its futile endeavour to work

out a plan of escape, Orloff's brain sought a temporary respite.

Freed from its unnatural tension, it naturally turned to the central idea of his life before Heather came into it. So, tramping up and down the wet, deserted decks, Zenski's picture of a soldier's chances rose before him.

Born in a land possessing little real individuality, and, indeed, in most things slavishly imitative of England, Orloff, like most of his fellow-countrymen, possessed little of that intense, if selfish, love of country common to peoples who have created an independent force in the world.

That, if need be, he would fight to defend his birth-place was true. But he had yet to learn that it was the only place worth fighting for, or for which a man can kill his fellow-men without becoming a murderer.

For the present, his chief ambition was to excel as a soldier, and the more he thought it out, the less did this appear practicable in Australia.

Zenski was right: active service alone meant his opportunity.

Possessed of about as much loyalty as his comrades who had rushed to the Soudan ostensibly to aid the mother-country, but in reality because they wanted to smell powder, Orloff felt few scruples as to which flag he followed. And now that his hopes of love seemed drifting to certain wreck, a strong repugnance for the comparative inactivity of Brisbane barrack life took hold of him.

Love gone, what use had he for idleness, save to mourn its loss? And could he sit down like a puling child to weep after this perished thing? The thought was madness. That he would never wholly forget he realized even now, but in the arms of ambition he might gain temporary oblivion, and if not, on the field of battle a soldier's death.

Carried away by his thoughts, he had taken no heed of time; but now, pulling out his watch, he noticed that all the deck-lights were turned off. Seeing a reflection on the skylight of one of the inner cabins, he walked towards it, and, stooping, he held the dial of his watch close to the glass. Then, remembering it was Harden's cabin, his eyes, impelled by a sudden fascination, looked down into the brilliantly-lighted cabin.

Suddenly brought in contact with the light, Orloff at first looked only on two ghostly forms, shadowy and indistinct. Then, as the mantle of darkness fell from before his vision, he saw a figure wrapped in white draperies move swiftly across the narrow room. With no wantonness of passion, but rather as one who treads the vales of sleep, the woman walked on to where, imperious yet eager, Harden stood; and now, no longer blinded by the electric rays, Orloff saw that it was Heather.

For a moment he stared as though turned into stone, then his teeth crunched through the amber, and his pipe fell with a crash on the glass. White and trembling, he staggered into the darkness.

CHAPTER IV.

ORLOFF BREAKS THE SPELL FOR EVER.

PHILIP ORLOFF sat in his cabin, waiting.

His black, disordered hair looked strangely dull this morning, and the lines about his mouth and under his heavy eyes were deep as those of an old man, for the devil we all have locked up in us had been struggling to get loose through the long night hours. Orloff had forced him back, but the effort had wearied him. With a strong man's egotism he thought he had conquered, but the devil did not: he only laughed to himself and waited.

After that glance when hope rolled like a parched-up scroll from before his eyes, his first impulse had been one of instant revenge. But on his road to consummate it, reason regained its sway, and he turned into his own cabin. In the dread vigil that followed he had reviewed the whole situation. Strong in his belief in Heather, he recognised that the guiltless must not suffer in order that he might punish the guilty, and, facing with merciless self-abnegation every possibility, he finally decided to give Harden one chance, and if he declined it, to force him into a duel, which could only have one ending. That he might be the one to fall, he recognised; yet, richly as the man deserved it, he could not bring himself to kill him in cold blood.

Morning came at last, and he rang and ordered his cabin-steward to tell Harden he wished to see him, and tired of all things, angry with God and hating man, he sat and waited. At last he pulled out his watch, only to put it back impatiently. The man he had sent for seldom breakfasted before ten, and it was now only a few minutes past nine.

Listlessly picking up a book that lay near his hand, he began turning over the leaves. What was written on them had no interest for him, he did not even take the trouble to read the words. Still, when he came to an uncut page, habit prompted him to rise and take from the shelf an antique dagger with a blade about six inches long, which he always used as a paper-knife. He had bought it at a curiosity shop in Naples, partly through the importunity of its Jewish vendor, but principally because a powerful magnet let into the hilt caught his fancy. He slipped the blade through the paper, and laid the stiletto down beside him as Harden walked in.

'What the deuce is up, old chap—off colour, eh?' inquired the visitor with rather forced gaiety. 'Some lark on?'

'No. I merely wished to ask you a question,' replied Orloff in a hard, dry voice.

'Devilish small provocation for dragging a fellow down here,' laughed Harden, dropping into a chair. 'Well, fire away—what is it?'

For a little Orloff looked at him, then said slowly :

'Do you intend to marry Miss Cameron ?'

At the words a startled look came into the man's shifting, restless eyes. Then, apparently satisfied, he replied :

'What business is it of yours, whether I do or not?'

'I have decided to make it my business, so answer me !'

At first an angry retort trembled on Harden's lips ; then, thinking better of it, he replied :

'Don't be absurd, Orloff! If the girl prefers me, surely that is her affair ; you heard what she said last night.'

'You forced her to say it,' retorted Philip quietly.

'My dear fellow, what humbug !' laughed Harden, encouraged by the other's calm. 'Women are "kittle cattle"; she happens to prefer me to you—devilish bad taste on her part, I admit, but, still, as I said before, that is her affair.'

'Admitting what you say to be true, you haven't answered my question. Do you mean to make her your wife ?'

'' 'Pon my word, I haven't thought about it.'

'Haven't thought of it ?' interposed Orloff savagely.

'No ; you see a fellow must do something to amuse himself on board ship, and she's a devilish nice little girl and all that. Still, you know, marriage is altogether a different affair. But, d—— it all, Orloff, this has gone far enough.'

'It has gone too far for you to draw back like this, you shuffling cur !' retorted Philip sternly. 'How dared you, in my presence, force the girl to say she loved you, unless you meant to marry her ?'

'Don't try me too far,' replied Harden, his eyes flashing with passion ; then, alarmed by the other's look, he added, 'I knew you were jealous of the girl, and I only did it for a joke.'

'Liar !' retorted Orloff ; 'you admit your power.'

Stung by the epithet, Harden sprang to his feet.

'You jealous fool !' he exclaimed ; 'believe what you like, but don't think I mean to stop here to be bullied by you !'

'Stop where you are,' growled Orloff, forcing him back in his seat, 'and listen to me ! Are you prepared to marry Heather Cameron when we reach Colombo ? By God, I will have an answer before you leave this chair !'

Silently the two men glared into each other's eyes. Helpless as a child, Harden suddenly thought of a way of escape.

'What if I say no ?' he asked, anxious to gain time.

'You must fight me when we reach land,' retorted Orloff grimly. 'And, remember, I will make no mistake if you do.'

As he spoke, Harden saw that he had him in his power. Struggling against the other's will, Orloff rose erect with an effort.

Still holding him with his eyes, Harden stood before him.

'Curse you ! I'll do neither !' he hissed, with malignant triumph ; 'I mean to amuse myself with her till she bores me. Then you can have her, and welcome.'

For an instant Philip seemed to regain command

of himself, but, pointing to the couch, Harden commanded him to sit down.

Powerless and inert, Orloff sank back. As he did so, his hand fell on the dagger-hilt that stuck out from between the leaves of the book.

Instinctively clutching it, a magnetic thrill passed through his body, and, springing to his feet, he drove it with the strength of madness into the heart of the hypnotist.

With a weird, inarticulate cry, Harden sank back in his seat.

Staring at the helpless mass that sat huddled in the chair before him, Orloff took no notice of the opening of his door. Stepping noiselessly in, Zenski lifted the head that lolled forward.

'Ah, Monsieur Harden!' he exclaimed. 'Poor devil! what wonderful creatures are the women!'

'He tried his cursed tricks on me, and I stabbed him,' said Orloff coldly; and throwing aside the dagger with a gesture of repulsion, he asked: 'Is he dead?'

'As mutton, to use the simile of my excellent friend Cameron,' retorted Zenski, locking the door.

'What are you doing that for?' asked Orloff. 'The doctor must be sent for at once.'

'It is a useless exertion.'

'Still, they must take this thing away,' insisted Philip.

'All in good time. But first I would have a little chat with you. May I smoke?'

'Heavens, man, how can you talk of chatting here?'

'Why not?—our friend will, I am sure, be discretion

itself. But to be serious, Philip; we may not have another chance. Why you have killed this man I don't know. Doubtless your reasons were excellent. But, unfortunately, the pig-headed authorities will fail to recognise them. I hate to be brutal to a man I respect; but, to be brusque, they will hang you.'

At the words the young man's cheek paled, but he replied firmly: 'I am prepared to accept the consequences of my act.'

'What, for a gaillard like that!' retorted Zenski. 'But time is short—I would save you from yourself. I was your father's friend: you are mine. But more than this, you are too useful to dangle from the end of a rope.'

'It is a degrading death,' said Orloff bitterly; 'but it must be faced.'

'Not so,' replied the Russian, bending forward and putting a proposition before the other in his own language. 'Agree to this, and I pledge my honour you shall escape. A Russian warship is in the bay; money will buy your way out of a stouter prison than this; and once free, a servant of the Czar has little to fear in the East. Quick! your answer? A diplomatist may hesitate, not so a soldier.'

'I will do it,' said Orloff coldly. 'I can't bring myself to die for ridding the world of such a miscreant.'

Picking up a pack of cards, Zenski scattered them over the floor. Then, ringing the bell, he said to the steward: 'Present Count Zenski's compliments, and tell the captain he is wanted immediately.'

Sitting on the couch, Philip remained silent. Presently footsteps again approached, and bowing to the officer who now stood in the doorway, Zenski said : ' At my friend Mr. Orloff's request, I have to inform you that he has had the ill-fortune to stab Mr. Harden during a dispute over a game of écarté.'

* * * * *

Late that night the mail-steamer entered the harbour of Colombo with Philip Orloff a prisoner in his own cabin.

When, however, on the following morning the officer of the watch made his rounds, he found the sentinel missing from his post and the cabin empty. Both had disappeared, leaving no trace.

Next morning the *Genoa* sailed for Australia, leaving Harden in the palm-shaded cemetery, powerless and unavenged, for his destroyer had vanished.

' Where do you think the ruffian has gone, Count ?' remarked Sir John Baggs as the island sank into the sea.

' To the devil, *mon ami*,' retorted Zenski with a weary shrug as he lit a fresh cigar.

BOOK II.

THE GATHERING OF THE STORM.

———•◦•———

CHAPTER I.

DICK HATTEN.

On a June morning of the year 1954, while the streets of Sydney are full of rain and umbrellas, in hotel bars, or crouching against the veranda-sheltered walls of sporting hotels, cunning-eyed, hard-faced men discussed the all-important question of whether the Grand National would be run or not.

Cowering under one of the arches of the Lyceum, a wretched, pallid-faced woman droned in a weary, ceaseless monotone the virtues of a bundle of laces that hung limp and unalluring on her outstretched arm. A gust of wind hurrying down the narrow street eddied and drove the thin, draggled print dress against her shivering limbs with wanton devilry ; but the men, heedless of the woman's tuneless plaint, hastened to swell the crowd that stood about the costly temple of the Goddess of Chance. Was she too respectable or too objectionable for the pity of humanity? Possibly both: civilization can forgive anything except a poverty that offends the eye.

Dodging among the nondescript mass who now blocked the pavement in front of Tattersall's, a wizened, barefooted gutter-snipe drove a brisk trade in race cards: his wares were more up-to-date. So was their cigarette-smoking, foul-mouthed vendor. Mankind is still full of a certain careless generosity for the quick-tongued, evil-hearted imps of their own creation. Later on, when they are old enough to be dangerous, they generally hang them.

In 'the Rooms' opinion was divided. Some held that the 'going would be right enough.' These last were, as a rule, men who had laid against the 'pots,' and who, not having to risk their necks over the fences, exhibited strong indignation at the proposed delay. At last the bell rang, and after a few seconds at the telephone, the secretary announced that the meeting had been postponed. Quickly the news spread to the street, and gradually the waiting assemblage of 'sports' melted away into bars and billiard-rooms.

Apparently satisfied with its morning's work, the rain had ceased. Following the stream, three men drifted out of the rooms and into the vestibule. Having lit cigars, they stood talking to a member of the ring, who chanced to be making his way upstairs.

'Can I book you another monkey, Mr. Hatten?' queried the layer of odds. 'They tell me your mare can't miss it—bar accidents.'

'That's just the devil of it,' replied Dick Hatten

anxiously; 'if this rain keeps on it's anybody's
race.'

'Nonsense! why, it's just into your hands; she's
fit, and likes mud as well as the best of them.'

'That's right enough,' answered Dick doubtfully;
'but how long are they going to ask me to keep her
fit?'

'About three weeks, I guess, from the look of it,'
grinned a wiry-looking, sun-tanned man standing
beside Hatten.

'Now, Mr. Johnson, don't you be spoiling business,'
laughed the bookmaker.

'Better take the monkey, sir; she's bound to
harden.'

'No thanks, Cohen; if I want any more I'll see you
in the paddock.'

'Very good, sir; recollect, it'll be level money, and
not too much at that.'

'If you have ended, let us go,' observed a short,
well-set-up man, whose white moustache and buttoned
frock-coat gave him a certain military air.

'Right you are, Count,' said Hatten. 'Come on,
Ted!'

As they stepped into the street, the woman with the
laces, like themselves, set free by the stoppage of the
rain, held out her sorry barter for life with wistful,
shrinking importunity.

Pulling a coin from his pocket, Hatten put it in her
hand, muttering apologetically as they walked away:
'Poor devil! she looked infernally cold.'

'*Mon Dieu!* you are a funny race,' grinned Zenski.
'You waste a fortune on messieurs the "books," and

then you apologize for giving a starving woman one shilling.'

'I suppose you have got your bit on Io, Count?' said Johnson, as they entered the Australia.

'With all due apologies to my friend here, I have my "bit" on that which with delightful naïveté you name the selling race.'

'Why, they are dead swindles,' exclaimed Johnson. 'You never get more than one trier for your money in one of those saddle-flaps.'

'In that lies the beauty of these races. I find out which is the animal on which the saddle does not flap. Then I smoke my cigar in peace. I prefer the horse which cannot lose to the grand animal which should have won. But I must write, so *au revoir*. We meet at lunch.'

Turning into the smoking-room, Hatten and Johnson began for about the hundredth time to win the Grand National. With both it was a subject of absorbing interest, for one of them it was a matter of vital importance; for while Johnson felt, as a sportsman and a Queenslander, the keenest sympathy with the only Northern representative in the race, his companion, apart from his wish to win, had risked all he had in the world on the result of the steeplechase.

Known from Port Darwin to Brisbane, Hatten had come to be regarded as the Admirable Crichton of the North. Creations of his skill with pencil and charcoal looked down from the walls of countless smoking-rooms; his verses were sung round camp fires from Port Darwin to Cobar; and tales of his feats, both over fences and on the backs of buck-

jumpers, were as household words in the Great Lone
Land of Australia. That he would some day do great
things was for ever prophesied. His dark, sun-bronzed
face, with its deep-set, penetrating gray eyes, somewhat aquiline nose, and resolute chin, betokened latent
force. His useful height and natural hardness of
condition, brought to absolute perfection by constant
saddle work, gave hostages for the success of any feat
he set his heart on accomplishing. In all things the
fates seemed propitious, but still the hard fact remained that Dick never seemed to get on. He had
done most things, and had done them well, but,
success achieved, he seemed to tire, and just when
duller men began, with tender care, to move along the
ball, at last come to their feet, Dick kicked it to the
devil and started after another.

About a year ago a new force had come into his life.
Isis Downs had long been a camping-ground of his,
its owner, Angus Cameron, and Ted Johnson, his
manager, both being old friends. By that part of
the world who held that Dick was a stanch believer
in the statement that it was criminal for a man to be
half an hour in the presence of a woman without
making love to her, Edith Enson, the daughter of
Cameron's housekeeper, was quoted as the real load-
stone which drew him to the Downs.

In this it was wrong. That Dick had played at the
game of flirtation with the girl was probable enough.
He was usually playful. But in his case it was
certainly not for 'keeps.'

When, however, Heather Cameron came back to the
station, Dick met his Waterloo. At first he was rather

bored with this tall, self-possessed girl with hair like
the reflection of a setting sun on a leaden cloud, and
hazel eyes full of searching light. She had such an
irritating way of saying nothing. In her presence
he began to realize that he was an utter fraud, and,
what was worse, he more than suspected that she
had arrived at the same conclusion. Acting on this
supposition, Dick, with a successful man's vanity, en-
deavoured to set himself right with her. In striving
to accomplish this he succeeded in interesting her,
and, fired by her attitude of masterly though unconscious inactivity, fell deeply in love himself.
Under the influence of the first real passion of his
life, Hatten, accustomed to succeed when he wanted
to, now began once more to look after the ill-used
ball he had so often had at his foot only to kick into
the limbo of human failures. Nominally he was a
squatter, but as the possession of a small cattle-run
on the Roper River, already mortgaged to a Sydney
Pastoral Financial Company up to what they considered its full value, presented few if any possibilities,
Dick cast round for something more tangible. Here,
once more, Fate seemed to hold out a straw; and,
with characteristic belief in his lucky star, he determined to grasp it. At a sale of yearlings in Sydney
five years ago, he had picked up 'for a song' a clean-
bred, likely-looking filly. As the youngster 'furnished'
in the forcing climate of the North, Dick conceived the
idea from her general appearance that he had got
hold of an ideal 'chaser.' A 'flutter' which he gave
her when two years old relieved his mind as to her
pace, and from then till she was five he never let her

face a starter's flag. In the meantime, however, he had taught her all he knew about jumping, and from constantly handling her himself had got her as tractable as a dog. As a five-year-old she began her career over timber, and, in justification of her owner's opinion and patience, carried his black jacket and scarlet cap to almost unbroken victory from Normanton to Brisbane.

Making allowance for money lost during the meeting, Dick was still a few hundred pounds on the right side after winning the Brisbane 'double.' Io was fit and well, and entered for the Grand National, now only about six weeks off, so, determined to follow up his good fortune, he finally decided to bring the mare to Sydney.

'I wish you had given her a "fly" for the "double,"' muttered Johnson regretfully, as he threw away a cigar-butt and began to fill his pipe. 'As usual, they haven't bothered to send anything really first-class from Melbourne, and half these local screws look like broken-down cab-horses.'

'I don't like doubles,' retorted Dick sententiously; 'the "books" are too sweet in laying them. Besides, Heaven knows what they might slop on me for a win under the new rules.'

'You could walk in on a buck-board.'

'Don't be too sure of that, Ted; it's easy to be king in one's own backyard. But, hang it all! look at the time; we must run up and tell Miss Cameron the races are put off.'

CHAPTER II.

WAITING FOR NEWS.

' SURELY they will not race to-day?'

The speaker—a tall, white-skinned woman with hair of gold—rose as she spoke and walked to the window.

The child, unformed alike in mind and body, who nine years before had brought to Philip Orloff the unwritten message of the gods, had now developed both mentally and physically into a fit companion for a lover such as he.

' Of course they will!' exclaimed a smartly-dressed brunette. 'The wretches never think of us. My dream of a frock is born to blush unseen in that stupid stand.'

'Ted can admire it, dear,' murmured Heather Cameron a little mischievously ; then, turning from the window, she dropped into a chair and, taking a racing-cap from the table, added : 'Do let me try this on you, Edith. It will not go right.'

Kneeling beside her friend, Edith Enson bent her dark head obediently, saying carelessly :

'Ted indeed! Why, his tastes don't soar above a
horse-cloth!'

While the two girls were talking, the third occupant
of the room—a stout, well-preserved old lady—sat
hidden from view by the morning paper.

Mrs. Enson was a widow, her late husband having
been a partner of Cameron's in the good old days.
Unfortunately, the want of character which had tended
to make of his wife a model British matron had a decidedly opposite effect in the case of John Enson.
Finding his wife absolutely colourless, and consequently woefully conventional, her husband first
chafed under her unimpeachable respectability, and
then somewhat illogically drank himself to death;
but before he died Enson succeeded in establishing a
reputation as a jolly good fellow, and in common
with every member of that selfish, and in many
instances utterly contemptible, fraternity, left his wife
and baby-girl little by which to remember him save
his debts. About this time Cameron, through the
loss of his own wife, found himself in pressing need
of someone to look after his own little daughter. For
the sake of the old partnership he offered the position
to Mrs. Enson, and ever since she had controlled the
domestic destinies of Isis Downs. Growing up together,
the two girls—Heather and Edith—though widely
apart as the poles in disposition, became more like
sisters than many who boast that tie; while in all
things save in actual relationship Mrs. Enson filled
the place of Heather's dead mother. Somewhat conventional himself, the squatter held the old lady in
the highest esteem as a model woman, and, if people

were to be believed, the daughter when she married would not be forgotten by her father's one-time mate.

As Edith began her somewhat contemptuous summing-up of her lover's tastes, her mother, having run her eyes over the agony column, found herself free to listen to what was going on.

'I am surprised at you, my dear!' she remarked severely. 'I am sure Edward is prouder of you than you deserve.'

'Possibly. But, then, some men are so good at hiding their feelings, mother. How would I look as a jockey, Heather?'

'Splendid, dear! But don't you think you are—well, a little plump for the profession?'

'Don't be spiteful—that's just like Ted. He says I want steady exercise every morning, the brute!'

'I wish Edward would remember that you are not a stable boy,' interposed her mother, in a voice of deep disgust.

'By the way, isn't it time they were back?' remarked Heather, glancing at the clock.

'Oh, they won't hurry,' grumbled her companion. 'Once let men get into their beloved racing haunts, and they'll gossip about condition, and pace, and "hot pots," whatever they may be, for hours. We are of too little importance to be worth a thought when horses are under discussion.'

'Well, I don't much wonder; I love a good horse myself,' murmured Heather reflectively. Then, as she looked out into the gloomy street, the girl added wearily: 'What maddening weather; I almost wish that we had stayed in Queensland.'

'It does seem a pity to miss our best three months
for a season like this,' admitted Mrs. Enson ; 'but
remember, Heather, it was your wish to come.'

'She's a humbug, mother ! don't take any notice
of her,' interposed Edith. 'Why, she's just dying to
see Io show them all her heels.'

'Her what ?' gasped the old lady.

'I know I am,' said Heather, her face flushing with
excitement. 'How the men from the North will
cheer if she does! They've all backed dear old Io !'

'I am afraid that foolish young man has risked
more money than he can afford,' remarked Mrs.
Enson, as she ran her eyes down the social column.

'He's put every penny he has in the world on the
mare.'

'How do you know, dear ?' queried Edith.

'Because Dick told me,' answered the girl, in such
a natural, matter-of-course tone that her friend concluded she was either very dull or very deep.

In reality she was neither. She certainly knew,
with the knowledge that comes to all women, that
Hatten was fond of her, and she returned this feeling,
but with one important difference. She liked him as
a friend ; he loved her as he had never loved any
human being. Still, as no word had so far fallen to
sweep away the sweet uncertainty of the present, they
remained but chums.

Just as Mrs. Enson was about to deliver a few
words of general wisdom founded on her past knowledge of men, Hatten and Johnson walked in.

'You both ought to be ashamed of yourselves !'
cried Edith, half in fun, half in earnest. 'A nice

time you have kept us in suspense. I suppose you expect us to get dressed in five minutes.'

' I am exceedingly sorry,' interposed Hatten, before his friend could reply. ' If any inconvenience has occurred, I am to blame. To be honest, we got on the subject of Io's chances.'

' And forgot all about us ?' laughed Heather.

' Not so. Merely forgot what time it was.'

' I fail to see the difference; but never mind. What is your news ?'

' The races are postponed till Saturday.'

' Are you glad ?'

' Well, yes ; on the whole I think I am. You see, though Io's a regular mud-lark, I don't quite know how she'd shape in a swimming contest.'

' I'm glad, too,' said the girl, with a look of comical despair at the cap. ' I would not have had it ready for you to-day.'

' Let's see how it looks,' said Dick, walking over to a mirror. ' Now, you tie it. Not quite so tight, please; you'll stop circulation. Ah ! that's a trifle loose; just a shade firmer, if you don't mind.'

Standing before him, the girl kept obeying his instructions with an anxious desire to please. She was evidently interested in securing a good fit ; but, despite his wish to think otherwise, that, he felt, was all—a somewhat poor result, he had to admit, after his elaborate and highly improbable story as to the loss of his old cap, which even now lay stuffed into a corner of his portmanteau. Still, it was something even to wear what her hands had made; they were kindly ones at least.

'When you young people have quite finished,' said Edith, who had apparently forgiven her lover's neglect, 'I wish to make a proposition.'

'We are all attention,' replied Hatten.

'It is that, in punishment for your sins, the pair of you take us for a drive this afternoon.'

'What do you say, mother?' asked Heather.

'I see I am in such a decided minority,' laughed the old lady, 'that I had better say I am delighted.'

'That's a good old soul!' said the girl; 'and I propose we go and call on Miss Io.'

'Agreed,' laughed Johnson. 'Come on, Dick, and let us hunt up a decent team; the last lot we had make me tired when I think of them.'

'Mind you pick quiet, respectable animals, Edward,' Mrs. Enson called after them.

'A nice thing to warn a man about who is going to explore a Sydney livery stable, eh, Dick?' groaned Ted.

CHAPTER III.

THE SMOKING-ROOM OF THE MIDAS.

THE smoking-room of the Midas was gradually filling. To-night those who usually had a cigar and then went out lit a fresh one, while men kept dropping in and forming into little knots in various parts of the lofty, richly-furnished room. Taken as a whole, they were a keen-looking lot of men; among them 'cute' faces were as common as intellectual ones were rare. In a word, they were fair types of the Australian plutocracy. Merchant princes (so called), squatters (or, to be more correct, men who managed their stations for banking and other institutions), an occasional politician, racehorse owners, and a nondescript contingent who neighed when spoken to on any subject, made up the well-dressed mob who lounged or sat about discussing horses, wool, and Russian designs. For the moment, at any rate, among the group who stood clustered round Sir Robert Blake, the intentions of the Muscovite claimed a foremost place. For months a shower of contradictory cablegrams had appeared in the daily press. But to-day

things looked decidedly stormy, for a Persian army
had occupied Herat—at least, so the cable asserted.

Sir Robert stood in front of the fire, a paper in his
hand, his spectacles gleaming like a pair of intoxi-
cated head-lights high up on his forehead. Over six
feet high, and well set up, he was undoubtedly the
most striking-looking man in the room. Though for
years a prominent politician, he was a comparatively
new member of the Midas, having changed his club
and his principles within the last six years.

' This comes of having a confounded Liberal Government in power!' exclaimed Sir Robert, with a fine
disregard for the fact that every Cabinet, whether
Tory or Liberal, had played into Russia's hands for
years past. ' These beggars mean making a spring
this time.'

' But, then, the cable is such a liar!' protested a
man half buried in an armchair. ' We've been
getting these scares off and on for years. I believe
it's all bosh.'

' What do you know about it?' replied Sir Robert,
glaring down at the last speaker.

Interruption always irritated him, but in the case
of this rather stout, self-satisfied-looking young man
it became unbearable.

' About as much as you do, Sir Robert, I suspect,'
retorted the sceptic coolly.

' Then you have more time and brains at your
disposal than I supposed,' replied Sir Robert rudely.
' I imagined both were fully occupied in teaching men
whose age should protect them how to manage their
offices and stations.'

The loud laugh that greeted this brusque retort was too much even for the man in the chair, and muttering, too low for his opponent to hear, 'Confounded cad!' he rose and left the field to the leader of the Opposition.

'They mean coming this time,' continued the ex-Premier, lighting a cigar worthy of his own proportions. 'This Persian business is only a "blind." The whole affair is as clear as day. Russia pulls the strings; Russian officers direct the advance; and while our Government are arguing the matter out with the Shah, the Czar will pour a hundred thousand men into the gate of India.'

'My dear fellow,' interposed a slight, rather commonplace man, who held the position of Minister for War in the existing Government, and in private life directed a large soft-goods emporium, 'you are as bad as these alarmists who for the last fifty years have been attempting to scare England into undignified and hysterical action alike unworthy of her traditions and present position. Rest assured the motherland will assert herself when the time comes.'

'Assert herself be d——d!' exclaimed Sir Robert. 'If she doesn't soon stop backing herself, she'll fall into the Indian Ocean.'

A chorus of indignant protest told the ex-Republican that he had gone too far.

'No man has a greater love and respect for England than I,' he continued; 'and feeling as I do, I'm not going to stand by without uttering a protest against a policy unworthy of a great nation.'

'For myself, I have no fear,' returned the Minister

4

for War. 'In the first place, Russia's power in the East is greatly exaggerated; and, further, I feel certain, as I said before, that England will assert herself when necessary. If Persia has really occupied Herat, doubtless a commission will settle the whole affair.'

'But what if Russia is, as I maintain, at the back of Persia?'

'My dear Sir Robert, you are a fire-eater! Please remember that England is a commercial nation, and it won't pay to go to war merely for a sentiment.'

'You've hit the nail on the head,' laughed Dick Hatten, who had just come in. 'Napoleon spoke too soon, that was all; we are a nation of shopkeepers.'

'Sir,' exclaimed the small man indignantly, 'where would England be to-day but for her merchant-princes?'

'In a more dignified position than that of the best-snubbed nation on the earth, possibly,' retorted Hatten carelessly. 'Hullo, Zenski! what are you up to?'

'*Mon ami*, I am listening,' retorted the Russian. 'Will you not join us? Here is a chair, and I can give you a passable cigar. Allow me to introduce you to my friend Mr. Alexis Dromeroff.'

The man who rose and bowed to Hatten looked, despite his clean-shaved upper lip, more of a soldier than a civilian. In age he might have been thirty-five—possibly was fifty—but the lines about his eyes and at the corner of his clean-cut mouth told that in knowledge of men he was patriarchal.

'My friend has just come from Russia,' Zenski

went on. 'Like myself, he has ideas of his own, and
so finds it conducive to his health to remain at a
distance from our great White Father.'

'Yes, Mr. Hatten,' said Dromeroff, in a low, well-
modulated voice; 'living under free British laws, you
little know what life in Russia means for the man
who dares to think for himself. Just when Siberia or
flight lay before me, my old friend's letter came,
telling me of this grand new land of yours, and—well,
I am here.'

'I'm sure we're very glad to have you,' replied
Hatten politely. 'I should imagine, from the way
Zenski speaks of it, that Russia must be a deuce of a
hole to live in for all parties. If you're a Nihilist, the
Government send you to Siberia; and if you belong to
the Government, the Nihilists send you to the devil.'

'Pardon, you mistake; I am not a Nihilist,' interposed Dromeroff quietly. 'I am what you would call
a Liberal.'

Before Hatten could explain, Sir Robert, who had
caught the end of the Russian's remark, said, with a
laugh :

'Then, I don't wonder the Czar objected to you,
Mr. Dromeroff. I only wish our King could make as
short work of our Liberal Government.'

'You surprise me, Sir Robert!' replied Dromeroff.
'I thought you were all democrats.'

'He is not to be taken *au sérieux*, Alexis,' interposed Zenski. 'Sir Robert merely suffers from irrita-
tion for the reason that he thinks the British Cabinet
have been too liberal towards Russia as regards
frontier lines.'

'Of course I was only joking, Mr. Dromeroff; and, allow me to add, we are quite ready to welcome all the Russians of your stamp who care to come and help us to build up a nation,' said Sir Robert courteously. 'Count Zenski has already shown us what your countrymen can do up North.'

'Bah! it is nothing,' said Zenski. 'I have built you a few railway-lines; anyone could do the same.'

'Not in the time.'

'Men and capital will do anything,' answered Zenski sententiously. 'Besides, the country is what you call easy.'

'What do you think about this occupation of Herat?' asked Sir Robert abruptly.

'If a fact—which permit me to doubt—and if attempted by Persia alone, it is madness; if carried out at the instigation of Russia, it is what you call "bluff."'

'But if so, with what object?'

'That I cannot pretend to explain. You forget I am as little in touch with St. Petersburg as you are. Perhaps the design of an ambitious General acting on his own responsibility; possibly to draw away all your available forces in view of another rush on Constantinople. Who knows?'

'What is your opinion, Mr. Dromeroff?' persisted Sir Robert. 'You, at least, cannot plead long absence from St. Petersburg.'

'True; but you will remember I of necessity know nothing but what I may have heard and read in common with the rest of the public. Personally, if my opinion is worth having, you are most welcome to it.'

'I would be glad to hear it, Mr. Dromeroff,' interposed the Minister for War, 'if only to convince Sir
Robert that the scare is not worthy the consideration
of a statesman.'

'Well, gentlemen,' said Dromeroff, hiding the keen
amusement he felt at the Minister's pompous mouth-
ing of the word 'statesman,' 'like my friend Zenski,
I am unable to explain why, but, nevertheless, I can
only put the movement down as—what shall I say?—
"bounce." That Russia would like well your rich
possessions seems but natural; that she at present
has any serious designs on them seems to me impossible. If I mistake not, she will want every available Cossack she can put in the field to defend her
Chinese frontier. The Pamir question can to my
mind only be settled by another war; and she has
learnt that China is not to be despised. Again, look
at what an invasion of India means—what risks have
to be taken hundreds of miles from her actual base of
supplies both of troops and war material. Believe
me, she recognises, if others do not, how different
fighting an English army, backed up by Indian troops,
is to conquering a few nomadic tribes badly armed
and worse led.'

'Just my opinion, my dear sir,' exclaimed the
Minister for War, with a triumphant look at Sir Robert.
'The British lion has only to wag his tail, and your
phantom disappears.'

'He's wagged his tongue so long that I doubt if he
remembers how to move any other part of his carcase,'
laughed Hatten.

'Russia must also remember,' went on the Minister,

ignoring Hatten's remark, 'that the first Cossack who crosses the frontier gives the signal for our gallant boys to rally round the dear old land; we've done it once, and we'll do it again.' As the speaker concluded, he rose and stood in front of Sir Robert like a soldier-bird defying an emu.

'Yes,' sneered the ex-Premier; 'and let me add, in the first instance, through no wish of your party, McFee. Still, so far I am with you, and permit me to congratulate you on adopting our idea.'

'And the country is with you also,' added an officer of the Soudan Contingent, noted as the man who, when asked to put his company through squad drill, gave the historic command, 'Men, fall in four thick.' 'The country is with you, sir.'

Before the warrior could end his remarks, a waiter entered with the last edition of the *Evening News.* 'The weights for the Melbourne Cup!' exclaimed a man, running his eye over a copy. In five minutes every man in the room, save the two Russians, was discussing the handicap, and Herat was forgotten.

'They are horses,' muttered Dromeroff contemptuously in Russian.

'Principally asses,' retorted Zenski in the same tone, lighting a fresh cigar, and handing his case to his companion.

CHAPTER IV.

THE DAY BEFORE THE NATIONAL.

EVER since the postponement the weather had begun to mend, the day before the meeting coming in with a clear sky and a fresh, drying wind.

In paper quotations Sardius held nominal pride of place for the big jumping event—partly because he represented Victoria, partly from the reason that he would be steered by the brilliant amateur, Jack Brewster. Still, in doubles Io was coupled with everything, and during the week a steady stream of money had 'trickled on to her' in the shops. The night before, in 'the Rooms,' a commission from Victoria, and the backing of two or three local horses, had enabled the ring to make a slight demonstration against the mare. But, rallying round their champion, the Queenslanders had stayed the 'rot,' and she left off only a point behind the first favourite.

There was one horse, however, who troubled Johnson and Hatten far more than the much-fancied Sardius.

Keenly alive to every move of the game, they had noticed that, although scarcely mentioned in the quotations, the books treated Satan with veiled respect, and that while no inquiries worth mentioning seemed to be made, a well-known old commissioner, with the square-toed half Wellingtons and white Newgate shave of a bygone age, quietly snapped up all fancy shots with unobtrusive regularity.'

On the track, Satan had done nothing worth remembering; but then, as Johnson remarked, 'that was no line; perhaps they preferred keeping it in him for the race; anyhow, the old boy could probably show them nothing they hadn't learnt long ago.

From the quaint, wizened mannikin who combined the offices of trainer and jockey, nothing was to be learnt. As a tout exclaimed after an hour's chat: 'D—— n him! when you've spent a quid moist'nin' his blooming old sucker, blow me if he ain't too dried up to pump anything but wind outer.' Of the latter commodity there was always an unfailing supply—but unfortunately he would blow on any point but the right one. On the hoary age and amiable domestic characteristics of 'the old 'orse' he was communicative to a degree, but when asked about his possible present chances, he would invariably remark sadly: 'Yes, he's been a hold dinger in 'is time at shearers' meetings, but that's gone by these many years. Amn't he a pore hold cripple?'

'Then why the devil do you bring him here?' Johnson asked one day.

' 'Cos it's the boss's orders.'

'Who is the boss?'

'A cove as lives up Grabben Gullen way,' retorted the old trainer.

'He must be a d——d fool!'

'Maybe,' the old man answered shortly; 'I never axed him meself.'

During the morning Hatten drove out to Randwick and had a look at the mare.

'She looks pink, Billy,' said the owner, as 'Billy the Kid' pulled off her sheet and exposed to view a shining mass of muscle and condition.

'My oath!' retorted the six-foot slab to whom this nickname of bygone light-weight days still clung.

'Had a good night?'

'You bet.'

'On her feed?' asked Johnson.

'She's never off it; stokes like a gin after a killing.'

While questioning Billy, Hatten had run his fingers over her tendons, and noted that his favourite's eyes and coat were both bright and lustrous. Io's lean, game head was set on the neck so as to give the wind-pipe full play, while a wither fine as a cutwater rose above the sloping shoulders. Her short, straight-backed, roomy barrel, well ribbed up, and terminating in quarters always sturdy, but now a concentrated mass of lifting power, rested on timber lithesome as steel, and sound as the day she was foaled. For though her hind-legs bore the marks of a rap or so against the rough split rails of 'Out Back' courses, she had run the gauntlet of the iron-bound tracks of the North without break or blemish. Just under sixteen hands, and black as night save for a star on her forehead, the mare looked a mistress to whom one might entrust both life and honour. Stepping again through the fresh, white-stemmed straw that

rose about her fetlocks, Hatten glanced into her feed-
box. As he did so, Io rubbed her soft muzzle against
his coat in friendly greeting.

'She knows me, Billy,' said Dick, stroking the
velvet nostrils.

'You bet!' Billy replied with great animation.

As they walked towards their cab, Hatten said
somewhat anxiously: 'I must win to-morrow, Billy.'

'My oath,' grunted the trainer.

'But,' went on his master impatiently, 'do you
think I can? If the mare goes down, every penny I
have goes with her.'

Stopping, Billy remarked fervently: 'Gor bloom
me!' then, after a pause, added: 'Look here, Mister
Dick, d'ye mind that day on the Flinders when you
met me with Matilda up, pig-jumping over them
blooming sand-hills, leading my blooming water-bag?'

'When you were on the wallaby, you mean?' said
Dick, with a laugh.

'Yes, per boot. Well, you gave me a lift on the
pack-horse and a pull at your flask, and we ain't
parted since, 'ave we?'

'No.'

'An' I've won you a lot o' goes?'

'You have, Billy.'

'Well, I ain't worked off that good turn yet, you
take it from me.'

'I suppose that means you're going to send the
mare out a winner to-morrow?' said Dick in a tone of
positive relief.

'My blooming oath!' remarked Billy, expectorating
solemnly.

CHAPTER V.

IN THE PALACE GARDEN.

MRS. ENSON and her daughter had gone out to spend the afternoon at the house of an old Queensland friend who was giving a garden-party as a sort of welcome to the Northern contingent.

Pleading woman's safest excuse when she wants to avoid any social function, Heather had remained at the Australia to battle with a 'sick headache.'

After a time the girl dressed herself for the street, and, coming downstairs, started to walk briskly towards the Palace Garden.

Restless and memory-haunted, the room, with its heavy hangings and colourless outlook into the narrow house-walled street, had grown hateful; she wanted to be alone, but not with such surroundings. The sunlight, the flowers, and the pulseless waters shining through fronded stems and rich tropical foliage, all were kind; so she went to them as one goes to a trusted friend—one with whom all secrets are safe, all sorrows sacred.

Reaching the gates watched over by the bronze statue of old Sir Richard Bourke, and guarded by two

Russian cannons now loaded to their muzzles with the orange-peel of an irreverent, if rising, generation, Heather entered the Palace Garden, walked down the broad pathway flanked with isles of scarlet and purple and gold set in seas of green, and halted above the basin where the marble boxers frown fiercely on each other. On her left, above the battlements of Government House, the Union Jack hung listless about its staff; away to the right the avenue of Moreton Bay figs rose like a rampart, glimpses of the old Domain showing through their stout gnarled boles; while above their crests the pinnacles of St. Mary's shot into the clear, translucent air. In front lay the gardens, bathing their feet in the blue Pacific.

For a little while Heather stood watching 'twixt sea and shore; then she passed on, down the roadway where the statues stand, to the great flight of steps. At their base she turned aside, and seeing an empty seat set close against a leafless trunk, sat down upon it and looked over the tree-heads out towards the sea.

We all live two lives. One a dim, uncertain existence, its failures and weaknesses lit up here and there by a pure thought, a noble inspiration. Its mission is to keep us from becoming utterly material, repellently brutish. The other—our everyday life, needs no explanation; as a rule, it is all that the mystic, the hidden life would teach us to abhor.

The woman sitting under the tree possessed, in common with her fellows, a dual existence; but, through no fault of her own, what lay hidden must never be revealed to the world, nor could she look on it herself with any feeling but one akin to utter despair.

In the days which had followed Harden's murder and Orloff's escape, memory, unchained by the hypnotist's death, came back to her. For long she lay in her cabin in the grief of a horror that had to be faced alone.

To her fellow-passengers, to her father himself, it was but the natural distress of a young girl suddenly brought face to face with the utter badness of a man she had favoured, if not actually loved, coupled with regret for the terrible end of another who appeared to have also awakened a certain interest in her.

To the child tossing in her narrow berth it was the death of all things bright and pure, the sudden rending of a veil white and spotless, the quick revealing of a gulf, its black, unfathomable depths unrelieved by a single ray of hope. The man she hated with a strength that a few days past her childless soul had been incapable of creating was dead, but the evil he had wrought would live for ever, for evil is immortal. The man she knew she loved was also dead—if not to life, at least to her; but his love would live, to be a crown of sorrow, yet to save her, for love, too, is immortal.

Thus Orloff rescued his twin-soul after all, and she rose up a woman pure in heart and determined to walk worthy of the man who would be to her for all time, not a murderer, but a judge; not an impossible ideal, but one who had smeared his hands with blood only that he might wipe away a stain from her own life. For though no word was spoken, no message

ever sent by him, Heather felt that Orloff knew all,
and that he understood. And in his keeping she
realized her secret was safe; nay, felt a certain sad,
indescribable joy that he should have the guarding of
it. Further, something told her they would meet
again, where or when she knew not, and that when
he came he would want her for himself, whether in
earth or heaven.

So she did not die; not that she cared to live, but
because she knew the manner of her death would have
seemed unworthy of him, and might part them for
ever. She lived, and as time moved on grew in some
sort to love life once more and face the world bravely,
for with the years her latent strength of character ex-
panded, and she took up her cross with firm hands
and marched on with the rest. Now for six years she
had lived this dual life, taking her part in the world's
joys and sorrows as other women take theirs, but
always keeping her heart for the coming of her hero,
and to-day he seemed very near her, and so she sat
alone gazing out upon the sea. Zenski had met them
at the theatre the night before, and had introduced
Dromeroff. In doing so, the old Russian had chanced
to say, ' Possibly my friend may know some friends of
yours, Miss Cameron; he has been a great traveller.'
In face of the fact that Heather had been wandering
half over Europe during the past six years, her father
having yielded to her wishes and again set off a few
months after their arrival in the *Genoa*, Zenski's supposition was natural enough.

To Heather, however, it seemed to conceal a deeper
meaning. Knowing the friendship that existed between

the Count and Orloff, she held a settled conviction that the Russian knew far more than he chose to tell of her lover's escape. Why she had arrived at this conclusion she could not have logically explained. Zenski never mentioned the subject of his own free will, and, if it was forced upon him, always professed to be as mystified as the rest. Still, the girl held, woman-like, to her own opinion, and now began to build strange, half-fearful hopes on the flimsy foundation of a diplomat's chance remark.

As she sat thus in a day-dream, Dick Hatten, searching for her, and duly admiring feminine comeliness wherever found, caught sight of a figure which seemed to warrant the exertion of a closer inspection.

Reaching the foot of the stairs, Dick thanked his possession of an eye for a pretty woman fervently, for now that he had rounded the flank of her sunshade, he discovered that he had found the woman he sought.

Moving noiselessly over the thick grass, he stood beside her before she was aware of his presence.

'A penny for your thoughts, Miss Cameron,' said he.

To his surprise, she rose to her feet with an exclamation, then, meeting his laughing eyes, sank back with a faint sigh of disappointment.

'You startled me out of a day-dream,' she said, somewhat sadly, it seemed to him.

'And I was not the prince you expected, I fear,' he replied a little bitterly.

'Well, no, you were not,' she answered with a frankness that argued ill for Dick. 'But then, you know, he only comes in dreams. Where have you left Mr. Johnson?'

'Oh, he trotted off to Mrs. Manson's,' said Dick, seating himself beside her.

'And why didn't you?'

'Well, you see, as Edith is there, he has a sort of duty to perform, which does not apply in my case, so when I found out from the clerk that you had gone for a walk, I thought I'd do a bit of tracking.'

'Why? did you think I'd get bushed?'

'Hardly that,' replied Dick uneasily; 'only I felt a bit unsettled, and I wanted to have a talk to a—well, to a friend.'

Ignoring his hesitation, she answered with kindly interest:

'I suppose you are anxious about to-morrow; how did you find Io this morning?'

'She's all right, thanks.'

'I do hope for your sake she'll win,' said Heather heartily.

'Then you do take a little interest in me—I mean in the mare?' asked Dick.

'Of course I take a lot of interest in both of you,' replied Heather, adding unconsciously, but cruelly, 'I'd be a poor Queenslander if I didn't.'

'Then it's only for the sake of the colony you want her to win?' replied Dick ruefully.

'Far from it; I admit I do want dear old Banana-land to be in front; but beyond that, I know all you have risked on the race, and how your heart is set on winning, and so, as your friend, I wish for your success from the bottom of my heart.'

That was the cruel part of it; as a friend she always was ready with her sympathy and good wishes, but Dick was keen enough to see that her feelings towards him never strayed over that cold, definite border-line.

'I have many friends,' he answered sadly. 'Heather, can you never be towards me all they are and something more? Forgive me if I say what had better have been left unsaid, but I must speak. All my life has been an aimless wandering—a weak, unworthy seeking after some new thing only found to be cast aside; I have been that most useless of human beings, a man without an object — that most hopeless of drifters, a sailor without a star. Now you have come into my life, and with you to guide me, I feel that there is a future yet to live for.'

As he spoke in low, disjointed, yet passionate accents, the woman at his side listened with growing pity to his words. And as his confession fell upon her ears, she could not help comparing it with the words spoken by Orloff the last time she ever heard his voice. Both men, she knew, were physically brave, but there comparisons ended.

Orloff had said, ' You are in need of a strong arm to defend and guide you; let it be mine.' The man beside her confessed his weaknesses, and asked her practically to defend him from himself and to guide him to a nobler life.

For a little she was silent, realizing how much she might be able to do, and further feeling that the man, for all his weakness, was worth it. She yet could hold out no hope. For one thing, could she in honour

5

take the place he suggested? But why trouble about
that? she was another's for all time; and that other
was braver and stronger and more worthy of her love
than this suppliant could ever be.

At last she said quietly, as one who fears to wound,
yet firmly, as one who would not be misunderstood:

'To pretend to misunderstand you would be unworthy of both of us. I know what answer you would
wish me to give, and I am sorry, sorry from my heart,
that you ever put me in a position to refuse to give it.
In all other things I will help you, and if a woman's
good wishes are worth having, mine are always yours.
Heaven knows I have yearned for such help before to-
day. I know you will hate me for talking like this;
but I must. I cannot love you, but let us be friends,
Dick.'

While she spoke, Hatten sat looking out over the
bay. From the decks of the warships the masts rose
dark and slender, crossed by the tapering yards; a
yacht with graceful lines floated like a water-nymph
near the shore, while midway between the tower of
Fort Denison and the garden parapet the oars of a
man-of-war's boat flashed in the sunlight as they rose
with measured swing. All these things he saw, and
yet he remembered nothing save the hideous shear-
legs that rose like a ghastly red scaffold above Garden
Island. This he never forgot, nor the fact that he
experienced a keen desire to hang its erectors on a
string from its triangular summit.

It was a defeat, he fully realized; nay, more, the
rout of hopes massed up behind the bastions of his
heart for many a day; and yet, so reluctantly do we

surrender a cherished desire, the man rallied his broken forces round one word. She had called him 'Dick.'

'I have been too precipitate,' he muttered brokenly. 'For the present I accept your offer to be my own familiar friend.'

Feeling it would be both prudish and unkind to cavil at his' conditional bargain at such a time, she made no demur, and thus from very kindness undid all that which had cost so much effort but a moment before.

'May I see you back to the hotel?' said Hatten, subdued, but full of fresh aspirations.

'Yes,' she answered, rising, and looking away past the tall figure before her into that land of dreams among whose filmy mists another figure seemed to stand and beckon.

'What are you looking at?' he asked in wonder— 'that ghastly gallows?'

With a shiver, she answered :

'No ; at that which lies beyond.'

CHAPTER VI.

ON THE ROAD.

In front of the Australia a four-in-hand stood, gazed at with a certain languid interest by a pack of cigarette - smoking infants, who filled in the time not occupied in disposing of ' c'rect cards ' by frank criticisms on the leaders' fore-legs and the driver's only ones.

Still, apart from some want of motive displayed in the man's tops as compared with the narrowness of his calves, and an indescribable stuffiness which seems to cling like a birth-mark about all vehicles for hire, the turnout in question was worthy of the occasion.

Dick and Johnson had secured it days before, having decided, after the manner of bushmen down for a spell, to live up to the traditions of their order while in town.

In the vestibule of the hotel a well - dressed mob stood comparing notes, while pulling on gloves and adjusting the hang of their field-glasses.

Globe-trotters, who would have been millionaires had half the checks displayed on their bodies been negotiable; a well-advertised star actor 'doing' the colonies, for the good and sufficient reason that he was 'done' at home; the vendor of a magic balm which, applied to the soles of the feet, cured deafness, and who averred that his mane-like head of hair was worth £200 a year to him; a sprinkling of Anglicized Australians, whose fathers had sold their souls in 'dummying' land, so that their offspring might acquire an Oxford training and an utter contempt for the old man—these, with sundry well-dressed women of all nationalities, made up the contingent which the Australia was about to send to Randwick.

As the Isis Downs party came down the marble staircase, the people below stared with more than passing interest at this last addition to their ranks. Edith, with her warm colouring and black hair, set off by a bright-gray tailor-made dress, with boa and toque of fur of a darker shade, looked like a joyous spirit of the night who had come to gladden the day.

Clad in that rich brown which in the sunlight glows with a golden radiance, its plainness relieved with deep borderings of astrakhan, Heather, white-skinned and hazel-eyed, with the hair and form of the Queen of the Morning, moved by her side in stately contrast.

As the girls, piloted by Mrs. Enson and Count Zenski, reached the hall, Hatten and Johnson, accompanied by Dromeroff and the rest of the men of their party, joined them.

'I do hope those wretched horses are quiet, Edward,' said the old lady anxiously; 'I noticed the leaders jumping about before we came down.'

'You needn't let that trouble you, Mrs. Enson,'
interposed Dick. 'That's all included for the money
—it's merely for effect.'

'Well, suppose we make a start?' suggested Johnson. 'It won't do to miss the hurdles.'

As he spoke he moved towards the steps, followed
by the rest. Swinging himself on to the box, he now
took the reins, while Hatten and the other men, after
helping the ladies into their places, clambered up
on top.

'Are you all fixed?' inquired Ted, straightening out
his team.

'Yes.'

'Now, don't be scared, Mrs. Enson,' whispered
the manager, as, dropping his whip lightly on the
leaders, they rose on their hind-legs according to
agreement.

Steadying them, Johnson got his wheelers going,
and the drag swung round into King Street, and away
past the statue and St. Mary's, at a good ten miles an
hour. Oxford Street, with its trams and miscellaneous
traffic, steadied Ted's pace considerably, but once past
the Captain Cook Hotel all was again plain sailing.

On either side, as they bowled along the straight,
tree-guarded roadway, crowds of footballers 'dribbled'
and 'passed' and 'collared' to the loud-voiced
applause of frantic 'barrackers,' while the bunting
floating above the Association Ground told that there
some special struggle for supremacy was taking place.

'You are a sporting race, Miss Cameron,' said
Dromeroff.

'Some ill-natured people say that we are nothing

else,' the girl replied. 'But don't you think, Mr.
Dromeroff, it is, after all, better to see too much play
than none at all ?'

'Youth is the time for play,' retorted the Russian,
diplomatically polite.

'Miss Cameron is very—what shall I say ?—Australian,' interposed Zenski ; 'and we are surrounded
by the same interesting race, so be careful, *mon ami.*'

Now they were in the thick of the stream of vehicles
bound for Randwick, and Johnson, tractable as his
team was, had his hands full.

'It's a bit different to steering out back, eh, Ted ?'
queried Hatten, as a bus axle broke just in front.

'You're right, old man,' muttered Johnson, steering
round the wreck. 'You can take the bearing of a
stump, and it won't fool you ; but these confounded
beggars line you, and jostle, and take the running as
coolly as gentlemen jockeys.'

'You are very personal,' said Heather, with a glance
at Hatten.

'Oh, Ned's only thinking of himself,' chimed in
Edith.

So, laughing and talking and chaffing, they rolled
on, giving their dust to the lumbering four-horse
buses and getting it back from the fast-trotting
American buggies, dodging the delivery-vans and
dodged by the sporting sulkies, racing the one or two
private drags that Sydney could boast, and admiring
the numerous well - horsed open carriages, where,
wrapped in arrogance which sought in vain to hide
their commonplace, sat Higginbotham's 'wealthy
lower orders.'

'What do you think of them, Zenski?' asked Hatten, as the Russian lifted his hat to his old friend, Sir John Baggs.

'Frankly, my friend,' replied the Count, who knew he could trust Dick, 'not much. They are the newest plutocracy in the world, and consequently the most objectionable.'

'How do you make that out?'

'Most simply. In America time has, in many cases, mercifully removed the original self-made man, and more refined association has rubbed the crude edges off his descendants. Here you seldom get beyond the founder of a fortune. For your fortunes are so paltry that, by the time your parvenu has brought himself into society, he has to drop out again for want of funds. But here we are; and, if I mistake not, the horses are going out for the first race.'

As Zenski spoke, Johnson wheeled his leaders into the carriage reserve, just as the discordant yet blood-quickening roar of the ring rose in that space behind the members' stand where men play pitch-and-toss with fortune and honour in the name of sport and in the guise of pleasure.

CHAPTER VII.

IN THE PADDOCK.

LEAVING the ladies in charge of three members of their party who meant to 'stand off' the hurdles, Dick and Ted hurried into the paddock, followed more leisurely by the two Russians.

'There they are,' said Zenski, as he and his friend took up a position beside a tree: 'commerce and law and medicine, masters and servants—even the Church, for aught I know—all are represented here: the world and his wife to pay tribute to a four-legged god through his chosen high-priests, the Levites.'

'In England, too, they think much of the race-horse; so do we, Zenski.'

'Here they think of nothing else; and that is one of the reasons why we have had so little trouble. Listen.'

As Zenski was speaking, a well-dressed, keen-looking middle-aged man coming from the Birdcage passed.

'One moment, Mr. Mills,' said Zenski, touching him on the arm; 'what is this I hear about Herat?'

Stopping, the man looked puzzled for a moment, then said in a tone of annoyance :

'Hanged if I can remember the nominations a bit! What about him ?   Is he scratched ?'

'So I hear,' replied the Russian.

'.Hope you haven't backed him,' retorted the other, adding, in a tone of friendly warning, as he turned away : 'Take my advice, and never touch 'em till after the weights are out.'

'Who is he ?' inquired Dromeroff curiously.

'A member of the Upper House,' said Zenski with a cynical grin.

As the winner of the hurdle-race turned up in Dart, a comparative outsider ridden by Jack Brewster, it naturally caused that brilliant horseman's mount for the steeplechase to harden in the betting.   Two minutes after the red flag was hoisted Sardius touched six to four, while, partly from the advance of the favourite and partly because of a rumour having gained ground to the effect that a well-known horse-owner and member of the committee had backed Satan, Io receded a couple of points.

Still the Queensland 'crowd' remained confident, for the mare looked fit as hands could make her, and her rider professed himself as confident of a favourable result.

As few of the Northern men were members, the whole party took luncheon at a reserved table under the stand.   Let moralists preach as they may, I wonder if friends can come together under gladder conditions than those of a race-lunch.   Given that the wine be mellow and the hearts be leal, I doubt it.   Too

early in the day to count the cost, the sordid side of
the question is as yet absent, while, the first blood
being drawn, the layers, whether the skirmish be for
or against them, are full of fight and enthusiasm.
Given the presence of two young and handsome
women both deeply interested in the same horse as
themselves, the man who is to ride and every other
man present a devoted partisan, and I can conceive
no closer bond of *camaraderie*.

Such were the spirits who now toasted Io and the
North amid the clatter of knives and the popping of
corks under the Randwick Stand. During the lull
that fell upon the paddock between luncheon and the
next race, Mrs. Enson foregathered with her friend
Mrs. Manson, leaving the two girls in charge of
Hatten and Johnson. Her daughter and the manager
of Isis Downs thoroughly understood each other, and,
despite Edith's habit of making light of Ted's horsey
proclivities, the girl really loved the good-hearted,
straight-going bushman. Recognising that it would
be some time before he could offer her a home, Johnson in no way attempted to clog her freedom of
action, shrewdly judging that in love, of all things,
coercion is worse than useless. That Edith fully
returned this magnanimity is doubtful, while that she
to a certain extent took advantage of it, Johnson
occasionally found to his cost. Still, on the whole,
all went smoothly enough, and to-day, as he walked
with her up and down the lawn, he fully realized how
good a thing it was to have for his possession this
winsome, warm-hearted daughter of tropic suns.

Hatten and Heather wandered farther afield, taking

advantage of the lessened crowd to look at the mare round which so many hopes centred. A weaker woman would have avoided Hatten altogether; one less earnest and honest would have made the fact of their being together appear to possess an embarrassment for her, whether it did so or not. With Heather all this was impossible. She had told him she had no love to give, and she meant it; she had, in place of what she did not possess, offered him her truest friendship, and in this, as in all things, she was sincere. Doubting his stability in all matters pertaining to deep human passion, she had little fear as to his quick recuperative power, and so, now that he had accepted what she offered, she felt that her best and kindest course was to simply ignore all that had passed, save only her latest compact. Though in this she had somewhat misjudged Dick, he, on his part, was too much a man of the world to rush on another certain defeat when every hope of ultimate success seemed to lie in delay. So, satisfied with the fact that if refused he had still retained his position, he, too, for the present, ignored all that had passed save the fact that they were firm friends, both deeply interested in the fortunes of Io.

Leaning against the rails of her stall, Billy the Kid kept jealous guard over his favourite. Seeing his master and Heather approach, the trainer's face brightened slightly under its casing of tan.

As a rule Billy strongly objected to women; at any rate, in connection with horse-racing. Some years ago he had remarked to Hatten, when discussing the hiring of a lad, 'Boys is the ruin of stables, an' socks

an' wimmin is the ruin o' boys,' and he meant it.
However, with Heather it was different. The trainer
recognised that she not only loved, but knew a good
horse when she saw one ; and this, coupled with the
fact that she had made a complete new suit for the
mare when Billy was last at the Downs, induced him
to waive his objections in her case.

Returning his clumsy, half-bashful acknowledgment
with a courtesy that was a part of her, Heather asked
if all was well with the mare.

'My o—beg pardon, my word, miss,' said Billy.
' She's had a great night, and '—throwing back the
sheet—' 'er coat's as shiny as yer own !'

'It does you credit, Billy,' said the girl, smiling at
his simile. ' I'm afraid mine never gets so well looked
after.'

'It's all a question o' elbow-grease, miss,' replied
Billy oracularly.

Here Hatten interposed, asking the trainer if he
had heard anything about Satan.

' It's whispered 'e did a great go last Thursday
mornin' with the weight up, but I don't think it,'
answered Billy. ' They got 'is measure to a 'air long
afore he come to Randwick, you take it from me, sir;
and they means backin' 'im for what they's worth, all
right. But never you mind; all you got to do is to
keep a hold o' the mare's head, an' don't let them go
too slow, nor yet take you too fast, and you'll d——
well lose 'em at the finish. Beg pardon for swearing,
miss,' stuttered Billy; 'I ain't been accustomed to
ladies as minds—I mean the mare likes me to swear
at 'er a bit.'

'Send her in a winner to-day, Billy, and, for the sake of the North, I'll forgive you,' said Heather kindly. 'Thank goodness, if she has learnt a bad habit, she can't express it.'

'She's in the first class, she is!' muttered Billy admiringly, as the two walked back towards the stand. 'But he'll never lead 'er in a winner, if I know anything about trainin'.'

As the horses went out for the Ransom Plate, the big flat event of the meeting, Zenski and Dromeroff, who had been captured by Sir John Baggs before luncheon, rejoined the party.

The Wonder, despite a career marred by frequent loss of form, again left the paddock an 'odds on' favourite.

'He looks head and shoulders above his field,' remarked Dromeroff. 'I think I must have a wager; it's better to buy money at a short price than to lose it at a long one.'

'Certainly, my friend,' retorted Zenski; 'I will go with you.'

As the two neared the ring, the older man added:

'Let well alone; when the price is too short, he becomes seized with a curious desire to inspect the tails of his compatriots. Come into the members' stand, and judge for yourself.'

The race needs little description; the Wonder, fighting for his head, lay out of position until entering the straight, then came only to be blocked; and, finally, after pulling out and coming round his field, just suffered defeat at the hands of a rank outsider by a length.

As the horse returned to the weighing-yard, looking
fit to go out again and run away from his field, an
angry crowd gathered round the railing, and treated
both horse and owner to a volley of hearty, ill-sound-
ing groans.

Standing beside his horse, the Wonder's master
looked with supreme contempt at the white-faced men
who hissed.

'Let them howl!' he said, loud enough for all to
hear. 'They have the fun, and I have the stuff!'

'He is a philosopher,' remarked Dromeroff.

'He would make an admirable Russian,' returned
Zenski admiringly, 'but I doubt if he is honest enough
even for us.'

CHAPTER VIII.

THE GRAND NATIONAL STEEPLECHASE.

THE last bell had rung out over the crowded course, and in response to its harsh, metallic summons the men on the boxes in the Ledger and the 'leviathans' of the paddock alike 'gave tongue.'

Layers, whether Jew or Gentile, shouted aloud their strident chorus of 'Ten to one, bar three !' 'Six to four, Sardius !' 'Three to one, Higho !' 'Who wants to back one ?' 'The field a pony, I'll lay, I'll lay !' and the public listened as though it were the refrain of some new, strange song, and backed their fancies, and their tips, and their dreams, with a childlike imbecility born of greedy hearts and sport-saturated heads. Threading their way through the pressing, shouting mass, the twelve competitors for the Grand National slowly filed out into the straight.

'Don't be in a 'urry, sir,' said Billy, who was walking beside Io. 'Last out, first in.'

As he spoke, Cohen, book in hand, rushed up.

'I'll lay you three hundred to one, Mr. Hatten. Remember, you promised to give me a turn.'

' Make it a point longer, Cohen,' replied Dick, after a moment's hesitation.

'It's a wager, four hundred to one hundred ; thanks, sir ; hope you get home.'

' I thought you said on Thursday it would be level money,' remarked Hatten a trifle uneasily.

' So it would,' replied the fielder ; ' only, you see, a commission's come in the last ten minutes, and they're backing Satan like water. There you are,' cried the bookmaker, hurrying away, as up from the ring rose ' Level money, Satan !' ' Three to one, Sardius !' ' Four to one, Io !'

Taking the bookmaker's place, Johnson laid his hand on Io's mane.

' For heaven's sake, be careful, Dick !' he whispered anxiously. ' Don't throw away a chance, old mate. The knowing crowd fancy they have a certainty in Satan, and they're just pouring it on to him.'

' So I can hear,' returned Hatten. ' Well, let 'em ; level money alone never won a race yet ; I've just put about my last pound on the mare, and if she stands up, I'll stretch his neck before I've finished with him.'

' Be patient, and don't forget Sardius,' said Johnson, as they reached the gate. ' You carry all I can afford to lose, and a lot some of our crowd can't.'

' What can I do for you, Count ?' asked a good-looking, well-set-up man, whose two clerks were booking wagers as fast as their pencils could travel over the paper. ' Better take a monkey about the mare,' he continued, as the other shook his head. ' All the Queenslanders are going nap on her.'

' What price Io ?' interrupted a fresh client.

6

'Four to one.'

'I'll take a hundred at fives.'

'Four fifty to a hundred, as it's a last wager. Thanks, sir. Book it to Mr. Jardine. Now, Count, shall I book you the same?'

'No, my friend; I never back the sex,' retorted Zenski.

'I'll lay you two to one, Satan, just for a bet, then,' exclaimed the bookmaker. 'They'll be away in a minute, and it's level money everywhere else.'

'You can book it!' said the Russian, as the gong gave the signal; 'I always back the devil!'

As the field for the Grand National drew up in front of the starter, the patrons of the Ledger, deserting purse mysteries and roulette tables, swarmed like ants into the stand, while up out of the paddock their richer brothers streamed into the flag-capped vantage-ground that faced the lawn. In the open land opposite the treble, humanity, balanced on the tops of cabs and family vans, looked over a fringe of heads whose owners clutched with eager fingers the white palings which guarded the track. At the corner nearest the winning-post the Northern contingent had posted themselves; and there Zenski and Dromeroff now joined them.

Skyward all was blue, while from the sea a light wind came, catching as it passed a perfume of heather from the sandy dunes. In the straight way the sunlight glistened on restless splashes of colour, cat-like muscles moving beneath shining skins and glittering steel. From the quick-pulsed stands hundreds of glasses flashed its beams.

As the horses breasted the machine a great silence fell over stands and flat alike. Then the barrier cut through the air, and amid a strange inarticulate roar the gong boomed over the level lands, and on the horses came.

From the jump the lightweights forced the pace, trusting to the dead going to account for the cracks. As they raced past the lawn, Hatten, hanging to the rails for the sake of the firmer going, glanced ahead for Satan's black jacket.

'He's not among 'em,' said Brewster, who lay beside him.

'A bit 'eavy, ain't it?' grunted a voice, and glancing over his shoulder, Dick caught sight of the lightweight's dark muzzle lying on Sardius's quarter.

At the first fence Tartar went round, but the rest of the field, jumping like 'tradesmen,' left it behind. Now they were off the course proper, and the going, though sound, was deader than ever; but scorning all question of elasticity, the front division raced at the water-jump, led by old Recruit, who, true to tradition, seemed determined to make the running while he stood up. Taking a good hold of the mare's head, Dick sent her at the narrow streak. Knowing it was new to her, he had let Sardius up on the inside, and now, to his infinite relief, Satan came up on her other shoulder. Standing feet away, she just saved herself with a scramble, while the favourite and Sardius, flying it without an effort, gained a couple of lengths. Satisfied to be over at all, Hatten now took a strong pull, lying twenty lengths behind the leaders as they galloped along the back stretch. Watching each other, the old man and Brewster began to improve their position as the already trailing field turned their heads towards the treble. With a rattle of hoofs and flashing of whips over raced the leaders, Satan and Sardius jumping neck and neck, both beautifully handled and both full of running.

Leading the ruck, Io faced the timber alone, and, fencing as clean as a stag, woke once more the cheer that had greeted the first flight. Still waiting, the Northern champion lay five lengths behind, as the favourites, moving through the shattered ranks of the light division, flashed side by side over the logs and began to close on the gallant Recruit.

'They've forgotten me,' muttered Dick, as horse after horse began to come back to him. Once over the fence at the bend, he, too, began to move up, and as Satan, leading Sardius by a length, rushed Recruit at the first of the treble and brought him down, Io ran up within half a length of the Melbourne horse, and led him over the last two fences amid the yells of 'Queensland for ever!'

Recognising that he must now make every use of his light weight, the old jockey on Satan drove his mount along in the hope of bringing down Sardius; and feeling that it was no longer wise to let the favourite away, Hatten, still keeping a big hold of the mare, led the Melbourne horse by a length over the jump opposite Oxenham's. Glancing back, the old man saw he had two to deal with, and trusting to his condition, he sat down on his horse to make the pace a cracker. As he did so, Sardius made a run, and closing with Io, the two, leaving the beaten field as though they were anchored, set sail after the light-weight. At the logs they were two lengths behind, and so they raced along the back; but at the next fence Satan struck heavily, and, falling on his knees, lost position. Locked together, Hatten and Brewster raced at the last fence but one—under the whip. As they rose, two tails flashed for a second high in air, then a thousand voices, hoarse with fear, uttered the dread cry: 'They're down!' Pale and white-lipped, the women turned aside. Then, their greed master-ing all of humanity that was in them, the backers of Satan yelled exultantly, 'The favourite wins!' for Sardius lay motionless, and the mare staggered to her feet alone.

'No, by Jingo!' muttered Johnson, between his teeth as Io rose and Hatten sprang up beside her.

Half dazed, the mare struggled to get free as the thunder of Satan's hoofs caught her ear, but running beside her, Hatten, with a supreme effort, vaulted on to her back, and, tossing the reins over her head, set her going before the favourite reached the fence. Still watching through his glasses, Johnson shouted: 'His reins are crossed, and one stirrup gone; my God, the palings!'

Maddened with the fierce excitement of the race, the heavy masses in the stands sent up a roar of exultation that was caught and carried on down the crowded railings and away over the teeming flat. Then in a moment all was still.

The paling fence lay not twenty yards in front of the man who, with reins crossed and stirrup gone, was driving Io at it with whip and spur.

Dead with a broken neck lay Sardius, stretched across his gallant rider, but Satan, blood-smeared and foam enshrouded, strode like an avenging fury not ten lengths behind; so, for a woman's bright eyes and the glory of the North, Dick let Io have her head, and, guiding her with whip and knee, drove her at the centre panel.

Did she know, this gallant daughter of a royal race? I deem she did; but be that as it may, with never a flinch or a swerve, ears pricked, and her eyes be-dimmed yet fearless, she measured her distance, and, rising above the wooden wall, landed with her face set for home, while the bronzed children of the North sent up a shout louder than the cries in dust-shrouded cattle-yards, for Satan had balked, and, even as they cheered, the mare flashed past the judge's box alone.

Carried away by the excitement of the finish, men and women alike had hurried down out of the stand, and Heather and Edith now found themselves stand-ing against the railing, close under the judge's box, surrounded by a jubilant crowd of Queenslanders. Keenly alive to a gallant action, Heather felt a genuine admiration for Hatten, as torn and dusty he now rode back towards the weighing-yard beside the clerk of the course, and followed by Satan, who had got over the palings at the second attempt.

As he rode in, flushed with the pride of victory, and greeted by the cheers of winners and losers alike, Hatten's eyes fell on the woman he loved standing beside the railing. Guiding Io to the picket fence, he pulled up beside her. Then, moved by a sudden impulse, the girl took a buttonhole of violets and

Frank Paton

THE GRAND NATIONAL.

To face page 80.

snowdrops out of her jacket, and, leaning forward, handed it to him. With no thought save that they were her gift, Hatten eagerly stretched out his hand and took the flowers. As he did so a murmur of warning rose, and a dozen hands were thrust out to stop him, while Johnson, springing over the fence, caught his arm, saying, in an audible whisper :

'For God's sake drop them, man !'

'No,' replied Dick, pressing them to his lips and then thrusting them into his jacket, 'I will not'— then, realizing the mistake he had made, he added : 'Surely no man would enter a protest on such grounds.'

Keenly watching, a smile of satisfied malice crept over the wizened face of Satan's jockey. 'The bloomin' swell 'as chucked it away, arter all,' he muttered.

'What !' exclaimed Johnson hotly ; 'would your owner be mean enough to take advantage of a woman's mistake ?'

'See here, mister,' retorted the old man ; 'we goes for the stuff, we does, and what's more, we means to get it. If you thinks you're goin' to rush a man the way your crowd did, and then kid the committee it was all along o' a nosegay, you're d—— well mistaken.'

Following the direction of the man's eyes, Ted saw the old bookmaker who executed the commission in favour of Satan talking to the member of the committee whom report credited with being his biggest backer. As he watched, the significance of what the old jockey had put forward struck him with crushing force.

For a few minutes the crowd waited for the red flag. Then, instead of the signal being hoisted, it was announced that the owner of Satan had entered a protest against the race being awarded to Io on the grounds that her jockey was interfered with before being weighed in.

CHAPTER IX.

THE PROTEST IS DECIDED.

On the Monday after the race, the A.J.C. committee sat to decide the protest entered against Io. The outspoken indignation of the public, and the private efforts of not a few prominent racing men, had alike failed to induce the owner of Satan to withdraw his charge.

'My horse is heavily backed,' was his answer to both argument and appeal, 'and I mean to go by the rules.'

Unfortunately on this point they were singularly clear, and as the member who was supposed to have plunged heavily on Satan put it : ' They would stultify themselves as a responsible body if they broke through a clearly-stated and most important regulation for the sake of sentiment.'

This settled the matter, and as a question of racing law the committee upheld the objection, and awarded the race to Satan.

As Hatten and Johnson walked out of the committee - room, Ted laid his hand on his friend's shoulder.

'It's a cursed shame, old chap,' he said, ' a cowardly
robbery. I wish I had the committee in nigger
country for about half an hour.'

Turning a face a trifle white, Dick replied coolly,
almost cheerfully :

' They couldn't help it, Ted ; every man of them,
bar Mills, would have given me the race if he could.
We have to thank him and that dog from Grabben
Gullen for the lot.'

' Well, we're in the soup, any way,' retorted Ted
ruefully, ' every mother's son of us ; but there, old
man,' as Dick started to apologize, ' none of that : you
rode like a hero for us ; it makes me mad to think it
was all for nothing.'

' You forgot my lady's gift,' said Dick lightly. 'Ted,'
he continued, ' you may call me as big a fool as you
like, but that bunch of flowers means more to me
than all I have lost.'

' Oh, confound your lady's gift ! I wish she'd kept
her flowers to herself!' exclaimed Johnson wrathfully.
' I didn't think Heather was such a fool.'

' Neither did I,' said Hatten absently ; ' but never
mind, I'm awfully sorry for all the fellows who backed
me, and I admit it's a bit of a facer ; still, it's not the
first. Let's have a drink.'

' Look here, Dick,' said Johnson as they drove out
later to Irish Town together, ' we know each other
well enough for me to speak straight : I've got a
hundred left ; will you go me partners in it for, say, a
couple of months ?'

' No, thanks, old chap,' answered Hatten ; ' as luck
has it, I find I have held on to enough to get Billy,

the mare, and myself up North again. But you've put me in your debt just as much as though I hadn't.'

'Nonsense!' muttered the bushman, anxious like all his craft to deprecate any imputation of generosity. 'What do you think of this talk about the Russians collaring India? It's not much in my line, but I heard them gassing about it at breakfast yesterday, and old Zenski said something about our sending another contingent. As you're a bit given to soldiering, I thought you might be on for going.'

'I gave that up years ago,' answered Dick—'in fact, ever since I was Lieutenant in Orloff's Mounted Rifles in Brisbane.'

'Was not that the chap who shot a man and escaped from the steamer at Colombo, the time Miss Cameron was coming out?'

'Yes,' replied Hatten, flushing slightly; 'and, say what they will, I'll swear the fellow deserved it. Orloff was a hot-tempered beggar, but as straight as a die.'

'People said at the time that he was jealous about——'

'People are idiots!' interrupted Dick, for this was a question he would never willingly discuss, both because he knew it was Heather's wish to let it die, and because, feeling there was much truth in it, it pained him. 'But about this contingent business; if it is got up, I won't be one.'

'Why, the last was a regular picnic!'

'That's right enough; and don't think I'm funking,

Ted; but the fact is, I fancy we'll be all wanted at home before long.'

'Why, the Unionists are dead to the world!'

'Perhaps. Cheeky as the beggars were, it would be better if they weren't,' replied Hatten seriously. 'I don't like all this land-grant, syndicate business, Ted. Queensland—at any rate, up North—is full of Kanakas and coolie scum. All the old squatters are either gone or are managing for a lot of Johnnies who never saw Australia, and don't care a rap for it so long as dividends come in.'

'It's a bit sick, I'll admit; but you know what a devil of a time the Unions gave us before McLoskie let in cheap labour.'

'If I'm not mistaken, old Zenski and that Levant crowd at Point Parker will give us a worse time still,' retorted Hatten. 'I don't cotton to these oily foreigners.'

'But, hang it, man! Zenski hates the Russian Government like poison,' exclaimed Johnson in astonishment.

'So he says,' retorted Dick suspiciously. 'But I wouldn't trust the sneering old devil as far as I could pitch him; and what's more, I'd like to see something more reliable between us and the Russian squadron than a lot of Kalmuck stockmen and coolie sugar-slaves.'

Just then the cab pulled up in front of Io's quarters, and Johnson forgot to reply as he caught sight of Billy's head stuck out of the horse-box.

With arms resting on the top of the lower door, the trainer watched his visitors' approach.

'Well, Billy, what do you think of it?' asked Hatten.

'I think they're a lot of pigs—not ordinary swine, but sandy-haired, long-tailed hogs, with manes on their backs!' replied the trainer, adding solemnly, as he spat over his left arm: 'Blast 'em!'

'How's the mare?'

'Barring bein' a bit cut about the stifles, and generally gravel-rashed, she's fit to go out now an' give that d——d mosquiter-chested waster three stone and a floggin'!'

Walking up to his favourite, Dick ran his hand lightly over her swelled stifles; then, caressing the head that she bent towards him, he said a trifle bitterly:

'You're all I've left, old girl.'

'What have I done, Master Dick?' muttered a voice at his elbow.

'Your best, Billy,' replied Dick gratefully. 'It was all my fault.'

'All a woman's tomfoolery,' grunted Johnson.

'See here, Mister Johnson,' said Billy. 'You know my general opinion of wimmin?'

'They're the ruin of boys and stables—eh, Billy? You're about right in this case.'

'Well, given in all about this affair, I don't include Miss Heather in no such opinion.'

'Why?'

'She ain't a woman.'

'What the deuce is she, then?'

'She's a Duchess; the King never knighted a better.'

Absurd as Billy's compliment was, Hatten's heart warmed towards him as it had never done before.

'You're right, Billy,' he said heartily. 'Get Io on board the mail to-morrow night, and next season we'll give them another taste of our quality without the chance of winning on a foul.'

CHAPTER X.

A PEEP BEHIND THE CURTAIN.

THE night after the Grand National Zenski and his friend, Alexis Dromeroff, sat over the fire in the former's room at the Australia.

'So the mine is about to be fired, Colonel,' said Zenski, who for the last half-hour had been a silent but attentive listener.

'Yes,' replied his companion; 'the work Peter left as a legacy is practically accomplished. The path that has taken centuries to tread, and which even in the last hundred years has cost Russia one hundred million pounds, has at last landed us within striking distance of Herat.'

'And——'

'And at the gates of India,' said the soldier, as he rose and walked up and down the room. 'Zenski,' he went on, in a voice low, but full of fierce excitement, 'what a prize lies at the feet of the Czar! Worth all the blood and treasure poured out on desert steppes, eh?—worth as much again!'

'But that is not India, my friend,' interrupted Zenski.

'It is its gate, and, thanks to English statesmen, we are in full possession of the ways which can bring us there quickly, and without trouble.'

'As a base it would be doubtless admirable, I admit,' remarked the Count; 'but we are not exactly there yet.'

'Not there,' retorted Dromeroff impatiently, 'when a Persian army practically led by Russian officers is there? Persia, liable to an attack all along the frontier, already Russianized in great part, and at best an inert mass ready for moulding as we wish, will hold it long enough, thanks to England's policy of masterly inactivity and settlement by commissioners, for us to make our spring at our leisure.'

'But suppose England alters her policy for one of action?'

'No fear of that!' laughed the Colonel contemptuously. 'Being commercial, they will bargain. But even so, as you well know, the mountain barrier between our outposts and Herat is all moonshine; nothing more formidable than downs crossed by roads nearly all practicable lies between us and the pearl of the East. When we won Merv and conquered the Turcomans, it meant not only prestige in the eyes of every nomad, but the possession of one hundred thousand of the best irregular cavalry in the world within a week's march of Herat. They have led the way to India before; as our vanguard, they will do so again.'

'Skobeleff's idea; but, remember, he is dead,' observed Zenski.

'He is,' replied Dromeroff sadly, almost reverently;

for to him, as to every Russian soldier, the conqueror of Geok-Tepé was a type to follow, a hero to worship; 'but others are left to carry out his dream.'

'It appears possible enough,' muttered the more cautious diplomat. 'We overcame more formidable difficulties in invading Turkey. The men who forced the Balkans should be able to march over the Paropamisus Downs in face of the Afghan forces, supposing them to be there at all, without much difficulty.'

'There is no difficulty,' said Dromeroff, 'for there is no barrier between Russia and India. The tribes are the least warlike, and the most amenable to our influence; the country is rich, and the road excellent; we have long given up the old hard track, and now can rattle along from the Caspian to Candahar.'

'From my despatches I understand that the massing of the Army of the Caucasus in the Caspian basin is complete.'

'The columns that are to invade India,' Dromeroff went on, 'will, as you probably guess, march *viâ* the Astrabad-Sarakhs road, and the parallel one from Astrabad *viâ* Meshed. On reaching the Hari Rud at Kusan the Astrabad force will leave the Paropamisus Hills on its left flank, cutting Herat off from India. Arrangements have already been made with the Shah to use the Golden Province as a line of advance and base of operations.'

'And how about the Indians themselves?' queried Zenski.

'They have been seen to. In the bazaars Russian prestige is common talk. Like Shere Ali, they begin

7

to think " the goat attacks, not the panther." Unlike us, as you know, England has been unable to identify herself with her Asiatic peoples. She dares not let them command her armies as we have done. Into her Civil Service they have certainly been admitted, but at what a sacrifice. Scorned by the members of the caste he has broken, shunned by his English fellow-officials, what a hell is that of the native civil servant! Again, thanks to her system of educating every villager, India is full of native demagogues railing at a Government which has educated, but cannot find billets for them. In such soil our agents have sown a magnificent crop. It is now ready for reaping. The advance of the Cossacks across the frontier will be the signal for a native uprising.'

' Then you reckon on getting the English army of defence between two fires ?'

' Simultaneously with the rush of fifty or one hundred thousand Turcomans and other Asiatic cavalry over the frontier under the banner of blood and booty, we expect the natives to rise at the rear of the Indus to the cry of "Freedom and revenge !"'

' Given that the native troops join the mutiny, I fail to see what the seventy thousand English can do even if massed to a man,' said Zenski.

' They can die, that is all,' replied Dromeroff, adding with a certain reluctant admiration, 'and they will. Summed up,' he continued, ' we have an uninterrupted chain of communication from the interior of Russia to the very gates of India. Besides the standing army of the Caucasus, one hundred and fifty thousand strong, we can get support from Odessa to Batoum in one day. With the water way and railroads now completed, we can carry troops from Odessa to Sarakhs in six days. On the other hand, the English, even with the railway complete to Pishin, are still four hundred and seventy miles from Herat. Our line of march is fertile, level and well watered. Theirs is through a country frequently arid, and menaced by tribes as likely to prove hostile as not. Twenty days from our present base will land us under the walls of Herat. It will take the English forty-seven days to arrive at the same point. With India disaffected, Persia under our thumb, and Afghanistan more or less under our influence, awed by our successes, and ever ready to follow the rising star, the fates themselves seem to guide our rush on India.'

'As a means to an end it is admirable,' said Zenski coolly. 'Had the pig-headed English given Constantinople to Alexander, it would have been all unnecessary.'

'Possibly. Still, remember we are a nation of conquest; and as Skobeleff said, "Without India, all the money spent in Turkestan is wasted, and the hide is not worth the tanning." Skobeleff merely saw in the invasion of India a means of drawing off the English forces while we seized Constantinople, *mon ami*. The same reason remains good to-day; is it not so? But what of my old friend Leroy?'

'Doubtless his letter has told you all that I can say; the authorities at Pekin, satisfied at last that Russia is the Power whose friendship is best worth having, will put no impediment in his way. Our

action during the Corean War in '94, and the late
operations on the Pamirs, are bearing fruit ?'

'To a certain extent, yes. Still, there are other
and weightier reasons. Doubtless the prospect of
our breaking into India is hailed at Pekin with satisfaction as being likely to draw off our attention from
their own frontier. They, I take it, judge that we
will hold what we win ; and as it is a richer country,
they naturally conclude that all our serious expansion
will take place southward. This practically means the
removal of a constant menace to their whole inland
frontier line. They, on their part, hopeless of breaking
through our cordon, look to Australia as their natural
prey. To the old Conservative section this idea of
fresh conquest is still hateful ; but the younger or
up-to-date party, educated abroad and filled with
the ambitions of the Western world, hold possession
of the Emperor's ear, and have filled him with a
desire to revive the glorious traditions of Genghis
Khan. With all this Leroy has had much to do. Ever
since, outwardly as an American soldier of fortune,
in reality as a servant of the Czar, he undertook the
reorganization of the Chinese army, he has been a
power. The fact that he played so active a part in
the Corean War has stood him in good stead, and
his success in suppressing the late rebellion, and so
winning the favour of the Emperor for Ching Tu,
the General nominally in command of the imperial
army, has naturally also gained him the friendship
of the Marquis. Fired by the accounts of how his
countrymen are ill-treated over here—accounts, I may
say, grossly exaggerated—and aware both by hearsay

and personal knowledge of Australia's weaknesses and
magnificent possibilities as an outlet alike for Chinese
rascality and industry, Ching Tu has eagerly taken
up Leroy's idea. Still, such is the magnificent
duplicity of the Chinese and the colossal gullibility
of the British officials, that nothing is suspected.
Outwardly Russia and China are ready again to fly
at each other's throats. The Russians are concentrating an army on the Caspian to occupy the Pamirs.
The imperial dockyards and arsenals are working
night and day turning out warlike material to resist
their old enemy. In point of fact, my dear Zenski,
as you know, our army is meant for India, and
a Chinese fleet is ready, once we draw off the
English squadron, to throw thirty thousand men on
Australia.'

'Leroy tells me the Chinese Government still
refuse to officially recognise his action,' remarked
Zenski.

'Yes,' laughed Dromeroff; 'they have taken a leaf
out of our Central Asian code ; he is only to be
acknowledged if successful. But it is too apparent ;
and if he fails, they will find it out.'

'If he once lands, he can't fail,' said the Count.
'Australia is to be had for the taking. The keeping
it, if England survives, is, *pardieu*, another matter.'

'With that we have nothing to do,' said Dromeroff
cynically. 'The invasion gives Russia a freer hand
by diverting the Chinese forces, and extends England's
already unwieldy defensive base. Will you be ready
for us ?'

'When you wish,' replied the Count, rising and

walking to a table on which lay unfolded a map of Queensland.

On the map the three great areas divided by watersheds were carefully traced, as also every railway line, road and town; positions also of artesian bores and distances between stages were all ticked off.

'The lines marked red are those which I have constructed,' remarked Zenski; 'but all these are practically in our hands;' and he went on, in cold, critical tones: 'It appears to me that the line from Normanton to Hughenden and Longreach, that from Normanton to Cloncurry, and the trunk-line from Point Parker *viâ* Bourketown and Cloncurry to Charleville, can all be utilized for strategic purposes.'

'They will be invaluable!' exclaimed the soldier, keenly following the dotted lines, ' if they will only let us make use of them.'

'They cannot help themselves,' replied Zenski. 'The whole country is practically held by land-grant railway syndicates and Melbourne and London corporations: all the properties worth mentioning are worked on the tributary system by means of cheap alien labour. The white population, never numerous, has, with the exception of a few poor whites, vanished. We hold by means of our grants the trunk-lines, and can transport a force from Point Parker to Charleville in fourteen hours sufficiently strong to hold it until reinforcements come up.'

'But how about supplies?' asked Dromeroff; 'remember, our attacking force will number at least thirty thousand.'

'The Levantine firm at Point Parker are prepared

to supply everything necessary both as regards war material and food supplies.'

'I know that. But supposing our base is cut off?'

'It won't be,' replied Zenski; 'but even so, nearly all the country intersected by our lines of advance is well grassed and watered. Cattle are to be got everywhere, and sheep are kept in the country round Cloncurry and Hughenden.'

'You are certain as to the water?'

'Perfectly. Where there was none our bores now provide a limitless supply.'

'We are bringing no horses. Will there be any difficulty in mounting the cavalry?'

'None; a sufficient number can always be reckoned on, and, to put the question beyond doubt, we have been collecting drafts for some months, ostensibly to open up a trade with India and Japan.'

'You are to be complimented, my dear Count,' exclaimed Dromeroff admiringly. 'On paper it appears as though the whole affair will resolve itself into a large picnic catered for by yourself.'

'Rather thank the admirable Sir Peter McLoskie, whose policy has made my work a pleasure,' laughed Zenski. 'But to return, when is the dash to be made? The last of my work will be complete in two months at most, and, if possible, I would wish that my Asiatic workmen should be utilized as food for powder.'

'What, Zenski, do you wish to give them a share of the plunder?'

'No, *mon ami*,' replied the director cynically; 'I

merely thought it would be a cheap means of disposing of them.'

'Anything to oblige you, Count,' grinned Dromeroff; 'three months should bring things to a head. When will you be ready to show me over the country?'

'We can start at the end of the week, and, as there is much of detail to work out, I will run over to China with you and see Leroy in person. Fill your glass, Dromeroff.'

'To the Yellow Wave!' said the soldier.

'And Sir Peter McLoskie!' added the diplomat.

CHAPTER XI.

WHILE sending Io by rail, as being less likely to knock her about, Hatten had booked a passage for himself in the *Barcoo*, sailing at four the same afternoon.

Johnson, whose leave and loose cash were alike nearly at an end, was going with his chum.

After lunch, while the two men were having a smoke over a last 'hundred up,' Mrs. Enson, Edith, and Heather remained chatting upstairs. Ever since she had been led out of the surging mob by Zenski half dazed and nearly mad with vexation, not at what she had done, but at the thought of its possible consequences, Heather had never ceased to bitterly regret her folly. It seemed as though she was fated to bring ruin on all who loved her. Orloff, the hero of her maidenhood, wore for her sake the brand of Cain, and now this glad-hearted, reckless wooer, who had asked in vain for a love not hers to give, had received from her hand defeat in the moment of victory, ruin in the guise of friendship. Yesterday the result of her action had been put beyond all doubt by the committee's decision. That Hatten had never by word or look reproached her—nay, rather, that he seemed to think all well lost in return for her ill-starred gift—only added new poignancy to her grief. His manner since the race had won her respect; his gallant ride her admiration, for, though it was but an exhibition of physical pluck, Heather's heart, being that of a woman of flesh and blood, went out to the daring horseman who counted her guerdon a recompense for every loss. Still, while all this was true, she knew that the man in shadow-land held all her love, and so the realization that Hatten had put a construction on her tribute to his bravery totally at variance with her real motives awoke in her a feeling akin to despair. Early taught the bitter lesson of self-restraint, and naturally averse from discussing such a subject, the girl exhibited to her companions nothing save a pardonable feeling of pain and annoyance in being the unthinking agent in losing for Hatten and others so much money. In talking of their friend's departure, the subject of Io's defeat again came up.

'I am sure,' said easy-going, fat Mrs. Enson in answer to an expression of regret, 'that the whole thing was sweetly romantic, but, ahem, a trifle indiscreet, my dear.'

'That I do not see,' replied Heather; 'it was purely my affair, mother, and, but for the consequences to Dick, I can't see what harm there was in it.'

This was really the keynote of the girl's character. So long as an action concerned only herself, and was in her own eyes harmless, she utterly refused to be the slave of conventionalism. Possessed of no particular force of character, Mrs. Enson naturally took refuge from all her perplexities behind the *convenances*. With her, to be natural was to be indiscreet, to be narrow was to be respectable. The old lady, like the majority of her fellow-matrons, was the result of an environment peculiar to the British nation.

'My child,' she went on, 'your one care should be to avoid being talked about.' Then, warned by the flush that came into the girl's white cheeks that she had touched an open sore, she added hastily: 'I am afraid both Edward and Richard lost large sums of money.'

'Pots,' interrupted Edith.

'Pots?' exclaimed Mrs. Enson, putting on her glasses, and gazing severely at her daughter. 'I was not aware that they speculated with cooking utensils on the racecourse.'

'Don't you know what I mean, mother?' laughed Edith.

'I regret to say that I do,' replied her mother sadly. 'Your slang is a sore trial to me. But if I did not make myself conversant with it, I would be unable to understand much of what you say.'

'Well, I apologize, mother!' said the girl, rising, and putting her arm round the old lady's neck. 'Why is this poor cat so sad?'

'There, Edith, that will do; I forgive you. And, Heather, you must not fret about your mistake; I can assure you that everyone I have spoken to is exceedingly nice about it.'

'See what it is to be a pretty woman,' murmured Edith.

'I hope those who have lost forgive me for a better reason than that,' said Heather simply.

'I am sure of it, dear,' interposed Mrs. Enson. 'Count Zenski told me your action reminded him of the days of chivalry, and awoke his highest admiration.'

'So I should think!' exclaimed Edith. 'Horrid old thing! Why, Ted tells me he backed Satan.'

'The Count is a perfect gentleman, and a man I greatly admire,' remarked Mrs. Enson with dignity. 'He never uses slang.'

'How do you know, mother? Remember, we don't understand Russian.'

'I must confess that, in spite of his cynicism, I can't help liking him,' said Heather. 'I think he shows us his worst side.'

'Well, you're both welcome to your opinions,' retorted Edith obstinately. 'But I can't endure him; I hate a man—a man—well, a man who swears in French. He's always *mon-dieuing* and *pardieuing*. I wonder what people would think if Ted or Dick gave the English version.'

'My dear,' said her mother, 'that makes all the difference. No one has a greater horror of profanity than I; but I understand foreigners of the highest rank always make use of such expressions. You will remember, Edith, our late cook invariably did.'

'And he was a count in his own land,' interrupted Heather, with a look at her friend.

'And took all our loose belongings away when he

left, doubtless to hang as curios in his Roman palace,'
added Edith, as the door opened and Johnson and
Hatten walked in.

'If you are ready, I think we will have to make a
move. It's after three, and the steamer pulls out at
four,' said Ted. 'Zenski and the other Russian
fellow are down below, so we had better take a four-
wheeler.'

Hatten remained silent. He could not help con-
trasting his own position with that of his friend.

'Come on, girls; let us put on our hats,' said Mrs.
Enson. 'How thoughtful of the Count to come and
look after us!'

'If he can manage yourself and Heather, I will be
content with Mr. Dromeroff,' murmured Edith mischievously.

'D—— these foreigners, Dick!' muttered Ted, when
the ladies had disappeared. 'I believe you're right,
they're worth watching.'

On board the *Barcoo* preparations for getting under
way were everywhere apparent. Dense clouds of
smoke poured ceaselessly from the black funnels, and
a constant stream of baggage-laden porters climbed
up the gangways. In the saloon Mrs. Enson was
giving Johnson a bewildering torrent of commands,
ranging from a solemn injunction as to how he was to
explain the race episode to Heather's father, down to
a charge as to his conduct with regard to sundry
setting hens. Meanwhile Dromeroff looked after
Edith with an adherence to detail that roused in
Ted's breast a desire to rescue her, even, if need be,
over his prospective mother-in-law's body. On the

upper deck Heather and Hatten stood looking down
into the dark, forbidding water. On its inky surface
things lost or cast away floated in hopeless, purposeless confusion. It seemed to both watchers that in
some sort below lay sketched a picture of their lives.

They, too, seemed born for failure—straws cast by
fate to wander helplessly over the sea of chance. For
the past half-hour few words had been spoken; both
were afraid to speak — the one because she feared
another avowal, the other because he distrusted his
powers of self-restraint.

At last the warning bell rang out, and, turning
towards his companion, Hatten took her hand in his.

'Heather,' he said huskily, 'am I still to drift on
like one of those goalless atoms—one of a great company, and still alone?'

Looking into his eyes, she answered softly and
sadly :

'Dick, I, too, am searching for my star; will you
bear me company?'

It was daring, but it did not miss its mark; the
man's hope died, but in its stead his nobler self arose.

'Heather,' he answered wistfully, 'I have found my
star ; and even if in searching for yours I lose it forever, I will bear you company.'

CHAPTER XII.

LADY BAGGS GIVES A DINNER.

SIR JOHN BAGGS was both an ex-Cabinet Minister and a member of the existing Parliament, and Lady Baggs was his wife. Sometimes, possibly, he wished she was not; but, then, wives are more difficult to drop than most other early associations. Not that her ladyship had not risen to the occasion. In point of fact, her expansion had been phenomenal. Perhaps the fact that she had seen so much of them in her young days had disgusted her with the 'lower orders'; but be that as it may, her ladyship's arrogance to the creatures who remained creatures was now only exceeded by her affability towards the creatures who, like herself, had become plutocrats. This was occasionally a little embarrassing for Sir John, as the masses managed to retain their memories, which did not matter, and occasionally voted accordingly, which did. In one respect, however, his wife was a distinct advance on the member for Frog's Hole. Being a woman, she had adapted herself to her new surroundings, and, so far as the conventionalities were concerned, passed muster as a lady, until one got to know her. Sir John, on the other hand, in the first five minutes told you he was a self-made man, and in the next ten made you wish to Heaven he had failed to create himself.

The arrival in Sydney of Sir Peter McLoskie, Premier of Queensland and high-priest of land-grant railways and cheap alien labour, had suggested to Lady Baggs the idea of showing off her husband's costly steam-yacht by means of a water-party.

Sir John, being largely interested in sugar-plantations, and consequently a warm admirer of the Northern Premier, gladly fell in with the project. In his eyes Sir Peter was a veritable champion, fighting for law and order as against anarchy and the annihilation of the sacred bulwarks of 'vested rights.' For Australia was practically divided into two hostile factions, one of which denominated itself Capital, the other Labour. One, because it possessed money, assumed that the national prosperity depended solely on its absolute ascendancy. The other, because it dug and delved, held as illogically that it alone possessed the right of shaping the nation's destinies. Distinct from, and disregarded by, both these opposing forces stood a vast number of people who, in the popular sense, were neither capitalists nor yet labourers. These, because they refused to admit that either of the above classes were of necessity the salt of the earth, were scorned by both. But for some inexplicable reason, while viewing with suspicion the blatant advocates both of capital and labour, this vast section, representing the real intellectual and creating power of Australasia, sat idly by, allowing itself in turn to be made the cat's-paw of both parties.

For the present Capital was in the ascendant. Labour, torn by a thousand petty jealousies, and led by men either wanting in administrative ability or unable to hold the confidence of the heterogeneous masses under their command, had hurled itself against the solid phalanx of wealth, only to fall back broken and more disunited than before. The silent despot, pitiless and strong enough to lead alone, and un-trammelled by the interference of petty agitators, had *not as yet* arisen, and so labour shouted its empty *threats* and shook its nerveless fists, and capital occupied both its wind and its hands in building up stronger barriers against the day of wrath. As a skilled engineer in this work of fortification Sir Peter McLoskie stood alone.

So the water-party was to take the form of a welcome, and to lend to it extra significance, the Premier, the leader of the Opposition, and other prominent social and political lights, among them Count Zenski and Dromeroff, were invited.

The lunch, served in the luxurious if somewhat floridly-decorated saloon of the *Aphrodite*, was worthy of its givers. As Zenski muttered to his neighbour, 'Who better should be able to create dishes than a one-time cook?'

Edith chanced to have Sir Robert Blake for a companion. Usually a delightful raconteur, he to-day started off on his favourite hobby, Russian aggression.

'I assure you, we may see them at any moment,' said he impressively.

'How delightful!' replied his listener cheerfully. 'I suppose, if they do come, furs will be all the rage; and they are so becoming, you know, Sir Robert.'

'You might find the Bear's claw less comforting than his fur, young lady,' retorted the leader of the Opposition, and then he changed the subject.

On one side of Heather sat Dromeroff, on the other the Minister for War. As McFee found it difficult to talk and eat at the same time, he invariably devoted himself to the more practical exercise. Thus the girl found herself given over to the Russian.

Unlike Zenski, Dromeroff, if cynical, seldom let his cynicism be seen, and, being a soldier, never neglected an opportunity of making himself agreeable to a pretty woman. As he had been everywhere, Heather soon found that many spots in the older world were known to them both. Still haunted by the idea that the man had possibly met her lover, the girl felt a singular interest in speaking to him, hoping that he might at any moment tell her something of the story her soul hungered to hear.

On the right of the host sat Sir Peter McLoskie. Stout and somewhat bloated, his face exhibited in a marked degree the characteristics both of command and fixity of purpose. It was the face of a strong man, one who to gain his ends would sacrifice much, possibly even that strange, impalpable thing called honour. At one period of his career he, like Sir Robert Blake, had posed as a Republican. Visionaries spoke of him as the possible president of a United Australia. But that was long ago. To-day he was Dictator of Queensland, and head and front of a powerful oligarchy, whose plantations covered the North, whose railways shot their snake-like arms far into the interior, and whose cheap alien labour created dividends unknown in the days when a white population existed. He was working out his destiny. Figs do not grow on thistles, neither could the cap of the Republican long sit on a head that might have belonged to a Roman Emperor. He was now expatiating to Sir John on the beauties of his policy.

'Socialism and anarchy are dead,' said he; 'the unions crushed, and, thank God, we have won back *the confidence* of the foreign capitalists. Trade was never so flourishing, for, through our introduction of cheap labour, the plantations have at last been made to pay.'

'I am aware of it, my dear sir,' interposed Sir John enviously. 'Here we are blocked at hevery turn. Last session my Bill to enable the Government to dispose of our existing railways, and so pay off our national debt, was thrown out on the second reading by a majority of ten !'

'Surely that was bad generalship ?'

'But, my dear sir,' protested Baggs, 'we couldn't persuade everybody.'

'*We* did. You remember the fuss there was about our Land-grant Railway Bill ?'

Sir John nodded.

'It was a big fight, but we won. Every man with a stake in the country fought nobly for us ; and what is the result ?' asked McLoskie proudly.

'Well, what is it ?' queried a Queenslander, who, though a friend, was politically opposed to the Premier.

'It is this,' answered McLoskie, glaring at his questioner : ' We have hundreds of miles of railway constructed for nothing, and, thanks to the introduction of coolies, the labour unions are crushed, while the profits from the sugar, coffee, and cattle properties are enormous.'

'And who gets them ?' asked the Queenslander dubiously.

'The capitalists, of course—the men who make a country.'

'And live out of it.'

Ignoring the remark, McLoskie went on :

.'You should be the last to grumble, considering the market we have opened up with the East for the Northern cattle.'

· 'I prefer not to be living in a suburb of Canton, all the same,' muttered the Northern man, one of the few left who could call his station and his soul his own.

'Isn't it possible to overdo this question ?' asked Sir Robert Blake. ' Clearly understand that I merely ask for information. I am sure you know me well enough to acquit me of all sympathy with unionism.'

'My dear Sir Robert,' answered McLoskie, 'practically it is only in its infancy. Of its beneficial results you can already judge. Eventually all Northern Australia must adopt our method. As you know, it is already in full force in that part of the Northern territory lately sold to England.'.

'With what result ?'

'A magnificent one. There, under the old system, a territory as big as Spain, France, and Great Britain, watered near the coast by navigable rivers, and in

many parts splendidly fertile, remained a waste, simply
because white labour refused to work it at a price
which would leave a margin of profit.'

'I always understood the climate was the great
difficulty?' hazarded a sporting doctor.

'It doesn't trouble the Chinaman, apparently,'
grinned McLoskie. 'The whole country has been
taken up by English and other capitalists, and
Kalmuck stockmen and coolie plantation hands are
working it for them. They only want our friend to
build them a few railways,' added the Premier, 'to
make it as big a paradise as our own Gulf country.'

'I am always at the service of the Australians,'
replied Zenski politely, 'in particular at that of Sir
Peter McLoskie.'

'I hope your company will reap as rich a harvest
as their enterprise deserves, Count,' said the Premier.

'Be at rest,' replied the Russian. 'I feel certain
that before long our traffic will increase amazingly.'

'Is there no danger of these aliens becoming a
menace to the whole of the colonies?' asked the
doctor who had before spoken.

'Bah! they are slaves,' exclaimed Zenski. 'A
crack of the whip will always frighten beasts of
burden.'

'The Count is right,' added McLoskie. 'From
them there is nothing to fear; their natural position
is in the North. If they are a menace at all it is to
the unions, and if for that alone we must retain them.
Once let the coolies go, and good-bye for ever to commercial prosperity.'

'You are right, Sir Peter,' said Zenski. 'And

what, after all, is the discontent of a few *canaille* as compared with the vast industries and vested rights you are fostering?'

'While I am quite with you, McLoskie, with regard to coloured labour for the plantations,' remarked the New South Wales Premier, a handsome, somewhat Jewish type of man, noted alike for his opposition to the new unionism and for possessing the courage of his opinions, 'still, there is no hiding the fact that your confounded Chinamen are spreading all over the Southern colonies. Personally I can see little to choose between the two classes of labour.'

'Then why trouble, my friend?' interposed Zenski. 'The Chinaman is cheaper and will obey; what more do you want?'

'Nothing from that standpoint, Count,' retorted the Hon. Henry Lewis; 'but while I am determined that this colony is not to be ruled by labour leaders, I am just as certain that the people will not tolerate its becoming a Chinese camp, and I am with them so far.'

'Then we must have federation,' suggested the sporting doctor, who was a bit of a humorist in his way.

For a moment there was a silence, such as falls when a crime is referred to in the presence of the perpetrators.

'I observe, gentlemen,' said Sir John Baggs, 'that our political discussion has driven the ladies on deck. I propose that we follow them.'

As Sir John had said, the ladies, and, indeed, most of the men, had silently stolen away, and now the small group who remained rose to follow.

'But what about federation, Baggs?' persisted the doctor as they reached the deck.

'Federation is in the hair, doctor,' replied the ex-Minister solemnly.

Graceful as a sea-bird, the sharp-prowed pleasure-boat moved on down the winding river. They had lunched in one of the inlets above the Brothers, and now steamed homeward past the broken column which rises out of the water, whose rippling waves have known the swift, strong sweep of many a stout-armed oarsman. Now the white monument of the dead and forgotten champion fades scarce swifter than his fame, and they are moving on with gardened villas on either shore.

As the *Aphrodite* swung round Dawes Point, a Government launch ran alongside.

'A message for the Premier!' shouted a man standing in her stern.

Lying to for a moment, the yacht again steamed on towards the Governor's stairs. Tearing open the envelope, the Hon. Henry Lewis glanced at its contents. On the deck the conversation had ceased. All felt that some strange, possibly fateful thing had happened.

Holding up his hand, the head of the Government read slowly:

'Can Australia supply 5,000 men if needed?'
            'DUNDAS,
                      'Viceroy of India.'

For a moment no one spoke. Then the Premier said, glancing at the leader of the Opposition:

' What do you think ?'

' Think !' exclaimed Sir Robert Blake.   ' Act, man !
—cable back "Yes." '

' Gentlemen,' said Zenski, ' although not of your
blood, permit me to call for three cheers for the flag
of the free !'

Moved by a common impulse, they cheered till the
stevedores on the ships ran to the bulwarks and the
men in the boats around them lay on their oars.
Then, led by Sir Robert, they sang the national
anthem, and the sailors on the warships took it up,
and the people on the shore carried it on.

So on sea and land his subjects shouted, ' God save
the King !'   Why, few of them knew, and less of them
cared.

' Will they be fools enough to do it?' whispered
Dromeroff amid the din.

' Why not ?' replied Zenski.   ' They suspect nothing,
and if they did, *pardieu*, these democrats would sell
their souls for a star.'

CHAPTER XIII.

QUEENSLAND IN 1954.

PROVIDED with free passes, Zenski and his friend
travelled north to Charleville on the Government
lines of New South Wales and Queensland. Here
the Count and his companion spent a day. As the
honoured guest of the Mayor, the Colonel was enabled
without cost or inconvenience to study from a military
standpoint the position and possibilities of a decidedly
uninteresting Bush town, while the managing director
received the reports of his engineers and personally
inspected the completion of an embankment, ostensibly to be used as sidings for spare trucks, but
which, with little trouble, could be converted into a
formidable earthwork. Though not yet complete in
detail, the line connecting Point Parker with Brisbane
was in reality open.

Untrammelled by all question of unionism, Zenski
had poured an army of Asiatic workmen into the Gulf,
and these, at a nominal wage, had carried his trunk-
line silently and swiftly across the eight hundred miles
of easy country that lay between the sea and Charleville.

Ever since the connections had become an established fact, one inevitable result began to show itself. Traffic started to ebb from the Government railways running towards the coast, setting in with no uncertain stream in the direction of Normanton and Point Parker.

As their reward for constructing this giant sucker, which, with its companion branches, only wanted time to divert all that produce to receive which millions had been spent by the State in building railways, dredging rivers, and constructing harbours, the combined syndicates had received two hundred million acres of the best land in Queensland.

Practically everything was gone save a strip along the coast already in great part held by other speculators, a few blocks hemmed in by the railway grants, and which were being rapidly bought up, and one . barren, hopeless corner peopled with disease and death—the God-forgotten 'No man's land' which buries its sun-scorched head in the sea at Cape York.

Built by alien hands, these railways were for fifty years the absolute property of the syndicates, while the lands through which they ran—saving only such intervening blocks as were not worth securing—remained the property of their constructors for ever.

Round Point Parker these enterprising capitalists had early secured every inch of ground, and on the shores of the Gulf a town had already arisen which bade fair to become the one city of Queensland. Under the new system, hundreds of thousands of pounds once paid by pastoral tenants had gone into the pockets of the syndicates. Legitimate squatting was dead. Individual effort in all industrial pursuits had ceased, but sugar-planting and cattle-raising flourished; for the Kanaka labourer and the Kalmuck stockman did more for a penny than the white man would do for a pound.

Queensland poured out a golden harvest, and law and order reigned supreme; but the harvest was for foreign consumption, and the peace was that which overshadows a land whose national life is sinking into the depths of forgotten aspirations.

After a day's stay at Charleville, the Count travelled North by special train, his luxurious private car with dining-saloon attached being the only weight behind the powerful electric engine.

Lounging in their comfortable chairs, smoking cigars from Zenski's special box, the two *soi-disant* victims of tyrant-ridden Russia followed their course on a map that lay spread on a table between them. At each point marked as a camp the train pulled up, so that Dromeroff might give an opinion as to its suitability. But in this regard there was little to cavil at, for Zenski, himself an old soldier, had picked each spot with an eye both for position as regards opportunities for defence and nearness to water. Wherever the latter was not naturally procurable, a bore supplied a limitless quantity. On either side of the line occasional mobs of cattle, horses and sheep were sighted, but except these and now and then a squat-faced, shaggy-haired Kalmuck stockman, no signs of life relieved the dull monotony of the level country. At every station Dromeroff noticed with satisfaction the presence of cattle yards, while in the absence of English officials, and in the ever-recurring camps of dark or yellow-skinned labourers, he soon recognised that Zenski's statement as to the invading force coming among friends was no empty boast.

'There will be practically no fighting until we pass Charleville,' said he, filling a glass of Chian wine.

'Not for the column that follows this route,' returned Zenski. 'That which starts from Normanton may meet more or less opposition at any point, but even it need fear nothing unless at Hughenden and Long-reach.'

'Then population is dense on that route?'

'So far as the actual route is concerned, no; for our own and other syndicates hold all the land between the two lines with the exception of Cameron's property, a co-operative settlement, and one or two small holdings. Danger, if it comes, will be from the direction of Townsville or Rockhampton.'

'Ah, I see; there are lines from these parts to our own?'

'To one of them,' replied Zenski. 'You will observe that the link between Hughenden and Charleville *via* Longreach is not in our hands; but that need not trouble you, *mon ami:* it is worked on the same system.'

'And what of those between Normanton and Clon-curry, and between Cloncurry and Hughenden?'

'To be used or left alone as we think fit,' said the Count. 'Our lines flank them, and there are not a hundred white men in the whole of the district.'

'Your firm has a splendid property,' laughed the soldier, 'and in Sir Peter McLoskie an admirable master. Will not all this mean the old story of killing the goose that lays the golden egg?'

'My firm is, as you know, indebted to me. Zuroff and Sons have a strong credit, but they could never have accomplished what they have done, both in bribery and construction, but for me; and I—well, again I say you know who stands at the back of Zenski.'

'But how does this fresh departure affect the original arrangement?—China is not Russia.'

'I admit,' returned the Count, 'that when first I had the honour to tender to the Queensland Government, it was to open up a back-door for Russia when wanted, and at the same time to present Zuroff and Sons with an investment which would enable them to pay not only the interest, but also to repay the principal if required.'

'And now?'

'And now, *mon Colonel*, China is about to take up that which Russia finds inconvenient, and in return for the help which Zenski and the Levantine firm can give her army of invasion, their possessions are to be held sacred—not by private arrangement, for we know the Chinamen, but in accordance with the secret treaty between Russia and the Emperor.'

'And should we fail, what happens then?' grinned Dromeroff. 'I am only a soldier, and know no more of your arrangements than is necessary; nor do I care. Still, it seems to me your firm is playing a risky hand—eh, Zenski?'

'We can hardly do that; but even so Russia can bear the loss. Win or lose, a blow will have been struck

that must further extend England's already weak line
of defence, and make the Czar's chance of winning
the Golden Gate more within the range of possibilities.'

'You are right, Zenski!' exclaimed Dromeroff.
'But for the glory of the Emperor, I would not lend
my sword to these cursed Chinamen. We are fighting
with halters round our necks for a set of dogs who
would sacrifice us without a thought if they could do
without our brains.'

'I understand that the Prime Minister is Leroy's
friend?'

'So he may be; but remember that Ching Tu will
not be with us. Still, don't think I wish to draw
back. The Czar asks nothing that his soldiers are
not ready to give; and, if we once escape the English
squadron, we can die for Russia.'

'The squadron will be seen to,' said Zenski
cynically. 'During the last scare they followed us
about like cats; they can be taken on another wild-
goose chase. As to your success, once landed that is
assured up to a certain point. Here they have no
military system worth the name. This contingent for
India will take away most of the officers who know
anything, and the best of their men. What is left
is a mob which will be led by men who as a rule
know less than many of the rank and file. As it
once was with your friends the Chinamen, a commission in Australia is simply a question of influence and
money.'

'The prospect looks promising,' muttered Dromeroff,
'if we can only depend on reinforcements. Thirty

thousand men can't hold a country like this against even a mob for long; they are bound to learn by defeat.'

'You are right, Colonel. For physically and in point of pluck these Australians are admirable; still, *pardieu*, when first you meet them, should you be so fortunate as to shoot all the paid instructors, the rest is easy, as these are indispensable to an Australian army.'

'In what way?'

'Because,' sneered Zenski, 'they so often have to tell their officers what to do. These same officers are too funny! For all the boast of Australian horsemen, half of them ride like tailors, while a big percentage know less of their manual than the rank and file.'

'You are joking?'

'Not so, my friend. The explanation is easy. Most of their mounted officers never see a charger save the docile animal provided by some livery stable for parade purposes. When not endangering that animal's ears with their swords, these gentlemen are busy in their offices and at their desks. Doubtless they are excellent at engrossing a deed or disposing of a line in slop trousers; as warriors they are useful only in providing cheap and innocent mirth for both their own men and the general public.'

'But, hang it all! you are stating exceptional cases.'

'Possibly,' retorted Zenski. 'It is an exceptional service, as you would find if you were in it.'

'I am glad to hear it,' laughed Dromeroff; 'and still it sounds improbable. With the material I have

seen, there should be no trouble in turning out a
first-class defence force ; while, whatever some of the
officers may do, I've seen even during my trip plenty
of men who can ride well enough for any cavalry in
the world.'

'So they can, *mon ami*, as you will doubtless find.
What they call their country troops are even now a
formidable irregular body, and here in Queensland
they have still the material left for magnificent light
cavalry.   But what use are these when the system is
rotten ?   First, they discuss every item of their
military estimates in Parliament, and so publish to
the whole world both their weaknesses and also their
absurd plans for curing them.   They order tons of
ammunition, and store it on a damp island.   After five
years they get some out, and are surprised because
it refuses to go off.   A local storekeeper in some
mountain region far remote from a railway desires a
red coat and sword so that he may go to the Odd-
fellows' ball as the Duke of Cambridge.   He commands many votes; to keep them the local member
of Parliament insists that the safety of the colony
depends on the formation of a corps at Budgeregar.
The Ministry must retain his vote, consequently the
opinion of the Brigade Office is set aside, and the
draper becomes captain of what with fine irony one
unfortunate commandant dubbed a Parliamentary
company.   Occasionally Parliament decides that military matters want a thorough overhaul.   Then they
appoint a' Royal Commission consisting of a general,
a retired pork-butcher, and an ex-Wesleyan parson to
draw up a report.'

'They are subtle humorists, these Australians,' sneered Dromeroff.

'Without being conscious of it. A few years ago, having driven their old Commandant to resign, they brought out a man from England who made the dry bones rattle. He told the officers what he thought of them, and he induced so many old colonels to resign that the people, seeing they were done out of their fun, refused to patronize reviews.'

'Then I suppose all you have said refers to a bygone age?' grumbled Dromeroff.

'*Not so, mon Colonel,*' sneered Zenski; 'they soon got rid of him. He trod on too many corns; he was accused of attempting to imperialize the defence force with the deep-laid design of carrying it away with him to India in his cocked hat. Possibly such was his idea. *Pardieu,* it doesn't much matter; for now they are moving heaven and earth to do the very same thing.'

'You have relieved my mind, Count,' muttered the soldier; 'he was a man well got rid of.'

'As you say, Colonel, he was too modern to be pleasant. Now things are as we should wish them; thanks to what they call the labour members and the retrenchment party, the forces of the colonies were never less effective. Personally I admit the logic of the poor devils of workmen; it would be indeed folly to foster an arm that might at any moment be used to crush them.'

'To their health, Count,' said Dromeroff, filling Zenski's glass and his own. 'Their argument is, as you say, admirable; what with the labourer's logic

9

and the capitalist's want of it, we have nothing to do but to take possession and keep it.'

'The first is easy,' remarked Zenski. 'As to keeping it, that will depend totally on whether England survives or not.'

Leaving Cloncurry behind, on the second day of their journey the Russians passed over the Gregory, a beautiful running stream winding through rich open plains; and from there to the Nicholson stretched an easy route through open forest fairly grassed. From the Nicholson, as they approached Point Parker, the country gradually became more difficult, thinly-grassed box and bloodwood flats, broken by barren, scrub-clad, gravelly ranges, taking the place of the level lands they had left behind.

'The country here wouldn't feed an army for long,' growled Dromeroff, as he glanced out over the cheer-less belt that encircled the town.

'Probably not,' said Zenski; 'but why calculate its possibilities? Spero, Aloysius and Co. can get you over that little difficulty.'

As he spoke, the train swept round a curve, and there, stretching along the shores of the Gulf, rose the vast warehouse of the great Levantine firm.

CHAPTER XIV.

DATING its rise from the commencement of the land-grant railways, Point Parker now ranked as one of the most important towns of Queensland. At the waving of the potent wand of commerce it had sprung into life on the desolate shores of the Gulf, and now both sea and land combined to force its more than tropic growth. In the holds of swift ocean steamers came all the costly luxuries of the Eastern world, to pass from its warehouses into the remotest corners of Australia, while on the wheels of Zenski's trains the raw produce of the province was carried to its wharves for transportation to the older worlds. Sitting by the gates of the sea, it bade fair to become a second Carthage, with none of that warlike spirit which wrecked the older city, but fed by even a vaster commerce than was borne into the African capital by desert caravans and silken-sailed galleys. Quick to recognise the possibilities that lay before so promising a commercial centre, and relieved as to all question of the necessary capital by the promise of a subsidy paid' down in return for certain services to be performed when occasion should require, the Levantine firm of Spero, Aloysius and Co. opened a branch establishment at Point Parker soon after Zuroff and Co. began the construction of their land-grant railways.

With the progress of the various lines, and the introduction of a wholesale system of alien labour, the industries of the Gulf country took a new lease of life. Individualism disappeared both in employer and employed; the syndicates daily absorbed more of the public estate. Fostered with fatherly care by Barlon's Land Bill, they were permitted to exchange their own special blocks for better areas, while another clause enabled Eurasians, Kanakas, and Japanese indented by the syndicates to obtain large areas in their own names and hand them over to their employers.

Unable to compete with the cheap labour of the East, the whites, never numerous, quickly disappeared. Unreasonable when the future was their own, it was now remorselessly taken from them. Overseers who transmitted unquestioned commands to unquestioning toilers had no places open for men who might strike at any moment. Work that was constant and cheap was what the corporations required to make the North a paying concern; so the white man was abolished, and ten aliens worked in his stead for less outlay, and, all things considered, with more satisfactory results — to the absentee syndicates.

First in the field, Spero, Aloysius and Co. rose with the improving fortunes of Point Parker. Six years ago they had introduced the fleet of the Levant and Red Sea Steamship Company to the shores of Australia. To-day their warehouses, wharves, and vaults, connected by tramways, stretched in unbroken succession along the shores of the Point.

Their vaults were said to be packed with tuns of Chian wine and other products of the Greek grape. As to the presence in the lower tiers of other merchandise of a more explosive and less palatable flavour, a discreet silence was maintained for the present.

Favoured guests, eminent Southern capitalists, patriotic statesmen making the grand tour, Sir Peter McLoskie, Sir Samuel Mitson, and others, always spoke with enthusiasm of the Mitylene Palace and the genial hospitality of the senior partner, Mr. Spero.

The firm was orthodox and devout in a marked degree. They had presented £50 to the district hospital, and £500 as an offering to the Church of England ; while the Pastoral and Financial Association in Collins Street, and the V.R.C., were both duly recognised ; in fact, everything truly English and in touch with capital was in evidence in their *carte de pays*.

But nothing was half so English as Mr. Simpkins-Thompson, Mr. Spero's coadjutor and partner.

To-night the firm were giving one of their justly celebrated dinner-parties.

Zenski and Dromeroff were to start in the morning for Hong Kong. During the week that had passed since their arrival from Charleville, the Russians had taken a run over all the other lines included in the scheme of attack ; and now, armed with a personal

knowledge of the country, Dromeroff was ready to get
back to Canton.

As a graceful *bon voyage* to his guests, Mr. Spero,
true to his character of a merchant prince, now
offered them a farewell feast.

The stranger within the gates of the Mitylene
Palace would be dull past compare who failed to
realize that here the influence of money was fully
displayed and vindicated.

The surroundings told of unlimited wealth, luxurious
taste, and generous hospitality towards men of the
right stamp, the appointments being alike picturesque
and gorgeous.

Lines of dusky faces in alternate scarlet and snowy
turbans stood waiting behind the chairs, each ready
to serve silently and swiftly the guest who chanced to
be his particular care.

On the table tropic flowers bloomed in dainty contrast, amid mimic glaciers of snow and ice, piled in
vases of aluminium, crystal, and gold. Silver-
mounted electric lamps filled the room with a soft,
mellow radiance, while from the space left open by the
sliding roof, a glimpse was caught of a star-shot sky
like a painting of the night set in a framework of
polished pine.

Through the lattice-work which hung between the
slender pillars of the eastern end, a perfumed breeze
from invisible punkahs rustled the scarlet hibiscus
and deep green foliage in their quaintly-carved jars,
and shook the rich tapestry and brilliant draperies
of Japan and Khorasan which, hanging above the
arches, let in faint murmurings of the sea.

Art and Nature combined to form an *ensemble* far exceeding in magnificence anything to be seen elsewhere in Australia. The *cuisine* was as far above antipodean aspirations as its altar of sacrifice. Here were venison and pheasants from Northern China, and beside them the dainties of the Bush and the plains, disguised with all the cunning condiments of Hindostan by the cultured skill of a real *cordon bleu* from the Faubourg. Besides these were Bush quails stewed in madeira, wallaby transformed into a dish of paradise, and desert custard served with the royal truffles that come from the banks of the Finke.

Mr. Spero presided at the head of the table; Zenski, always at home in Mitylene, acted as croupier, while the bluff and burly Simpkins-Thompson sat in the left centre among a lot of jolly fellows, globe-trotters with the Carlton Club *imprimatur*, primrose enthusiasts in the greenness of youth, quaffing Moet to the Finke truffles, and one or two solemn and deferential representatives of Sydney mortgage companies. On the right side of the table, opposite Simpkins-Thompson, sat the nobodies in particular: pastoral clients under the screw, chance visitors, and overlanders from beyond the telegraph line.

Such stragglers were always invited—the clients in order that they might be suppressed and sat upon by the ornate talk of the junior partner and the magnificence of the surroundings; outside strangers beyond the business network, because they served to spread over the plains and wastes the wealth of the firm and their great power as capitalists.

Dick Hatten, *en route* for his ill-starred cattle-station, had chanced to drop into Point Parker a few hours before, and now found himself sitting beside a neighbour, who had just come in from the 'Territory.' From Donald Farquhar of Deeside, Dick heard little to promote appetite. Things on the Roper were going to the devil, said the Scotchman.

But as that had been their normal state for years, and as his own run was mortgaged past redemption, Hatten called philosophy to his aid, and decided to spoil the Egyptians, if only in the matter of truffles and champagne.

Overlanders and pioneer squatters are used to live upon salt beef, Johnny cakes and quart-pot tea; so the glow of pleasure may be imagined with which Donald Farquhar found before him, placed reverentially by an attendant in a scarlet turban, a grouse-pie and a mutton ham.

'The Dee, the Don, Balgounie Brig black wall, the heather-scented breeze from the Braes of Mar,' all passed over him with the memories of his youth and the sniff of those Highland viands. As Lord Byron once felt far away among the isles of Greece, Donald thought he had got among first-rate folk, and he devoted himself with fervent loyalty to the moor-cocks and sheep-shank. Mr. Simpkins-Thompson was now addressing his remarks to a Sydney youth in elaborate evening dress, who ran a brick wool store on the shores of Port Jackson. The wool-broker's manner betokened the most profound deference. It was not every day that he was privileged to sit down with such representatives of capital, and he hoped to extend his connection and pass over some Northern accounts to Spero, Aloysius, and Co.

'Yes, my dear Mr. Hodson,' said Thompson, with a real Yorkshire accent and manner, 'I assure you the thorough English character of the McLoskie policy is becoming plainer every day, and nowhere do you find that policy so highly approved as in Pall Mall, sir, and the midland counties, sir. If you have the Tory interest, sir, the county families, sir, and the hunting men at your back, you have all England, sir, and no other opinion is worth a whiff of tobacco. I was in the shires last season ; Hodson and I met in one hunting-field, near Northampton, nine owners of Gulf property drawing incomes through our firm of from eight to twenty thousand a year. They had got their estates through our agency, and without coming to Australia or putting themselves to the slightest bother. Their profits in sugar, coffee, and cattle reach them yearly through the Levant Company ; while under our supervision the routine of their estates goes on, worked by boss tributors from the North and coolie labour contractors. We have in our books now forty clients of this stamp. Results like these show the true statesman, and I tell you, sir, the Queensland Premier has saved Australia with his land-grant railways and Asiatic commerce and labour.'

Here Mr. Thompson's fist came whack down on the mahogany, making the plates and crystal rattle.

'England, sir, is the real home of capitalists and the storehouse of capital, and the true people of England can count their thousands by tens and twenties.

I assure you, my dear Hodson, it makes me sick to hear the infernal trash they talk in the old colonies, about settlement and colonization, and farming and other rot. I say with the late Admiral Boggs, the founder of Townsville, and the father of the plains of promise — I say so with that venerable patriot and bank director : " It is capital that must have the land, sir, and must have the sea and everything else, sir. Squatters and selectors are d——d paupers, one and both—boil 'em down, sir—wind 'em up and have done with them—it's the greatest mercy to such infernal crawlers. Let 'em go into the soda-water and billiard-marking line or drive a dust-cart, and make an honest living, and be d——d to 'em !" '

Hatten was getting interested in this blatant John Bullism—especially the version put in the mouth of the late Admiral Boggs.

' Did Admiral Boggs really say that, Thompson ?' he inquired, with a broad grin of disbelief, ' or is it only your Eastern imagery ?'

Innocent of intent as the question really was, it apparently struck home with most unpleasant force. Thompson's bloated face took even a deeper tinge, and his answer, when he made it, was not up to his usual form. When his nerve failed, his speech lost the bluff English intonation, and savoured of the Lubeck steamers, and the Odessa Coin Exchange, and other polyglot centres. But being a stout, florid man, and well up in club and racing talk and Stock Exchange jargon, he seldom broke down. In the present instance the collapse, slight as it was, was not lost upon Hatten, who laughed more heartily than discreetly.

Round Zenski the subject of the Kanaka trade was under discussion for the benefit of a new man who had secured a plantation through Spero, Aloysius and Company.

'*Mon ami*, it is an admirable system,' remarked the Count, 'if only the *pauvre* devils would not die so quickly.'

'Is that a fact, sir?' asked the sugar-planter. 'Some years ago we sent a lady from England to see into this matter, sir, and on her return she assured us in the *Times* that the Kanakas were treated splendidly, and were as happy as Sunday-school children.'

'Doubtless,' laughed Zenski; 'I remember her. She was a most charming lady, and, unlike most of her sex, singularly modest in the matter of luggage.'

'Then how do you reconcile your statement with hers?'

'If you had a pig-pen, and knew the inspector was about to arrive, what would you do?'

'Clean it, I suppose.'

'Precisely; that is what my estimable friends did. *Pardieu*, you English are too comical, with all respect to your great nation; you want to find out particulars about a mob of savages practically without women of their own, and only able to speak through an interpreter paid by their masters, and you send a woman who can't speak their language, and who, if she discovered half their immoralities, dare not for very shame's sake print them.'

'Then you think the system bad?' asked the Englishman in surprise.

'Pardon me, I consider it admirable, as I said before. They are only slaves, and not fit for a better destiny. I am only tickled at the naïveté of your grand newspaper ; such innocence is refreshing.'

'Then what would you advise ?'

'Coolies, my friend—they last longer; besides, the Kanaka will soon be like the Moa. In twenty-three years 43,000 have come to Queensland ; of these 26,000 returned, about 9,000 died, and 9,000 more are not accounted for. They are apt to become too sickly for sugar-growing, and a trifle expensive as manure.'

Gradually the guests had begun to straggle out on to the marble colonnade that overlooked the Gulf. Those who remained were Spero's particular friends, men like himself, interested only in the creation of wealth.

Gathering round the junior partner, and relieved from the restraint caused by the presence of strangers whose tastes were unknown to them, they became natural. Led by Simpkins-Thompson, his particular coterie vied with each other in the narration of dubious anecdote. They were an average company, neither better nor worse than their fellows.

Still, their wit was grosser than that of scholarly men, and, unlike theirs, totally unrelieved by any suggestion of art or intellectual ideal. But for the costly silver, the glittering crystal, and the faultless get-up of its occupants, a listener might have supposed that he was witnessing the jollity of a band of factory hands during the dinner-hour. Practically such was the case. Most of them were men who, to use the cant phrase, had been the architects of their own fortunes.

For some, possibly, this definition in its best sense was applicable enough, with, of course, this reservation, that a number of innocent people are invariably sacrificed during the erection of any large structure, whether of gold or stone. In most cases, however, land-grabbing, bogus banks, syndicates, and mining speculations, in which the promoters sold the general public experience at boom prices, were the chief factors in the creation of the capitalists of the party. But whatever the means, it was in nine cases out of ten a rush for the spoil, and such being the case, those engaged in it had seldom either time or inclination for polishing the mind while gilding the body.

So these plutocrats brought their early coarseness along with them—not because they were worse than other men, but simply because the law of evolution demands more time for working out its ends than an ordinary life can give.

After midnight, when the last guest had gone, the partners, accompanied by Zenski and Dromeroff, entered the cabinet where they held their secret conclaves.

'Look here, Bourouskie,' said Spero irritably: 'you do too much the Tory Englishman. You over-act the part. That *schimmil* with the black moustache was laughing in your face. What is his name? Hand me the register. Yes: "Hatten, Richard, Roper River. One thousand seven hundred cattle mortgaged to the Pastoral Finance Company, £2,600." Lucky Hodson is here! Give him a cheque for

£3,000, including margin to cover expenses, and get
him to wire for an assignment of the mortgage. Mr.
Hatten is not wanted on the Roper River. See that
he is turned out quick, and let one of the Kalmuck
herdsmen look after the cattle. Grinning, d——d
Socialist! cheeky pauper with his paltry cattle! Now,
have you got that down ?'

Getting an affirmative nod from his junior and now
totally subservient partner, Spero went on :

' Well, is your report ready for the steamer ?   Bring
it in an hour, and I will enclose it to the house at
Smyrna. Wait a moment, Bourouskie : there is something I nearly forgot. Tell the Hetman to get all the
cattle with cancer and pleuro drafted out for shipment
to Thursday Island—they will answer well for the
British commodore's contract. It is easy to sell
anything to the officers of her Majesty's commissariat.'

As Bourouskie went out to finish his report, Zenski
remarked to the senior partner :

' Waste-paper, Spero, *mon ami*, if all goes well ; but
let him make it out—he is useful, doubtless, but the
canaille irritates me : I would sooner have a last look
at your wine-vaults without him.'

Touching the panelling with his finger, a door
opened silently, and, taking up a hand-lamp, Spero led
the way down a winding stair.

Following their leader along a narrow tunnel, the
two men soon stood in a vast catacomb of cellars—
below the surface, but dry and airy.

' You have a large stock of wine ?' grinned Zenski,
pointing to rows of casks that disappeared in the
darkness of the vaults.

'Enough to blow the whole of Queensland into the China Sea,' laughed Spero.

'And the batteries?' asked Dromeroff.

'Come with me, Colonel, and I will show you where we keep them very nice and warm,' replied Spero, moving on into the gloom.

BOOK III.

THE LULL BEFORE THE HURRICANE.

———◦◦◦———

CHAPTER I.

ISIS DOWNS STATION.

A HOT September sun had dropped red as a blood-
dyed targe behind the clouds piled up against the
western horizon as Dick Hatten came in sight of the
head - station. From the coolibahs which fringed
the watercourse just left behind, the dust-shrouded,
thirsty leaves hung motionless, while from one solitary
chimney on the ridge ahead the smoke rose straight
into the voiceless air. For the last quarter of a mile
Dick's mount had evinced a fresh interest in things in
general, and now, as the house came into view, he
pricked his ears and began to pick up the hoofs that
for the last few hours had dragged wearily over the
hard, Mitchell-grassed Downs. Similarly galvanized
by the near prospect of a spell, the old groggy-legged
' cutting-out ' horse who carried the swag now closed
up his distance, jogging cheerily almost abreast of his
mate.

Sitting loosely in his saddle, with bent back and with feet rammed home in the stirrups, Dick pulled stolidly at his pipe.

True to his threat, Spero had taken over the mortgage, and with it in his possession had made short work of the mortgagor; and now Hatten found himself minus even the nominal ownership of his station, and practically with no assets save Io and the two horses now carrying him and his belongings to Isis Downs. As things had chanced, his future troubled him little.

Heather was lost to him, and this being so, what fate might have in store had little real interest for the man whose one ambition to succeed had been prompted by the prospect of asking her to share his altered fortunes.

For his personal wants he had no fear; a good all-round man need never starve in Australia, and without any undue egotism Dick knew he was that. Since he had last parted from Heather on the deck of the *Barcoo*, Hatten had often thought of the strange, apparently impracticable promise to which he had committed himself.

In the presence of a beautiful woman the man who loves her is apt to promise much; nay, if he has in him aught of chivalry, she has but to ask to receive all that he can proffer—save honour.

From Dick, Heather had required the performance of a task not only hard in itself to accomplish, but whose realization could only be brought about by an act of supreme self-sacrifice. Many a man under the circumstances would have left these wandering planets

10

to conjoin, or forever revolve in different orbits as chance directed. Not so Dick; he meant to keep his compact to his friend, even although his reason told him it was unattainable, for his heart dominated his mind. This illogical but potent organ urged him on his platonic quest, only that in its own time it might break in pieces the cordon which, in the unsatisfying guise of friendship, held him apart from the woman he loved. Like most men, however, Dick had little knowledge of his own heart, and so he rode up to the horse-paddock gate resolved to treat with Heather from a purely platonic base. Pulling up, the latest victim of finance companies looked with friendly interest at one of the last strongholds of the purely squatting class. Rising from the crown of a low, rocky ridge, Isis Downs head-station presented all the appearances of a small Bush township.

In common with most of the early squatters, Cameron had begun life on the Flinders nearly thirty years ago in little better than a hut. This had been added to as necessity arose, then deserted for a more pretentious building, which in its turn took unto itself wings and wide heat-defying verandas. The old house still stood, having been converted into a bachelors' barracks and smoking-room by its builder, in recognition of a sentiment which refused to allow of the destruction of a habitat hallowed by the memories of the past. At the back of the main building were clustered that miscellaneous collection of stables, stores, and men's huts, which as a natural consequence sprang into existence round the head-station.

Isis Downs looked strangely homelike from where

Dick sat, surrounded by the dust-cloud which had followed the pack-horse, and now hung in a lazy column all down the winding track. The gray *pisé* walls and white-painted roofs of the long rambling building relieved his eyes, scorched with the glare of the Downs. As he looked, he caught the faint glitter of waterdrops on the rough reed-mats hanging from the façade. Behind those broad verandas lay infinite possibilities of shade. To the green foliage of the garden the sunflowers lent here and there a golden radiance, while over the *pisé* walls masses of scarlet and purple bougainvillea ran like a flame. Wrapped in thought, Hatten sat looking at the scene before him till a flutter of wings, accompanied by the discordant grumbling of turkeys driven above their pace, roused him out of his abstraction.

Glancing to the left, he saw a flock of these persistent wanderers hurrying homeward. Some distance in their rear waddled an apparition, monk-like in its proportions. The one vestment of calico, bound midway by a belt, which served to mark the location of a long-since-fleshed-up waist, suggested that the wearer belonged to the gentler sex, though this supposition was hardly borne out by the heavy blucher boots and dissipated felt hat which completed the turkey-driver's attire.

As the birds flew over the fence, their captor looked with a certain lazy curiosity at the horseman.

' Hullo, Maggie !' shouted Dick ; ' how are the hens getting on ?'

' Faix, you'd better ax the turkey-cock !' retorted old Margaret, with chilling indifference. Then, recognising the laugh that followed, she rolled towards the gate, exclaiming as she neared Hatten : 'Augh, glory be to Gad if it ishn't Misther Dick, wid a beard on him loike a goat !'

'Draw it mild, Maggie,' laughed Dick, as he shook hands with the old hen-wife ; 'three months' stubble, that's all. How are they all up at the house ?'

' Augh, foine, Misther Dick. The masther's got the rheumatiz, poor man ! but, God be praised, the spotted pig have the most beautiful litter yer ever clapped eyes on. Then the missus is in grate heart entoirely. Faix, phwat wid all the clutches doin' noicely and that auld Roosian Count, she's as lively as a coult. Augh, an' I forgot Masther Ted an' Miss Edith an' the cockatoo—bad cess to him for a crass-timpered divil—is all in the best of health, the saints be praised !'

' I'm glad to hear it,' said Dick when the old woman stopped. ' And Miss Heather ?'

' Augh, now, Misther Dick,' grinned Maggie, with a knowing wink, 'faix, wouldn't you like to ax her swate silf ?'

' So I will when I see her.'

' Av coorse ; but I mane by yerselves loike.'

' What are you driving at ?'

' Divil doubt ye, how grane you are !' exclaimed Maggie. ' But plase yourself ; I seed Miss Heather in the saplins beyant, and maybe she's there yet. Bad scran to 'em, I musht take a wheel out of them contrairy hens.'

As the old woman toddled off, Dick passed through

HEATHER AND IO.

To face page 148.

the gate and cantered towards the clump of trees to which Maggie had pointed.

On the further side of the timber belt he found Heather. The girl stood beside Io, one hand resting on her slender neck. Pricking her ears, the mare uttered a friendly whinny.

The graceful proportions of the thoroughbred and the woman's faultless outlines, backed up by a clump of flame-clad coral trees, appealed at once to Dick's artistic sense; but even as he looked, the cold glaciers of platonic friendship slipped headlong from about his heart, melted into the consistency of water by the warm realities of the picture.

Swinging out of his saddle, he clasped her outstretched hand, then, as he felt the contact of the soft, lithe fingers, a thrill went through him, magnetic, passion-compelling—supreme in power, and yet conceived in weakness. So for a little he stood still holding her hand, but saying never a word. Then, looking into his eyes, she said :

' I'm so glad you have come back.'

But there was no tremor in her voice, only the mellow ring of a friendly greeting. What more could there be ? he asked himself; and yet it all seemed such a mockery, for, despite his philosophy, he knew that Dead Sea fruit must be his portion, and now he further realized that platonic friendship was but a poor sauce for such a banquet.

Heather intuitively understood somewhat of the struggle that was in progress, and so, not because she was indifferent to his pain, but rather for the reason that she realized the cruelty of prolonging the situation, the girl began to tell him of her life since they had parted.

As he ran his hand fondly over Io's mane, the mare rubbed her muzzle against his shirt.

'You see, she's true to her old love,' said Heather; then, noticing the man's cheek flush, she added: 'I've been riding her every morning lately, and, see, there isn't the sign of a sore on her back.'

As she spoke, Billy, bridle on arm, came towards them. Seeing Dick, he remarked:

'Got back, I see, boss. Fine day, ain't it?'

'It's been a hot one, at any rate, Billy. I'm glad the mare's all right.'

'Look here,' said Billy in an awed tone; 'it knocks me bandy. According to orders, Miss Heather's been riding her reg'lar, and blow me if she's got a scald the size of a pin's 'ead on her back.'

'Then I've surprised you, Billy!' laughed the girl.

'You've upset my calculations clean, miss,' replied the trainer. 'The motter o' my life has been never to lend a woman or a sky-pilot a 'orse, unless you wants him skinned—prepared for a fastin' contest, or ridden to death without interference from them cruelty-to-animals coves.'

'Then you'd give me a mount, Billy?'

'Blow me if I wouldn't!' said Billy earnestly. 'Your hands is light, and you sit square—'anged if I see what's to stop you, barring the—beg pardon, I'll look after the mokes, Mr. Dick,' concluded Billy, slipping the bridle over Io's head and jumping on her back.

Left to themselves, the two walked slowly towards the garden-gate.

Dick had passed the time of life when it is considered excusable to allow one's feelings to become a public nuisance, so he talked to the girl at his side on matters pertaining to all things save the one desire that lay nearest his heart. Zenski, he found, had been to Isis Downs with a cattle-buyer, who was securing large drafts to be delivered at the various railway-stations about the end of the present month. During his visit the Count had, it seemed, paid considerable attention to Mrs. Enson, and, as Heather remarked, visions of becoming a countess now began to take tangible form in the old lady's mind.

'By Jove, I wish he would marry her !' laughed Dick. 'For if things go as I fear they will, it might be convenient for you to be able to claim connection with the Count.'

'Do you mean in the matter of free passes on his lines ?' laughed Heather.

'No,' replied Hatten quietly, 'in the matter of saving your lives.'

As he spoke, the girl looked at him with some alarm, not certainly at his words, but because a certain suspicion of sunstroke flashed into her mind.

Guessing what her manner meant, Hatten said :

'Don't be alarmed ; I'm not dangerous. I suppose what I said sounds mad enough, but I fear there is a lot of method in it.'

'What do you mean ? I detest mysteries.'

'I suppose I shall only confirm your opinion of my insanity, but nevertheless I feel certain in my own mind that your friend the Count is well worth watching.'

'Why?' asked Heather coldly, for she liked Zenski, and rather resented Hatten's imputation.

'Because he is not what he professes to be,' retorted Hatten stoutly.

'Then what is he?'

'If I am not vastly mistaken, a Russian spy.'

'Don't be absurd, Dick!' laughed Heather. 'Is it likely the Russian Government would choose a man they have practically outlawed for such a post?'

'We have only his word as to the banishment both of himself and his friend Mr. Dromeroff,' retorted Dick.

'Since that day on the *Barcoo*, Ted looks with grave suspicion on poor Mr. Dromeroff. He seems to have made you a convert.'

'Perhaps from his point of view Ted isn't far out, either; but my suspicions date farther back.'

'Surely this is petty, Dick,' said Heather. 'I thought you were above the old English prejudice against foreigners. I admit that it seems unfair to drive out all our white people for the sake of these wretched coolies, but Sir Peter McLoskie is to blame for that; and remember, both English and Australian firms, more shame to them, are employing cheap alien labour quite as readily as Count Zenski.'

'I admit all you say, and, believe me, they will yet pay back in blood all they have won by this cursed system of slavery. Thanks to McLoskie, the North is an open door for the first invader who thinks fit to anchor in the Gulf.'

'But what has this to do with the Count in particular?'

'Everything. His railways are worked by men who have no interests here, and who, I believe, are merely tools in his hands. He is hand-in-glove, despite all he may say to the contrary, with the infernal half-breeds who have just sold me up, and who are absorbing fresh stations every day.'

'I know it is all wrong,' said Heather, indignant for her friend's sake. 'But isn't Mr. Thompson an Englishman, Dick? Not that that makes it any better for you, poor old fellow!'

'He's no more English than Zenski. I bowled him out at that dinner Spero gave Dromeroff. In point of fact, I fancy it was for that very reason they took over my mortgage and hunted me.'

'Then what do you think it all means?' asked the girl in puzzled tones.

'I don't quite know,' admitted Dick; 'but this is what I fear. War with Russia seems inevitable; the massing of English troops on the Afghan frontier, and the request for our help to do garrison duty and act as a check on the natives, all point to a grave crisis. Now that five thousand of our best men have gone, what is to prevent Russia making a dash on us?'

'But you forget the English fleet, Dick,' said the girl in some alarm.

'They, I fear, will have more than they can well manage elsewhere. Remember, Russia has France at her back, and both their fleets are now formidable in these seas.'

'But even so, don't you think they would confine
their attack to our capitals?'

'Undoubtedly they would make a demonstration
both at Brisbane and Sydney; but my idea is this:
that once past the China squadron, they would throw
their main force on Point Parker, be received with
open arms by Spero, Aloysius and Co., and find a
swift and easy roadway on Zenski's lines clean into
the heart of Queensland.'

'Oh, Dick!' exclaimed the girl, convinced in spite
of herself by Dick's earnestness; 'and what then?'

'A fight against terrible odds, with a horde of blood-
thirsty savages,' muttered Dick grimly.

'Surely you have told the authorities what you
think?' exclaimed Heather, now as full of certainty
as before of doubt.

'The authorities,' laughed Dick bitterly, 'are too
much in love with the whole beautiful scheme that
has made all this possible to listen to me. I should
be treated as a madman or a fool, who wanted to
have revenge for the loss of my station.'

'Mr. Musgrave must have some such idea in his
head,' said Heather; 'for weeks past they have been
putting Fort Mallarraway in a state of defence;
everyone thinks they are mad, but now I can see
what it all means.'

'Musgrave is no fool,' said Dick in a tone of relief,
'as we may all find soon enough; but God help us if
he alone is wise.'

'That reminds me, the Government have let Count
Zenski a contract to fortify Point Parker, so they
must have their suspicions.'

'Yes, I know they have,' retorted Hatten contemptuously; 'they are paying him to build batteries that will never be completed to defy the Russian advance, but which may later defend a hostile base.'

As he spoke they passed from under the trellises, and moved up the steps on to the veranda.

'Welcome back to Isis Downs, Dick!' cried Cameron heartily. 'Thank God, the infernal banks and finance companies haven't put it out of my power to give shelter to a friend yet!'

'Perhaps they're preserving you as a specimen of an extinct race, sir,' laughed Dick, as he shook hands with Mrs. Enson and Edith.

CHAPTER II.

A WELL-NIGH EXTINCT SPECIMEN.

ANGUS CAMERON was one of the few squatters left in Australia who, after a pastoral career of forty years, was able to boast that he had never owed the banks a sixpence. When the Act of 1861 gave the Pastoralists of New South Wales one of two alternatives, Cameron, then a station-holder in the parent colony, decided to move on in preference to selling his manhood to the banks and his soul to the devil in securing his lease-hold by means of dummying.

Still following out the squatter's true destiny, he eventually found himself owner of Isis Downs, where, thanks to climatic influences and distance from any of the land-grant lines, he was still practically left alone both by selectors and the Government. Thoroughly long-headed in the management of both sheep and cattle, and with neither money sunk in land nor interest on borrowed capital to cripple him, Cameron had for years been a comparatively rich man. On paper, safe investments amounting to £30,000, and a net return from the station of £2,000, certainly did look paltry beside a Riverina freehold valued at

£300,000, with a rent-roll of £30,000 a year; but when
it is remembered that the return from the Riverina
property barely paid interest on the mortgages
rendered necessary to create it, and that Isis Downs
owed no man a shilling, it will be seen that Angus
Cameron had little, if any, the worst of the deal.

On the introduction of the Act of 1861—a measure
avowedly to enable an industrious class of farmers to
settle on the lands of New South Wales—members of
Parliament who had been elected as friends of the
landless poor strained every nerve to provide efficient
weapons by which squatters could defeat and ruin the
very men they had pledged themselves to protect.
Filled with an insatiable land-hunger, the whole
community wallowed in every kind of dishonesty.
False declarations were made daily alike by squatters
and selectors. Fraud, perjury, subornation, and
bribery were universal. Any man who refused to do
as his neighbour did, or to lend his name to a lie
when wanted, incurred certainty of social enmity.
Truth and honour ceased to be considered virtues in
dealings connected with the public lands. And in
this fearful wreck of national honour the individual
squatter disappeared for ever. In his stead shadowy
syndicates sprang into life from among the festering
garbage of broken oaths and shameless trickery which
now permeated the whole land system of the colonies.
Stations grew larger and fewer; millions of improved
acres became as complete a blank in respect to human
existence and national well-being as a mangrove-
swamp or a worked-out mine. All signs both of
family life and local wealth disappeared. Of the

thousands of bales of wool and flocks of wethers sent off these properties, in many instances not the value of a sheep skin remained in the colonies ; as improvements were extended, both the management and labour were economized, so that upon millions of acres homestead life was represented only in the shape of a meagre cottage for the manager, and a filthy, pot-house hovel outside the horse-paddock.

A well-known land expert writing in 1893 thus describes a town in the richest pastoral district of New South Wales : 'A Riverina town frozen in by station purchases, with a peacocked paddock held in the name of an English loan company at the end of every street, and no sign of rural or suburban life.'

The same writer, referring to the old squatters of Queensland, says : 'There are no such squatters now. In country taken up lately, the universal system of absentee business ownership, the enormous holdings in the hands of financial bodies, and the employment of the native police, have impressed one common character upon frontier relations with the blacks ; namely, that of irresponsible, callous cruelty.' In Queensland in 1954 the aboriginals had practically dropped out of the question. Rum, opium, and prostitution had, to all intents and purposes, swept them out of existence. All else touched on by this old writer had, however, become intensified not only in Queensland, but throughout the whole of Australia. The bank crashes and universal depression of the year 1893 had brought land matters to a crisis, and now, with of course the exceptions which must naturally in all cases occur, pastoral and agricultural Australia lay bound and helpless in the hands of bowelless foreign syndicates, who squeezed out her life-blood, and gave nothing in exchange save a hopeless race of utterly worthless, if nominally cheap, jackaroos, and an equally hopeless and cheap, though less useless, horde of alien labourers.

To again quote a passage applicable to the whole of inland Australia : ' It is certain that in the western half of New South Wales it would be impossible for purposes of defence to enroll a single squadron of Bush cavalry mounted on their own horses.' Such was the state of affairs which obtained in Australia in September, 1954, intensified so far as the North was concerned by land-grant railway syndicates and unlimited coolie and Japanese labour.

As Cameron was his own master, he only employed white men ; but while refusing to cut down wages, he as firmly declined to be dictated to by the unions. Still, such was his general character for hospitality and straight-dealing that he remained popular with both capital and labour. No swagsman was ever refused rations and a ' doss ' in the travellers' hut at Isis Downs, and no stranger could ever say that he had been turned away from the head-station, though many a one discovered that it was far easier to get into old Cameron's house than to get out of it. They didn't dress for dinner at Isis Downs. As its owner said : ' Men can't carry dress-clothes droving, and I don't care to adopt the plan of the Bathurst potentate who bought up a job lot so that he might be able to provide guests who came unprepared.' Neither did they provide lady's-maids. On one occasion this

caused serious inconvenience to a visitor. This young
lady's father, from being a draper in a small way,
suddenly developed into a Southern wool king. Intent
on gaining an *entrée* into English society, the eminent
financier had just concluded an arrangement with an
embarrassed member of the aristocracy, whereby, in
consideration of the payment of all his debts and a
liberal income, the needy one undertook to face his
relations with the squatter's daughter. The young
lady, in the course of her 'starring engagement,'
chanced upon Isis Downs, where she electrified
Heather by requesting the loan of her maid.

'I assure you, dear,' said she, 'I don't really know
how to dress myself.'

'She never did, poor girl!' laughed Cameron when
he heard of it; 'but I little thought that when she
used to look so dowdy in the store she was only
working out an aristocratic destiny.'

CHAPTER III.

UNDER THE WISTARIA.

AFTER a whisky-and-soda with Cameron, Hatten made off to the barracks. On his way he caught sight of four or five men lounging in front of the store-door, and, stepping up, looked in. A figure in leggings and moles, with his shirt-sleeves rolled above the elbows of a pair of sun-tanned, sinewy arms, stood behind the counter pouring sugar out of a pint into a dirty calico bag.

'Well, what the devil do you want?' grunted Ted Johnson impatiently.

'A little civility,' retorted Dick; 'or, if you can't supply that, five minutes on the grass.'

'Why, Dick, old man, I didn't know you with that confounded stubble!' exclaimed Ted, jumping over the counter. 'Put it there, if it weighed a ton!'

As the friends shook hands, Dick said:

'What! turned storekeeper? Where's Ewan?'

'He went over to the Fort to see about a horse-muster they're talking about. Just dodge into my diggings, and when I get rid of these swaggies, I'll be with you before you can say "knife."'

11

As Hatten looked at himself in Johnson's glass, he felt that in retaining the stubble, which now stood out in hedgehog-like bristles, he was doing himself less than justice. Then, as he thought of his platonic *rôle*, he muttered : 'Hang it all ! what does it matter ? And still,' mused Dick, with a fine assumption of purely disinterested feeling, 'that isn't the way a man should look at it ; heaven knows, women allow us enough latitude, in all conscience, but I think they have just cause to draw the line at my impersonation of a badly-scraped pig.' Following out this train of thought, Dick began to rummage for his friend's shaving-tackle.

'So that's your little game !' laughed Ted, entering the room just as the searcher drew a razor from the toe of a wellington boot.

'Hullo, Ted ! Fact is, I was too lazy to look up my own. I know you don't mind, old chap.'

'Not a bit,' grinned Johnson, as he pulled his shirt over his head, 'as long as you've finished when I'm through with my splash.'

As Johnson returned from the bathroom, Dick demanded wrathfully :

'What the devil did you plant this infernal old hoop for ?'

'Why, what's up ?' said Ted, looking at his friend's blood-stained throat. 'Had a row with the good old animal ? She's a daisy, if you take her right.'

'Take her right, be hanged ! The miserable thing can't cut, and as to scraping it off—well, look at me.'

'Man alive, she's a demon on corns.'

' So this is your corn-cutter you've palmed off on me ?' growled Dick with strong disgust.

' The fact is, Dick,' laughed Ted, producing another razor, ' the fellows have given me such a devil of a time boning my razors, that I had to lay for them. I'm sorry you fell in; but, Lord! isn't she a beauty ?'

' For skinning a man ?'

' For giving some of those beggars a love-of-God shave,' retorted Ted, as he carefully returned the razor to its hiding-place.

As the men dressed, Dick's treatment by Spero, Aloysius and Co. was fully threshed out.

' I have nothing left bar Io and the two stock-horses,' said Hatten.

' You've been as close to bottom before to-day.'

' Yes; but Queensland wasn't a slave province then. A poor white man has no show here at present. I think I'll cut it.'

' Lots of time to think about that when we're tired of you, Dick,' said Ted heartily.

' Well, yes, if old Cameron doesn't mind, I'll put in a few weeks with you, and then strike out West.'

While he was speaking the gong sounded, and the two men walked out.

' Under the wistaria, I suppose ?' said Dick.

' Rather; it's as hot as an oven inside,' replied Ted, leading the way into the space formed by the main building and the wings.

During the summer months the dining-room at Isis Downs was practically deserted. At Heather's suggestion the distance between the wings had been spanned with battens supported by light wooden pillars, and over this framework she had trained wistaria after the fashion of the Japanese. Under this lavender-tinted canopy dinner was now served.

Cameron, white-bearded, ruddy, and straight as a lance, sat at the head of the table. Jovial, self-reliant, and hospitable as an Arab, he well represented a type of pioneer fast passing away. Opposite him Mrs. Enson, in black silk and lace cap, presided over the teapot with even more dignity of manner than usual. To Dick she already appeared to be living up to the future possibilities.

The two girls, dressed in white, relieved only by the silver buckles of the belts that bound their blouses, formed a restful contrast to the glistening rotundity of the older lady.

With Edith and Heather on either side of him, Hatten felt that, if not with all things content, he was at home once more. Having given an account of his adventures since last they were all together, and having heard in return the various little items of local interest which the ladies had stored up against his return, Dick asked after their neighbours at Fort Mallarraway.

'You're just in time to see for yourself,' said Edith. They are going to have a big horse-muster, and Mr. Musgrave wants Heather and myself to go over and help.'

'The three of you should be equal to six stockmen at least,' laughed Cameron; 'only I'm afraid you'd talk too much to be trusted with the "tailers"—eh, Edith ?'

'From all I can hear, the men are no better,' retorted Edith. 'At any rate, I don't want to mind the stupid " tailers "; we'll do the running-in for you.'

'Edith,' remarked Mrs. Enson severely, ' you will do nothing of the kind; you have purposely misunderstood Mr. Musgrave's slipshod method of expressing himself; what would—ahem—what would the young gentlemen think of you?'

' Ewan says the girls over there ride like fun,' persisted Edith.

' I fail to grasp the full meaning of Ewan's simile,' retorted the old lady. 'But I am determined that while I am alive you shall ride like a lady, not like a stockman.'

Stepping into the breach, Dick remarked :

' Your nephew is late, sir?'

' The girls I expect, Dick,' began Cameron, when a tall, raw-boned young Scotchman walked up.

Shaking hands with Dick, he took a seat.

' Well, what news, boy?' asked his uncle.

' They expect you all over next week,' replied the new-comer, with a slight ' burr ' in his slow, deliberate speech. ' Save us, but they're building a fortification yonder !'

' Not before it's wanted,' interposed Hatten; 'these confounded Russians mean mischief, or I'm vastly mistaken.'

' Talking of Russians, have you seen or heard anything of that delightful Mr. Dromeroff?' asked Edith mischievously.

' Not since I had dinner with him at Point Parker. By the way, he wished to be remembered.'

'Did he?—how nice of him! I wonder if we will ever see him again—he was so amusing.'

'It's the trade of all these foreigners,' growled Johnson; 'probably your friend is an absconding valet.'

'Edward, remember he was a friend of the Count's,' said Mrs. Enson reprovingly.

'Whatever he was, I wish he'd look us up again,' retorted Edith; 'even a gentlemen's gentleman is preferable to nobody.'

'Passing over your contemptuous reference to myself,' laughed Dick, 'I think I may safely say that you will see him again.'

'You know I didn't mean it, Dick,' said the girl quickly. 'I was only talking nonsense; but, joking apart, I am glad we are to see Mr. Dromeroff. When do you think he will be here?'

'Very soon, I fancy,' replied Dick uneasily, anxious not to say too much before so ardent an admirer of the Count as Mrs. Enson. Then, turning to Heather, he asked how they all meant to go over to the Fort.

'Father will drive Mrs. Enson; and now that you have come, Edith and I will ride over with you and Ted—that is, if you don't mind?'

'Splendid! You will ride Io?'

'I would like to,' interposed the girl; 'but won't you want to put her into work again now that you are back?'

'If I did, what better work could I put her at?' replied Dick; 'but don't let that trouble you, she is not going into training yet awhile.'

'I'm so glad,' said Heather; 'she and I have become quite chums, and she is as gentle as she is good.'

'I am glad you are so well matched,' murmured Dick as the ladies rose.

.

CHAPTER IV.

HATTEN SPEAKS OUT.

THE smoking-den at Isis Downs was originally the dining-room ; in fact, the only reception room of the old slab station-house. Now the worn-out shingle-roof was covered with iron and the earthen floor boarded, yet about its low, white-washed calico ceiling, deep, high fireplace, and broad cobweb-hung veranda, an aroma of early squatting life still clung. The calico-lined walls of the room itself were covered with various sporting prints culled by Ted Johnson from English illustrated papers. Spurs, a stock whip or so, and an old navy cutlass, all played a part in its adornment, while in the spaces left Dick Hatten had sketched in charcoal various prominent racing and political characters, including Billy the Kid and Sir Peter McLoskie. To-night, when the men had filled their pipes, Cameron suggested the veranda ; so, dragging out their canvas-backed chairs, the four settled down to that most soul-soothing of all smokes, an after-dinner pipe.

' What's that you were saying about fortifications at Musgrave's ?' asked Cameron, glancing at his nephew, a young Scotchman about a year out, but who, like most of his long-headed race, was already able to do a lot of station work over and above his nominal billet of store and book keeper. 'I thought the report about that tomfoolery was conceived in Billy's brain.'

'Far from it. Musgrave has one of those "Bees," as they call them, working hard at cutting trenches, putting up both earthen and wooden breastworks, and generally making the place a fort in reality as well as name.'

'Poor old chap, he's mad, sure enough! What do the others think of it? Do they expect the shearers to besiege them?'

'From the way they're drilling and pushing on the work, they appear to fear something a lot more serious than union troubles,' replied Ewan Cameron earnestly.

'And they're right,' exclaimed Dick, rising to his feet and knocking the ashes out of his pipe. 'Pardon me for saying it, sir, but you are all asleep; you are sitting on a mine with the slow-match already burning, and so far as I can see, the Mallarraway people are the only ones up North who realize the fact.'

'Bless my soul, Dick! have you gone daft too?' laughed Cameron; 'what are you talking about, man?'

'Listen to me, sir,' said Dick calmly; 'since I have been away, five thousand of our best-drilled men and most of our capable officers have sailed for India.'

'Jingo humbug, I admit,' interposed Cameron. 'Still, it will give the lads a big picnic and a better training than fifty camps.'

'Do you think that England would incur all this
expense—for, say what people will, her share of the
cost will be enormous—unless she really wanted them?
I say, no.   Believe me, the probabilities of a Russian
advance on India have got beyond the stage of rumour
this time.'

'A big war does look likely,' admitted Cameron.

'To my mind it is inevitable.   The death of the
Emperor has split the Austrian Empire into fragments; Italy is bankrupt through her effort to remain
in the Triple Alliance.   Disaffection is rife in India,
and Germany is beggared with her enormous military
expenditure.   All this we know.   What better chance
for France to wipe out Sedan while her ally Russia
opens the gates of Constantinople by way of an attack
on India and Australia.'

'I don't quite follow you,' said Cameron, still
sceptical, but with a growing interest.

'Don't you see that Russia's object must be to
extend, and consequently weaken, the English line of
defence; in point of fact, to draw every man she can
from Turkey, her central point of attack?   We know
that she has been prepared to rush down on India for
years; and now that France has given her a naval
station off Siam, and that New Caledonia is open to
her as a base for operations against Australia, what
is to prevent her either singly or in conjunction with
France from making a swoop on us?   There is no
disguising the fact that both their fleets in these
waters are now formidable.'

'You're not far wrong, Dick,' admitted Cameron
after a pause.   'But still, what have we to fear

personally? All this would at most mean an attack on our capitals.'

'Don't be too sure of that, sir,' said Dick quietly. 'What is to prevent a squadron, who once got through or slipped the English fleet, from throwing a few thousand men into Point Parker? And, further, for the sake of argument, supposing Spero, Aloysius and Co. and Count Zenski were in collusion, what is there to stop the invading column being landed in the centre of Queensland before the authorities at Brisbane know anything about it?'

'Good God, man! what are you thinking about?' gasped Cameron.

'Possibilities,' retorted Dick, 'which may become realities; and if they do, heaven help us all! For, thanks to McLoskie, the whole of the country they would march over is in the hands either of absentees or of men who, if my suspicions prove correct, are already in Russian pay. As to the population, who would under other conditions form the backbone of our defending force, nothing need be said—they are all either coolies, Kanakas, or Japanese.'

'I hate this infernal slave policy as much as any man; still, I can't go the length you do,' said Cameron; 'such an invasion appears to me outside practical possibilities. Naturally you are sore with Spero, and I don't blame you; but still——'

'Don't misunderstand me,' interrupted Dick. 'I have a little score to settle with him, I admit; but what I am now saying has nothing to do with that. When last at the Point, I bowled out Mr. Simpkins-Thompson; the fellow is a Russian Jew, for all his

posing as a Tory John Bull. This may appear trivial
to others; to me, taken in conjunction with other
matters that have lately come under my eyes, it has
a big significance.'

Further startled by this new development, Cameron
snatched like a drowning man at a straw.

'But, Dick, the Government are fortifying Point
Parker, and have given Zenski the contract for the
earthwork. Surely they are not so blind?'

'So far as Zenski is concerned, as bats!' sneered
Dick. 'They are the high-priests of capital, and
Count Zenski has laid too big offerings on its shrine
in connection with the Queensland railway contracts
for them to dream of doubting so good a customer.'

'Dick, you are unjust! McLoskie has his faults,
but you go too far.'

'Hold your own opinion, sir, and I will do the
same,' retorted Dick; 'all I ask is that you say
nothing of this conversation, for, even if it all comes
out as I say, Count Zenski and others may have time
to make it unpleasantly warm for me in the law courts
before the dénouement. Afterwards, none of us need
hope for much quarter, if, as I suspect, they will use
Asiatics for the invasion.'

During the discussion Ted and Ewan had smoked
on in silence. On Johnson, Dick's remarks had little
effect; he had heard some of them before, and rather
looked on Hatten as slightly 'cracked' on the subject.
On the Scotchman, however, they made a deep impression; for, apart from Hatten's evident convic-
tions, they were in great part a reflex of what he had
just heard at the Fort, and now, summing up the

matter, he came to the conclusion that much more lay behind them than his uncle would admit.

'What do you think about it, Ewan?' said Cameron as he put his pipe away and turned to go into the house.

'It reminds me a wee bit about Pompeii,' drawled the Scotchman. 'I think we might do worse than move out of reach of the eruption, uncle.'

CHAPTER V.

UNDER THE FLAME TREES.

LEAVING the smoking-den, the four men joined the ladies on the front veranda. From where they sat the garden lay wrapped in silver light, while out beyond, in the horse-paddock, the trees threw their long trails of shadow over the ripe dun grasses.

Skyward, no thought of cloud dimmed the fair face of the night, where swimming in azure depths a soft September moon looked down from among the glittering constellations on a resting world.

After a few minutes' chat, Ewan excused himself on the plea of making up the day-book; and then, at Edith's suggestion, the younger people started for a walk, leaving Cameron and his old friend to discuss 'langsyne.'

The old squatter enjoyed these chats far more than his companion. To him they recalled the one gleam of romance in his long, practical life. Talking thus in the gloaming, his gentle wife became again something more than a memory, and the full strong voice now and then grew strangely husky, as he told of those days when together they had watched over the wee baby-girl, sleeping in her rude box cradle. At such times as these the squatter felt full of doubt as to the future. Strong as he was, he knew that he was growing old, and that in a few years he, too, must rest beside the mate who had waited for him so long in the Garden of Sleep. The transition itself held no fear for him—nay, rather the elements of a supreme content; but what could he tell the yearning mother of the wee baby she had left for him to cherish? Could he truthfully say that all was well with her? He knew he could not. In the past his selfish heart had almost rejoiced when Orloff, its one rival, had madly sacrificed himself, and left his one ewe lamb to cheer his lonely life. But now, when he realized that he, too, must soon leave the child of his affection to face the world alone, the old man would have given all he possessed to know that she was safe in the arms of a husband who would take up his trust. Of late his thoughts had turned on Hatten, as the one man in whom Heather appeared to take an interest beyond that of a mere conventional friendship, and little as Dick satisfied his hopes, he yet felt that, did his girlie think well of him, he would be wrong to oppose a man who, however far he fell short of his practical ideal, was in all things a gentleman. Money, fortunately, she did not require, and so Cameron began to accustom himself to the picture of Heather marrying Hatten, and weaning him from his present purposeless existence to a more useful life.

With the idea of Heather's marriage, Mrs. Enson was fully in sympathy, and of late she seemed even inclined to waive her commonsense objections to Dick.

In fact, the old lady appeared to be possessed of a keen desire to marry off both the girls as soon as practicable. The part of these evening chats, to which, however, she evinced a growing distaste, was that which treated of a period bringing into unpleasant prominence the question of her own age. As she repeatedly remarked to Cameron, ' The past is too painful a subject for me to linger on.'

Rendered uneasy, in spite of his disbelief, by Hatten's statements in the smoking - room, the squatter asked his companion whether she thought Heather really had any feeling beyond mere friendship for Dick.

' Heather is a puzzle to me, Angus,' replied the old lady ; ' sometimes she speaks of Richard in a way which leads me to suppose she has, and then, when I suggest such a thing, she looks so utterly surprised that I am forced to the conclusion that I have been mistaken.   What do you think yourself ?'

' My dear Prudence, I don't know anything about women,' exclaimed Cameron.

' Few men do,' sighed Mrs. Enson.

' How about the Count ?' asked Cameron slyly.

' Ah, he is a man of fine discernment,' murmured Mrs. Enson.   ' Now, *he* says Heather has never forgotten that dreadful young man Orloff.'

' Does he ?' muttered Cameron.   ' I remember Zenski and he were great friends.'

' Yes, poor Count ! that is one of his biggest regrets ; he says he was never so deceived in any man.'

' He seems to take you more into his confidence than most people,' hazarded Cameron.

'He tells me everything,' said Mrs. Enson, adding coyly: 'He calls me his affinity.'

'The deuce he does!'

'Ah, yes; to me all his plans are confided, all his hopes for the future of this his adopted land explained.'

'Indeed!' drowsily.

'I sometimes think I may be a little old.'

'Nonsense!' muttered her companion sleepily. 'Let me see, you were twenty-seven when you married Enson, and he's dead about twenty-five years: that would make you a trifle over fifty, Prudence. Why, you're good for another twenty years yet.'

'Angus, what do you mean?' gasped Mrs. Enson. 'Your memory must be failing.'

'Tut, tut! of course, now I remember, you were thirty.'

'I was barely twenty,' retorted Mrs. Enson with dignity. 'I don't care about myself, for, thank goodness, my appearance bears out the truth; but I am surprised at your attempting to make the poor girls older than they really are.'

'Well, I apologize,' muttered Cameron, his voice thick with sleep; 'what does it matter how old you are if you feel young?'

'It's all for the Count's sake,' simpered Mrs. Enson. 'Angus, I feel I should confide in you as my oldest friend. The Count has told me he is lost without a companion. Whenever he is near me I feel his eyes are resting on my face; when I suggest a younger girl he tells me fruit must be ripe before it satisfies

12

the palate of an epicure.   Now, how would you
interpret this charming allegory ?'

For reply a deep snore came out of the recesses of
Cameron's chair.

'Soulless creature !' snapped Mrs. Enson, rising
and walking indignantly past the sleeping squatter.

While the conversation on the veranda was going on,
the two girls and their companions strolled on in the
moonlight.   At first they kept together, but once
through the garden-gate, Ted and Edith fell behind.
For a time Johnson maintained a morose, not to say
cynical, attitude towards the world in general, which
keenly amused his companion.   Knowing her lover
as she did, his pessimistic utterances sounded about as
real as the thunder of a stage storm.

'Look here, Ted,' said she at last ; 'I know what
it's all about, and I apologize.   I don't care if Mr.
Dromeroff is in Siberia.'

'I hope he is,' growled Johnson fervently.

'Don't be a goose ! why shouldn't I like him if I
wish ?'

'I detest foreigners,' retorted Johnson somewhat
illogically.

'Well, on the whole I agree with you,' laughed the
girl, ' so let us make it up.'

At first Ted stood on his dignity, but in the end, as
generally followed, she twisted him round her well-
shaped little finger, and he humbly asked to be forgiven
who but a few minutes before had grave doubts about
granting forgiveness.

Then they talked about the future as true-hearted
lovers do, and builded their little castles of pleasure

with the good old fatuous faith which has obtained
since the world began.

' Your mother was so nice to me when I talked to
her of our wedding the other day, Edith,' said Ted
as they turned aside and walked towards the river-
bank. ' I believe she'll be really glad to see us
married.'

' I'm sure she will,' retorted Edith a little sadly.
' Do you know, Ted,' she went on, almost in a whisper,
' I'm afraid the dear old mother is going to make a
fool of herself.'

' Why, has she bought scrip ?' exclaimed Ted.

' Worse than that.'

This was a ' staggerer,' for Johnson understood
Australian mining morality, and anything worse than
falling into the hands of a mining broker nonplussed
him. At last he said with awed hesitancy :

' She has not taken to drink ?'

' No, you old stupid !' cried the girl, laughing in
spite of herself at Ted's expression of concern.

' Then what has she done ?' demanded the manager.

' She's fallen in love with that horrid old Count
Zenski, or thinks he's fallen in love with her. Isn't
it awful, Ted ?'

' Oh, is that all ?' laughed Johnson. Being in love
himself, he felt thoroughly cosmopolitan on the
subject.

' It's too much : I won't have the hateful old thing
for a stepfather, so there ! And besides, I feel sure he's
only making a fool of the mater, and that's worse.
Oh, the whole thing is too ridiculous !' exclaimed
Edith, stamping her foot.

'Well, if what you say is a fact, you won't have him for a father, that's certain,' grinned Ted.

'Don't make fun of it; it makes me vexed enough to cry; the mater's over fifty, and her hair is growing darker every week, and now she wants to take up tennis and riding again.'

'If all Dick says is true, she might do worse than marry the Count,' blurted out Johnson. And then, despite Hatten's request of silence, he allowed himself to be pumped dry. The following day, during a passage of arms with her mother on the subject of the Count, Edith forgot her promise of secrecy, and so in due course Zenski heard Dick's opinion of him.

Not noticing the loss of their companions, Heather and Dick walked on as by a common consent in the direction of the clump of coral-trees. Questioned as to his future plans, Dick told her of his proposed trip out West.

'Here there is no chance for a man, and if there were, I can't bear the idea of settling down to the hopeless monotony of a super's life,' said he. 'I feel I must have action, or I shall rot. Some time ago I read in Favenc's book of the possibility of rich country in the heart of what they call the Great Desert. As Favenc says, these flying camel trips have been practically useless, and if Major Warburton was right about wild geese flying over his camps, then it follows that there must be water somewhere in the heart of Western Australia.'

'And you mean to try and find it, Dick?' said Heather.

'I do. Billy, I know, will go with me, and with him

and a couple of black boys who know the country, I mean to succeed on horseback where these camel expeditions have failed.'

As he ended, they reached the flame trees, now flooded with the moonlight, and looking into the dark, firm face, dignified with the majesty of a strong resolve, Heather realized that she had misjudged him. He might have once been weak ; to-night she discovered that he could also be strong.

To her there was something heroic in this wild quest. It appealed to her as a deed attempted amid all the alluring pageant of war could never have done. He was about to attempt the noblest form of physical adventure, exploration, and her heart went out to him standing there hopeless and penniless, but still determined to play his part fearlessly and well.

Then the vision of the dangers he was about to face rose before her.

' Dick, think well,' said she ; ' what if you never find the water ?'

' I will do my best,' he answered simply.

' You will die !' she exclaimed, and a note of self-reproach rang through each word. ' Dick, this is no time for false shame. I feel that could I have given you another answer you would never have thought of this mad expedition. Is it not so ?'

' It is,' he answered huskily.

She looked so fair, with the moonbeams revelling among her radiant hair, that his strength forsook him, and he spoke the truth when he felt a lie would have been more noble.

For a little there was silence. He had answered

not as she hoped, and still as she expected. Then
she spoke slowly and as if in pain :

'You know I love another man—you have promised
to help me find him—and so you must know that my
love is not mine to give.'

'Heather,' he interrupted, 'for God's sake don't let
this phantom stand between us. Orloff can never
come back to you : do you think that if he were alive
he would have sent no message ? My love, do not let
this cold, impalpable presence hold us apart for ever.'

She knew that even if Orloff were dead his love was
still alive, and so at last she said :

'Mad, unreasonable as it may seem to you, Orloff
holds me bound by ties which even the grave cannot
break.'

'Let me but have you here, and I will give you to
him in the world beyond if it is your desire,' he
pleaded in a voice of passionate appeal.

'I cannot,' she answered strangely. 'Dick, you
are too much of a man to ask me to betray both of us
with a lie.'

Then, as he was about to speak, she cried in a voice
of despairing bitterness :

'Believe me, I am not worthy of your love !'

He knew that all was over ; that the one pure
passion of his wandering, reckless life could never
wake responsive fire in the heart of the woman who
stood beneath the flame-clad corals, so full of pity
that she hated herself because she could not love.

Looking into her face, he said slowly : 'Now I
know that I have no hope.' Then, with terrible
earnestness : 'But this I swear : Could one so pure

as you have by any strange mischance become in the eyes of the world unworthy of a passion such as mine, even had some sin cut you off from all human kind, my love would have bridged the gulf.'

In this supreme moment, when unconsciously Hatten spoke as though he knew of her sorrow, and in the same breath let her see that even had it been a sin he yet would forget all for her sake, Heather's heart went out to him.

'Forgive me,' she faltered, overcome by the grandeur of his passion; 'I know that I am cruel and ungrateful, but, Dick, I can't be false to you—to my own heart. I do love you, but not in the way you wish. Surely, when your love is so noble, you can give it to me in the sacred name of friendship?'

'I love as a man,' said Hatten slowly, 'and you have again asked a hard thing of me; still, for my love's sake be it so. I accept your friendship as a more precious gift than the love of other women.'

Taking her hand in his, he kissed it, as, stepping from under the coral-trees' red flame, they walked homeward through the moonlit paddock.

CHAPTER VI.

PROFESSOR HEINRICH JANSEN.

PROFESSOR JANSEN had been a well-known figure on the northern coasts of Australia for some months. He was both philosopher, naturalist, musician, and litterateur; but as he travelled *en prince*, and gave excellent whist and dinner parties on board his rakish, slate-coloured steam-yacht, his intellectual fads were forgiven. A poor man possessed of the Professor's inquisitive, not to say prying, disposition would probably have been arrested as a spy. In his case, however, the eccentricity of genius was the name given to his investigating habits by the leading men who enjoyed his hospitalities. As he was apparently in no need of financial help, Sir Peter McLoskie had lately appointed him to draw up a report on Pearl-shell and Bêche-le-mer, so that the Professor, apart from his standing as a man of means, now commanded an official recognition as well.

Through the medium of irreproachable cigars and unlimited whisky-and-seltzer, Jansen had made a bosom companion of Mr. Peter Smith, Post-Office Inspector for the Government of Queensland, and through that somewhat bibulous official possessed the run of all the local post-offices. The Professor's knowledge of telegraphy was indeed remarkable, as he had proved on more than one occasion, when the local line-repairers and operators were nonplussed.

Though, as a Finlander, a subject of Russia, being a philosopher, the Professor looked with contempt alike on a Czar who risked explosion for the sake of power, and on the Nihilists who courted death in an attempt to overturn one tyrant only that another might be set up. So to his well-balanced mind the fairness of British rule appeared incontrovertible, particularly that part of it immediately presided over by Sir Peter McLoskie.

Being a man of artistic tastes and manner of life, the ornate splendour of the Levantine firm of Spero, Aloysius and Co. rather repelled him, while with Zenski, the great contractor, he professed to hold little in common.

Speaking of these commercial magnates, he was once heard to declare: 'While trade is doubtless admirable, I hold the right to buy supplies and railway-tickets without fraternizing with their vendors.' And the men who listened, all traders themselves, laughed loud and long at the distinguished visitor's admirable logic. Of late the Professor had spent most of his time on the pearlshell ground near Thursday Island, but, as it happened, on the day after Hatten's arrival at Isis Downs, he and Zenski met at one of the hotels in Normanton. During the progress of the *table d'hôte* meal Jansen and the Count took little notice of each other, but, nevertheless, about ten o'clock that night a visitor came on board the yacht, who, on being shown into the cabin, threw aside his slouched hat and cloak, and, slapping the Professor on the shoulder, remarked, ' Well, what news, *mon brave ?*'

Regarded physically, Jansen hardly bore out the title. There was, in fact, nothing warlike about his rather stooped figure, while the face, covered with a straggling, ill-kept beard, and further hidden by a pair of omnipresent glasses, gave little promise of a martial spirit.

Lady admirers said he was so artistically negligent ; men with no soul for genius dubbed him confoundedly dirty. The Professor himself remained impervious to all criticism. He candidly admitted that the one cold of his life was caused by his falling into the water ; his appearance vouched for the fact that he had since avoided any such accident.

Rather wincing under his visitor's touch, Jansen pointed to a chair, saying, as he pushed a box of cigars within reach :

' You grow too English, Zenski. But I am glad to see you ; there is much to talk over.'

Lighting a cigar, the Count leant back lazily.

' We are ready,' said he. ' *Pardieu*, I hope no hitch occurs. If it does, we will have a nice lot of horse-flesh and cattle on hand. Besides, I hear these co-operative *canaille* grow suspicious, and you know how that spreads.'

' What matter ; up North, at least, it will have no brains to feed on. We are among our own people,' sneered Jansen.

'You forget all we risk,' retorted Zenski.

'Not I; and, what is better, I can show you there is no risk. Leroy is ready, and, if all goes well, his fleet will be in the Gulf by the end of the month. I will see that you know to a day in ample time.'

'How about the cables?'

'That I will see to. Thanks to Monsieur Smith, I am in touch with all their system, and can tap where I require.'

'Have operations commenced yet?'

'They have. The Russian advance on India is an established fact by now. The Franco-Russian fleets have only to draw away what is left of the China squadron, and the road lies open.'

'When are the cables to be cut?'

'All but the one from New Caledonia will be seen to next week.'

'How about the attack on Hong Kong?'

'It is to be made simultaneously with the sailing of Leroy's expedition.'

'Don't forget the overland line from Thursday Island.'

'Never fear, my friend; it will be tapped.'

'I wonder if they will swallow our cables *viâ* New Caledonia?' grinned Zenski.

'Poor devils! what choice have they?' replied Jansen. 'All other communications will be cut off; and, after all, we will only cable that which is likely to happen.'

'Set them on the *qui vive* all round the Southern coasts; we must keep their forces scattered at any cost.'

' The flying squadron now lying in Noumea will see to that; all you have to do is to land General Leroy and his savages in the centre of Queensland, *mon* Zenski,' chuckled the Professor, as his companion rose.

CHAPTER VII.

FORT MALLARRAWAY.

FORT MALLARRAWAY was an organization of recent growth. In reality it was a product of the conflicts between capital and labour, and it would not be incorrect to describe the basis of this institution as 'co-operative settlement.' At the same time, the aspects of the organization were manifold, and to call Fort Mallarraway a co-operative station would be as incorrect as to describe the Knights Templars as a benefit society. The association combined originally the functions of a club, a joint-stock company, and a co-operative body. The times were fast turning it also into a social and military power. Disgusted with existing social conditions, a hundred men belonging to that class who stand midway between capital and labour, and who set more store by brains than either money or muscle, had put £100 apiece into a common fund. With part of this sum they purchased Afton Downs, an immense pastoral property which had fallen into the hands of a financial company. Thanks to general mismanagement and the depression of 1893, the syndicate was glad, after getting rid of everything salable, to dispose of the bare country for a nominal sum to close the account.

Once in possession, the new owners drew up a constitution.   The settlement was governed by a committee of three, controlled by a President, and elected by ballot to hold office for twelve months. Besides the executive, sub-committees to deal with the various duties of the settlement were appointed. These had to submit their reports to the central authority.   To further expedite work, a combination named the ' Bee ' was instituted.   Whatever a man's special work was, as soon as a Bee was announced, he dropped his stockwhip or his hammer or his pencil, and hurried to the spot where the general muster was proclaimed.   These Bees were determined upon by the executive committee, but never except upon suffi-cient grounds.   No member, however, was exempted from attending except for obviously necessary reasons, so that after such reductions from their strength, the executive could always throw a body of sixty or seventy men on any spot where the emergency existed.   These Bees told in keeping up wholesome good-fellowship and club feeling, for when the President was often seen driving a plough, and his *confrères* of the execu-tive yoking a team of rowdy steers or handspiking a log, the rest of the members had practical illustration of the fact that in both work and profit the principle was share and share alike.

Official salaries and fees were rigidly tabooed, so that as each man held a full equal share as a pro-prietor, his pride and interest reconciled him to any work he had to take in hand.   The question of unequal brain-power was easily met. It was laid down that if a man did contribute to the common fund the work of his brains as well as of his hands, he gained immensely more than he contributed by the voluntary work of the ninety-nine other brains concerned. The conditions of original membership were simple in the extreme, the subscription being £100 cash down, and the time of service five years. The shares were non-transferrable at the end of that period, except to the association.

When the pioneers took possession of Afton Downs, they turned the old station-house into a species of club, and this became the central camp of the association. Soon after the commencement of operations, a limestone grit was discovered in the bed of a creek, and from it a splendid artificial stone was cast in moulds. Now, after a lapse of nine years, the new club-house, and most of the members' cottages which clustered round it, were all built of this marvellous concrete. At the end of the first five years a reconstruction became necessary at Fort Mallarraway. The shares of the original proprietors who had completed their term of service remained their unincumbered property, to be devised by will, or at their death to be inherited by their next-of-kin. In order to carry on the work they had begun, the club as a body decided to adopt one hundred apprentices, to be balloted for by the shareholders. These apprentices, distinguished as 'No. 2,' were bound under articles to serve for five years, and at the end of that time all who were qualified by a certificate of good service were to be incorporated, and to receive a subsidy in the form of live stock, working plant, and necessaries to enable them in their turn to form a new ' co-operative settlement.' This new arrangement was agreed upon on January 1, 1950, and so far as the work was concerned, there was every prospect of things going on well, but how to meet household wants puzzled the executive. The ladies of the club ended the matter. With their girls and boys, they professed themselves ready to take over all domestic arrangements, the only stipulation they made being that ' No. 2 ' should live barrack fashion and attend to their own quarters themselves, of course taking their places at the common tables, which were free to them as they were to their predecessors.

Fort Mallarraway got little goodwill either from capital or labour. The representatives of finance invariably pourtrayed the members as a mob of paupers trying to make a living in a manner adverse to the interests of capital, and they had expected for years to see the ' concern ' forced into the market and sold for a song. Nevertheless, the club went on without their property appearing in any list of mortgages. The stony Downs on the Afton, forty miles across, kept sheep and bred horses in a manner not equalled by any of the pastoral syndicates in the North, while the open flats and valleys of the main river, besides carrying a herd of model Devons, showed a seemingly boundless extent of irrigated cultivation. With no mortgagee to satisfy and no wages to pay, the owners of Afton Downs were equally independent of the Government, the banks, and the labour unions.

Starting at daybreak, the Iris Downs people neared

the Fort, so called from the strategic nature of its surroundings, at about eight o'clock. Cameron and Mrs. Enson occupied a hooded buggy drawn by a pair of half-breds, who on occasion did duty as wheelers in the light four-wheeled waggon which served as a drag. The two girls, accompanied by Ted and Dick, rode as before arranged, while Billy and a couple of stockmen and a black boy brought up the rear-guard.

As the party moved on over the broken, lightly-grassed Downs, cut here and there with deep, rock-bound ravines, the white buildings of the Fort rose above the plain, glistening in the morning sun. Built on the crest of a strong stony ridge, from a distance they presented all the appearances of a well-appointed and admirably situated fortress.

When about half a mile from the basalt eminence on which the buildings stood, Hatten and his com-panions caught sight of a swarm of men clustered round some bullock teams, a steam locomotive, and machinery of various kinds. At first Dick was puzzled to comprehend the nature of the work in progress, then, guided by his old military experience in the militia, it flashed on him that the lines of strong fencing with solid block houses at the gates and angles, backed by deep trenches, formed part of those fortifications of which Ewan had spoken. Before him rose a line of iron-bark and box logs, set after the fashion of a Maori pah, and as he rode up under them, he noticed that the outer line stood between two trenches, and that the stakes, while loose at the bottom, were securely bound together by chains along

13

the top. Higher up, the square, loopholed, concrete cottages afforded excellent cover for riflemen. 'It's ingenious,' mused Dick admiringly. 'This palisade, while letting balls through without injury to itself, should stop any rush if well defended.'

'Dick Hatten, by Jingo!' said a voice near him. 'Why, where the deuce have you sprung from?' and a man whom he had not noticed walked up, and, raising his hat to the ladies, greeted him warmly.

'Thank you, Nugent. What's up? are you going to muster?' grinned Dick.

'I believe you. There will be a muster, but we want to keep them *out* this time.'

'I think we will ride on, Dick,' said Heather, who had realized all through the ride how painful the situation was for both of them. 'I know you have a lot to say to Mr. Nugent.'

As his companions cantered off, Dick dismounted.

'Wait a minute, old chap, and I'll go up with you,' said Nugent, turning to supervise the opening of a new trench.

A little later, as they walked on together, the Mallarraway man again asked what had brought Dick back.

'I had a row with Spero, Aloysius and Co., and they got an assignment of my mortgage from the Pastoral Finance Company, and have turned me out. I expect some Kalmuck super is in possession now,' replied Hatten bitterly.

'They'll turn every white man out of Queensland, if we don't look out!' exclaimed Nugent. 'But, by G—! we mean to give them a hard nut to crack.'

'So I see. You must be spending a small fortune over these works.'

'Fortune! why, we are not spending a penny. Well, I suppose work does cost money. In our case, however, it costs nothing to speak of. All you see going on here has been worked out on paper for some time. I got an official note yesterday appointing me captain of the Bee, and the papers handed me contained complete directions; all that I am carrying out is the mechanical part. Any donkey who has hands and eyes can do that. The only skilled men I want are the bullock-drivers and the engineer. Mere manual labour is thought precious little of by us, Hatten, old man. We learn in our society that the real work is done by brain and skilled science. Physical details are completed by steam-power, bullocks, horses, and boys in the apprentice stage. Stay with us a few weeks, and you will learn how, under co-operation, clubbed thought and knowledge are the real motive forces. Men who can do nothing but work with their hands and use a shovel or a pair of shears we don't want. One of our apprentices is worth two such ordinary men any day.'

While Nugent was talking they reached the head-quarters, and, after a visit to the bath and bachelors' quarters, Hatten was taken up a high stair which opened upon a flat roof, whereon were situated the President's and committee room and other offices. President Musgrave, a tall, sturdy, somewhat stern-looking man of about sixty, received his visitor cordially.

'I know you by name, Mr. Hatten, and I am

particularly glad to see you at this time,' said he.
'There is much that I wish to speak to you about;
however, come on to breakfast; we will have plenty
of time for a chat afterwards.'

The party who sat down to breakfast in the lofty,
skilfully-ventilated dining-hall of Fort Mallarraway
was a small one. Nearly all the men were down at
the Fortification Bee, where all meals were provided
for them, while most of the ladies had already breakfasted, and were now either teaching the children or
engaged in the multifarious duties of the immense
establishment.

Mrs. Musgrave, a delightful old lady, who combined
the progressive spirit of the present with the gentle
courtliness of a past decade, presided over the tea
arrangements, while her two daughters waited on
their guests.

'I can't allow this,' protested Cameron; 'it is our
duty to serve.'

'If you were one of us, Cameron,' laughed Musgrave, 'you would understand that we all serve each
other.'

'I suppose your servants have struck, Mr. Musgrave,' said Hatten, who had but a confused idea of
their internal arrangements. 'I hear the same story
wherever I go. Do allow me to be Ganymede.'

'No, no, Mr. Hatten! it is the girls' allotted work,
I can assure you. We have had no servants such as
you speak of for years. Apart from the difficulty of
keeping them, our women realized that paid servants
could hardly be expected to take much pride in work
in which they held no real interest. So now we do it

all ourselves, and feel healthier and better for it. Don't you see, we now have an important mission to fill, for if the men provide the raw material, our skill turns it into wholesome food for them.'

After breakfast, while the ladies all took a share in straightening up, Musgrave and the three men returned to the roof of the club-house.

'Light your pipes,' said the President, as they sat down under an awning. 'I mean to take a holiday in honour of your visit.'

Before them stretched a magnificent and far-reaching view of undulating downs, broken here and there by deep ravines sunk below the general level of the country.

An occasional bottle-tree with a bole like a water-jug, and crowned with a tuft of kurragong-like leaves, and here and there clumps of gorgeous corals, relieved the flatness of the landscape, while belts of coolibahs marked the winding course of every creek. Between the club-house and the western outworks stretched a deep ravine, heavily grassed, and watered by a natural spring.

'What the deuce are you up to?' asked Cameron, pointing with his pipe in the direction of the works. 'Is it for protection against the shearers' union, or do you mean to revive the old border days?'

'I know you think I'm mad, Cameron,' replied Musgrave quietly; 'most people, unfortunately for themselves, share your opinion.'

'I for one do not, sir,' interrupted Hatten.

'No; Dick is with you heart and soul,' laughed Cameron.

'I am glad of it!' exclaimed the President, looking keenly at Hatten. He knew well by hearsay of Dick's universal popularity with all the younger bushmen, and, judging from appearance, he saw in him the beau-ideal of a guerilla leader.

During the talk that followed, both Cameron and Johnson began to realize that perhaps they had been mistaken.

Musgrave held proofs of which they could hardly doubt the authenticity, and which, placed side by side with some of Zenski's late actions, gave a most unpleasant colour of suspicion to the whole business.

'Have you communicated with McLoskie about this matter?' asked Cameron.

'Repeatedly; but as you know he and I don't row in the same boat, and as the men I doubt are all friends of his, he has either ignored or pooh-poohed my warnings. The best I have been able to do was to get a supply of small arms and rifles and four light guns a few months back, on the plea that the unions meant to burn us out.'

'Poor devils! cheap labour has cooked their goose up here,' remarked Cameron.

'Practically, yes. Still, there are enough of them left to make the excuse hold water. These arms I still have, and above the ammunition supplied, we are laying in a good stock on our own account.'

'Have you any idea of when we may expect these infernal Russians?' asked Johnson, now quite won over to Musgrave's view.

'No; but they may come at any moment. Russia, as you know, has occupied Herat, and though no formal declaration of war has been made, it can only be a question of weeks, perhaps days.'

' I doubt if Russia will be polite enough to observe the rules of the ring if she can gain a first advantage by breaking them,' muttered Hatten.

' You are right ; therefore we may expect trouble at any moment. Could you collect a body of irregular horse if required ?'

' I fancy so,' replied Hatten. ' There are still a lot of fellows about Hughenden and scattered through the district who can both ride and fight, but how about arms ?'

' I will do all I can in that way,' said Musgrave. ' If you can guarantee a couple of hundred good men, we will see that they have something to handle. If the Government won't help us, we must help ourselves, eh, Cameron ?'

' I am with you,' replied the squatter. ' It may mean nothing—God send it does—but on the off chance be prepared, and I will stand in with you in the cost.'

' Spoken like a man. Now suppose we go down and have a look at the work,' said Musgrave heartily, rising and leading the way to the staircase.

CHAPTER VIII.

THE HORSE-MUSTER.

RECOGNISING the hopeless deterioration of Australian horse-breeding, the owners of Afton Downs early determined to try and get back to that weight-carrying, stout-hearted strain which had of late become replaced by the weedy, slab-sided flyer. In most parts of the colonies the old stock-horse, unequalled for both intelligence and endurance, was rapidly growing extinct. Wholesale racing, with its attendant evils of big handicaps and light-weights, had brought into existence a miserable class of weeds, admirable as a medium for betting, but ruinous as regards the future of the breed. With direct communication opened up to the East, the demand for horses suitable for remounts became intensified ; the only trouble was where to find them. Determined to make capital out of the insane folly which permitted brutes only fit for pigs' food to be used as stud-horses after their miserable legs had broken down under burdens of six stone, Musgrave had collected after infinite trouble a select band of mares, and as mates for these a couple of Arab stallions were imported. This nucleus

of a stud was turned out on a part of the run joining
Isis Downs.

As the paddock in which they ran contained over
twenty thousand acres, they were practically as free as
the early squatters' herds. Still, the ring-fence formed
a more satisfactory boundary than the blazed tree-line
or dividing-range of past days, and offered less induce-
ments to neighbouring stockmen to brand a few clean-
skins who had wandered in among their ' bosses' '
mobs. At the present time there were a promising
lot of about two hundred four-year-olds fit for the
market, and Musgrave had decided to have them
handled, not, however, so much with the object of
selling, as to provide remounts for his own men should
the occasion arise. On the morning after Cameron's
arrival the muster took place.

It was a poor affair compared with the grand old
musters of the past, for most of the stations round
were now worked solely by Kalmucks and other aliens,
and Musgrave for many reasons decided not to ask for
their help.

But apart from this, the muster really died with
the introduction of fenced runs. In the days when
only an imaginary line divided stations, stock naturally
got more or less mixed. When branding-time arrived,
each man came for his own, and sometimes for as
many of his neighbours' foals as he or his men could
manage to secure by superior finesse or more unblush-
ing prevarication. Starting at one station, and taking
each of the adjoining runs in turn, the muster was an
affair of weeks. To it all sent a contingent, and at it
the best and bravest of the country side outvied with

each other in deeds of daring horsemanship and feats with rope and brand. What men they were, these old stockmen !—lean-flanked and bearded, with eyes like hawks, and hearts as hard as their sun-tanned, sinewy hands. Men ready, if required, to rope a young one over night and ride him at daybreak ; not one of the half-starved poddies one sees rough-riders winning reputations on to-day, but a colt fit to buck through his tackling, and then go out and carry the man till dark who was able to sit on him. What horses they were !—stout-barrelled, iron-legged ' lasters,' as short behind the wither as they were long in front of it ; horses who worked day after day on no better feed than grass, and raced up beside the swiftest outlaw when the whips were cracking. To see the old stock-horse jogging along behind the ' tailers,' scarcely noticing the spur, one who didn't know points might easily have been pardoned for calling him a moke. But once let a mob get going, and it took a good man to hold most, and a better to sit on many when their noses were on a bullock's rump, and he turned in his own length.

' Cutting-out ' horses used to be led out to a cattle-camp so broken down and ' crutchy ' that they could hardly walk without stumbling; but once at work, what wonders they were !—quick as lighting, sure as death, and game to the last. The bullock they were once ' laid on to ' never got back into the mob if once he left it.

Now, in most parts of Australia the muster was in reality a thing of the past, and the stock-horses and their riders lived only in story. The bushman of the day rode round boundary-fences on a hybrid creature, having as much in common with the gelding of the past as the wooden structure on which clothes are dried. After all, it was as well; the mount was worthy of its rider, for men who called innocent gambolling bucking, and whose reins were either dangling about their horses' chests or held on a level with their own mouths, were better fitted to jog at the trail of a flock of old ewes than to ride on the wing of a mob of wild horses. ' Out back ' Australian horsemanship still lived, but in the country, where sheep and farming had driven out cattle and horses, the bush - rider was a shameless fraud, who traded on the memories of the past. Doubtless the average Australian still rode better than the average Englishman, simply because the latter seldom got the chance to ride at all. Still, this is certain : under changed conditions the wonderful horsemen of Australia were growing fewer and fewer, and were now, with certain brilliant exceptions, only to be found where surroundings still remained in which to create them.

Taking out enough quiet horses to act as ' tailers,' a dozen men from the Fort, accompanied by Dick, Ted, and their stockmen, rode out early in the morning to where the horses ' ran.' Rounding up the ' tailers ' in the bottom of one of the ravines across which the mobs were accustomed to ' make,' the party, leaving half a dozen men in charge, rode off in threes.

' You ought to drop on some the other side of that bald hill,' said Jackson, one of the Mallarraway men, pointing to a flat-topped rise about five miles away.

'Right you are,' said Johnson, as he, Dick, and Billy rode off. 'Now, mind you "tailers" don't go to sleep.'

'Did you ever know the beggars do anything else?' laughed Dick.

Making a big sweep, the three came in well at the back of the hill.

'They're sure to be down on the flat,' said Ted, who knew the country.

Riding on to the crown of a rocky ridge, they came on a mob of about thirty resting under some corals. Silently as they had approached the wild horses heard them, and now as they topped the rise ran neighing round a white, bloodlike-looking stallion. Giving a trumpet-tongued snort, he tossed his long tangled mane and raced off like the wind, followed by his companions.

'I'll take the lower side,' shouted Johnson. 'Don't let 'em break back, Billy!'

'No blooming fear!' grunted Billy, as Ted shot past him, while Dick, who did not know the lie of the country, ran up on the other wing.

Galloping straight from point to point, Johnson met and turned them whenever they tried to break through, while the crack of Billy's stock-whip rang out above the clang of the horses' hoofs as he forced the mares and foals up into the mob. Afraid to lie off too far, Hatten raced well up on the other wing.

Down a rock-bound ravine they dashed, the stallion still in front, but met on either side, and pressed too close to double, they galloped up its broken face, and on over the open downs straight for the square-topped

hill. The foam flying from their leaders' manes fell
like snow on the sweat-stained coats of the weary
mares as they neared its base. Breasting it gallantly,
the mob, tossing back dust and stones from their
flying hoofs, reached the crown. Then for a moment
they wavered, but Billy's whip rang out, and tossing
their manes they charged down the farther side.
Racing round either shoulder, Ted and Dick, sitting
well back with feet rammed 'home' and hands held
low, shot up on both flanks, as Billy, giving the
'Barcoo back cut,' drove his horse down the face of
the hill. Running wide, then closing up, the three,
with practised generalship, steered the wild horses
straight for the ravine in which the 'tailers' were
placed. As they neared it, all their stock-whips rang
out in warning, and closing on the chase, they drove
them over its edge. Down into the gully the horses
plunged as a chorus of yells and stock-whip cracks
rose above the thunder of hoofs and neighing of the
tailers.

'D——n them, they're asleep!' shouted Ted, as
they saw in a flash the mob burst through the
'tailers,' carrying most of them away with them up
the other side.

Cursing the men, just mounted, and now vainly
attempting to block the rush, Ted and Dick drove
spurs into their blown horses, and, nursing them up
the rise, gave chase. Luckily the country was good,
and gaining half a mile by one of Johnson's short-
cuts, they again met the mob, and turning them with
their whips, drove them back into the 'tailers,' now
rounded up and well backed by Billy and the men.

'What the devil were you up to?' demanded Dick savagely, as he loosed the girths on his reeking horse.

'Oh, shut up!' growled one of the delinquents; 'the fellow you left behind has just given us about as much as we can stand already.'

'Been reading out their characters—eh, Billy?' laughed Ted.

'My oath!' drawled the trainer.

About four in the afternoon the musterers started for home. Steadying the mob on a bit of good country, Dick, Ted, and Jackson moved on ahead, followed by the horses, while the rest of the men jogged on the wings and kept up the stragglers. Sitting loosely in their saddles, the stockmen discussed the chances of the day to a running accompaniment of hoof-beats and the whinnying of foals and neighing of the stallions.

Tired limbs could now be stretched at leisure, and reins still damp with sweat let hang on drooping necks, for the smoke-rings which coiled lazily above each pipe told that the work of the day was done. As they guided the horses between the wings of the stockyard, which stood at the head of the valley commanded by the entrenchments, Cameron and Musgrave, accompanied by Zenski, drove up.

After a look from the top of the fence, the Russian remarked carelessly :

'You have a few fair remounts among your horses, *mon ami;* they are for India?'

'I'm not sure,' replied Musgrave curtly.

'If it will save you any trouble, possibly I may be able to find a buyer for a few of them.'

'You are very obliging, Count,' remarked Musgrave suspiciously.

'Not at all,' laughed Zenski; 'self-interest, I can assure you; *ma foi!* I am but what you would call touting for business.'

Hearing in Hughenden various reports as to the work going on at Fort Mullarraway, Count Zenski determined to judge for himself. Everyone voted the Afton Downs people a crowd of lunatics, and with this opinion Zenski cordially fell in — in public. Privately, he considered that there was enough of method in their madness to warrant a personal inspection.

Much as Musgrave detested the Russian, he yet felt that to show his dislike would be both useless and unwise, so on his arrival he was received, if not with cordiality, still with all due politeness. That he was not wanted struck Zenski at once, but this troubled him little ; he had come for a purpose, and so long as that was gained the feelings of his hosts towards himself were matters of perfect indifference. The fact that even Heather met him with a certain restraint roused the Count's curiosity, and induced him to cultivate Mrs. Enson with even more *empressement* than usual. From that lady he soon learned all he wanted to know, and considerably more than was likely to prove advantageous to Hatten should Dick ever fall into his hands. During the afternoon the Russian made it his business to inspect as much of the scheme of defence as could be viewed from the roof of the club-house.

Musgrave's politeness utterly refused to allow of

his guest's nearer approach on the plea of the intense heat; and as Zenski had no wish to appear suspiciously interested, he had perforce to be contented with this somewhat distant view.

While professing indifference as to the colts, Zenski had determined to buy up all the four-year-olds if he could manage it. He was moved to this determination by the double motive of wanting good mounts for the invading cavalry, and desiring to keep them out of the hands of the defending force.

That night, after considerable finessing, Zenski made an offer for the whole draft. As he put it, their trainage to Point Parker would cost his firm nothing, so he could afford to be liberal. This liberality first took the shape of an offer of £10 apiece, but at last, as Musgrave remained firm, Zenski made a final bid of £20 a head on a three-months bill. Under ordinary conditions this was handsome enough, but to Musgrave and Hatten the conditions sounded both ominous and ludicrous. If they were right in their supposition, both felt it would be a hard bit of paper to collect.

'I admit the offer's not a bad one, Count,' said the President after a little thought; 'but I regret to say I must ask you to let it stand over until after our annual meeting, three months ahead.'

'*Pardieu*, that is not business!' muttered Zenski. 'In three months I may not want your horses, *mon ami*; what then?'

'I doubt if you will, Zenski,' replied Musgrave, so significantly that the Russian dropped the subject.

BOOK IV.

THE WAVE BREAKS.

—◆—

CHAPTER I.

A STORMY PETREL.

LEAVING the brilliantly-lighted piazza of the Mitylene Palace, two men walked slowly down to the pier that stretched out into the dark waters of the Gulf. On either side of the broad rail-shod causeway, electric lamps shone like giant fireflies, throwing their prismatic rays far out into the gloom and cresting the lazy ripples with coronets of silver.

Here and there groups of townsmen lounged or sat on the pier, either idly smoking or discussing local scandal and the latest cablegrams with that hopeless lassitude and utter ennui common to European-Asiatic life. Moving among them, Afghan hawkers and Chinese fruit and cigarette sellers supplied the local colour of an Eastern picture.

Standing on the approach, the two men looked out along the pier. Turning and waving his hand towards the wretched hovels that clustered round the warehouses, Zenski said in French :

14

'The foreground is already of the East.'

'So is the middle distance,' replied Spero, as they walked past a mob of scarlet-turbaned hawkers.

'With luck Leroy should be able to provide an admirable background before morning,' sneered Zenski.

'Yes, this is the twenty-fifth of September; if Jansen has made no mistake, the flotilla is due,' said Spero in a low, anxious tone.

'*Peste*, how could he mistake?—his message reads distinctly: "Both flotillas past all danger; should form junction at latitude 12°, longitude 140°; look out for me to-morrow night."'

While they were speaking they neared the end of the pier, and, standing against the railing, looked silently out into the dark, moonless night. As they watched a light rose faintly out of the gloom.

'Some fishermen,' muttered Spero.

'Not so, *mon ami*,' returned Zenski, as the light grew rapidly brighter.

Then, as they waited, their eyes caught a phosphorescent gleam on either side of the advancing beacon.

'It is Jansen,' whispered Spero; and as he spoke the Professor's yacht ran up beside the pier, and the man of science climbed up the steps and stood peering into their faces from behind his glasses.

Galvanized into some amount of interest by the arrival of a strange boat, the people on the pier began to crowd round the three men; but recognising that further pretence was useless, Zenski and Spero followed Jansen back into his cabin.

'Well?' exclaimed the Count, as they entered.

'I have come direct from Leroy,' replied Jansen;

' the wing which came round the north of New Guinea ran through Torres Strait safely, and I believe unseen.'

' Thanks to electricity and slate-coloured paint,' grinned Zenski.

'At the point agreed on the two flotillas joined. Making allowance for the extra speed of my yacht, Leroy should be off Point Parker before daylight.'

' Had they any trouble getting through ?' asked Spero.

'None. As you know, Leroy had concentrated twenty thousand men at Port Arthur, with which, in conjunction with a powerful fleet, he was supposed to be about to operate against the Russian forces in maritime Manchuria, while Ching Tu was massing a formidable army to defend the Southern ports. A week before war was officially declared, the Russo-French fleets made a demonstration before Hong Kong, which practically drew off the British squadron. As soon as the coast was clear, the Chinese fleet shipped Leroy's column and ran out to sea. A day or so later, the allied fleets having drawn the English squadron into the Gulf of Siam, Dromeroff, with ten thousand of Ching Tu's picked Kalmuck cavalry, slipped out of the Southern ports. The massacre of the English and attack by Ching Tu on Hong Kong were to follow, but of these Leroy has no information.'

' Then neither of the fleets met any opposition ?'

' None worth the name.'

' The English squadron must have had its hands full,' muttered Zenski.

' Doubtless,' retorted Jansen. ' Still, you must not forget that our transports are built for speed ; under equal conditions they can outpace the unwieldy English ironclads. In this case they have had a long start as well.'

'*Pardieu!* the fates fight for us,' laughed the Count. 'Now, even if they do come, we can give them a warm reception from the batteries I am building for my good friend Sir Peter.'

'Are they nearly completed?'

'Yes; the guns are here ready for mounting, and our merchant prince is even now entertaining the distinguished engineer who is about to take over the work.'

'Leroy should indeed be obliged,' sneered Jansen; 'not only do you build him batteries, but you provide him with a skilled officer to pass them.'

'*Ma foi!* had we not better return?' said Zenski. 'Bourouskie may get drunk himself in trying to bring our gallant Colonel to a similar condition.'

'He dare not,' muttered Spero. 'Still, we have much to do between now and daybreak. Do you come with us, Jansen?'

'No, I have other work to do.'

'Doubtless the cables are seen to?' said Zenski.

'All are cut except that from Noumea,' replied the Professor. 'I myself sent the last message from Port Darwin.'

'What was its import, *mon brave?*'

'War declared; be prepared for Russian or French attack on capitals.'

'What chivalry!' laughed Zenski. 'You deserve hanging for your devotion to Sir Peter, Professor. Adieu; we will be ready to welcome *Monsieur le Général* and his Mongols.'

CHAPTER II.

THE COMING OF THE MONGOLS.

THE sea-birds sleeping on the dreary surface of the Gulf rose screeching from their wave-rocked slumber, for fiery-eyed monsters, swift and silent, were moving relentlessly over the waste of water.

At intervals a sharp word of command rang out, spoken in a tongue that was old before the Western world rose out of chaos, and in response men with the broad yellow faces and coarse black hair of those fierce nomads who followed Genghis Khan sprang to obey. The lights, falling on them as they worked, lit up their features with ghastly distinctness. From their cruel lips flowed a song, discordant, fear-compelling, which, as it floated out over the sea, filled all the air with its awful cadences.

For a space the half-wakened birds hung motionless, caught in the thrall of the demon chorus, then, uttering startled cries, fled into the night.

To Jansen, going to meet them in his yacht, a vision of the old blood-limned days arose. From such beings and in some such guise must have rung out the dread Raven's song. Then, when he remem-

bered who and what they were, he realized that
silken-sailed galleys, with glittering shields and triple
banks of oars, were not for demons such as these.
Such a song should only come from betwixt the folds of
bat-like sails, and up out of the bowels of dragon-prowed
junks.   To-night it rose above the decks of swift,
low-lying, smokeless cruisers, armed with the latest
weapons of the Western world.   It was the battle-cry
of Tamerlane shouted by warriors such as his; but, in
place of the bow and spear, they held in their relentless, clawlike hands the weapons of a civilization
which had risen and marched on while his race stood
still.   The Mongols, after a sleep of centuries, had
awoke at last.   Still brave as lions, enduring as dogs,
and rapacious as wolves, they had shaken off their
death-like stupor and again taken up the glorious
traditions of the past.   Cunning as foxes and far-
sighted as ravens, they had learned by defeat, and
now, following out their policy of making use of their
enemies, were led by a renegade, who could be
destroyed when he had fulfilled their purpose.   Strong
as ever in their belief in their absolute superiority to
all mankind, and armed with the very weapons which
in the past had brought about their humiliations,
they were coming under the old banners of blood
and fire to avenge past insults and win new possessions.

In answer to Jansen's signal, the leading vessel
slowed down.   Running alongside, the Finlander
spoke for a few minutes in Russian to an officer who
had come to one of the ports, then sheered off and
disappeared.   Walking down into the gun-room, the

officer knocked. Absorbed in thoughts that, from his knitted brow, were at best full of anxiety, the only occupant took no notice of the summons. On the table before him lay a map on which he had been marking different routes with a pencil which still lay between his fingers.

The cavalry sabre lying on a chair, and his striking half-Russian, half-Eastern uniform, told that he was a soldier still. Apart from these signs, General Leroy could hardly have been mistaken for a civilian.

Broad-shouldered and deep-chested, with dark eyes that never flinched, either at the ping of bullets or the frown of another, with lips devoid of sensuality, but almost cruel in their firm, close lines, and with a large though delicately-cut nose, he looked essentially a leader of warlike men. His age was always a subject of dispute among his comrades. For while his close-cropped hair was white, his heavy moustache and strongly-marked brows remained black. The lines about his mouth and under his eyes were those of a man who had either lived hard for years or else long in a short space of time; but in all matters of endurance he was still in his prime.

Roused by a second knock, the General called out in the full, strong voice of one accustomed to utter words of command:

'Enter!'

Obeying, the officer saluted.

As he did so, Leroy rose, and then his great height became apparent. As a comrade had said to him, 'He was not only born to command men, but savages.'

' Well, Redski, what is it ?' he asked.

' Jansen has returned, General; he wishes me to convey to you that all is ready both at Point Parker and Normanton.'

' I expected as much; Zenski never fails in detail.'

' Jansen also instructed me to announce, General, that the division for Normanton must leave us in an hour.'

' Inform the Admiral, and signal Colonel Dromeroff to come on board when the squadron lies to,' said Leroy, dropping again into his chair, and pulling the map towards him.

Swiftly the slate-coloured monsters glided past Cape Van Diemen, then a signal-light ran up the solitary mast of the Admiral's ship, and the fleet lay to. Picking up Dromeroff, Leroy's second in command, Jansen again ran alongside. This time, however, he came on board, and, walking up on the bridge, began to explain certain matters connected with the tides, while Dromeroff hurried down into the General's cabin.

Dressed in uniform, and now wearing a moustache, the Colonel had thrown aside all semblance of the persecuted civilian who had given the members of the Midas so frank an opinion on the war scare.

' The time has come for us to part company,' said Leroy. ' Is there anything upon which you are not clear ?'

' Nothing, General; everything is prepared for landing the moment our ships drop anchor; and piloted by Jansen, a hitch seems impossible.'

' See that it is impossible,' retorted Leroy. ' I look to you in this matter, Dromeroff.'

' I accept the responsibility.'

' And will share the glory of success, my comrade !' exclaimed the General. ' I leave all in your hands ; only, remember, it is not a question of we *may* win—we *must* win, Dromeroff.'

' I know it. From the enemy we can expect no quarter, and these devils of ours would turn on us like wolves in the hour of defeat.'

' Possibly !' muttered Leroy. ' Still, I doubt it; nevertheless, let us not give them the chance,' said the General. ' Are your rafts and landing bridges ready?'

' They are now putting them together.'

' Dromeroff, I know these men,' said Leroy. ' How cruel and brutish they are when the lust of blood is on them !'

' Are not all men alike ?' sneered the Colonel.

Disregarding the question, Leroy continued:

' About the men it would be folly to trouble. They will give no quarter, so they can expect none; but I command you—and remember I will be obeyed—save the women and children.'

' I can but do my best,' growled Dromeroff. ' But how can I be everywhere ?'

Recognising the truth of his officer's remark, Leroy replied:

' I leave our honour in your keeping, my comrade; and now, *bon voyage.*'

Clasping each other's hands, the two men stood looking into each other's eyes. Both felt they were standing on the edge of an unknown abyss, in whose depths lay hidden the elements of disgrace and fame. Both were soldiers of fortune, men reckless of most things, and yet, as the Mongols' devilish chorus floated down from above, a sense of the awful scourge they were about to let loose fell upon them.

Then, realizing the madness of such thoughts at this eleventh hour, Leroy caught up his sword, and, striding to the door, exclaimed :

'To your ship, Colonel ; are we not the servants of the Czar ?'

Standing on the bridge beside Admiral Frampton, a thick-set American, who had originally been a midshipman in the United States navy, Leroy watched the Normanton flotilla, led by Jansen, disappear. As the last light merged into the darkness, he turned to the pilot who stood beside him :

'When should we be off Point Parker ?'

'In a couple of hours, General,' the man replied.

'Won't you have to slacken down when we get on the coast ?' asked Frampton anxiously.

'I have reckoned on that,' said the pilot ; 'but we can run up to twenty till we are off the harbour.'

On board each transport the work of preparation went on. Directed by officers claiming every nationality, but among whom Russians predominated, the Celestial warriors toiled with that dogged endurance which has made their race hated, and was yet to make it feared.

Rafts which, when loaded with infantry, could be towed ashore by steam-launches, and floating-bridges on which to land artillery and the staff-horses, were being transferred from the holds and laid in sections on the decks with a mathematical exactness which told of perfect preparation.

Forward the different detachments were forming for a final inspection. Armed with the latest types of rifle, some of them capable of discharging a hundred rounds per minute, and provided with light, bullet-proof uniforms, a dress long known to the Chinese, but now brought to a high state of perfection by Western skill in Eastern pay, the men, both in physique and discipline, utterly belied the popular idea of Chinese soldiery. With the miserable market-gardener and the fossiker known to Australia these warriors had little in common. They were Mongols, possessing the same physical strength and capacity for endurance that made their ancestors the most formidable soldiery in the world, and Kalmucks, who had revived the old Manchu saying that 'A man's sole duty is to ride a horse and to bend a bow.'

Realizing that the institution of trade relations with their neighbours must mean in one form or another the loss of those territories which at present admitted the sway of the Bogdo Khan up to the Pamir and the Karakoram, the Conservative party at Pekin had at last decided that the only chance of retaining them lay in taking one side or the other in the coming struggle between Russia and England. Led by Ching Tu, and saturated by that potent Russianizing process with which the Muscovite seems able to influence even the most hostile of Asiatic peoples, the younger Chinese party threw all their weight on the side of Russia. Fanned by Leroy and other secret agents, hostility to England grew more intense, while the accounts of Australia brought back by the Chinese themselves not only filled their countrymen with a feeling of revenge, but also with the more potent desire for conquest. Still, as befitted the most subtle diplomatists of Asia, even when a Russian policy was agreed upon, its ends were jealously hidden from the world. Until the day the flotilla sailed, Russia and China professed to be preparing to spring at each other's throats, and, with consummate trickery, Leroy was placed under arrest on the ground that, although an American soldier of fortune and instructor to the Chinese forces, he had once served in the Russian army.

Standing on the bridge, General Leroy looked down on the men he was about to hurl on a continent upon whose vast expanse they would be but a speck. Still, this troubled him little; he well knew that in its colossal limits lay its impotency, and that once the barriers were forced, numberless thousands were ready to rush in through the opened breach. That many of these would never see the promised land he well knew; but even if a few thousands left their bones to pave the narrow waterway, there were plenty to take their places. Then the thought arose, But what if England cuts off all further reinforcements? Casting it aside as unlikely, at any rate, for the present, Leroy conjured up another picture. Ambition was his god, and now it seemed to him that this deity held out a prize worthy for a soldier to grasp at, even if Death sat in the other scale.

Ching Tu, he well knew, aimed at becoming viceroy of this new world, did victory crown his arms; but now that no fealty to Russia stood in his way, Leroy, backed by the brain-power without which this huge engine of destruction must go to pieces, felt that in his hands Australia's destinies lay. Other chiefs of the Mongols had become kings of the lands their swords had won; why not he? Absorbed in his dream, the wild, barbaric chant of the workers below fell all unheeded, when suddenly a cry rang out, which as it rose swelled into a roar, wolf-like in its fierce desire. Starting, he looked ahead, and there, shining through the darkness, gleamed the lights of Point Parker.

CHAPTER III.

COUNT ZENSKI WELCOMES GENERAL LEROY.

SOME revellers staggering through the deserted streets caught gleams of fire moving over the surface of the sea. In the dull, gray light it seemed to their uncertain eyes that constellations of suns were rising out of the depths, but the watchers on the roof of the Mitylene Palace saw in the advancing flashes the lightning that presages storm and death.

Tossing his cigar over the parapet, Zenski rose.

'Come, *mes amis*,' said he gaily, 'our distinguished visitors are here; let us live up to Australian tradition, and give them welcome.'

As he spoke, his two companions walked to his side, Spero calm and anxious, Bourouskie trembling with a half-fearful unrest.

'God help us if these savages get out of hand!' the latter muttered.

'*Pardieu!*' sneered Zenski, 'we are between the devil and the deep sea if they do; but fear not, Leroy is an admirable wild-beast tamer.'

Just then a stream of fire rushed through the gloom, followed by the dull boom of a cannon. Reverberating over the water, it woke the echoes with its dull thunder.

' Leroy's signal !' exclaimed the Count. ' Come, the landing has begun.'

As the three men hurried towards the pier, a motley and excited mass began to fill the streets and pour down towards the water. Here and there a white, scared face stood out for a moment among the dusky, gesticulating crowd, then disappeared for ever.

Surrounded by a bodyguard, the Russians at last reached the pier. As they did so, the sun, rising above the horizon, shot flaming rays skyward and seaward, and there, standing out against the blazing background, floated the Chinese fleet, the Dragon standard waving from each peak. Already rafts packed with men began to move shoreward, and in answer to the Mongols, the crowds who lined the bay sent up a dread, inhuman yell.

Staggering through the press, a half-drunken planter pushed aside a powerful coolie with an impatient curse. Suddenly drawing his knife, the Chinaman drove it into his assailant's chest. As the man fell back, a stream of blood spurted out of the wound into the face of his murderer, and, moved by one common impulse of slaughter, the hybrid, downtrodden slaves became brutal avengers.

Rushing back into the streets, they began to kill with the indiscriminate hate of wild beasts, and, drunk with slaughter, dared to stain with their bloody feet the piazza of the Mitylene Palace. On its marble pavement stood three machine guns, trained to sweep the approaches, backed up by a detachment of heavily-armed Kalmucks. Zenski knew his men, and had instructed Spero to collect all the townsfolk worth saving over-night, and also to get up the guns, and provide a sufficient force to hold the palace against possible assault. Awed by the armed force, the mob hesitated for a moment, then, impelled by the demon of greed, rushed on. Waiting until the compact mass was within fifteen paces of the muzzles, the officer gave the word. No sound drowned the coolies' wild yells, no smoke hid their outstretched bloody knives; but when the watchers on the roof again turned their fearful eyes down on the square, it was littered with the dead and dying.

Terrified by the voiceless reaper, the mob rolled back into the narrow streets, uttering fierce cries of rage, while the Kalmucks, rushing from behind the guns, bayoneted with wanton devilry the wounded wretches writhing on the slippery pavement.

Recognising that defence was impossible, many of the inhabitants had fled at the first alarm; but so sudden was it all, that the majority opened their eyes only to gaze into the faces of devils mad with lust and carnage, and sworn to offer up womanly purity, prattling babyhood and helpless age on the altar of a blind, unreasoning revenge.

While these scenes were being enacted in the streets and houses of Point Parker, a launch left the side of the Admiral's ship, and, steaming rapidly through the heavily-laden rafts, approached the pier. Sheltered by a silken canopy sat Leroy, dressed in the magnificent costume of a military mandarin of the highest class. Round him stood his staff, all,

like himself, soldiers of fortune ready to stake their
lives against the prizes of the game of war. On the
right of the General sat Commissioner Wang, a mandarin of the first grade, and one deep in the confidence of the Marquis Ching Tu. Dressed in a
yellow silk coat heavily bordered with fur, and with a
chain of priceless pearls hanging over his breast, the
Commissioner rivalled Leroy in the splendour of his
costume. From under his red-buttoned hat looked a
face stolid as that of a sphinx, save for the scarce
veiled cunning that lurked in his oblique, half-closed
eyes.

Ostensibly Leroy's civil colleague, Wang was in
reality a spy sent to watch over Ching Tu's interest.
From the first the General had fathomed his mission,
but, while fully meaning to blow his brains out the
first time he dared to interfere with his plans, he had
decided to pay all due respect to Wang while he
remained passive.

The infantry, forming with machine-like precision
as they landed, now stood drawn up under their
different standards ready to salute the commander-in-
chief.

As Leroy's barge reached the stairs, the guns on
the cruisers rang out their dread applause, and the
warriors on the rafts and transports took up the
fierce pæan.

Startled by the thunder of the artillery, the coolies
in the distant streets paused in their work of rapine,
and the fugitives struggling in the mangrove-swamps
forced their way with nerveless hands deeper into
their dark, noisome depths.

15

Obedient to Redski's command, the troops already formed presented arms, and at a sign from their officer the Kalmucks watching from the roof of the Mitylene Palace ran up the Dragon standard as, followed by his staff, and greeted alike with shouts of triumph and shrill cries of despair, General Leroy sprang up the steps and stood on the pier.

Stepping forward, Zenski held out his hand:

'Welcome, *mon Général,*' said he gaily, adding, too low for those behind to hear: 'Welcome home once more, Philip.'

At the words Leroy started, and a dark flush tinged his cheek; but, recovering himself, he grasped the Count's outstretched hand heartily.

'Thanks, Count. Allow me to present you to my colleague, his Highness Commissioner Wang.'

Then, turning to Redski, his chief of staff, he asked if the railway-station, public buildings and batteries were occupied.

'All has been attended to, General,' replied the officer.

'Signal the transports with the artillery and staff horses to come alongside the pier, and see that the artillery and stores lying in the warehouses are transported to the railway-station at once. The battalion for Charleville must leave within an hour.'

Saluting, Redski stepped back.

'How about the transport trains, Count?' asked Leroy.

'Four can be ready at five minutes' notice.'

'Good! Let platforms mounted with automatic guns be attached to the front of each engine.'

'They are prepared,' interrupted Zenski.

'How about the horses?'

'Five hundred are here for shipment,' grinned the Count. 'Doubtless, however, you will take the lot. Others are ready along the line.'

'Let the squadrons who have horses be mounted as soon as the chargers are disembarked,' ordered Leroy, 'and with them round up these coolie dogs I see prowling about.'

'Yes, sire,' replied a squat Kalmuck cavalry officer.

'Put them to work on the batteries, and shoot down any hound you catch with blood on him,' exclaimed Leroy sternly.

'*Pardieu!* General, you will have no workmen left,' sneered Zenski.

'Ah, I am right,' said Leroy; 'these scoundrels have broken loose already.'

'*Peste!* what did you expect?' retorted the Count with a shrug; 'has Asiatic war so changed since Scobeleff's campaign?'

'I will have no massacre of women,' replied Leroy, 'and I will hang any man who either allows or takes part in such barbarity. These are my wishes; see that they are obeyed.'

Glancing at his staff so fiercely that the incredulous smile faded away on their lips, Leroy turned on his heel. 'I will expect your report, Redski, in two hours at the Mitylene Palace,' he said. 'Now, Zenski, I am at your service.'

Stepping into a carriage that was waiting, the party drove off.

'The General has grown tender-hearted suddenly,' muttered one officer to another.

'Bah !' laughed his comrade ; 'if he carries out his orders he will shoot more of us than the enemy. Believe me, he will soon learn neither to hear nor to see ; our tigers are tireless killers.'

'But bad discriminators,' grinned the first speaker.

CHAPTER IV.

COUNT ZENSKI AND PHILIP ORLOFF.

PUNCTUAL to time, Colonel Redski rode up to the Mitylene Palace.

In the streets, the shrieks of women and the despairing curses of men had given place to the measured tramp of feet and the dull rumble of wheels. The masters of yesterday were dead, or in full flight, and McLoskie's cheap alien labourers were now at work on the batteries, or engaged in transferring baggage and warlike stores from the wharves and warehouses to the Mongol camp. In the yards built to receive drafts of remounts prior to shipment to the East, the Kalmuck cavalrymen were already handling the chargers which were to bear them on their march to the South, while the three squadrons who had brought their horses were patrolling the streets and driving cattle into the camp.

Pulling up among a group of orderlies who were holding staff-officers' chargers, Redski dismounted, and, throwing his reins to the Kalmuck who accompanied him, ran up the steps and entered. Pushing his way through the crowd who filled the reception-room, Redski, after a moment's parley with the sentry, entered Spero's cabinet.

At a table covered with papers sat three officers writing, while, walking up and down the room, Leroy, now dressed in uniform, dictated orders with practical speed and conciseness. Looking up as his chief-of-staff entered, the General said sharply: 'You are punctual, Redski.'

'Your orders were that I was to be here within two hours, General,' replied the Colonel simply.

'Good! And your report?'

'Major Hoffman, with a battalion of infantry, two machine batteries, and a squadron of dismounted cavalry, has started for Charleville. Trains following will drop troops of cavalry at all stations where horses are collected, and these, with automatic guns mounted on trucks and propelled by engines, are instructed to hold communication clear between Charleville and our base.'

'The line must be held at all costs,' muttered Leroy, glancing at a map. 'Hoffman can't hold Charleville long without reinforcements.'

'Nearly all the workmen are aliens, and they will turn on their masters as they did here,' replied Redski confidently.

'Admitted; still, help will come from the direction of Brisbane.'

'If Dromeroff has as little trouble as we have had, a part of his force should be able to form a junction with us at Cloncurry to-morrow.'

'True, and from what Zenski says, he can't possibly fail. Keep pouring men into Charleville as fast as the train service will allow,' said Leroy. ' I will leave for Cloncurry to-morrow.'

Bowing, Colonel Redski retired as the chief of the Commissariat Department entered.

' Well ?' demanded Leroy.

' Everything is as Count Zenski promised,' replied the officer. ' Cattle are plentiful, and I have organized an admirable camp service from the coolies and other scum.'

' Are they obedient ?'

' Most,' grinned the Commissary-General. ' I had occasion to shoot a few, and while I regret the waste of powder, I have to report that the effect has been excellent.'

All day long the work of disembarkation went on, and so perfect had been the preparations of Zenski and his colleagues, that at nightfall the Mongols were encamped beyond the town, ready on the morrow for a forward movement. While the streets still echoed to the tramp of hostile feet, the dining-hall of the Mitylene Palace was filled with guests, but to-night Mammon had given place to Mars. The smug and peaceful apostles of wealth had gone, and in their stead sat the directors of a destructive force soon to sweep away for ever their boasted thrift and hoarded capital. McLoskie, their great magician, had waved his wand, and, in response, land-grant railways and dusky slaves had risen to fill his followers' coffers and swell their dividends. Heedless of the disappearance of their race before the spread of a helot population, the votaries of capital seized with insatiable greed acre after acre, never reckoning who should defend their heritage did the spoiler come. Blinded with the conceit of riches, the plutocracy said in their hearts : 'Soul, thou hast much corn laid up for many years; eat, drink, and be merry.' But an outraged God woke suddenly, and made answer : 'Thou fool! this night thy soul shall be required of thee.'

The firm of Spero, Aloysius and Co. were banqueting General Leroy and his colleague, Commissioner Wang. In place of the sombre black of commerce, glittering uniforms reflected the glow of the lamps, and echoes of war filled an atmosphere long saturated with the dull jargon of trade.

When the dinner was over, leaving Spero and his partner to escort Wang to his apartments, Leroy and Zenski turned into the cabinet where so many schemes had been matured.

'The compact made on board the *Genoa* has been fulfilled at last, Philip,' said the older man, offering his case.

Taking it, Philip Orloff carefully chose a cigar, and lit it before he spoke. When he did, there was a certain bitter ring in his voice as he replied :

'I never dreamt that it was to be kept under such conditions.'

'What matter ? the object is the same.'

'It is the means I dislike. These men are savages.'

'Russian or Mongol, it is all the same, *mon ami*,' retorted Zenski. 'Is it not better to be the commander of a Chinese army than a brigade-major in a Russian ? If you win, the ball is at your feet; you can be what you make yourself.'

'You forget that I have a colleague, or, to be frank

with you, a spy, in Commissioner Wang; I am to take the risk, the Marquis Ching Tu the glory, of this enterprise.'

'If you are fool enough to allow it, *mon brave,*' laughed Zenski. 'But that I know you are not.'

' Not if I can prevent it, I admit,' replied Orloff.

Well knowing that when Zenski smuggled him on board a Russian warship in the harbour of Colombo he saved his neck from the hangman, Philip had always retained a strong friendship for the old diplomatist. The fact that in return for his services Zenski had demanded the betrayal of his country had long since faded from Orloff's memory; for though born in Australia, he was in reality a Russian. Thanks to Zenski's influence, he had received nothing but kindness from the General into whose service he had been admitted after his escape. Fortunately for Orloff, his new commander was a man quick to discern the stuff of which good leaders are made, and so Philip's future had not been marred by want of opportunity. Speaking their language, and full of the same blood as the men among whom he had found a refuge, it would have been strange if Orloff had not become one of them. This was what had really taken place, and now in all things save place of birth Philip Orloff was a subject of the Czar.

Thanks to the outbreak of hostilities between China and Japan over the Corean difficulty, Orloff had an opportunity for seeing active service within a few months of his escape from the *Genoa.* For when in their extremity the Chinese authorities were forced to call in the aid of European soldiers of fortune to reorganize their military system, the Russian General under whose command Orloff found himself promptly picked out the young Australian as the man for the hour.

So it happened that Philip offered his services to the Mongol Emperor, ostensibly as an American free-lance, but in reality as a servant of the Czar, free to fight for China so long as the Dragon throne wanted his sword, but, at the same time, sworn never to forget that Russian interests must take precedence of all others, and that his first duty was to carry on that subtle Russianizing process by which his leaders hoped yet to permeate even the impassive Mongolians.

During both the war and internal rebellion, Orloff did such good service for his new masters that for the past three years he had held the highest military position in China possible of attainment by an alien.

Still, while given up to ambition, and clearly realizing the splendid possibilities which lay ahead of his present adventure, he felt more and more that he would willingly surrender his chances to know that the army which lay outside the town fought under the Eagle standard. Savage as the Russian soldiery were, they were not all barbarians, and Orloff's soul revolted at the thought of the butcheries which he knew must accompany the march of these Mongol invaders.

While afar off he had stilled his conscience by the thought that it was, after all, for the glory of the Czar. Now that he stood once more on the land that had given him birth, and saw in the rapine of the morning a pretaste of the scourge he was letting loose, a strange feeling of kinship awoke in him and filled his soul with shame. Crushing it back, he again called ambition to his aid, and now with a certain feeling of relief he began in a guarded fashion to discuss possibilities with his old friend. Personally Zenski was both ready and willing to fall in with his plans, for, as he reasoned with himself, he was far more likely to reap rewards under Orloff's rule than under that of a China- man, who, judging from his spy, was just as likely to behead his tools when done with as not.

Far into the night the two men talked, for, apart from his own personal designs, Leroy had much to question the Count upon. As regards his enterprise, Zenski's report was most favourable. Leroy's own line of march until he reached Charleville could not, according to the Count, be seriously opposed, and, when Dromeroff had sacked Normanton, there was nothing to stay his advance until he reached the high stony tableland at the head of the Flinders Valley.

'Where are we to find the enemy, Zenski?' laughed Leroy.

'*Pardieu!* you will come to him in due time,' grinned Zenski. 'And Dromeroff may have brushes after he leaves Hughenden; but, after all, the real fighting must take place at Charleville or beyond.'

'Not before?' queried Leroy.

'No; you cannot call this an enemy's country,' replied the Count, pointing to the map. 'Thanks to McLoskie's policy, there are no settlers left for at least two hundred miles. Colonization has ceased, *mon ami*. This country is either in our hands or held by Melbourne and London corporations. Both classes of property are worked on the tributary system through labour contractors in Macao and Hong Kong. Cheap labour grew too popular for McLoskie's promise to be kept, that aliens were only to be used for field-work on the plantations, and now the sweepings of Chinese prisons are brought up wholesale, landed at the Gulf, and sent to their destinations under Kalmuck overseers.'

' The people would not have stood it in my time !' exclaimed Leroy.

' As there is no white population, and no press except our own, there is no fuss,' replied Zenski. ' Besides, the bosses and managers know how to keep things quiet in their own way.'

' They have given themselves bound into my hand !' exclaimed the General exultantly.

' You have but to advance, *mon brave*,' chuckled Zenski. ' The railway-lines are open, and the few officials and managers who wait for you can easily be disposed of. Our Intelligence Department, as your Commissary-General informed you, has arranged for the wants of the imperial forces, and horses and cattle are ready mustered all along both lines of railway.'

As Zenski finished speaking, there was a pause. Instinctively the Count knew what was in his com-panion's mind ; in fact, he had been waiting all the evening for the question which Leroy appeared to hesitate to put.

Rising at last, the General leant his hand on the mantelshelf.

' Where is Heather Cameron ?' he said slowly.

' At Isis Downs.'

'Ah, it will be in our line of march.'

'Hardly; still, the cavalry are sure to loot it,' replied Zenski. 'But doubtless the Camerons will seek refuge in Fort Mallarraway.'

'Seek death, you mean!' exclaimed Leroy. 'Zenski, they must never be allowed to get there, or God help them.'

'God help them if they do not!' retorted the Count.

For a little the General stood thinking. In all the years that had passed, he had never forgotten the love for which he had risked so much, for though he had worshipped at the shrine of ambition, he had admitted no mistress to find a shelter in his breast in the name of love. In the days that followed his escape he had decided, with the egotism of a strong-willed man, to put this fair picture far from him. Between Heather and his mental sight a veil of blood arose, rendering the vision of his lost love shadowy and indistinct, for, justify himself how he would, he felt that Harden's death had raised up a barrier between him and his heart's idol. Arguing thus, he had decided that, even could he return acquitted in the eyes of men, he yet could never dare to dim the whiteness of Heather's life with a companionship such as his. For a time Orloff held to his determination, aided by the excitements of escape and the manifold promptings of military ambition; but such aids are of little avail when the object of a man's affection remains pure in his own eyes. To a man betrayed, ambition has before to-day become a paramount passion; to Orloff it grew daily less effective, just as a powerful specific loses its potency before the advance of an incurable disease.

Marching over desert steppes, or watching in the face
of a wakeful enemy, the memory of Heather never left
him, and at last the very force with which he had
sought to kill his passion suggested the means by
which he might again make of it a living reality.
A soldier's life under semi-barbaric conditions had
gradually produced a mental deterioration in Orloff.
War at its best is a return to primeval conditions,
and so its disciples insensibly grow to regard all
things from a less exalted standard than other
men.   Through Zenski Orloff learned that Heather
was still unmarried.   Knowing what he did, this
would once have appeared only the inevitable condition of a woman such as he held Heather to be,
but now it came to him clothed with a subtle significance.   She still loved and was waiting for him.
Subject to be hanged for murder, even although his
act had been that of a judge, he could never hope to
meet her as Philip Orloff; but as General Leroy what
boundless possibilities might he not offer at the feet
of his queen! So, by a strange freak of fate, Heather's
influence became the chief propelling force which
urged Philip Orloff to undertake the conquest of
his and her native land.   Rousing himself from his
reverie, Leroy stepped to the table and began to look
over the map that lay on it.

'How far is Isis Downs from Cloncurry?' he
asked.

'About two hundred miles.'

'Why the devil didn't you get Cameron to take his
daughter South?' exclaimed the General.

'I am not his keeper,' retorted Zenski.   'And

even so, I thought you wanted her in your own hands.'

'To save her, yes—and now it must be done. I will start a troop under an officer I can trust to secure them before they get into that cursed fort; well-mounted men should be able to reach Isis Downs from Cloncurry in twenty-four hours.'

'Possibly,' assented Zenski. Then, remembering that Hatten had called him a spy, a title to which the Count strongly objected, and further anxious, if possible, to wean Leroy from a pursuit which he felt was full of possible dangers to the expedition, he added: 'You may rest easy with regard to Miss Cameron, for, if I mistake not, she will be well cared for.'

'What can her father do if these savages come on them?'

'Little, I admit; but her *cavalier servente* is not wanting in resource.'

'What do you mean?' exclaimed Leroy in a low, fierce voice. 'By God! be careful, Zenski; remember I love this woman.'

'So does Dick Hatten. Pardon if I expressed myself badly,' added the Count, seeing he had gone too far.

'If we are to remain friends, make better choice of your similes,' retorted Leroy. 'Who is this Hatten?'

'He was once in your troop in Brisbane, I understand.'

'Ah, I remember; so he is my rival?'

'*Pardieu!* he would like to be, at any rate.'

'Then, Heather does not love him,' said Leroy confidently.

'She has not made me her confidant,' retorted the Count. '*Ma foi!* I have had other matters to attend to. Why not let this woman marry whom she will, Philip? Once already she has brought you ill-luck; why tempt fortune again for her sake?'

'Because I still love her.'

'Bah! you talk like a schoolboy,' exclaimed Zenski impatiently.

In this infatuation he foresaw the possible wreck of the whole enterprise; for, knowing Orloff, he realized that once under the thraldom of this woman's presence, its leader was no longer to be relied upon.

'Why should this matter trouble you?' said Leroy coldly. 'I have not asked your advice, nor do I need it.'

'You were glad of it once, Philip.'

'Pardon my ingratitude, Zenski!' cried Leroy, dropping his hand on the Count's shoulder. 'I have not forgotten; but in this affair I will not be guided. Call it fate, folly, what you will, I must go on.'

'Then I will say no more,' muttered Zenski, shrugging his shoulders irritably. 'If this woman brings you to ruin, she will have only lived up to the traditions of her charming sex.'

'You have forgotten the history of many women,' laughed Leroy.

'If so, I have remembered that of one man,' retorted Zenski cynically.

'Yourself, Count?'

'*Ma foi!* no; Mark Antony, *mon Général.*'

When at last the two parted, Leroy rode back to the camp; a soldier himself, he always lived among the men he led, sharing their hardships, and often joining in their rough amusements. Physically superior to most men, and always as ready to reward a gallant action as to visit with relentless hand an act of cowardice, he exercised a potent sway over the half-savage soldiery who fought under his banner. To-night, late as it was, he rode round all the outposts, and after that sat for awhile smoking in his tent. Then, remembering that he had to start for Cloncurry at daybreak, he threw himself, dressed as he was, on his stretcher, and, with a soldier's economy of time, fell asleep.

CHAPTER V.

THE NEWS IS CARRIED SOUTH.

On the afternoon which saw the streets of Point Parker full of armed and hostile soldiers, Frank McLean sat reading in the wide veranda of the old house at Cape York. Beside him lay two books, 'The Nomadic Hordes of Central Asia' and 'The Eastern Question in Australia.' Having led an isolated life for years, his mind had naturally turned to the questions rising in the near future. After doing his full share of pioneering and adventure, he had arrived at that stage of life when a vigorous, wholesome-minded man naturally uses his brains more than his muscles. Still, in fertility of resource and contempt for danger, he was the same youth who, twenty years before, had carried out a daring journey from the head of the Burdekin to the north-eastern extremity of Australia, through an unknown and difficult country swarming with hostile savages. Barefooted and in rags, he and his brother, accompanied by a few young fellows of the right stamp, and a group of black boys with no better weapons than the guns slung on their backs and the tomahawks held in their hands, had conquered the manifold horrors of that drear 'no man's land.'

Since that day pearlshelling among the coral reefs, scrub-shooting, and rambling through the islands and coast country, had found him work, and had enabled him to acquire a large knowledge of the savage races and the fauna and flora of the Pacific. Yet, though generally living alone, Frank was no misanthrope. Whenever a mail-steamer rounded the Point at Somerset, the eight-pounder before the old veranda belched out its salute, and whoever landed got a hearty old-time Australian welcome. This afternoon his mind ran upon the contents of the books beside him, in connection with the endless contradictory war rumours which filled the colonial papers.

Suddenly the gate flew open, and a little man rushed on to the veranda.

'Well, Archie, what's up?' inquired McLean, looking his visitor over with calm surprise.

'The wire's cut!' gasped Archie.

'Cut, is it?' grunted the veteran pioneer; 'mend it, then!'

For answer the little man stamped with vexation.

'Why, you little beggar, don't you bring yourself to an anchor, and get back your wind,' suggested McLean coolly.

Archie Scrimour was an ill-formed, excitable dwarf in appearance, but, like many another manikin, he possessed both brain and heart enough for a gallant cavalier. He was at present agent for the Somerset Station, and being very fond of McLean, he had come to consult him with regard to his discovery.

'Look here!' said his placid host, pouring out a stiff dram of Uam Var, 'swallow this physic, and then you'll be able to tell what you've got to say.'

Watching his patient swallow the dose, Frank started him with:

'Well then, Mr. Scrimour, reel it off.'

'The wire was cut two hours ago. I'm not surprised; for my suspicions have been awakened by many things that have come to me in a way I need not explain. I've been tapping for cipher correspondence the last two days, and I have just worked it out. Look here, you know something of cryptograms. Well, it comes to this, that a force is at this moment landing at the Gulf. My reading of the cipher is confirmed by the very last wire that came from Thursday Island. A pearlsheller reports that he saw, three days ago, a flotilla of steamers steering south, near Cape Arnheim. I believe that by this time every wire, both on the coast and inland as far as Cooktown and Charleville, is silent.'

McLean was a good listener, but he was not given to unnecessary speech. Blowing a silver whistle, a gray-headed black boy answered his signal.

'Eulah,' said his master, 'send the boys at once to yard the horses, and ask Mr. Walker to get up steam in the launch, and then come to me.'

As Walker, the engineer, came in to report himself, McLean looked up from the ciphers.

'I am not a bit surprised, Archie,' said he. 'Walker, I'll be ready to start in three hours. I will take a couple of black boys. Get what Kanakas you need for stokers. Help yourself to whisky.'

As the engineer walked away, McLean said :

' There is not much time to arrange, Archie ; but I was actually brooding over what was likely to happen when you came in, and I think I've the right plan in my head. It is this : You will go straight along the line, mending the wire and forwarding letters to the right people on your road ; I will send Eulah with you, and a young active boy, and will give you what horses you need. Finch, McDonald, Herbert and Fraser, will all help you with horses and messengers. Of course you will leave your assistant here to keep up communication ; meantime, I shall go full steam to Cooktown, and start things there. Now I'll dictate the letters, and you write them.'

By two in the morning the letters were written, Archie with the black boys was off to mend the line and raise the country, and McLean's launch was steering South, cutting the smooth waters of the Darrier Channel with impatient prow.

CHAPTER VI.

A CLOSE SHAVE.

FOUR days before the attack on Point Parker, Ted
Johnson drove Edith and her mother from Isis Downs
to Cloncurry, where he had business.

Thoroughly alarmed by his visit to Fort Mallarraway,
Cameron had suggested on his return that Mrs. Enson
and her daughter should visit Brisbane, urging among
other reasons that it was absolutely necessary in face
of Edith's approaching marriage. To this arrangement the older lady was only too ready to agree, but
when Cameron spoke to Heather about accompanying
them, he was met by an absolute refusal, nor could
any arguments alter the girl's determination. Filled
with the liveliest apprehension for the future, the old
squatter used every means in his power to alter his
daughter's resolve. But Heather remained immovable;
she would wait, she said, and keep house for him until
everything was prepared, and then they could go down
together to be present at the wedding.

Driven to desperation, her father pointed out the
possible dangers to which she might expose herself by
remaining with him, but this only the more fixed her

in her desire to stay. Besides, as she argued, might there not be even greater risks in Brisbane? At last, won over by her loving entreaties, Cameron, with a heart full of misgiving, gave his consent, and Johnson drove off without her.

As Ted stood with the two women on the Cloncurry railway - station, waiting for the train that was to carry them South, Edith, in wistful, strangely tender words, begged him not to long delay his coming. But sweet as her request sounded to the lover, long accustomed to her changeful humours, it at the same time filled him with a sense of future evil. To Mrs. Enson, who, strong in her fealty to the Count, scouted all thoughts of danger, the trip held out nothing except pleasant possibilities. But Johnson could see both in Edith's regrets for the absence of Heather, and in a certain reluctance to go, which now began to possess her, that her mind was, like his own, oppressed by a sense of impending disaster. As he said good-bye at the carriage-door, the girl hesitated for a moment, then, leaning forward, kissed him passionately on the lips. A fat man sitting in the corner noted with languid interest the tear-dimmed eyes, and bent a little forward, but the shriek of the whistle deafened his curious ears, and only her lover heard the faint ' God guard you, Ted !' that came from the red, trembling lips.

Walking back to his hotel, Johnson was struck, as he had never been before, by the preponderance of coolie labour. Everywhere an alien tongue fell on his ears. In the past, 'John' had often been a fruitful subject for amusement and chaff, but to-night each stolid, expressionless face filled him with aversion and distrust. As obedient slaves their worth was undoubted, but as men to defend the result of their toil they appeared to the manager beneath contempt.

Walking into the telegraph-office after dinner, Johnson noticed one of Zenski's Kalmuck overseers reading a message. As the man thrust it into his pocket, it by some mischance fell to the floor. Glancing at it insensibly, Ted noticed that the message was both long and written in cipher.

Trivial as the incident was, the manager could not dismiss it from his mind, and even in his broken, dream-disturbed sleep, the man's cunning, half-fearful glance, as he picked up the telegram, lowered on him with startling distinctness.

Just as the dawn was breaking, Johnson got his four-in-hand hooked to, and drove out of Cloncurry. Reaching the railway gates, he found them closed against him, and cursing the stupidity of the keeper, he was about to open them himself, when the rumble of a train coming from the North warned him to get his Bush horses into clear ground. Wheeling his leaders, he moved back about a hundred yards and waited. Presently the train came in sight. Occupied at first with his horses, Johnson had no time to watch its approach, but just as it flashed past he looked up. In front of the engine, mounted on a platform, was a machine-gun of some kind, and round it stood three or four men in uniform. In a moment it was gone, and then truck after truck, packed with armed, savage-looking troops, moved past the thunderstruck watcher. Suddenly the cipher message recalled itself to his mind, already prepared for all that was most unexpected. 'The Russians!' he gasped; then, as he looked again, a certain resemblance to another race struck him with irresistible force, and he exclaimed: 'No, by heaven! they're Chinamen of some sort.'

As he uttered the words, the thought of Edith rose before him. 'Thank heaven, she's on the Government line by now,' he murmured. 'But what of those left at Isis Downs?' He realized that he must warn them without a moment's delay. What if the train to Hughenden was, even as he sat idly there, hurrying down on his friends another horde of savages?

Gathering up his team, he again drove towards the gate, but even as he did so, a volley of musketry rang out in the direction of the station, followed in quick succession by a dread chorus of yells and screams of fear and despair.

'Open the gate!' shouted Ted, as the man in charge came forward and leant over the bar; but the fellow only shook his head and grinned. 'Curse you! are you deaf? open the gate!' repeated Ted.

In the distance he could hear another train. 'I'm trapped,' he muttered, as he once more turned his horses' heads. Filled as the one which had preceded it, the second train rushed by, some of its occupants taking flying shots at Johnson. In the distance he could see a crowd of coolies running after a man; stabbed in the back, he fell in the dusty road. Now they caught sight of the waggonette, and, yelling like fiends, ran towards it. In less than five minutes they would be on him. 'I must jump the gate, or I'm a gone coon,' muttered Johnson.

Springing to the ground, he whipped off his near leaders' collar and harness, then, cutting the reins short with his knife, jumped on his back. Now the coolies were not twenty yards behind him, and guessing his object, the gate-keeper stood waving his arms in the crossing. Taking hold of his horse's head, Johnson drove his heels into his ribs, and sent him at the bars.

Balked by the keeper's gesticulating, the leader, good jumper as he was, began to waver, but giving a yell that made the man spring aside, Ted drove his knife into his horse's ribs. Mad with pain, the leader rose in the air, and pulling him almost on his haunches as he landed, his rider sent him at the farther gate. With a crash and a scramble he got over, and working himself into his seat, Johnson galloped on without looking back — to spread the dread news that the spoiler had come, and that Cloncurry and Point Parker were given over to demons of blood and lust.

CHAPTER VII.

'HATTEN'S RINGERS.'

WHEN once convinced by President Musgrave that the
danger of attack from the Gulf was not only possible
but probable, Cameron had thrown himself heart and
soul into the question of defence. Hearing on his
return from the Fort that McLoskie was expected at
Longreach, he made it his business to meet him, and,
while avoiding all reference to Zenski's possible
treachery—as a useless waste of argument likely to
defeat his object with the Minister—the squatter
placed before the Premier the absolute want of
organization in the North in the event of a Russian
landing.

As white labour had become superseded both in
the townships and on the stations, the various volunteer companies, both horse and foot, had gradually
dwindled away, until now, what with migration and
that inability to stick to anything which forms so
strong a characteristic in the modern Australian, the
defence force of the North was little better than a
name. Aware that all this was both known and

disregarded by McLoskie, who, now that he had no unions to intimidate, looked on the volunteer forces as a useless expense, Cameron decided to make a personal matter of his request. Though politically opposed to Sir Peter, in private life they were still friends, and, being a wealthy man with undoubted influence, Cameron knew that he could ask a favour with fair chances of its being granted. Approaching the subject from a billet-seeker's standpoint only, the squatter described how Hatten, a protégé of his own, had lost his station, and was now without work of any kind. Then, touching lightly on war possibilities, rather as a joke than otherwise, he reminded McLoskie that Dick had already held a commission in the Mounted Rifles. Being an Australian politician, the Premier rather admired Cameron's cool advocacy of his friend's claims to loot the Treasury.

'Then you think the Northern Mounted Infantry want reorganizing, eh, Cameron?' said he.

'Most undoubtedly.'

'And Mr. Hatten seems to you the right man to do it?' chuckled the Premier.

'I know of no one better fitted; and, besides, it will not be a bad move politically to give an Australian a show in the service.'

'My dear Cameron,' replied McLoskie with dignity, 'I, as you should know, am actuated by a man's merits, not his nationality.'

'Of that we have had ample proof,' replied Cameron. 'Still, in this case I think you will have little trouble in deciding.'

'None, my dear fellow,' said the Premier graciously.

'.It is, I assure you, a pleasure to oblige any friend of yours.'

So it happened that Dick Hatten was appointed Staff-Adjutant to the Northern Mounted Infantry.

Throwing all the weight of his personal popularity into the scale, Captain Hatten began his work of reorganization, only to find how well-nigh hopeless a task lay before him. Many of the best men were gone, and of those who still had their names on the roll, the greater part were utterly disheartened by the apathy and neglect of the Government.

Backed by Cameron's offer of horses, Hatten, however, succeeded in enlisting a troop of cavalry from among the managers and men still left in the Isis Downs district, and, through Cameron's influence, their services as volunteers were accepted.

When, however, Hatten sent in a requisition for fifty sabres, he was informed that there was not a spare sword in the colony, and that he must wait until they were ordered from England.

Apprised of the state of affairs through a paragraph which had slipped into one of the papers, a speculative Jew, who had bought up a collection of old Waterloo swords, came forward and offered to do business. But of this Dick heard nothing until a few months later, when the Government were glad to secure them at famine prices.

How to arm his men puzzled Hatten, and still to let them disband was not to be thought of. At last an inspiration seized him, as he sat furbishing up his old sabre, the only weapon of offence in the whole troop.

'I'll make 'em lancers and chance it!' he exclaimed.

'Where are you going to get the lances from?' asked Ewan Cameron slowly.

'Never you mind, Ewan!' retorted Dick. 'I'm going to do it in spite of the infernal fools down in Brisbane.'

'Mallee sticks pointed and hardened in the fire,' laughed Ewan incredulously.

'No,' answered Dick; 'any straight sticks I can lay hands on, with shear blades riveted on their ends.'

At the next parade Hatten put the situation before his men.

'The authorities are unable to send us a sword under four months,' said he; 'if I am right in my reckoning, we will have to fight in less than two. Will you sit idly waiting, or will you arm yourselves?'

After a pause, one of the men said:

'We are willing enough, but how can it be done?'

'There is only one way that I know of,' replied Hatten. 'There are cases of old shears in the stores at Hughenden, and odd packets lying about most of the stations. Now that the machines have taken their place, the store-keepers will, I dare say, let us have them for the asking. Let each man get a pair, break off one blade, and level down the shoulder so that it will offer no resistance when being withdrawn, then sharpen the back and rivet the handle on to a strong, light shaft of wood, and he will have an Australian lance, not as well finished, certainly, as an English one, but quite as reliable as most of them.'

Struck by the originality of the idea, the men took it up on the spot.

'Let each man carry the second blade in case of a break,' said their officer, as he dismissed them.

'My oath! we'll tomahawk 'em like blooming ringers,' shouted Billy the Kid, as Dick rode away.

And so the Isis Downs troop won the name of 'Hatten's Ringers.'

Putting in the night at a friend's diggings, Hatten started before sunrise for Isis Downs, intending to reach Hughenden the same evening. Making good use of the morning, he and Billy rode up to the horse-paddock at about breakfast-time. Leaving the trainer to shut the gate, Hatten jogged slowly on. Heather's refusal to go South had caused him as deep concern as Cameron, for while admiring the filial love which impelled her to stay by her father's side in the time of peril, he wished with his whole soul that the old squatter had insisted on her departure with the rest. In his mind visions rose of the woman he loved given over to the unspeakable barbarities of brutal Cossacks, or at best slain by some friendly hand. For all that he knew, his might be the very hand marked out for this gruesome act of mercy. A clatter of hoofs woke him from his reverie, and glancing over his shoulder, he saw a man racing up the track. Something in the appearance both of horse and rider seemed familiar, and turning his horse, Hatten waited. Leaving a cloud of dust behind his flying hoofs, the horse passed Billy like a flash. As he did, his rider shouted something to the trainer, who now also put spurs to his mount. Now he was within a hundred yards of Dick, and, with a feeling akin to fear, the Adjutant recognised in the reeking horse one of his trooper's chargers, and in his wild, ragged rider, Ted Johnson.

Waving his arm, Johnson shouted hoarsely :

' They've landed.'

' What—the Russians !' exclaimed Dick as Ted pulled up.

' No.—Chinamen !' gasped Ted.

' How did you hear ?   There must be a mistake.'

' I didn't hear ; I saw them myself, man.'

' Where ?' asked Hatten, beginning to think his chum had ' gone off his head.'

' Coming into Cloncurry yesterday morning.'

' My God ! you don't mean that, Ted !' exclaimed Hatten.

Then Johnson told him how he had got Edith and her mother away, and described what he saw next morning at the railway gates ; how he had ridden bare back all that day and night to bring the news, and how his gallant horse had dropped dead close to the very house which Hatten had left a few hours ago.

' Ferguson lent me his to come on with,' concluded Ted ; ' now, what's to be done ?'

' You're a brick, old man !' said Dick admiringly; ' go and have a sleep, and then rouse the boys.   I must push on to Hughenden.   God only knows if another batch of these devils may not be down upon the town already.'

' Sleep be hanged !' growled Johnson ; ' wait while I have a drink of tea, and I'm with you.'

'No,' said Hatten after a moment's thought; 'I can't afford the time, and you can do better work by remaining.'

'You are my superior officer,' replied Johnson, who now held a commission in the Isis Downs troop; 'only, for God's sake, let me do something!'

'Get the other waggonette and a team ready for a start at a moment's notice, and explain matters to Cameron,' said Dick. 'Then ride out and tell all the men on this side to muster at Isis Downs to-morrow with the best arms they can rake up. I will warn Musgrave as I go past, and will send Billy back to-night with final orders.'

Putting his horse into a brisk canter, Hatten rode past the house, followed by Billy, while Johnson rode up to the stable to tell his news and obey his chief's commands.

CHAPTER VIII.

THE ESCAPE.

WHEN first Johnson told his story, Cameron sat as a man stunned. Then, as he realized that the horror which filled even his sleep with anxious dreams had come, the old squatter became possessed by a feverish anxiety to place his child beyond the reach of fiends, who he now knew were more to be dreaded than the Russians themselves.

Heather, while experiencing that fear which under such conditions must strike the heart of every woman, crushed back her first impulse of terror for the sake of the trembling old man, who took her in his arms and fell into a passion of self-upbraiding.

Powerless to offer comfort, Johnson slipped out of the room, and, calling a black boy, ordered him to run in and stable four harness horses. Then, going into the buggy-shed, he began to oil a waggonette, generally used as a ration-cart, but now the only trap left in which to escape. While he was tightening up some bolts, Cameron came up to him.

Now that he had got over the first shock of surprise, the old squatter was once more the self-reliant pioneer. From the first his only fear had been for his daughter, and now the girl had succeeded in imbuing him with a hopefulness as to her future which she hardly felt in her own heart. Helping Johnson, and discussing with him future possibilities, Cameron decided that they had little to fear from the direction of Cloncurry. From the Hughenden side, however, always supposing a force was advancing from Normanton, both men agreed that danger was likely to come. Though off the direct line of march, the enemies' scouts were nearly certain to reach Isis Downs on their foraging expeditions.

'If we don't hear from Hatten to-night, I will start at daybreak for Longreach with Heather,' said Cameron, 'and send her by train to Springsure; where she ought to be safe with the Westlys.'

'I'd go whether I heard or not.'

'You're right; then I can be back all the sooner to strike a blow for Queensland with you all,' exclaimed the old man.

'Never mind us, sir,' said Johnson; 'you look after Heather; we'll fight all the better if we know you're out of harm's way.'

'I never shirked work this fifty years, and I'm not going to do it now,' replied Cameron stoutly.

After a hurried lunch Johnson started away to deliver Dick's orders. As he had to call at the man's place who had lent him the horse, he rode it and led another on which to get back. All the hot afternoon he cantered over the treeless, broken Downs, delivering his call to arms, and at last, about eleven at night, began to again draw near Isis Downs. Now that his

work was over, weariness began to creep into the
man's iron sinews, and to lie like a leaden weight on
his eyelids.   Jogging along with his bridle-reins lying
loose on his neck, the stock-horse made a bee-line for
home, and at last, worn out with the fatigue and excitement of the past two days, the manager fell asleep
in his saddle.   Retaining his balance instinctively,
Johnson slept on for a couple of miles, when his horse,
like himself overcome with weariness, stumbled.

Losing his balance, Johnson fell forward.   Then,
roused by the shock, he pulled himself together, and,
shaking his horse up, looked round.   A glance told
him that he was passing a bend of the stony creek,
and that he was still six miles from home.   Just as
he hit his heels into his mount's ribs again, he caught
a strange, eerie sound rising from the other side of
the creek.   Filled with a certain curious desire to
solve the mystery, he fastened up his horse, and,
crouching down, crept to the edge of the bank.   As
he looked cautiously through the coolibahs, a flame
shot up on the farther side, while the guttural murmurings became more distinct.   A camp of strange
beings was close to him.   Half of them were still
mounted, the others were cutting up the carcases of
a couple of bullocks.   In the firelight he could catch
the gleam of arms, and as the blaze rose between
him and the butchers, their broad, yellow faces and
coarse masses of hair stood out with ghastly distinctness against the sombre background.   They were
Kalmucks, men such as he had seen flash past him
two mornings ago at Cloncurry.   How they had
come, he took no time to think.   Their presence was

enough for him. Judging from those he could see, Johnson reckoned there were at least fifty in sight; how many more might be round the bend he wasted no time in trying to discover. Great God! others might be at Isis Downs even now. As this thought flashed through his mind, he crept back noiselessly to his horse, and, blindfolding him, led him carefully past the light. Once out of earshot, he jumped on his back, and, driving home the spurs, raced for his life in the direction of Isis Downs.

Taking Cameron into the smoking-den, Ted told of his fearful discovery. To the squatter the news was both unexpected and appalling. In the face of the enemies' near presence, could he dare to travel South unprotected as he was? while, on the other hand, Hatten's letter, brought from Hughenden by Billy, told of approaching peril. According to Hatten, the town was full of vague rumours of trains from Normanton crowded with troops, of telegraph-wires cut, of the horses mustered in Spero's yards along the line being mounted by savage horsemen, and also whisperings of fire and slaughter, repeated, but not believed. As all telegraphic communication with Normanton was blocked, Hatten warned Cameron to be prepared for instant flight South, and expressed the opinion that bands of mounted devils might appear on the Downs at any moment. He was busy rallying what forces he could muster, and in throwing up a defence of fallen timber; but, as he had no artillery and few arms, he had no hope of holding the town, and intended, after feeling the enemy, to fall back on Fort Mallarraway.

In face of Hatten's message, Cameron had decided to start at daybreak; but now that Ted had come on Kalmucks within six miles of the station, this determination appeared more than foolhardy. At last it was decided to make for Fort Mallarraway; then if, as they hoped, Hughenden was still safe, Heather could be sent by train to Rockhampton. If not, her chances among its defenders would be greater than if pursued by the savages, with no bigger escort to protect her than Isis Downs could provide.

Now that the danger was at their very doors, the two discussed every possibility with the calmness of brave men conscious of their peril and determined to throw away no chance in their efforts to escape from it.

At Heather's earnest request it was decided that she should ride Io. Knowing how Dick valued the mare, the girl insisted that she should not be left behind, and, as she explained, she would be safer on horseback than in the waggonette. As it was, the trap would be well loaded, for, besides old Margaret and the two other girls, their belongings and an extra supply of firearms and ammunition must be carried in it.

Outside, the moonless sky was now covered with heavy, riftless clouds, and the night had settled down as black as pitch. Still, something had to be done at once, for the Kalmucks would certainly strike the main station track after sunrise.

Besides Cameron and Johnson, there were only Ewan, Billy, and a priceless black boy, named Micky Nerang, at the house. The plan of escape was soon arranged. First, Io was saddled, and then, after one silent embrace from her father, Heather rode away under Micky's guidance, parallel with the road, but not upon it. Muffling its wheels, the men then dragged the waggon across the creek, and left it about half a mile off the road. They could do little more till dawn. Heather, led by Micky, could creep on at a foot-pace in comparative safety, but those who remained had perforce six hours of black darkness to get through. An hour before the dawn, the men led the four horses over to the waggonette, and hooked them to.

'You'd better come up on the box-seat with me, Maggie,' said Johnson.

'Bedad, is it the Chows yer boltin' from?' demanded Maggie, with strong disgust; 'by the powers! oi'd foight tin of them yaller divils meself.'

'That's all right; now please hold your tongue,' muttered Johnson. 'When the fighting's about to begin, I'll let you know.'

Cameron had insisted upon Ted driving, both because he was a singularly cool and masterly whip, and, further, for the reason that he felt it his duty to guard the rear.

'I mean to see the last of the old place,' he said in answer to Ted's protest, 'so say no more about it. When there is a streak of light, jog on; then, when you can see, let the horses go for twenty minutes. That will give you a good start. After that nurse them; don't go above seven miles an hour. We will be within two miles of you, and one of us will race up as soon as it is time to make a rush. Remember that you have twenty miles to go ; still, a stern chase is a long one, and if these devils can knock fifteen miles an hour out of their horses, this team if put to it can do twelve. If we are run close, let Heather ride for it while we block the road and make the most of our cartridges.'

There was another reason why Cameron had decided to stay. In the cellar of the house was stored a stock of firearms and ammunition intended for the use of the Isis Downs troop. These warlike supplies had been purchased by Cameron privately, and it had been his intention to have given them out to the troop as a surprise at their next parade. This was now impossible, but the old squatter had decided to pro- vide a surprise for all that. He had determined to tempt the enemy to make an assault upon the house in force, and then to blow them into the air. Rude dummy figures, constructed during the long night hours, stood on the veranda and at the windows, while loaded guns, securely strapped to the posts, pointed down the road, with wires stretching from their triggers to the clump of azaleas where the horses stood.

When all their preparations were completed, Cameron, Ewan, and Billy, now brought to the broad level of brotherhood by this common danger, drank a last solemn ' cup of kindness ' in memory of the old house.

Then they sat in the growing light and watched. At last Cameron lifted his finger, and pointed to the swell of the Downs to the south. A black cloud was drifting over the surface as if blown by a hurricane.

Presently the dark mass began to resolve itself into distinct atoms.

'Hadn't we better make tracks, boss?' muttered Billy.

'Take it easy,' replied Cameron coolly; 'we must let them sight the bait, lad.'

As he spoke, the old man rose, and with his companion walked up and down the long veranda. When the horde was within about a quarter of a mile they caught sight of the moving figures, and came to a halt, yelling like all the fiends in hell. Then one half began to sweep round in a half-circle, while the other dismounted and dashed straight for the veranda.

'Now for it,' said Cameron, as the three men crawled among the azaleas.

Mounting their horses, Billy and Ewan sat, holding in their right hands the wires connected with the rifle triggers.

Now Cameron was also in the saddle.

As a score of wild figures jumped into the veranda, he gave the signal, and three rifle-shots rang out above the hoarse shouts of the Kalmucks. Then, as the assailants poured in, the squatter pulled the wire he held in his own hand. In an instant the roof of the old house parted in a blaze of fire, and from the blackened sky timber, wreckage, and fragments of human bodies fell earthward in gruesome confusion. Driving spurs into their plunging horses, the three men galloped away unnoticed.

'Ewan,' said Cameron, as soon as they had got under cover of the creek, 'go ahead, boy, and keep

Ted moving; this blow-up won't stop these fiends
long.'

Johnson had driven so well that he had picked up
Heather and done nine miles of the road before
Ewan pulled him up. Heather was now riding in the
waggonette, while Micky Nerang was cantering beside
it, leading Io.

In a few words Ewan told what had happened,
but on the subject of advice as to pace he held his
tongue. The young Scot did not see how they could
be doing better. The team was fresh, and had to be
held, for Ted was saving them for a rush, if wanted.
Pulling his horse into a walk, Ewan kept steadily on,
watch in hand. It was a close calculation of miles
and minutes. Seventeen minutes after the waggon
left him, Cameron arrived at full gallop. 'Ted's
about two miles ahead!' said his nephew.

' And these hell-hounds are not above two behind!'
exclaimed Cameron. 'Gallop on, and push Johnson;
he's sure to lose time at that infernal pinch this side
of the Fort.'

Riding desperately, the young Scotchman caught
the waggon up again just five miles from their
destination. But again his cool, practical brain
warned him not to interfere. 'If Johnson makes the
rush now,' he reasoned, ' will the horses be fit to face
the pinch, and to do the last two miles? He is doing
well, and will be at the top of the hill in less than
twenty minutes, and the Kalmucks must be at least
three miles behind us. I'll let him gang his ain gait.'

In less than ten minutes Cameron was once more
beside him.

THE ESCAPE.

To follow page 286.

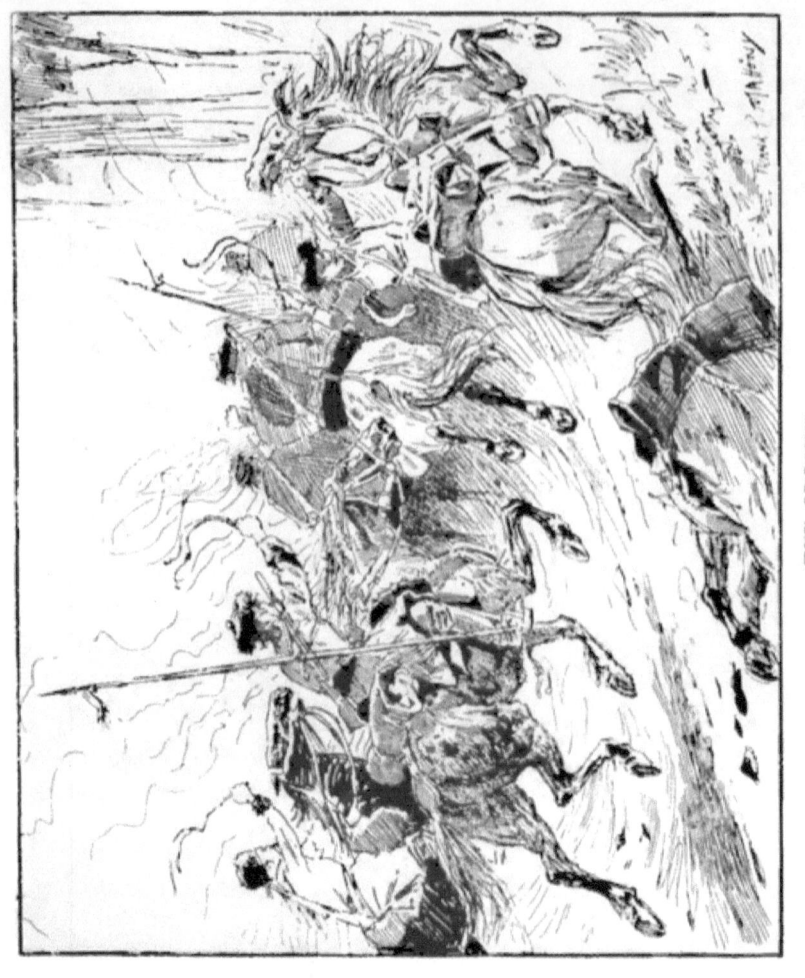

THE PURSUIT.

To follow page 288.

'They're within a mile of us!' shouted the squatter, his eyes blazing with apprehension. 'Tell Johnson to race for dear life!'

Thoroughly alarmed, Ewan again galloped on, scarcely daring to breathe until he reached the foot of the rocky rise.

Heather was again mounted, and was climbing up the steep ascent after Micky, while the team was beginning to crawl up behind.

'Thank God; he's done the right thing,' muttered Ewan, driving his horse up the hill.

As the waggonette neared the top, distant sounds of pursuit fell on his ears, and turning his horse on the summit, he caught sight of Cameron and Billy racing not five hundred yards ahead of a cloud of dust, out of which rose the gleam of steel and the shadowy forms of the yelling Kalmucks. Gazing from his vantage-ground, the reckless horsemanship of the savages appalled Ewan. With spurs like knives, and quirts of hide dripping with blood hanging from their wrists, they forced on the unhappy animals they rode until they stumbled and fell, dying under them. Then, with practised quickness, they changed their saddles, and mounted the spare horses which, after the manner of their race, many of them led. On the pinch they left a trail of crippled and dying horses, and many of the riders fell behind; but some twenty or thirty still held on, galloping up the steep face of the rock.

As soon as Cameron and Billy came up, the three men raced on for their lives. A mile ahead they met two scouts from the Fort. They had just seen a lady

and a black boy, followed by a trap driven hard.
The thunder of hoofs now showed that the Kalmucks
were upon them, and round the edge of a patch of
scrub they came at a whirling gallop. With one
common impulse the five men poured their rifles into
them, and spurred off, sending their revolver bullets
into their faces as they raced for the Fort. As they
dashed up to the stockade, Johnson and Heather
passed through the gates, and a volley from the
picket drove the men sent by Leroy to capture
Heather reeling back out of fire, uttering fierce yells
of disappointment and rage.

CHAPTER IX.

THE SACKING OF HUGHENDEN.

THE rumours of which Hatten had spoken in his letter
to Cameron were only too true. Normanton had fallen
into the hands of Dromeroff. Taken utterly by surprise, and totally unprepared to oppose a serious
attack, the volunteer force and white population
fought desperately, but without cohesion, with the
inevitable result that they were cut to pieces, and the
savage soldiery provided with a pretext for the per-
petration of a general massacre.

Despatching a column by rail to effect a junction
with the Charleville reinforcements at Cloncurry, and
another to occupy Croydon, and hold the line from
there to Cairns, Dromeroff advanced on Hughenden
with his main body of troops. Undeterred by any of
Leroy's scruples as to the treatment of women and
children, Dromeroff, while professing to obey his
General's orders, secretly let it be understood that his
object was to create a reign of terror. Relieved from
the fear of possible punishment, his savage cavalry
carried out their commander's wishes with fiendish

completeness, sparing neither sex nor age in their onward march.

Soon after daybreak on the morning of Cameron's escape from Isis Downs, the first of Dromeroff's trains approached Hughenden.

Determined to give the women and children a chance to escape, Hatten had torn up the line about a mile from the town, and thrown up a rude breastwork of trees. Behind this feeble defence he had posted all his available force, but as he was totally without artillery, and short both of small arms and ammunition, he recognised that at best he led a forlorn hope.

Stopping the train some distance from Hatten's barricade, the officer in command of the attacking column began to derail his infantry. Forming them under the shelter of some timber, he led them on, while the Maxim gun in front of the engine poured a heavy fire over their heads into the breastwork. Afraid to waste a shot, Hatten ordered his men to lie down and wait. Advancing in open order and firing as they advanced, the Mongols came within fifty yards of the breastwork. Then, just as they closed on their centre and charged, Dick gave the word, and an iron hail poured into their crowded ranks. For an instant they wavered, then, rallying to their leader's call, rushed on once more. But again a volley met them, and breaking, they fell back on their supports. As they retired, about fifty mounted men armed with Dick's lances charged their flank. But, opening on the advancing horsemen, the Maxim gun swept them down beneath a withering fire. Unable to withstand

the shower of bullets that rained on their shattered
ranks, the cavalry melted away, leaving two-thirds of
their number on the blood-smeared ground.

Glancing between two logs, Hatten could see
another train sweeping round the bend.

'It's all up,' he mused despairingly. 'God send
they've got the women away.'

In front the enemy were preparing for another
attack. The defenders could see the Mongols' officers
fiercely gesticulating.

'I hope they won't give the other beggars time to
outflank me,' muttered Hatten grimly. He had his
wish, for, scorning to wait for help against so in-
significant a foe, the Mongol commander, sword in
hand, led the assault.

Again Dick's rifles rang out; but pistolling any of
their men who wavered, the officers still urged them
on. In another minute they were beneath the breastwork, and, following their leader, they rushed it at
the point of the bayonet. Fighting for their lives
and their women's honour, the ill-armed townsmen
fought like heroes, and many a yellow-faced Mongol
fell back with his brains dashed out beneath their
fiercely-wielded rifle-butts. Hatten met the Russian
who led them face to face as he landed over the
barricade, and with a swift downstroke split his skull
before he could articulate his shout of victory. But
even as he fell another took his place, and, overmatched both in discipline and arms, Dick's green
levies gave before the Mongol bayonets, and then,
seized with panic, broke and fled. Borne back by the
terror-stricken crowd, Hatten made desperate efforts

to rally enough to cover his retreat, but his men were deaf alike to curses and entreaty.

'Jump up, Captain!' shouted a voice beside him, and looking round, he saw one of his cavalrymen holding a horse, and surrounded by a dozen other troopers.

Springing into the saddle, Hatten galloped off towards the railway-station, followed by the remnant of the Hughenden Mounted Rifles. On the platform confusion reigned unchecked. One train packed with women and children had started, and another had just run in. As Dick rode up, the crowd on the platform rushed to the carriages.

'Women and children first!' roared Hatten, as half a dozen men, mad with drink and fear, crushed through the press.

'You be d——d!' growled one of the ruffians, dragging an old woman from her seat and springing into her place.

Jumping off his horse, Hatten made for the carriage, followed by half a dozen troopers.

'Come out of that, you cur!' he said sternly, but the man did not move.

Stretching out his hand, Dick laid hold of his collar and dragged him out. As he landed on the platform, the man drew a knife and lunged at him, but before he had time to strike, Dick sprang aside, and, whipping out his revolver, fired. Throwing up his arms, the man fell to the ground, and holding the smoking revolver in his hand, Hatten shouted, 'By God, I'll serve every man who doesn't come out of the train the same way!' Backed by his troopers, their Adjutant now restored some sort of order. It was heart-breaking work at best. Here a woman begged him to find a child she had lost in the crush, while another implored him on her knees to allow her husband to remain. Sisters clung to brothers, and mothers cursed him for holding back their sons to die on the Mongols' bayonets. But firm to his resolve, Hatten allowed only women and children to enter the carriages, and at last, amid wails of sorrow and curses of despair, the train moved out of the station.

An engine drawing a mixed collection of trucks now drew up. It was the last train, and the station seemed more crowded than ever. As it stopped, Hatten realized that the firing was perilously near, and now a blood-stained, wild-eyed crowd began to mingle with those already waiting. This time no human power could stay the wild rush for ignoble life. The Mongols were at hand, and each panic-stricken wretch thought only of himself.

Rushing to the gates, Hatten determined to hold them with his life. Little as he cared for the safety of some of the men, he remembered that there were still women among them. Fighting his way through the press, followed by a few gallant comrades, he nearly reached his goal; but when only a few steps from the entrance, a fresh rush of fugitives swept him aside, and on their heels panted the red-handed children of death.

Dragging him with them, the troopers forced their way to the side-gate, where their horses stood as yet unnoticed by the Mongols.

Realizing now that all was over, Hatten mounted

with the rest. For a moment his eyes took in the whole fearful scene : the screaming women pushed back by frantic men only to fall on the bloody bayonets of their foes ; the children tossed from point to point in wanton devilry. Then his ears caught the shriek of the whistle and the fearful cries of those who were being ground to death between the wheels and the bloody pavement, and over all rang the yells of the Mongols as they thrust their bayonets into the passing trucks, and dragged back struggling women by their hair from the still open doors. In a moment it all passed before him, but instantaneous as it was, its gruesome impression never faded from before his eyes.

'Let's get, Captain,' muttered the man who had saved him before.

Tearing his eyes away from the awful picture, Hatten saw a crowd of Mongols and coolies running towards them.

'Thank God, here are some devils to kill !' he muttered grimly as he drew his sabre.

Sitting home in his saddle, he waved it above his head and shouted 'Charge !' Weary with slaughter the Mongols scattered before their rush like chaff, and without looking back, Hatten and his troopers galloped away towards Fort Mallarraway.

CHAPTER X.

In Fort Mallarraway a feeling of doubt and unrest pervaded every breast. Ignorant that the Kalmucks, who had so nearly captured Cameron, had been sent by Leroy for that special purpose, the men in the Fort naturally concluded that they were but the scouts of a larger body. At any moment the enemy might be down upon them in force, and so the outworks were manned, and every worker attached to the establishment was called in.

During the morning, Colonel Collins, the newly-appointed Chief of the Defence Commission, and his colleague, Major Keith, called to inspect the Fort on their way to Hughenden. The Government, it appeared, had at last awoke to a certain sense of possible danger, and had sent the Colonel up North to inquire personally into the disquieting rumours that were in the air, prior to submitting a report to the Minister for Defence.

Totally unaware of the real state of affairs, both officers were thunderstruck at the news which awaited them. The enemy they had been sent to prepare

against in the improbable event of his coming had
already landed. And the men they were privately
instructed to snub as a lot of insane meddlers were the
only ones who seemed in any way prepared to oppose
his advance. That the landing was really a fact was
amply proved both by Johnson's experience at Cloncurry and Hatten's letter from Hughenden; while
Cameron's escape further demonstrated that the
whole of the country between the two great trunk
lines was practically overrun by hostile cavalry.

Fully convinced of the gravity of the situation,
Colonel Collins decided to at once wire Sir Peter
McLoskie, and asked Musgrave to provide him with
a messenger to ride to the nearest station on the
Hughenden-Longreach line.

'It will be useless, I fear,' replied the President.
'The line is in Zenski's hands, and you may depend
your message will be blocked.'

'Then you think the Count is in collusion with
the attacking force?' exclaimed Collins, now full of
respect for the opinion of the man he yesterday
looked on as a fool.

'I am sure of it; all inland communication is cut
off before this. Sir Peter will hear from below
Charleville long before you can let him know.'

'You are right,' interposed Major Keith; 'we must
do the best we can on our own responsibility.'

'I have half an hour while the horses feed,' said
Colonel Collins; 'then we must push on to Hughenden.
Meantime, I would like to have your opinion.'

'Such as it is you are welcome to it,' replied
Musgrave, leading the way into the committee-room.

Taking his usual seat at the head of the table, Musgrave began :

' I assume that you wish to deal with the defence of this part of the colony ?'

The Colonel nodded.

' Of course our preparations form a portion only; still, they have their value. To throw further light on the subject, I propose to ask Mr. Cameron and one or two other gentlemen well acquainted with the country to join us.'

After the men spoken of had taken their seats, the president resumed :

' Our works you have already seen ; to defend them we have a couple of hundred men well armed and fairly drilled, and all provided with good horses. We have also four machine-guns, such as they are, and enough ammunition to last for a fortnight. If help does not arrive before, we must then cut our way out. I intend to send all our women folk to Hughenden to-day, where Hatten will meet them and send them on to Townsville.'

While Musgrave was speaking, the two officers, both old army men, listened without comment.

When he had ended, Colonel Collins began :

' It appears to me that the whole of the Gulf country may be considered already in the hands of an enemy—whether Russian or Chinese matters little, for in either case they are formidable. Facts are well known here pointing in this direction, which will not be readily understood in Brisbane, and they are so notorious that it is idle to discuss them. The only way to have defended Normanton and Point Parker was to have sent there by train a strong force of infantry and artillery months ago, and also a squadron of gunboats by the Barrier Channel. As it is, there is no possibility of making a stand beyond Hughenden. Well, we have reached this point: what can be done at Hughenden?'

'There is the usual company of volunteers,' said Johnson, 'commanded by a very decent fellow, a contractor by trade—no doubt he'll do his best; and about two dozen men, nominally belonging to the mounted rifles, good enough horsemen, but seldom mustered.'

'I have this from the official report, also that there are a few mounted police,' said the Colonel. 'Such being the small force available, is there any prospect of defending Hughenden? The ordinary colonial township is hardly capable of protracted defence. By felling all the trees around as abattis, manning the windows of houses, and barricading the streets, a strong force of good riflemen might cause an enemy serious loss and delay his advance; but no such town could be saved ultimately from troops with artillery.'

While the Colonel was speaking, the door had opened, and now Hatten, with a sabre-slash on his cheek and with his uniform torn and bloodstained, walked into the room. Rising to their feet, all stared aghast at the new-comer.

Saluting, Hatten said in a voice hoarse with fatigue and rage:

'You need not trouble about the defence of Hughenden, Colonel. The town is in the hands of the enemy, and every man, woman, and child who has not escaped has been slaughtered.'

For a little there was silence. With the fall of Hughenden all hope of saving their women by flight was practically extinguished.

The Colonel was the first to speak.

'Did you succeed in communicating with the officer in command at Longreach, Captain Hatten?' he asked.

'No, sir,' said Hatten, a trifle bitterly; 'Count Zenski's station-masters were in the way.'

'You of course wired Townsville?'

'I did; but got no reply. Probably the line was cut; however, the trains that got away before the town was taken will give the alarm along that line.'

'My God!' exclaimed Cameron, full of fear for his daughter's safety. 'We are trapped.'

'Not yet,' said Collins. 'Why not let all the women be got away South by a forced march through the centre of the country flanked by the trunk-lines.'

'You forget, sir,' interposed Hatten, 'the cross-line between Longreach and Mayne River Station. If I am right in my calculations, the enemy, having full use of the telegraph lines, will attack Longreach simultaneously from Hughenden and Mayne River.'

'Gentlemen,' said President Musgrave, 'as Mr. Cameron says, we are trapped. How do you propose that we should act?'

'Here the outlook is hopeless,' remarked Major Keith; 'no serious organization is possible with such scanty material.'

'We should, however, be able to reckon on help from the coast by railway or otherwise,' said Collins.

'You are right, Colonel,' said Musgrave, placing a map on the table to illustrate his explanation. 'The

Townsville Railway intersects a country of gold-fields and cattle-runs containing even yet a fine, hardy population ; perhaps one thousand men might be expected by this line. Later on a smaller force may be expected from the North.'

'These could operate on the enemy's flank,' muttered the Colonel ; 'but I doubt if they will be strong enough to break through and relieve you.'

'Then,' said Keith, 'it comes to this—the only position between the lines fit to offer a real resistance is Fort Mallarraway.'

'Yes,' said Collins ; 'here we must make our stand. Every man drawn off from the general advance of the enemy gives our comrades behind one chance the more. So, gentlemen, let us fight them while the powder lasts.'

'And then blow up the Fort and cut our way through the yellow devils !' muttered Hatten grimly.

'You are right, Hatten. This army of Asiatics, even if officered, as is probable, by Europeans, must be fought to the last. The idea of surrender must not be entertained for a moment. No terms would be kept by them. The officers have little power over the savages they lead, and all experience shows that the last excesses and extreme horrors of war must be expected from such an army. As at Hughenden, so everywhere : neither sex nor age will be spared.'

As the Colonel spoke, President Musgrave glanced at Cameron. The old squatter's cheek was pale, but his lips were set. Face to face with the inevitable, he was once more the dauntless bushman, ready for all things save his child's dishonour.

Rising, Musgrave said :

' I agree with every word spoken. Every girl and boy capable of firing a shot must be given the chance. Further, I consider it will be necessary to speak very plainly to the women. In spite of us, they may fall into the hands of these savages. Every woman should carry a weapon, and, besides, have poison upon her, so that protection from worse than death may be assured.'

For a moment the old man stopped, then went on in a voice husky and broken :

' If our women carry their fates in their hands, their husbands and brothers will fight with at least one weight of horror off their hearts.'

By virtue of his official rank, Colonel Collins had every right to assume command of the Fort, but recognising that President Musgrave was the natural leader of its garrison, he courteously offered to assume a subordinate command.

' No, Colonel,' replied Musgrave ; ' you're a soldier, and I'm not. I'll look after the commissariat, and see my fellows carry out your orders, but you must lead them.'

About an hour after Hatten's arrival, fugitives from Hughenden began to arrive, and a little after mid-day the greater part of the Isis Downs troop rode in.

Finding the station-house blown up, and dead Kalmucks scattered about the burning ruins, the men had pushed on for Fort Mallarraway. As they reached the outposts, Hatten and Collins met them.

' I see you've christened your new lances,' said Dick.

' We came across a body of about thirty savage-looking devils four or five miles back,' replied Lieutenant Ryan, ' so I charged them on spec. The beggars showed fight, but we were too fresh for them, and when they tried to clear, their horses were so done that we ran every mother's son of them down.'

' Did you make any prisoners ?' asked Collins, anxious for possible information.

' Devil a one ! the boys reckoned they had a hand in burning Cameron out, so we just practised on them with the new pig-stickers.'

' How did they act ?' asked Hatten.

' Didn't I tell ye, Captain, that we took no prisoners ?' grinned Ryan. ' What better proof could ye ask of the success of your invention ?'

As the day wore on, odd fugitives still kept coming from the North, all full of the same gruesome story. The coolies had joined issue with the enemy, and helped in the general massacre that followed Hatten's departure. So far no women had come, while the men reported that, once clear of the town, they had seen no signs of the enemy. Dick understood only too well the absence of the former, while the fact that the Kalmuck cavalry had not reached Hughenden explained the rest.

On all sides the task of completing the works went on with machine-like rapidity. Naturally, the opportunities for effective resistance to troops without heavy artillery were excellent. On the south side of the ridge on which the main buildings stood stretched a rocky ravine watered by a permanent spring. Protecting the farther edge of this valley rose a palisade,

with a ditch on either side, while a similar defence
ran along the northern base of the hill, the two lines
being connected by short barricades. At the four
corners of this parallelogram stood bastions built of
concrete and stone, on which were mounted the four
machine-guns, placed so that they could sweep the
face of either front.

As the roof of the club-house commanded the whole
position, Colonel Collins erected a breastwork of sacks
filled with earth inside the parapet, from behind
which the riflemen could fire over the defenders on
an approaching enemy.

Under Dick's direction, the horses were picketed in
the ravine below the enemy's line of fire, and as there
were over four hundred tons of hay and ensilage, the
question of fodder for them and the stock wanted for
the commissariat caused no uneasiness. In Dick's
mind the question really was, Could they hold the
position long enough to use it all?

At four o'clock everything was prepared for the
defence, and the men, divided into companies, were
ready to rush to their posts the moment the signal was
given.

Nugent and Ryan commanded on the east and
west barricades, while Major Keith and Johnson had
charge of the two main palisades. Hatten retained
his position as Adjutant, and Colonel Collins directed
the whole defence.

As the hot November sun, glowing like a shield of
molten copper, sank into the sullen western haze,
Colonel Collins and Hatten joined Cameron and his
daughter on the roof of the club-house. All day long the

girl had been working with the rest loading cartridges and preparing bandages. This last was gruesome work, but, as Mrs. Musgrave said, not to be avoided on that account. Their defenders were about to face death, and they must be prepared to bind up their wounds. So these women set about their task, and, in providing for the wants and pains of others, managed to put aside for the time the thought of the dread alternative which lay before them.

Leaving his commanding officer to talk to Cameron, Dick walked to the northern parapet with Heather. Again they were alone; but to-night no word of love fell from his lips, and yet to-night he loved her with an intensity before unknown even to himself. In a few hours he might, for all he knew, be beyond all reach of human passion—dead in the trench which stretched like a long narrow grave beneath. But even this grim prospect troubled him little; it was what must follow when the Mongols rushed over his and his comrades' bodies that filled his soul with horror for Heather's fate, and with a strange yearning love, such as comes to a mother watching by the death-bed of her first-born.

Awed by the near presence of an unutterable danger, the girl spoke rather of the past than the present, but at last the dread reality of her peril forced itself upon her, and she spoke of the coming foe.

' Dick,' said the girl almost in a whisper, ' I want you to promise me something.'

But knowing what it was, the man said never a word.

' ' Mr. Musgrave has told us that if the worst comes we must kill ourselves.'

' It won't come to that while I live,' muttered Dick hoarsely.

' I know that, you brave old fellow!' said the girl trustfully; ' but even you can't do what may be impossible, and, Dick, I hate the thought of killing myself. I know it's weak, but I dread it; and so, when all is lost, I want you to save me. If I must die, let it be by your hand.'

' You have asked much from me, Heather,' replied Hatten huskily, ' and for the love I bear you I have striven to obey; but this is more than I can do.'

' For the sake of your love grant this last request,' she pleaded; ' your aim is sure, mine may fail, and then God help me.'

For a long time he stood silent, looking out into the blazing west; then he said slowly: ' If I am alive I will do what you ask.'

' Do you see something moving on the horizon line?' exclaimed a voice, and turning, he saw Colonel Collins pointing towards the north.

Taking the Colonel's field-glasses, Dick looked steadily out over the Downs; then he said quietly: ' Horsemen of some sort.' Again putting the glasses to his eyes, he handed them to Collins with an exclamation.

' There are women and children running in front of them!' exclaimed the Colonel. ' One has fallen; now she's kneeling over her child. My God! the wretches are butchering her! They've caught up to the rest. Ah!' and the strong man winced as

if beneath a blow. 'The devils are cutting them to
pieces! Hatten!'

But Dick was gone; and almost as the Colonel
called him, his voice rose from below ordering his
men to saddle.

Hardly delayed by their work of murder, the
Kalmucks galloped on towards the Fort, and now the
watchers could catch the glitter of their lance-heads
as they swept over the Downs.

For a little they were puzzled by the standard
carried by the leading trooper. Then with a thrill
of horror they realized that it was a girl's head stuck
on the point of his spear! Her long hair, streaming
in the breeze, glittered fitfully in the dying sunlight
as the ruffian waved his lance with a gesture of
defiance. Behind him raced a yelling horde, some
bearing trophies such as his, others with human
heads dangling from their stirrups. Splashed with
blood and drunk with slaughter, on they came, their
broad, squat features, tangled elf locks, gleaming
eyes, and shark-like jaws, combining to make up a
picture worthy of the hell they were sent to create.
When about two hundred yards from the outworks
they halted, and, uttering a yell of defiance, wheeled
about.

As they did so, 'Charge!' rang out, and sword in
hand, Hatten, followed by his troop, dashed out of
the Fort and away over the Downs.

FRANK FELLER

THE YELLOW WAVE.

To face page 286.

CHAPTER XI.

A SACRIFICE ON THE ALTAR OF AMBITION.

AT daybreak on the morning after his interview with Zenski, Leroy started for Charleville, drawn by an electric engine capable of running up to one hundred and fifty miles an hour, and reached Cloncurry at a little after six o'clock.

Here everything was quiet. The officer commanding reported that the inhabitants, taken utterly by surprise, had offered a sharp but futile resistance; that the coolie labourers had joined issue with his forces; and that, as a natural consequence, the whites were either dead or flying before his cavalry. In the yards at the railway-station a troop of Kalmucks were hard at work handling horses, while the coolies of the newly-organized camp-service were slaughtering cattle and sheep as they were driven in by the various foraging-parties.

As soon as he heard his officer's report, Leroy ordered him to at once despatch a picked squadron, under the guidance of one of Zenski's overseers, to Isis Downs. Determined that there should be no mistake, the General gave his orders personally to the Kalmuck officer. He was to bring back all the women he found there unharmed to Cloncurry, as the price of his own head.

At mid-day a telegram came through from Dromeroff, announcing the fall of Normanton and the despatch of a column by rail to Cloncurry.

A message received from Major Hoffman had already described the taking of Charleville. The Major, it seemed, had landed his force in the suburbs of the town before daybreak, and had occupied the railway-station almost without striking a blow.

As at Cloncurry, the Asiatic population turned on their masters the moment they realized the state of affairs, and so rendered all hope of resistance vain.

With regard to the scenes which followed, Major Hoffman maintained a discreet silence, merely stating in his telegram that those who escaped would be certain to spread the news, and that, in view of the fact that the surrounding population was a large one, reinforcements were urgently required.

Fully aware of Hoffman's critical position, Leroy had already taxed the train-service to its utmost in pouring fresh troops to his support, and the following morning, his mind at rest as to Dromeroff's success, he started for Charleville himself.

As the powerful electric motor drew him swiftly through the flat, lightly-timbered country which lay between Cloncurry and Charleville, the General recognised that, long as his line of communication was, its defence need trouble him little.

On either side of the railroad stretched the grants of Zuroff and Co., uninhabited save by the company's alien stockmen and station hands. And even beyond this radius he knew that cheap labour principally obtained.

Queensland depended for her brawn and muscle on inferior races, none of which, save perhaps the Japanese, were prepared to fight for their masters. These, Leroy knew, would resist his followers to the last, through their fierce hatred for the Chinese. But as they were peaceful coolies, ignorant of war and totally without arms, their presence caused him no uneasiness.

As Leroy entered the Warrego district, the country became absolutely flat, nothing deserving the name of even a hill breaking the sameness of the landscape.

Here wheat began to take the place of grass, but as its production was wholly in the hands of the Japanese, the increase in population made little actual difference. Round Charleville, however, and along the Roma-Brisbane line, a number of small proprietors made a living either by wheat or vine-growing. These, in most cases, worked their own properties, and so employed little coloured labour.

From these men danger was to be expected, but even from them only after they were supplied with arms and provided with skilled leaders. At present they were no more fit to face Leroy's machine-guns and automatic rifles than were the gallant Matabeles who fell fighting for their country before the Maxims of the English invaders, who differed only from the Mongols in that they cloaked their designs and justified their actions under the twin catch words of English hypocrisy, ' God and free trade.'

19

Satisfied that communication with his base was secure, Leroy still recognized that his front must soon be attacked by all the force Queensland could place in the field. That the other colonies would also send contingents he well knew, but those would hardly arrive before Dromeroff's columns formed a junction with his own.

In face of the increased numbers and hostile character of the inhabitants below Charleville, any advance, even if reinforced by Dromeroff's columns, must be made subject to the risk of having his line of communication with the North cut, and so, as all the hope of further surprise was ended, Leroy had decided to form an entrenched camp at Charleville, and there to await both the arrival of the enemy and his own supports.

At about four in the afternoon the special ran into the town. As the train slowed down, Leroy could see from his carriage that the town had been not only taken, but sacked. Above the corpse-strewn ground and blackened, fire-gutted buildings, a heavy canopy of smoke hung. Still, beyond an occasional harsh word of command, and the measured tramp of the pickets, no sound of war fell on the General's ears. The shouts of the pursuers, and the screams and curses of those who fled, were alike hushed. Leaving the carriage, Leroy walked through the encampment. A believer in deeds, he was more at home amid the action of war than when taking part in its pomp. Still, knowing the value of effect on Asiatics, he was quite ready, as at Point Parker, to gratify his followers' love of parade when necessary. Now he wanted to judge for himself as to results, and so he came absolutely unannounced.

The encampment in which he now found himself presented the appearance of a collection of small forts. The 'Kian Ping Sin Chi,' or manual for Chinese soldiers, ordains that each company of one hundred men is to form its own encampment, which is to be fortified by a trench and rampart. Recognising that under this system the men (who were unencumbered with tents) not only obtained a considerable amount of shelter, but also held a position secure against surprise, Leroy adopted it as being peculiarly well suited to present surroundings. The Commander-in-Chief found Major Hoffman personally directing the erection of the earthworks which were to enclose the camp. The Major, an intelligent-looking, middle-aged man who wore glasses, had been cashiered from the German army for duelling, and now used his skill as an engineer of the first class in directing the wakening intelligence of the officers and men of the Dragon throne.

Apprised of the General's arrival, Hoffman walked to meet him.

Dropping his hand on his officer's shoulder, Leroy exclaimed heartily, and so that all might hear :

'*Mon camarade*, you have done well! With such officers and such men, I have but to order and it is done.'

Gratified at such words from a man who never depreciated the value of his praise by 'over-supply,' Hoffman bowed. Then he said quietly :

'*Mein Gott, Général !* it is easy to obey with only an unarmed mob to dispose of.'

'Our quickness alone has accounted for this,' replied Leroy. ' Now we must be prepared to meet an enemy worthy of our steel. The day of surprises is over; that of action draws near.'

'I know it, and am preparing. In a week from now, if properly garrisoned, these works will be impregnable, unless the attacking forces use melanite bombs.'

' Bah! I doubt if they will have enough powder to supply their infantry,' sneered Leroy. ' Besides, I only mean to use the works in case of a repulse. We will fight their raw levies in the open, Major.'

As they talked, the two men mounted a railway signal-box, whence they could look over the whole expanse of level country. Already lines of fortification commanding the Charleville-Brisbane Railway, Zenski's line, and the artesian bore were beginning to rise. Belts of myall and gidyea rose here and there above the dead level of landscape, and along the course of the river barren sand-hills lifted their sun-scorched summits.

' It is an ideal battle-ground on which to meet green troops,' muttered Leroy; ' they must fight with no natural features to cover their retreat or interfere with our advance. What possibilities for cavalry and horse artillery !'

' With the Northern line in our hands, and the river held as I mean to hold it, our position is secure either as a base from which to strike or a defence to cover retreat.'

' You are right, Hoffman; but let us not expect retreat.'

'I do not,' replied the cautious German ; 'never-theless, I will be prepared for it.'

'Again you are right : a leader must be prepared for everything. I leave the question of defence in your hands, Hoffman ; and, remember, if I trust much, I expect much.'

Guarded by detachments of Mongols, gangs of Europeans and Japanese toiled at the earthworks ; for Hoffman had saved all the prisoners left after the first onslaught, not from motives of mercy, but in order that he might utilize them in the construction of his fortifications. Under a burning sun and kept to their hateful task by brutal overseers, the wounded and heart-broken wretches slaved on without hope, and impotent even to exact vengeance on the destroyers of their homes and loved ones. Here and there one weaker, or perhaps stronger, than his companions sank under his load, and found beneath the bayonets of his guards rest from his dishonoured labour. But, recognising the loss entailed by killing the workers outright, the Mongol officers soon ordered another punishment, and the prisoner who fell to the earth either from exhaustion or a desire for death, was flogged to his feet by their quirts of hide. Reinforced by fresh batches of prisoners brought in by the Kalmuck scouts, and helped by crowds of friendly coolies, the gangs worked ceaselessly, and as the sun, hot and relentless, sloped westward, the hated task of raising up a defence against their own countrymen began to take definite shape.

Keenly as he had looked, Leroy had seen no women among the gangs ; but, questioned on the subject,

Hoffman admitted candidly that in the attack many
of both sexes were butchered. Knowing the wanton
savagery of all troops suddenly let loose, Leroy felt that
he was powerless. His officer declared that he had
done his best, consequently there was nothing more
to be said. He might have thought differently had
he known that Hoffman, going on the cold-blooded
principle that women prisoners were undesirable,
had issued an order that no woman was to be made
prisoner, leaving all question of detail to his men.

Over an after-dinner's smoke in Hoffman's quarters,
Leroy heard his officer's report. The artesian bore
included in the lines of defence gave a daily supply
of three million gallons of water. In the country
already occupied, large quantities of wheat were
almost ripe, and would consequently soon be available as a food supply ; while cattle and sheep were
both easily procurable. Every horse seen had been
secured by the small body of mounted men at his
command, and now he was in a position to put a
considerable force of cavalry in the field when their
mounts were handled. Flying columns, each with a
machine-gun attached to the engine, had been pushed
on to occupy Thargomindah and Cunnamulla, and to
hold the South Australian line as far as completed ;
and detachments of sappers were busy blowing up the
Charleville-Roma Railway for as great a distance as
circumstances would allow.

' You have lost no time, Hoffman,' said Leroy.

' The surprise was absolute, and I have made the
most of it ; but the enemy is sure to rally, and I must
have more cavalry to hold what I have won.'

'You shall have them as fast as the trains can carry them,' replied Leroy. 'As to our opponents, even if they have horses, they have no arms. For the present, nothing but guerilla operations need be feared from them, and before they can possibly organize, our columns will have concentrated.'

'When may Dromeroff be expected ?'

'All his infantry and artillery will come on by train from Longreach to Mayne River, and from there along the main line. The cavalry will march from Longreach to Charleville. They are all provided, as you know, with waterproof, air-tight bags, capable of holding full equipment for horse and rider, so there need be no delay even if the country should be flooded.'

These bags, which floated buoyantly with their loads, and could be towed after the men and horses to whom they belonged, allowing them to swim unencumbered, only weighed between two and three pounds each. General Leroy had adopted them, as he held that rivers should prove no hindrance to cavalry who might be ordered to explore land on the opposite side, and who, if unprepared, must suffer great loss in men and horses.

'Then we may look for them in ten or twelve days ?' said Hoffman, running off the distance on the map.

'Twelve at most. I leave in the morning to operate from Mayne River in conjunction with Dromeroff. The attack on Longreach should take place to-morrow.'

'There may be fighting there?'

'Possibly. The chances are that the alarm has reached them, and the country on the Barcaldine-Rockhampton line is thickly populated. Still, what can they do? Like all the rest, they have no arms and little, if any, organization.'

'Later a flanking force may be expected, however.'

'Undoubtedly!' said Leroy, as he rose. 'It will entail the leaving of a strong column at Longreach to keep our line of communication with Normanton intact.'

Though night had fallen, the dull sounds of explosions still went on, for Hoffman was destroying all houses that chanced to stand outside his defence lines.

Lighting a fresh cigar, the engineer said: 'I must go, General; my presence is necessary on the outworks. Do you accompany me?'

'I have despatches to attend to,' replied Leroy; 'when they are written I may follow you.'

Left alone, the General wrote rapidly for a time; then, sealing up his letters, he sat back in his chair, and smoked hard. Now that his work was done, thoughts of the woman he loved filled his brain. Would the Kalmuck succeed in his mission? As a picture of the dangers that lay in Heather's path rose before him, Leroy cursed himself for not obeying his first impulse, and going for her himself. Now that he could think it out alone, he realized that all would be well lost so that she was saved. But despot as he was, holding in his hand the lives of thousands, he knew that even his power had its limits, and that one false move might break the spell with which he controlled the fierce spirits who fought under him; and, then—well, then chaos.

'No,' he muttered as he rose, 'if only for her sake,
I must not now turn back; as their General I can
at least protect the woman I love. With my fall
she must share the fate of others.' Reaching the
street, Leroy walked slowly on towards the river.
He had no wish to rejoin Hoffman; the half-fearful,
wholly - hateful glances of the wretched workers
scorched him. He had looked on many such a scene
unmoved in Asia, but then the prisoners there were
only having meted out such treatment as they had
often meted out to others. Here they were beings
born under the same skies as himself; perhaps among
them slaved men who had been schoolmates of his
own. One old man had looked into his eyes with a
glance of half - recognition that very afternoon as
he struck up the arm of a Kalmuck who was cutting
the bent, weary back with a bloody quirt.

Now he remembered where he had seen the face;
it was years ago in his own father's house; the old
man had patted his boyish head and given him some
trifling present. God! it was awful! He was a
modern Attila without the old barbarian's excuse,
the wielder of a scourge wet with the blood of men
who had called him friend, and blasted by the
dishonour of women who belonged to the same race
as his own dead mother. Appalled by the recognition
of his own baseness, Leroy moved on through the
deserted, ruined street. Unquestioned by the pickets,
who recognised even in the gloom the tall form of
their leader, Leroy reached the river-bank. For a
little he gazed into its black depths, then turned
away with a shudder. In its foul bed he knew many

a woman lay who had sprung into its cold embrace with the bloody finger-prints of the ravisher staining the white freshness of her wind-tossed robe.

Wandering aimlessly and conscience - stung, he found himself at the open door of a deserted house. Without thought or purpose, he walked into the ruined hall, and then, impelled by some strange force, pushed aside a torn mass of drapery and stepped into the room which opened on the farther side.

Hanging from the ceiling, a lamp still burned, shedding a dim flood of light on the bed-clothes and broken furniture, which lay scattered over the floor in hopeless confusion.

The occupants had evidently turned it down when going to rest; possibly someone was sick, and so they had feared to put it out altogether.

Still holding a revolver in his hand, a man lay on the floor, his head split almost to the chin, and across his body a middle-aged woman reclined in a huddled mass. Stretched across the tumbled bed lay two young girls, their white limbs bruised and bloody— in their eyes the print of that despair which flashed through their scarce-opened lids into the faces of their destroyers.

One child's poor fingers still clutched fragments of white drapery; from the other the spoilers' lustful hands had torn aside all covering, and now naked and dead they lay before his eyes.

The open door of an inner room told whence they had come and who they had been. Less fortunate than those now sleeping in the ooze and drift of the river, this wife who had fallen asleep in her husband's arms, and these two winsome maidens, perchance lulled to rest by dreams of love and life, had suddenly awakened to see husband and father cut down by murderous hands, and to feel a breath worse than that of death upon their faces.

Now all was over, for Hoffman's brutal order had given them the only boon left for such as they to pray for.

Silently Leroy took in the whole fearful scene, and then the strong man covered his face with his hands, and sobbed aloud in unspeakable agony.

Ambition, the goddess of his idolatry, had brought him face to face with this supreme sacrifice, and now that he saw the offering which she demanded for her altar, he realized as he had never done before the awful price which must be paid to win and hold her favour.

[300]

CHAPTER XII.

THE DEFENCE OF LONGREACH.

WHEN Leroy left the ruined house, his first impulse
was to at once confront Hoffman; but as he hurried
towards the outworks this resolve first weakened, then
was put aside. Knowing his soldiery, he recognized
that what he had just seen was possible of accom-
plishment in spite of all that his officers could do.
He had Hoffman's assurance that he had done all in
his power to prevent needless brutality, and he felt
that, under the circumstances, he could take no other
course but to believe his statement.

Standing gazing on the murdered girls, the man's
numbed but not yet dead nobility of character rose
for a moment superior to the grosser passions which
of late years had crushed it back into dim, almost
forgotten, recesses of his being. Filled with righteous
wrath, he was prepared to measure out punishment
on the heads of the killers—ay, even if the sword-
strokes which let out their miserable lives cut from
him the allegiance of the army he led.

But now, as he walked towards Hoffman's quarters,
ambition once more asserted its potent sway; he was

still filled with rage, pity, shame, but all these feelings now ran their course subject to the cold guidance of reason.

Emotions such as prompted his first impulse were the peculiar property of women, and of men unencumbered by supreme responsibilities ; but he was a soldier, a leader before whose grasp vast possibilities lay, and so he must thrust aside this ghastly detail on which he had chanced as impracticable of solution by ordinary methods. A quarrel with Hoffman was not to be thought of, while the discovery of the actual criminals was worse than hopeless. Above all, would he be justified, when face to face with the enemy, in risking disaffection among his followers for the sake of such a quixotic quest ?

Reason answered, No. And at last, falling back on the old ground that Heather's safety was bound up in his remaining absolute leader of the Mongols, Leroy turned into Hoffman's quarters determined to keep what he had seen to himself, not as a matter of willingness, but as an act of expediency.

In the morning the Commander-in-Chief returned to Mayne River junction, where everything was in readiness for the movement on Longreach. At Charleville no symptoms of serious attack as yet manifested themselves. During the night small bodies of horsemen had come into collision with the outposts, but beyond this the scouts reported that there were no signs of the enemy within touch. So Leroy left Hoffman to complete his works with little danger of opposition, at any rate for the present.

On reaching Mayne River station, the General found

that all communication between his advanced posts and Longreach was cut off. This was of little importance as regarded touch with Dromeroff, for the line from Hughenden *vid* Normanton and Cloncurry was open. Still, it meant that the alarm had been given.

A telegram from Dromeroff confirmed Leroy's fears. The enemy was on the alert, and had begun to blow up the line from Winton.

Warned in time, Dromeroff had pushed on a column supported by a Maxim gun, which now held the road to within ten miles of Longreach. Acting on his own responsibility, the officer commanding at Mayne River had despatched every available truck, crammed with men, to support the flying column which had started the night before to cover the Mayne River road.

The latest news from the Point informed Leroy that this column had succeeded in holding the railway as far as the Thompson River, and that the bridge was for the present safe, the enemy being unable to face the fire of the Maxim guns.

Wiring Dromeroff to push on at all hazards, and so divide the defending line, Leroy started for the front with every man he could find rolling stock to carry.

The officer in command of the Longreach volunteer detachment had received a wire from Rockhampton on the night Leroy reached Charleville, to the effect that a warlike force of some sort had landed in the Gulf, and was advancing by rail. How far they had got the message did not say. It had come from Cooktown, where Frank McLean had arrived, and only contained the meagre information he himself possessed. Regarding it as a hoax, the Lieutenant did nothing beyond sending a reply asking for something definite. An hour later he got his answer from Townsville, announcing the sacking of Hughenden, and almost before the instrument ceased ticking, a further telegram came to the effect that Charleville was in the hands of the invaders. Following this, the bewildered Lieutenant received orders from the officer in command at Rockhampton to get away all the women and children, and to destroy both lines of railway as far as practicable. This done, he was to hold the Rockhampton-Longreach railroad with all the men he could muster, until such time as support could reach him.

Placed suddenly in a position calculated to test the resources even of a trained veteran, Lieutenant Jones held the message in one hand, while with his other he scratched his head. Then, after the custom of his countrymen, he walked into the nearest bar and had a drink.

Being in private life a draper, who combined extreme affability (some people called it servility) with a nice discriminating faculty as between good and bad marks, Mr. Jones had thriven amazingly, and now called his shop an emporium, and himself a merchant importer.

Left to follow his natural bent, it is probable that he would have rested content with aldermanic honours, and the privilege of adding the magic letters J.P. to his name. Personally, he had no cravings for blood, nor did he pine to lead the Longreach fencibles to the

muzzles of the enemy's rifles. In fact, to him
might have been applied the remark made by a
certain colonel to a Sydney military commission,
when he said that it seemed to him impossible to
combine the fierceness of the soldier with the tame-
ness of the clerk.

Mrs. Jones, however, thought otherwise. This
misguided lady had conceived the idea that, if her
husband became a lieutenant, she must of necessity
be entitled to call herself Mrs. Lieutenant. Being
already brigadier-general in the Jones household, this
settled it. The local member was rather heavily
represented in the debit column of the emporium
ledger, and so, as a natural consequence, when the
position became vacant, Mr. Jones was gazetted on the
legislator's recommendations.

During the piping days of peace things went fairly
smoothly with Lieutenant Jones, under the watchful
supervision of the Government drill-instructor.

Thanks to that obliging 'non-com.' he passed his
examination in a way which made it hard to understand why he always allowed the sergeant to whisper
the word of command before uttering it himself. But
as he shouted liberally, his men let this peculiarity
trouble them little. Longreach was too hot a hole
for the working out of abstruse problems.

But now war had come, and it was a ' line ' in which
the soft-goods man had had no actual experience. In
his perplexity he naturally turned to his guide,
philosopher, and friend, Sergeant Hegarty. That
respected relic of the British army was, as luck would
have it, reclining on a bench in the bar, an empty

pewter in his hand, the froth from its late brimming measure frosting his moustache, and gleaming like a star on the crimson expanse of his nose.

Walking up to the instructor, Lieutenant Jones shook him. At first only a grunt rewarded his efforts, but as the shaking continued, the sergeant rose to a sitting position and demanded thickly what the deuce he wanted. Then seeing who it was, he added affably: 'Hullo, Jones, old cock, I don't mind if I do.' Passing over this familiar mode of address, Jones stood the necessary drink, and then led his 'non-com.' into a private room and read him the telegrams.

Roused by the message, the old soldier sobered up instantly. 'Faix, Captain,' said he, 'it's the divil to pay, an' no pitch hot, right enough.'

'But what am I to do?' asked Jones feebly.

For a moment Hegarty looked at his superior with pitying contempt, then he answered stoutly:

'Obey orders, Captain.'

'But how?'

'Get the wimmin and kids away, and foight the divils, av course.'

'But I never fought in my life.'

'Bedad, then, you can't begin earlier,' grinned Hegarty; 'an' by the powers it will be a hell of a tussle intoirely.'

'Don't you think we'd better retire?'

'Is it guardin' the wimmin ye mane?' asked Hegarty; 'not in the face of these orders, Captain. You send a couple of engines along the lines to feel for the inimy; if there ain't any to be had, bicycles 'ull

20

be better than nothing. Manetime I'll rally up all the buoys.'

Before daybreak, thanks to Hegarty's exertions, the alarm was spread, and every man who chanced to have a weapon was under arms.

Roused to some sense of duty, Lieutenant Jones now lost no time in carrying out his sergeant's suggestions; and as fast as was practicable every woman and child was removed into safety.

Warned by the pilot engines of the near approach of the enemy, the townsmen began to tear up the line, only to be driven back by the Mongol advance columns. Ill armed, and totally without artillery, they now had to fall back across the river.

Barricading the streets, and filling the houses with riflemen, Jones and Hegarty then waited the attack. About five o'clock in the afternoon it began. Standing on the barricade, the old sergeant said grimly:

'Nothin' but the Almoighty or reinforcements can save us, buoys; but, tare an' ages, is it the loikes of us is goin' to run afore a lot of d——d cabbage-growin' chows! Lie down, buoys,' he added as the fire opened, 'and blaze at 'em betwixt the chinks.'

Not knowing when reinforcements might come up, Leroy poured a heavy fire from his machine-guns into the barricades and then ordered a general advance.

Protected by their cover, the defenders had so far lost few men, and thanks to Hegarty's orders, 'to fire low, and at something,' the Mongols suffered heavily as they rushed to the assault. Still, though their ranks showed many a gap, the infantry never wavered.

Their General's eyes were on them, and closing each break in their line, on they came.

'Give the yaller-bellies the cold steel fur it!' roared the sergeant, as the Mongols charged the breastwork.

Then, sword in hand, he leaped on the barricade. Inspired by their leader, the volunteers met thrust with thrust, while those who had no bayonets clubbed their guns and rifles, and battered at the heads of the Mongols, with the grim strength of despair.

Mad with the lust of battle, Hegarty fought in the foremost ranks. Bayonet clashed against bayonet, and men trampled over each other in their fierce haste to slay. Then, just as the defenders began to give ground, a chance shot struck the Mongol leader, and he fell. For an instant his followers wavered, and seeing their indecision, Hegarty waved his sword above his head, and, leaping over the breastwork, yelled :

' They're licked ; intil 'em, lads !'

Borne back by the resistless rush, the Mongols gave way, and then, missing their leader's voice, broke and fled.

' Back under cover, buoys,' shouted Hegarty as the Maxims again opened fire.

' Well, Captain,' muttered the sergeant, as he lay down beside his officer, ' how do ye feel at all ?'

' Right enough,' replied Jones, who had fought with the best, and who had sense enough not to object to his sergeant's assumption of command; ' only I've broken my sword.'

' More power to ye,' whispered his companion; ' it must have been a grate sthroke intoirely.'

'But it wasn't,' replied Jones irritably; 'I just leant on it when I slipped, and it snapped—a weapon I gave six pounds for, too.'

'That's nothing,' grinned Hegarty, 'oi've had me own bayonet turn roun' from a nigger's brisket, and job me in the jaw, before to-day. Hullo, here they come again!'

As he spoke, a man ran up.

'Our powder's nearly out, Captain,' he said.

'What's to be done?' asked Jones helplessly.

'Hould this barricade without it,' roared Hegarty, his Irish blood up. 'Eh, buoys?'

But the men began to murmur, and Hegarty himself saw its utter madness.

'We'll give 'em one more taste of our quality while the powder lasts, then retrate while they're in confusion,' he suggested.

A cheer told him they were ready, and then silently they waited the coming foe.

During the afternoon a train from Barcaldine had brought up the local company, and a body of picked civilians who had rifles of their own. These, under their own officer, were posted in a position to oppose Dromeroff's advance, and if possible prevent him from turning Jones's flank. Like all the rest, however, they had little ammunition, and their supply had already been lessened in order to provide the men facing Leroy with a few extra rounds.

Hearing the sound of firing from the north-west, Leroy determined to carry the barricade before Dromeroff arrived.

Not to do so was alike repugnant to his pride and calculated to impair his prestige.

Besides, to let this paltry force defy him would not only lessen the enemy's opinion of their opponents' courage, but would be certain to fill the Mongols with doubts as to their own invincibility.

Riding to the front of the re-formed companies, their General put himself at their head. Taking no notice of their wild shout, he pointed to the barricade, and, putting his charger into a walk, advanced towards it, his sword resting in its scabbard.

Keeping up a continuous fire with their automatic rifles, the Mongols continued their forward movement under a hot discharge from the breastwork and houses. When less than a hundred yards from the barricade, Leroy's horse fell under him. Springing to his feet, the General drew his sword, and, giving the word in a voice that rang out above the roll of the musketry, he dashed on, followed by his troops.

Again Hegarty leaped on the barricade, brave as a lion, and as before his men fought like devils. For a moment the bayonets met, and the whirling rifle-butts sank with dull thuds into shattered skulls. Making straight for the old sergeant, Leroy engaged him hand-to-hand. Never flinching, Hegarty parried his fierce thrust. But useless was all his valour against the first swordsman of his day. For a little the swords rang against each other, then, breaking down the gallant Irishman's defence, Leroy swung his sabre aloft like lightning, and with one mighty downstroke cleft him to the chin. Tossing his arms, Hegarty fell back on a pavement of dead and dying, and, following his advantage, Leroy sprang over the breastwork, followed by the Mongols, and the position was won.

Leaderless and broken, the defenders fought no
more. Panic-stricken, they fled before the dripping
bayonets of the foe, only to meet Dromeroff's victorious
column. Outflanked, the weary survivors became a
helpless mob, and the retreat a merciless butchery.
At the railway-station Leroy and Dromeroff met.

Sheathing his sword, the General grasped his
comrade's hand.

'Well met, *mon brave!*' said he. 'Save all the
prisoners you can; they are too useful to break good
bayonets on.'

'*Pardieu!* you are right, General,' exclaimed
Dromeroff; 'but these tigers have tasted blood.
Still, I will do what I can.'

That night the two commanders held a consulta-
tion.

There was much to discuss; but both were men of
action rather than words. Dromeroff told all that
had happened since he parted from his chief in the
form of a concise report, and Leroy, in a few words,
explained his future plan of campaign.

While discussing Fort Mallarraway, Leroy discovered that the squadron he had sent to capture
Heather had failed in their mission. A survivor had
been picked up at one of the stations about mid-day,
who declared that the whole party had escaped into
the Fort.

Dromeroff had left orders for the cavalry to invest
it. But now that Longreach was taken, he proposed
attacking it in earnest with artillery.

'It must be stormed,' admitted Leroy. 'Such a
position in our rear is of course impracticable.'

' It shall not exist two days from now,' remarked Dromeroff confidently.

Hiding the keen interest he felt about the matter from his second in command, Leroy said carelessly :

' I will see to it myself; I want to personally inspect Hughenden; you have enough to do here, *mon Colonel.* Longreach must be put in a position of defence, and your forces pushed on for Charleville without an hour's delay. So leave this small nut for me to crack.'

So it happened that Leroy went North, while Dromeroff remained at Longreach to fortify the position and personally superintend the advance of his columns.

CHAPTER XIII.

THE SIEGE OF FORT MALLARRAWAY.

An hour after Hatten left the Fort at the head of the 'Ringers,' the watchers on the roof of the club-house caught sight of the returning troop. At the entrance to the barricade Colonel Collins met his Adjutant, who reported that he had come up with the Kalmucks after a short pursuit. Hampered by the unbroken state of their mounts, the murderers were easily dispersed, though offering a stout resistance when brought to bay. A few had managed to escape, as Hatten feared to put too big a distance between himself and the Fort, but with these exceptions every savage had been destroyed.

During the night all remained quiet, but the following afternoon the scouts reported that the enemy's cavalry was advancing in force from the direction of Hughenden. A couple of hours before sunset they swept into view, their lance-heads and sabre-blades glittering above the level lands. Halting his main force out of range, the officer in command rode forward to reconnoitre.

'Let me make a dash at the beggars, Colonel!'

exclaimed Hatten. 'If I can get in between them and the main body they're ours!'

'I can't risk it, Hatten,' replied the Colonel; 'your fellows are full of fight, but they're a bit green yet. If they once got going, you'd never stop them, and then good-bye to the whole troop.'

While the two men were speaking, the reconnoitring party rode within a few hundred yards of the northern defence line, and halting, their leader began to inspect the works through his glasses.

'Damn his impertinence!' muttered Collins. 'Swing round that gun and try a pot shot, Keith.'

But the Kalmucks' leader had not used his glasses for nothing, and before the gun was round, he wheeled his horse and galloped off, followed by his companions.

'Don't fire!' shouted Collins; 'we can't throw away a shot.'

Apparently satisfied that the position was too strong to attack unsupported by infantry, the cavalry commander now began to make a reconnaissance of the surrounding positions.

Whenever the enemy chanced to come within range, the rifles on the roof of the club-house rang out; but beyond these occasional reports and the answering yells of the Kalmucks, no sound of war broke the stillness of the sultry day.

Just before sunset a column of infantry joined the besieging force.

Too short of both ammunition and men to assume the aggressive, Collins and his officers watched the Mongols raising up their mimic fortresses on the northern point. With practised skill, each company soon enclosed itself with a breastwork, from above which its particular standard flapped lazily in the evening breeze.

On the south the cavalry hung like a cloud.

'They mean to have us,' said Musgrave, glancing uneasily at the deliberate preparations of the enemy.

'Thank God, there isn't a field-gun among them!' muttered Collins, closing his glasses. 'Without artillery they can only starve us out.'

'Unless it rains again within a week, they'll be starved out themselves,' retorted Cameron hopefully; 'the surface water lying about won't last a force such as theirs long.'

Hatten, who was standing by, said nothing; he felt it would be cruel to kill the old man's hope, but both he and Collins well knew that the arrival of guns was at most only a question of hours.

That night every man slept at his post; that is, if anyone within the Fort slept at all. The women certainly did not. Filled with the near reality of a peril, supreme, and yet so abhorrent that they shrank from discussing its awful climax, the women, when their work was over, sat round Mrs. Musgrave. At times, when Hope's lamp burns dim, and the hollow echoes of Death's implacable footsteps draw near, mankind insensibly calls upon its God. Face to face with a foe who will not be denied by human skill, man, be he ever so gross, recognising that Death laughs at the material, turns his eyes at last to the spiritual.

It is our *dernier ressort* in face of the inevitable.

The act of a coward probably, still, but for all that and because of it, intensely human. For a like reason we draw nearer to one better than ourselves in moments of extreme peril. Perhaps we deem it is well to leave for the unknown in good company.

To-night the women gathered round old Mrs. Musgrave, and, after the manner of their kind, prayed; for the old saw 'that men must work and women must pray' still held good, at any rate in emergencies such as the present.

All women pray, if it be only to ask God to keep them beautiful; but most of these gathered round the President's wife were honest, pure-souled girls and wives who asked for help as from a trusted guide rather than a forgotten and dimly-understood power. Unlike the majority of humanity, they did not regard God as on a par with a nauseous if potent drug, only to be sought after in extremes, and to be carefully avoided with returning health.

Out in the darkness the men waited behind the barricades.

Now that the infantry were up, Collins knew that an attack might be made at any moment, if only to feel the strength of the besieged. Beyond the defences a few lynx-eyed black boys were acting as scouts, so that a surprise was well-nigh impossible.

Fearful as to the alertness of his willing but raw material, Hatten spent his time in going round the works, and at last, just about that gloom-clad hour when the night begins to die, he entered the north-west bastion.

Round the gun the men were lying discussing the enemy, and emphasizing their arguments with original and more or less ingenious profanity.

'Good God!' exclaimed Billy the Kid with more fervour than actual reverence, ' you don't mean to tell me that I can't belt six bloomin' chows!'

'We shall see when ze time arrive,' replied the old Frenchman with whom he was arguing.

' Look here, Frenchy, d'ye take me for a· bloomin' waster?' asked Billy hotly.

'*Non, non, mon brave!* it is you who take ze Mongol for one.'

' So he is '—stoutly.

'Pardon, it is not so.   Ze man you vill have to fight is not vat you would call ze common chow.   If led as these are by European officers, he's nomber, he's obedience to authority, and he's personal bravery must make him almost irrezestible.'

' How the blazes do you know ?'

' I have met ze gentleman years back in Tonquin,' replied the old soldier quietly, ' bayonet to bayonet. Doubtless, *mon beau* Beeley, you will soon likewise be able to joodge for yourself.'

' I ain't much up in these 'ere jobbers,' growled Billy; 'but I'll back myself to shoot mosquitoes on the wing agin any blarsted chinkie in the push.'

' Go on; what yer given' us?' sneered a Hughenden man.

·'Send I might live,' retorted Billy, ' and I'd take these Johns with the bare " mud-scratchers "—one down next come on.   Gor blow me! ain't they got chests like drinks o' water!'

'I was talkin' about your shootin',' drawled the man who had last spoken.

'Right; and you'll have the straight wire about it, too,' said Billy. 'A couple of months ago, on the Downs, I went out to get a duck for the missus. Well, on the t'other side of Scottie's Lagoon, I sees a dozen roosting in a line along a coolibah log. Slipping a ball in, I says to myself, "Blowed if I don't knock the heads off the lot!" Down I drops ; but just as I pulls the blarsted trigger, a blarsted branch falls plump across the barrel. "Blarst it !" says I. But so help me never, when the smoke clears I sees every bloomin' duck still there a-flapping and quacking like mad.'

'Get on !'

'As true as I live!' protested Billy; 'I runs across, and what d'ye think I finds ?'

'That you'd been havin' a dream.'

'No bloomin' fear ! I finds the ball had hit the log just below the ducks' feet, and blow me if they hadn't all fallen into the split it made! Then it closed and caught 'em, so I rings their necks and fetches the lot home. Didn't I, Capten ?'

Billy never got Hatten's answer, for even as the words were on his lips, a rifle-shot rang out, and almost simultaneously the bugles sounded, and broad streams of light shot from the summit of the club-house far into the night.

As the electric flashes fell upon them, the Mongols sent up a deafening yell. But held in hand by their leaders, the men behind the defences remained silent.

On the northern front the attacking infantry now

poured in a terrific fire from their automatic rifles, all
the more appalling in that no report drowned the
fierce hail of bullets which beat against the logs.

'Wait for them, men!' shouted Keith; 'this devil's
tattoo won't hurt much.'

While the infantry were advancing, the cavalry
now dismounted, and, armed with their carbines,
made a determined attack on the southern barricade.

Pursuing similar tactics to Keith, Johnson let them
blaze away and waited. Meantime the men on the
parapet of the club-house lay behind the bags glancing along their barrels.

'Surely they are within range, Colonel?' exclaimed
Musgrave.

'Possibly; but I want every shot to tell,' replied
the Colonel.

Emboldened by the silence, the Mongols now began
to close for their final rush. Then the Colonel said
sharply, 'Now, men, let every bullet mean a yellow
devil! Fire!'

In an instant the roof of the club-house was enveloped in smoke, out of which rushed red tongues
of flame.

Sword in hand, the Mongol officers led on their men,
who, galled by the riflemen's fire, now rushed on the
barricades with yells of defiance and rage.

Directing the full force of his attack on the northern
front, the Mongol commander made a furious demonstration against the gate. When the Mongols were
less than a hundred yards from the outer ditch, the
men behind the palisades opened fire. Met at point-
blank range, the enemy fell in scores; but, splendidly

led, they still came on, thinned by each successive discharge, but undaunted. At last they reached the ditch and began, in face of the defenders, to throw their storming bridges across at points where the fire was slackest. But now the machine-guns opened fire, and raked both in front and on either flank by foes they could not see, the stormers fell back on their supports.

Knowing that the Commander-in-Chief would be with him on the following morning, the officer in charge of the besiegers was keenly anxious to carry the Fort before his arrival. The repulse first sustained showed him that this was no easy matter, and that, to be successful, he must be prepared to sacrifice his men without stint. This, however, cost him no uneasiness. Accustomed to Asiatic warfare, the question of human life never entered into his calculations, save as a means to an end.

His soldiers' present use was to win him the favour of Leroy, by carrying the position which delayed the advance, so he decided to again attempt it without regard to the certain and necessary loss which must ensue.

Inside the Fort a feeling of exultation prevailed. The dreaded enemy had been hurled back almost without the loss of a man, and now the one desire of the defenders was to sally out and complete his rout. In spite of what their officers had said, the Mongols were only Chinamen—mongrels like all their countrymen. At least, so the majority of the men behind the barricades thought, and said, flushed with the excitement of their first and, as it happened, successful 'brush' with an actual enemy.

Permeated with the sickening and indiscriminate adulation which England had poured over all things colonial during the past ten years, these undisciplined warriors most illogically deemed themselves invincible. Had not imperial commandants and successive governors told them so ? And now actual experience came to prove it.

Crowding round their officers, the men demanded to be led against the enemy.

Recognising that he was in some sort to blame for this insanity, Colonel Collins hesitated. But, not handicapped by the memory of past parade orations, Dick Hatten answered them.

'Don't be a lot of damned fools !' said he. 'You fight well enough behind cover. Stop there !'

As he spoke, the rifles of the scouts again rang out.

'To your posts, men !' shouted Collins. 'Fire low and keep your heads !'

Taking advantage of every inequality in the ground, the Mongol stormers again crept on through the gloom ; but again the quick-eyed blacks sighted the advancing columns, and firing their rifles, the scouts retired under the cover of the palisades.

As the first report fell on his ear, Musgrave sprang to the electric battery and connected the current. Then, as the whole wild scene became lit up, he looked over the parapet.

The Fort itself was enveloped in a cordon of smoke, out of which incessant tongues of flame rushed, followed by that dread crackling chorus which belongs peculiarly to Bush fires and volleys of musketry.

Beyond the circle of smoke, but ever drawing

nearer, crept hundreds of shadowy forms. He could see the light glint on their rifle-barrels as they brought them to the shoulder, yet neither smoke nor sound came forth from the phantom tubes. Still beneath him he could see an occasional man sink forward, or spring upwards, in his death-agony, and about his ears the ping of passing bullets told the watcher that death lurked in the voiceless rifles of the foe. Now little space remained between the smoke-cloud and the enemy. With his night-glasses he could catch the wolfish glare in the stormers' eyes, as, treading over their dead companions, they rushed on the points of the flame-tongues.

A gleam of sword-blades, a red light on the bayonets, a wild mingling of shots and fierce, hoarse yells, then a cloud of smoke, and Musgrave saw nothing more.

Mad with the riot of the battle, the old man grasped his sword, and rushed down the stairway and on to the barricades.

This time the stormers reached the palisades. Reckless as to death, and led by men whose trade was war, fatalism and the lust of plunder rendered them fearless as tigers who have tasted blood. Standing on the narrow space before the hanging logs, they thrust their bayonets between them, and tore fiercely with their fingers at the swaying timber.

Meeting thrust with thrust, the defenders hurled back each yellow face into the already corpse-strewn ditch. As before, the brunt of the attack fell on the northern point. But this time the Mongol leader, leaving the southern line almost unassaulted, con-

21

centrated every available man in an attack on the four bastions. This he was able to do under comparative cover from the nature of the ground.

Forced to defend their guns, the men in the bastions were unable to keep up a constant fire across the northern face, and taking advantage of this, the Mongols kept up a desperate assault on Major Keith's line of defence.

Suddenly above the tumult, a blare of trumpets rang out, and like magic the Mongols melted away.

Blackened with smoke, and with their clothes torn with bayonet-thrusts and stained with sweat and blood, the defenders watched the retiring enemy in grim silence. No word of following them fell from the firmset lips ; each man had realized, in the minutes just past, that Death fought in the forefront of the foe, and that now they must wait for him—if needs be, yield to him—on the ground where they stood. In the ditch at their feet, and on the trampled grass beyond, lay a ghastly company, some with arms rigidly in air, others with legs drawn and fixed, and many with trunks horribly distorted by the final muscular action at the last moment of life. There lay Major Keith, and not far away President Musgrave knelt, semi-erect, one knee against a bank of earth, his arm laid on the low breastwork in front. In the hollow of his other hand lay a rifle.

Kneeling down, Hatten put his hand over Keith's heart. 'Gone, poor chap!' he muttered. Then, rising, he laid his hand on Musgrave's shoulder. 'The Colonel wants you, sir,' he said. Then, as the President did not move, he leant forward, and looked

into his face. A dark mark in the centre of the
forehead, from which an ugly discoloured substance
oozed, made answer for the old man. 'My God!'
exclaimed Dick. Turning to some men who were
removing the wounded, their Adjutant ordered them
to place the body of the father of Fort Mallarraway
in one of the cottages, and then hurried away to the
club-house.

CHAPTER XIV.

THE STORMING OF THE FORT.

As Hatten passed the dining-hall, now converted into a hospital, he met Heather.

Through the half-opened door he could hear an occasional stifled groan.

Looking into the girl's face, he saw reflected there the manifold pains of others, and hesitated for a moment before he could bring himself to entrust her with one more burden. Quick to notice that something was amiss, she said anxiously, 'What's wrong, Dick?' Then, as he remained silent, 'Is it anything I can help you in?'

'Yes,' he replied, almost brusquely. 'Mr. Musgrave is dead, Heather, and I want you to tell his wife.'

At his words the girl's cheeks paled, and she half lifted her hand, as though to ward off some unseen possibility. Then she said, 'I will tell her, Dick. Good-bye;' and, passing into the room, she was gone.

On the parapet Hatten found Collins, Cameron, and the other officers.

The Colonel was looking in the direction of the Mongol camp.

Turning to Hatten, he asked:

'What do you make out of this last move?'

'The arrival of field-guns,' muttered the Adjutant, as he dropped his glasses.

'Then it's all over with us,' groaned Cameron.

The others made no reply, for all felt that practically this was what it amounted to.

The arrival of the guns had been most opportune for the Mongol commander. Little as he cared for waste of life, he was just beginning to realize that possibly it would be all in vain so far as taking the Fort was concerned, and he well knew that Leroy would not forgive failure under such circumstances. With the coming up of the artillery, a way was opened out of his dilemma, and now he was busy getting the guns in position to batter a breach in the northern defence line. This accomplished, he had no fear for the result, as, with the reinforcements which had accompanied the siege-train, he felt the assault must prove successful. For the defenders the outlook was utterly hopeless. With their numbers thinned, and hardly enough ammunition to last for two more days, the position was desperate even before the arrival of the artillery. Now it was simply untenable. Melenite bombs would sweep their feeble defences away like straw, and without these aids resistance was not to be thought of seriously. To reckon on relief from the coast they all recognized was hopeless. To stay where they were meant certain death, and to attempt to cut their way out held few possibilities of escape, in a country overrun by a watchful enemy, even if they succeeded in breaking through the besiegers' lines.

Still, this last alternative offered a chance of escape, feeble as it was, and so Colonel Collins decided to take it.

'Hatten,' said he, as the others by their silence signified their acquiescence, 'I leave all matters of detail in your hands. You will collect all the ammunition and arms not actually wanted, and store them in the cellars under us. Let all the horses be saddled, and when the enemy again opens fire, place the women in the centre of your squadron, and slip out between the two eastern bastions. Before you make your dash, the guns will open a passage; after that your swords must keep it clear.'

'And you, sir?'

'I will hold the position long enough to give you a start; then blow up the Fort, and do my best to follow.'

For a moment Hatten hesitated. His first impulse had been to accept a charge which he knew would include Heather. But now all his soldier's instincts urged him to stay and guard the rear.

'Let me remain with you, Colonel,' he said firmly; 'and put Lieutenant Johnson in my place : he knows the country better than I do.'

'As you wish, Hatten,' answered Collins; then, turning to Johnson : 'You will take command of the squadron. Once clear of the enemy, your Bush craft will be your best protection. Don't trouble about the rest of us. Your orders are to save the women if possible; if not, to shoot them rather than let them fall into the hands of the enemy.'

As Johnson turned away, Hatten whispered something to the Colonel.

Nodding, Collins called after the Lieutenant:

'Mr. Cameron will accompany you.'

During this discussion and arrangement of a plan, the old squatter had sat on one of the sand-bags, taking neither part nor interest in what was going on around him. Musgrave's death had stunned him. The other men, much as they regretted the loss of the President, had too much anxiety on their shoulders for the living to brood over those past human help. But to Cameron this passing away of a man old as himself was fraught with a dour significance. Old men see the reaper nearing themselves with vivid distinctness through the eyes of their dead companions, no matter how they have died.

Roused by the Colonel's mention of his name, Cameron looked up. Then, following out his late train of thought, he asked:

'What are you going to do with poor old Bob?'

'Put him over the magazine,' replied Collins grimly.

'It's the spot he'd have picked,' muttered Cameron, rising and walking to the stairway. 'Don't forget to send his body after his leal old soul.'

Left alone on the roof of the club-house, Colonel Collins again brought his glasses to bear on the enemy.

But now, though the dawn had given place to morning, the gloom had grown so intense that all distant objects were little more than blurs on the surface of the Downs. Above the northern horizon a bank of clouds, flushed with pale-red, rose swiftly in dull, leaden masses through the dense impervious haze which now enwrapped the new-born sun with sable coverings.

Near where the Colonel stood, the flag hung motionless about its staff. But skyward a swift strong current carried the storm-clouds up from their northern fastnesses. Behind the guns he could see the Mongols swarming like ants. Turning, he glanced into the ravine. All the horses were saddled.

'If the artillery only brings it down, it's all in Johnson's favour,' muttered the Colonel, as he signalled his bugler to sound the alarm. 'God send it falls in bucketfuls!'

Below everything was ready. Helped by Nugent, Hatten had packed all the explosives so that their full effect would be felt. Johnson and Ryan had seen to the horses.

Warned to prepare for flight, the women had retired to their rooms.

'We must do our best to help the men who are trying to save us,' said Heather. 'Let us take off our dresses and put on trousers and coats. If we ride like the rest, we will have a better chance in every way.'

Suitable as the suggestion was, it was not allowed to pass unchallenged. With some women habit is strong as death, prudery more deeply ingrained than love of life.

'Horrible!' gasped one Hughenden matron, celebrated for the generous display of her charms at balls and dinner-parties. 'I would sooner die than let a man see me in trousers.'

'My troubles, whether they see me in pants or stockin's,' snorted old Margaret, 'but, bedad, if we've got to roide straddle-legs, git me a pair of throusers, Miss Heather, or bad cess to it; it's rheumatics o'ill be catchin' in me legs.'

While Margaret was speaking, a knock sounded at the door. Opening it, Heather saw Hatten standing in the passage.

'Are you ready?' he asked.

'No, Dick.' Then the girl said : 'Can you lend me a pair of trousers and a coat?'

'Who for?' he asked.

'For myself,' she answered.

At another time he might have laughed, but now he merely answered, 'Yes,' and, running off to his room, got them, and handed them to her.

'I thought I would be less trouble to you with these on,' she said simply as she took them.

Then it all flashed on him.

'You've cut the knot about saddles,' he said in a tone of relief; 'are the rest going to do the same?'

'Some of them don't like to.'

'Rubbish!' exclaimed Dick, indignant to think that any woman would not follow Heather's lead. 'Tell them the orders are that every woman who is not prepared to do what you have done will be left behind. We can't risk lives for the sake of a lot of prudes.'

Then, as she turned to re-enter the room, he took her hand.

'Good-bye,' he said, in low, almost expressionless,

tones ; it is only the actor who can afford to let his heart speak in the inflection of his voice.

'But I will see you again ?' she said, looking into his face. 'You are to guard us ?'

'No,' he interposed; 'Johnson commands the squadron.'

As he spoke the bugles rang out.

Dropping his sabre, he leant towards her. Striking the floor, the scabbard filled the lofty passage with hollow echoes.

'Twice I have asked for what you cannot give, girl !' he whispered with fierce yearning. 'Now let me hold you in my arms, kiss you on your lips, and I will weary you no more.'

For an instant he stood with outstretched arms. Then she stepped forward, and, winding his strong arms about her, he kissed her full on her trembling mouth. Holding her from him, he looked once into her eyes, and then, snatching up his sword, rushed down the corridor.

Determined, now that the guns had come, to carry the Fort before his General's arrival, the Mongol leader, in less than an hour after the last attack, again opened fire.

With the firing of the first gun, Collins ordered the women and children to be placed on the horses.

'Where's Mrs. Musgrave ?' exclaimed Johnson, as he put his charges in the centre of the squadron.

'Mother was with us when we left the house,' said one of her daughters, hastening to dismount.

'Stay where you are, my child,' said Cameron ; 'I know where your mother is.'

Filled with foreboding, the two girls slipped off their horses and ran after the old man.

Pushing open the door of the room in which Collins—true to his promise—had placed the father of Fort Mallarraway, the squatter stepped in.

On a stretcher Musgrave lay, still distorted as when Hatten had found him, but now in place of a rifle his wife rested on his outstretched arm.

On the table stood a glass, some glittering particles still clinging to its side.

Lifting his hat, Cameron said reverently, ' She has obeyed his last commands.'

Then raising the girls, who had thrown themselves on their knees beside the dead, he led them out and back to where the rest of the sad company waited.

Fierce gusts of wind now swept over the level Downs, and angry peals rang out of the troubled sky, as if in answer to the dull booming of the Mongol artillery.

Unable to judge of what was behind the defences by reason of the dead level of the surrounding country, the Mongol chief was ignorant of the fact that the besieged had horses within their barricades. So to farther extend his line of attack, he still used his cavalry as infantry. Massing his stormers behind the guns, he opened fire with ball on the northern defence line.

Spreading his men as much as possible, Hatten ordered them to lie in the trench. At first it seemed as though the palisade would prove equal to the occasion. An odd post splintered or broke, but as a rule the swinging timber glanced aside and let the balls rush through. With the bastions it was different; already the flying splinters of stone told that the enemy had got the range of the north-western one.

'I can't wait any longer,' muttered Collins; 'if they disable the other gun, half Johnson's chance is gone.'

Leaning over the parapet, he gave the signal to his waiting lieutenant, and, forming his men into the shape of a wedge, Ted led them down the ravine.

As the squadron neared the barricade, a blinding flash lit up each rock-bound crevice, and, splitting asunder, the storm-cloud hurled sheets of water and fragments of ice in the faces of the Mongols.

Rushing into the depression below the barricade, the dismounted Kalmucks crowded for shelter, and, swarming round their guns, the men in the bastions fired into the huddled masses at point-blank range.

Caught between showers of hail and bullets, the besiegers broke and fled.

'Down with the gates!' yelled Johnson, and, sword in hand, he dashed out of the Fort and up the end of the ravine, followed by his squadron.

Away from their chargers and blinded with the rain, the Kalmucks who attempted to bar the way fell, trampled under the flying hoofs, and before the men who had charge of the horses were able to force them up against the storm, Johnson was through the lines and out of range of the enemy's carbines.

Side by side, Heather and Cameron had shot through the barricade; but in the wild gallop up the rock-shod ravine, with shots pinging past their ears, and lumps of ice falling about their heads, father and daughter lost sight of each other. Just as he mounted the crest of the gully, Heather's horse, struck by a chance bullet, staggered on his knees and fell.

Rushing up to the prostrate rider, a Kalmuck officer lifted his sword. Then, as he hesitated for a spot at which to strike, a rush of wind carried away Heather's hat, and, caught in the hurricane, a cloud of golden hair drifted over the sodden ground at his feet.

Almost as Collins gave the signal for Johnson to make his rush, the enemy, quick to notice the little effect produced by their fire on the palisade, began to shell it with melenite bombs.

'It's all over, Hatten!' shouted Collins above the din of the storm. 'Call off the men, and let us make a dash for it!'

Shrouded by the rain, the defenders left their posts unobserved, and mounted the horses held for them in the ravine.

As they did, the bombs began to hurtle overhead, and one, striking the palisade, tore a gap in its timber. Through the breach they could see the Mongols rushing on to the assault, hear their yells rising shrill above the wind.

Running into the club-house, Hatten lit the fuse, then, jumping on Io's back, he wheeled her down the ravine.

Rallied by their leaders, the Kalmucks had now closed in on either side, and as Dick and his comrades charged through the breastwork, the enemy poured their carbines into their packed ranks. With a gurgling cry Collins fell from his horse. On either

flank fierce eyes gleamed from masses of wind-tossed
hair.   In front the lightning played on waving lance-
heads and shortened sword-blades.   Then, up from
the 'valley of the shadow of death' rang the word
'Forward!' and standing in his stirrups, Hatten
buried himself in the midst of the Kalmuck horde.

Clear of the melée, the officer who had found
Heather dropped his sword-blade, and stooped over
her.   As his eyes fell on the girl's face, an evil smile
played about his mouth, and lifting her in his arms,
he hurried towards a clump of low scrub that rose
above some rocks.   As he neared the cover, a roar
deeper than the boom of artillery, more awe-compelling than the thunder of heaven itself, shook the
ground over which he hurried.   Startled, he dropped
his burden, and wheeled about to see the club-house
lifted from its foundations and hurled in a thousand
fragments through the air.

Roused from her stupor by the explosion, Heather
half rose ; then, as she saw the Kalmuck's wolfish eyes
looking down on her, she staggered to her feet and
fled.   With a curse the cavalryman sprang after her.

Galloping towards the fight, an officer heard the
womanlike cry, and wheeling his horse, rode towards
the strange figure who had given utterance to it.

As he rode up, the Kalmuck again caught his prize
in his arms.

'Halt!' exclaimed the horseman sternly.

Saluting, the Kalmuck answered humbly :

'A man who was attempting to escape, sire.'

'Liar!' fiercely retorted Leroy, for it was the
Mongol General.   'It is a woman!'

'I was saving her,' muttered the trembling slave.

'Liar again!' thundered his chief. 'You have deserted your post to destroy her!'

'Mercy!' pleaded the Kalmuck.

'You shall have it,' said the General grimly. 'The knout is the punishment for cowards, but I will blow your brains out.'

As he spoke, he drew his revolver and fired, and falling forward, the Kalmuck dropped at his feet.

Unable to understand a word of what was said, Heather, now that her senses were coming back, felt that her rescuer's voice was strangely full of the cadences of the past. But with the shot consciousness again left her, and she sank to the ground beside the dead man.

Kneeling, Leroy rested the golden head on his knee, and began to open her collar. As he did, the beauty of the face enchained him. Opening her eyes, Heather looked up into his, and then in a moment he knew her.

Dressed as a boy, and changed from a child to a woman, she was still the twin soul for whom he had dyed his hands in blood and forfeited all hope of Heaven's forgiveness.

'Heather!' he exclaimed, holding her face close to his.

Then the look of puzzled wonder rolled away out of her eyes, and she whispered, nestling to him with the trustfulness of a child:

'Philip, you have come back at last. Oh, my darling! I have waited for you so long—so long!'

CHAPTER XV.

THROUGH Orloff's veins the blood surged for a moment, then rushed back to his heart, while his hands trembled, not with the enervating ecstasy of desire, but because his whole body had become suddenly charged with subtle magnetic thrills.

Rising from beneath the grosser materialism which had crushed down his other and better self for years, the divine spirit of his one pure passion now came forth to greet its long-lost *alter ego.*

As he looked into the girl's eyes, he became conscious of something gone from him only to be replaced by a purer quantity newly come, and, bending his head, Philip Orloff placed his lips reverently on those of the woman who lay in his arms.

Over the pallid whiteness of Heather's face warm-tinted shadows waxed and waned. Then, in the supreme moment when the current of love's twin forces became united by actual contact, both became conscious of a coming together of vital essences. For as in chemistry the particles of two bodies, impelled

by the irresistible law of affinity, unite and blend, so
is it in the human organism.

Women fair as Heather had moved with alluring
reluctance across the stage of Philip Orloff's life. A
man in many things more noble than he had sued
with passionate devotion for Heather's love. But
wanting each other, these two could be satisfied with
nothing less.

Impelled by an attraction founded on the inner-
most chemical properties of their own beings, and
proceeding from the same sources as the organic
processes of life itself, this man and woman, formed
by nature for the reproduction of life in its highest
form, could no more unite with any foreign entity
than nitrogen can with platinum—could no more
remain apart now that circumstances had brought
them together than oxygen and potassium.

Goethe expresses in a single word this essence
of love. It is *Wahlvermandtschaft*, or elective
affinity.

But of all this Philip Orloff was ignorant. He
knew he loved Heather; her own words proved that
she reciprocated his passion. Still, the question in
his mind was, Will she be prepared, when she knows
all, to hold fast not only to Philip Orloff, but also to
his dual self, General Leroy, the leader of a host of
demons, from which he, in the guise of his original
being, has just rescued her ?

In Heather's mind a sense of restored possession
dominated all else. Accustomed to view the coming
of her hero from one standpoint only, she for the
moment utterly failed to connect her lover with his

surroundings. The words he had spoken to the Kalmuck were unintelligible to her, and the latter's death, if it told anything, pointed to the fact that Orloff came in the character not only of a saviour, but also of an avenger.

Rising, Orloff lifted her to her feet. The Fort was now a mass of ruins, showing dimly out of the drifting clouds of smoke, while in the distance an occasional rifle-shot woke dull echoes. Through the riven palisades masses of Mongols poured, intent on plunder, but where the two stood all was silent. Realizing the nearness of their peril, the girl caught Orloff's arm.

'Let us go, Philip,' said she; 'these wretches will see us, and '—glancing at the dead Kalmuck—'then even you will be powerless.'

'There is nothing to fear,' he began, and stopped. Dare he reveal himself? Not yet, he decided. 'You are right, darling,' he continued, in the tones of a man doubtful of his words. 'You are knocked up, so I will. put you on my horse, and we will get out of their sight.'

Lifting her on to the back of the charger, who had waited with trained intelligence beside his master, Orloff handed Heather the reins, and, pointing to a clump of scrub that rose about a hundred yards from where they stood, he walked on beside his horse. As they moved towards the cover neither spoke. In moments of extreme peril thought takes the place of speech. The fact that he was beside her was enough for Heather—at least for the present—while the falseness of his position made Orloff only too glad to avoid by silence the risk of an explanation which, inevitable as it was, he still feared to anticipate. As they rounded the corner of the scrub-belt, Orloff's quick eye fell on the body of a man lying under the meagre shadow. Taking hold of the bridle, he sought to turn his charger's head, but Heather had already seen ; and now, filled with apprehensions which each moment helped to develop into certainties, she slipped off her horse and ran towards the body.

Roused by her cry of recognition, the wounded man rolled over on his back.

Already his eyes were dim, and sweat-drops, which gather when Death has his grip on men of strong vitality, hung about his forehead.

'Father!' cried the girl, dropping on her knees ; 'you are not wounded, you are only tired! Philip, help me to lift him, and he can ride in place of me.'

Orloff knew she was deceiving herself ; still, he bent down and placed his arm under Cameron's head.

'I can't see you, dearie,' gasped the old man ; 'but it's your voice. Who is with you, child ?'

While he was speaking, Orloff drew a flask from his sabretache, and, raising the dying man, poured a mouthful of brandy down his throat.

'It's Philip—Philip Orloff, father,' answered Heather. 'Now will you come with us ?'

Revived by the spirit, Cameron stared at the man who knelt beside him. Glazed though his vision had become, he saw that he was in uniform of some kind. Unable to distinguish it, Cameron, like his daughter, at once concluded that reinforcements from the South had arrived.

Deceived by her father's manner, Heather began to feel some real hope.

'Philip has saved me, father,' she said caressingly. 'Let us get you away before these murderers come back.'

'I am past all that, darling,' whispered Cameron huskily. Then, with sudden energy : ' Go before the savages murder you ; before they can reach me I will be past even their vengeance !'

Heedless of his commands, the girl knelt beside him, kissing his hot, clammy hands, and murmuring passionate words of love.

On the other side, Orloff, conscience-stung, still held up the wounded man's head, and, in response to the latter's gesture, again put the flask to the old man's lips.

Then Cameron, rousing himself with a supreme effort of will, said :

'Philip Orloff, I am going to give a charge into your hands. Heather has always loved you. You have killed a man, and so—— But let that pass, I have no time for explanation. The man I would have asked to guard her is gone—dead, for all I know. You have saved my darling's life. Promise me before I die that you will be to her, in the terrible days which lie before you both, what I would have tried to be.'

Laying his hand on Heather's shoulder, Orloff was silent for a moment, then he began in a broken voice:

'Sir, I swear.'

'I am content,' gasped the old man; 'your word is enough. Kiss me, child—I am going !'

Even as her mouth rested on his own, Cameron's

eyes grew fixed, one long shiver shook his limbs, a crimson tide stained Heather's lips, and her father was dead.

With one common impulse both rose, and stood looking down on the dead man.

Then, walking to her side, Orloff took the girl in his arms. Resting her head on his shoulder with a gesture alike of sorrow for the father she had lost and trust in the love she had found, Heather sobbed with all the bitterness of one who has lost something which can never be exactly replaced, no matter how long the loser may search for its counterpart.

Filled with a strange dull wonder with all things, Orloff stared into the face of the man who had unwittingly handed the thing he loved best on earth into the keeping of his slayer's leader.

Suddenly a sound of galloping hoofs recalled both to a sense of their surroundings. Turning her head, Heather saw a troop of Kalmucks racing towards them. With a gesture of fear she clung to Orloff. Then, with that supreme self-abnegation which makes certain women divine, she moved in front of both her father and her lover.

With a yell of triumph the Kalmucks rode straight at the pair.

'We are lost, Philip!' whispered Heather.

'I may be, darling,' he answered with terrible intenseness. Then, stepping past her, he held up his hand with an imperious gesture.

Without waiting for the word, the troop pulled their horses on their haunches, and, jumping from his reeking charger, their leader came towards Orloff.

Saluting, he said : ' Pardon, Monsieur le Général.'

Struck by the effect of Philip's presence, and now able to understand the officer's words, Heather turned to her lover a face full of puzzled wonder not un-mixed with doubt.

Face to face with the inevitable, Orloff determined to meet it alone.

' You will ride round to the camp,' said he, ' and bring back a horse for this lady, also a stretcher. *Allons !*'

Saluting, the officer again mounted, and, wheeling his troop to the right, galloped away.

' What have you to do with these men, Philip ?' asked Heather, her mind now full of terrible possi-bilities.

' I am not the man you once knew, and loved !' he answered hoarsely.

' Not Philip Orloff?' she exclaimed, looking into his face, and now noting with a feeling akin to pity that it bore the impress of an act done years ago in her service. ' Then who are you, Philip ?'

For answer he looked into her eyes, took her hands, then dropped them, and said in a voice of bitter, yet proud self-contempt : 'I am General Leroy, the leader of the Mongols.'

Lifting her hands as if to ward off a blow, the woman stepped back.

' Hate me, kill me, if you would do your country a service !' exclaimed Orloff, drawing a revolver from his belt and offering it to her ; ' but, for God's sake ! don't look at me like that !'

For a moment it seemed as if she would take him

at his word, for, glancing at her dead father, she took the offered weapon.

Standing in front of her, Orloff waited. Half raising the revolver, Heather looked on its shining barrel. Her father's death, her friends' slaughter, the ruin of her country—all alike cried out for vengeance; but a passion stronger than any one of these—ay, more powerful than all other human forces combined—rose to confront her first stern impulse, and, throwing the weapon on the ground, she exclaimed, 'I dare not kill the man I love!' and fell at his feet.

CHAPTER XVI.

THE CALL TO ARMS.

On September 24 the intelligence that war had been declared, accompanied by a warning with regard to possible attacks on capital cities, reached Adelaide by the overland line.

This was the message Professor Jansen had in reality sent before cutting off all communication with Europe.

Deceived by the frequent cry of 'Wolf!' the various Australian Cabinets had grown to regard war-scares with an equanimity which even the demand for help from India had failed to seriously shake. Cabinet Ministers excused the financial side of this expedition, on the grounds that it must tighten certain silken bonds which were supposed to unite the colonies with the mother-country, and which, through defective tying or shoddiness of material, required periodic bracing up. The general public, as was its wont, shouted when the soldiers marched away, and then began to laugh at the whole affair. But neither the people nor their advisers deemed the question of hostile attack of sufficient importance to call for special investigation as to present means of resistance.

Occupied by indecent scrambles for office, and arduous efforts to shield or whitewash various members of their respective bodies who had overstepped the bounds of legal honesty, the Parliaments of Australia found little time in which to do anything more useful than flood the pages of Hansard with hopeless twaddle, in which the worker was deified as a god by men who valued him only as a beast of burden on which to ride to place and power.

Standing in the relation of an unknown quantity, the various Labour parties sold their support to either faction in return for value received in the form of concessions; and this system had naturally produced a condition of legislative immorality without precedent in the annals of history. In the excitement of this political debauch, the question of defence dropped out of sight. So long as the Governments of the day had enough men to overawe the working classes when they became openly rebellious, they were satisfied. Naturally the labour members would have displaced even this force were it in their power to do so, but, recognising that this was impossible, they contented themselves with effectually blocking the introduction of any scheme which promised to render it more effective. Moulded for obvious reasons on imperial lines, the Australian war offices were little in touch with the national pulse, and the military service of the colonies now held little in common with its natural aims and objects.

The news that war had actually been declared,

produced an immediate and spontaneous revival in
military matters.   Men who had left the various
companies and troops, either disheartened with existing conditions or weary of the dull monotony of drill,
crowded to again enrol.   Every regiment in Australia
could have been raised to double its war-footing in a
week but for the one fact that, when the officers
commanding made application for arms, it leaked out
that they could not be obtained.

Driven from office by what he considered a trick,
Sir Robert Blake now realized that his opportunity
had come.   Rising in his place in the House, he put
the following questions without notice to the Minister
for War :

'1. Is it a fact that there are no rapid-firing field-
guns in the colony, and that in consequence 16-
pounder muzzle - loading siege - guns have to be
used ?

'2. Is it not a fact that the Soudanese had better
guns in 1885 than our forces have to-day?

'3. Is it not a fact that, while the returns in the
official report show that there are 321 rounds per gun
available for the 25 - pounders, there are only 76
rounds actually in stock ?

'4. Is it true that there are only 100 rounds each
for the twenty 6-inch guns?

'5. Is it not a fact that 2,220,000 cartridges imported
from England were stored in a damp magazine, and
that in consequence of this the powder in the 1,800,000
which remain is defective ?

'6. Has not rifle practice been curtailed through
shortness of ammunition, and is it not absolutely true

that the Government has barely 400 rounds per man for 4,000 troops ?'

Naturally the Minister refused to answer Sir Robert's questions without reference to his departmental head, but the Leader of the Opposition could see that he had the Government cornered.

The following day he had an interview with the leader of the Labour Party, and that gentleman, despite the fact that he had consistently opposed any increase in the military estimates, professed himself ready to give Sir Robert a block vote if he moved a vote of censure.

Personally the question interested him little, but the existing Government had refused to support a measure which was very dear to the hearts of his followers. This the Labour Leader had set before Sir Robert as the price of his party's vote, and Blake had pledged himself to its support.

In due course the Minister for War attempted to answer Sir Robert Blake's questions, and failed.

Then the Leader of the Opposition tabled a formal motion of censure, which, coming from him, the Government could not ignore. Just before the debate opened, the Premier received a telegram from Sir Peter McLoskie announcing the landing of the Mongols at Point Parker, and asking for immediate help.

Recognising the nearness of the peril, the Hon. Henry Lewis implored the House to go to division without debate. But amid cries of ' Gag !' a dozen members sprang to their feet and demanded the right to speak to the motion.

Sir Robert Blake's speech was brief and to the
point. He showed the absolute rottenness of the
defence system, pointing out as an instance that the
submarine-mine field, which constituted the outer line
of defence for the town and port of Newcastle, was
situated only a quarter of a mile from the battery
and town itself, and showing that, as modern cruisers
carried ordnance capable of throwing projectiles seven
miles, the enemy's fleet could lie beyond the marine
field, and shell both battery and town in perfect safety.
'This obsolete form of defence must be situated as in
New York—at least seven miles from the position it is
meant to defend—to be worth anything at all !' he
thundered, ignoring the fact that his Government had
in reality sanctioned the construction of this very
work on the eve of their last defeat. Knowing he had
nothing to hope for from the Labour Party, the
Premier contented himself with pointing out this fact
to Sir Robert, and after a short, bitterly sarcastic
speech, in which he threw the whole blame of the
existing state of affairs on the Opposition, he again
begged the House to go to a division, and sat down.

Now a rush of meaningless sound filled the
Chamber. Australian members of Parliament invariably show a callous indifference for the Divine
warning, 'Beware of vain repetition'; and to-night,
with foes gathering on the sea and the ring of armed
and hostile feet echoing on their borders, they shouted
their inane and disjointed ravings in the reporters'
weary ears, as if no graver issue than the repeal of
the dog-tax hovered overhead. Three days later a
blear-eyed, dishevelled House recorded an adverse vote

against the Government, and, thanks to the abolition
of the absurd custom of Ministerial re-election, Sir
Robert Blake took his seat as the head of a fresh
Government. Goaded to a sense of its responsibility,
alike by public and press indignation, the Legislature
promised the new Premier loyal support.

With characteristic impetuosity, Blake had immediately wired McLoskie an offer of help; and now
the question arose, how was he to fulfil his promise?

The Indian contingent had taken away the pick
both of his officers and men, and those who remained
were barely sufficient for local defence. Port Stephen,
Port Hacking, Newcastle, and Botany, were all practically open for a hostile landing. Then there were
the larrikins and unemployed, to be reckoned with.
The latter had during the debate made an attack on
the Chinese quarters, and Sydney was, as a natural
consequence, already almost in a state of siege.

To further complicate matters, not only was Sir
Robert unable to satisfy McLoskie's urgent demand
for ammunition, but he could not get sufficient to
supply his own men. The one powder factory in
Australia was at present at a standstill. In supply-
ing the orders of the Victorian Government they had
used up all their tubes, and, now that communication
with England was cut off, were unable to obtain fresh
supplies of cartridge alloy. Weakened though the
fleet was by the absence of the vessels which had
accompanied the contingent as a convoy, Blake now
looked to this arm of service as his main line of
defence.

He was to receive a rude awakening. In an interview with the Admiral of the station, that officer informed the Premier that imperial orders took precedence of colonial demands. Interests affecting England's very existence were at stake, and, much as he regretted the circumstance, the colonies must rely for defence solely on themselves. He had orders which necessitated his immediate presence elsewhere.

Blocked at every turn, the Premier met the House with a firm front. Thrown on his own resources, he rose to the occasion, and stood revealed as the self-reliant man of years ago. Suppressing with a contemptuous gesture the howl of abuse which his news brought forth, he announced his intention of ordering all the Northern troops to advance at once to McLoskie's help.

Filled with bitterness at Blake's attack, McFee, the late Minister for War, now rose to a point of order.

He quite appreciated the Premier's difficulties, and his own desire was to aid him in every way. Still, his respect for constitutional methods forced him against his inclinations to challenge the Premier's right to order these men across the border. By the military Act each man was sworn in to serve in his own colony only. This being the case, he must ask the Premier to remember that they were Englishmen, and as such must resent, ay, fight to the death, any infringement of that glorious birthright of justice and liberty which had been handed down from father to son.

Full of resentment against McLoskie for his treatment of the Labour question, the Labour members, despite their leader's recent promise, took up McFee's

objection; while one gentleman, who had striven for
years to bring about the abolition of camels, sought
to show, in the course of a long and fervid speech,
that the present state of affairs could be easily traced
to the continued presence of these alien animals in
the Bourke district.

After the debate on McFee's objection had lasted
for two days, Sir Robert Blake informed the House
that he thought they had better save what breath
remained for possible future contingencies.

The Northern troops had volunteered to a man, and
so effectually disposed of all constitutional difficulties.

What had occurred in Sydney found a counterpart
in each of the other colonies. The drain of supply-
ing men to the Indian contingent had in all cases
practically completed the disorganization of their
military systems; and now, with no navy to depend
on, and barely enough ammunition for purposes of
purely local defence, the various Cabinets found
themselves utterly unable to send either men or
material to Queensland.

Following the example of Sir Robert Blake, they
now called on the people to find those means for
defence which their obsolete and Parliament-
dominated war offices were powerless to provide.

On all sides the answer was the same. Capital
and labour, face to face with a supreme peril, put
aside their natural hatred, and stood united to fight
for their children's lives and their women's honour.
Thinned by voluntary migration to Africa and South
America, and driven out by the cheap labour both
of the West and the East, the working-classes of

Australia had not improved either numerically or physically with the advancing years.

The capitalistic classes, exposed alike to climatic influences and the iron law of environment, had similarly degenerated. The large body who stood midway between the two extremes of the social zone alone retained their full vitality.

Still confronted with a danger which threatened the very existence of the race, the whole community became galvanized into warlike life, and cried out for arms with which to drive back the Mongols into the sea. Again the Cabinets had to reply that they had none. Thrown utterly on their own resources, the people armed themselves as best they could, and while Leroy was busy concentrating his splendidly-equipped and admirably-led army at Charleville, an ill-armed, undisciplined, heterogeneous, but desperately-in-earnest mob began to collect on the Queensland border.

When first the news of the invasion reached Brisbane, McLoskie's life was in imminent danger. Angry crowds seethed round the Premier's office and the Houses of Parliament, and demands for the body of the arch-traitor, as the Premier was now called, penetrated to the Chamber itself. .

Rising, Sir Peter McLoskie placed the position before the House. Scorning to attempt the defence of an impracticable position, he demanded the support of every section in the hour of national need : later they could deal with his Government as they thought best; for the present, a united front could alone avert disaster. 'Whatever you may think of me personally,' said he, 'you know I am no coward; and every man who refuses to stand by me to-day is alike a traitor to his party, his country, and the sacred cause of womanly purity!'

Recognising the truth of his words, and, while they hated him, swayed by his potent individuality, even his bitterest opponents were silenced. And so by reason of the very magnitude of the peril which many considered he was responsible for bringing upon them, the Opposition struck no blow, and the Premier, who had risen as a criminal, sat down once more a dictator.

CHAPTER XVII.

WHILE the various Australian Cabinets, awakened from their long dream of false security by the ring of mailed knuckles on their very gates, were vainly attempting to organize an effective scheme of defence, the invaders went on with their work of concentration almost unopposed.

Three weeks after the Mongol landing at Point Parker, the flotilla had returned, bringing a reinforcement of twenty thousand troops, and every week fresh swarms of Black Flags kept pouring in over the undefended ocean way. With the arrival of the fleet, Leroy learnt that Hong Kong was now in Ching Tu's hands, that the Russian army, thanks to internal revolution, had forced the Himalayas, and that the English forces, their supplies cut off by thousands of Indian fanatics, must either fight under conditions which rendered victory almost impossible, surrender, or starve. Desperately short of men, the Viceroy had summoned every available ship for the defence of India, and now, as a last resort, every sailor who could be spared was being used for land operations.

Under these circumstances, the road to Australia was of necessity left open, and an unlimited supply of men placed at the command of the Mongol commander. Relieved from all anxiety as to support by this development, Leroy now assumed the offensive on his eastern flank.

Thursday Island, Cooktown, Townsville, and Rockhampton, were successively occupied. In each case the inhabitants did all that men could do, handicapped by want of both organization and ammunition, but at best the defence was a useless waste of brave men's lives. Driving the ill-armed guerilla bands before them, the Mongols now practically held the whole of Queensland as far as latitude 25°.

Leaving ten thousand regulars, and about an equal number of primitively armed pirates and camp-followers, to hold the conquered districts, Leroy waited with forty thousand splendidly-equipped troops and a horde of picked irregulars, at Charleville, for the enemy to attack him. The country around was admirably adapted for supplies, and, while resting on his own base, he was anxious to fight the enemy as far from theirs as possible.

That the Australians meant to attack him was evidenced by the fact that his cavalry had, within the last few days, come into collision with their outposts. Determined to know exactly what he had to meet, Leroy made a reconnaissance in force. Now, he knew that the enemy, besides being numerically weaker, was, save for a nucleus of infantry, artillery, and cavalry, composed of raw levies, armed with obsolete rifles and ordinary sporting guns, while the

brush he had with their advance column told him
that the men's personal bravery, evident as it was,
would hardly compensate for the peculiar modes of
strategy of some of their officers.

The Australian army had now arrived within
striking distance, and so Leroy moved out of camp
and took up a position from which he could attack.
Holding that men lose self-reliance by lying behind
earthworks, he left his entrenchments with a feeling
of satisfaction. In common with another celebrated
general, his rule was, 'Always attack; never wait to
be attacked.'

This, in the case of Asiatic troops, may seem a
risky policy; but Leroy knew his enemy, and recognised that, even supposing the personal dash of his
troops to be inferior to that of the Australians, their
better arms and discipline more than placed them on
an equality with the opposing army.

The night before the battle, Count Zenski sat in the
General's tent. The old diplomatist had observed
much during the past three weeks which, in his eyes,
more than qualified the outward triumph of his one-
time protégé. He had seen this man, about whose
future success so many of his own plans centred,
staking every prize ambition had poured with such
lavish profusion at his feet for the sake of a woman.
And so, hopeless as he considered Orloff's madness to
be, he had ridden out from Charleville to-night to
make one last effort in that most sacred cause—his
own self-interest.

With the present state of affairs, Orloff was as little
satisfied as the Count. In the three weeks that had

gone by since his revealment to Heather, the man had undergone a process of reincarnation, in which he had become gradually clothed with some of the cast-aside robes of his old nobility. Philip Orloff was still General Leroy in name, but the instincts of the Mongol leader were daily giving place to the re-awakening aspirations of the original man.

True to the confession over the body of her father, Heather had found it impossible to banish her love for Orloff. The announcement of his real position had shattered the ideal of her youth with the brutal swiftness of a lightning flash, and, standing amid the ruins of this self-constituted image, she deemed that the substance of love was buried beneath its pieces. But in the days which followed, when, in response to her wish, Cameron was laid at rest beside the love of his youth, and she realized the dread completeness of her loneliness, her heart turned, despite all efforts of will, towards its *alter ego*, for natural mutual attraction is a law of nature, and not to be thwarted by artificial conditions, be they ever so powerful.

Too proud to attempt to palliate his present position, Orloff had left Heather utterly alone from the first. While travelling in the same train to Charleville, he had never approached her carriage, and on arrival there, while seeing that she had every luxury, and the attendance of some of her own countrywomen, he studiously avoided forcing his presence upon her. In a formal note written before their journey South, he placed the position clearly before her. Wretch, he said, as he must ever appear in her eyes, he still meant to keep his promise to the dead, but in such a way as to inflict as little pain as possible on the living. She had nothing to fear, and all her wishes would be carried into effect where possible; but he would never intrude himself upon her unless she wished it.

At first the girl thanked God for even this mercy, but a time came when she asked him to come to her. A woman's heart is ever an unknown quantity, and in her solitude many things fought for Philip Orloff. The past was still peopled with the memories of his self-devotion ; the present, clouded as it was with his awful sin, held much which she began to wish explained. His tenderness when first he found her, his despair when he had to reveal himself, the delicacy which marked his absolute avoidance of herself, all pointed to the fact that he still loved her. That she loved him, all her self-loathing was powerless to blot out of her mind, and so at last she wrote a note and asked him to come to her. From that hour Philip Orloff began to dominate General Leroy, and in the days which followed, the influence of a new force became evident in the character of the Mongol leader.

It was the knowledge of this, and of the effect it was already beginning to exert on his future plans, which had determined Zenski to speak plainly to-night.

Knowing well the nature of the man with whom he had to deal, Count Zenski made no immediate reference to the real object of his visit. Lighting a cigar, he sat on a camp-stool discussing to-morrow's chances with his companion, who filled in the pauses by glancing over a rough sketch which lay spread out on his knees. Rising at last, the Count stretched his cramped legs.

'Your sitting accommodation is execrable, Philip,' he grumbled. 'With permission, I will make use of your stretcher.'

As Orloff nodded, Zenski threw himself down on the narrow bed.

'*Pardieu!*' he growled; 'I wonder you inconvenience yourself with this instrument of penance while dry ground is available.'

'See what being a railway director may do even for an old soldier,' laughed Orloff, adding with a sneer: 'You should have stayed with my colleague, Commissioner Wang; he more affects feather-beds than hard knocks.'

'I have but just left him,' retorted Zenski. 'He is most unobtrusive, and has no desire to interfere with your plans.'

'Not when danger is ahead,' interrupted Orloff, with bitter contempt. 'Later he will doubtless be more in evidence than myself.'

'If you win, *mon brave.*'

'I must win.'

'You are confident, Philip,' replied the Count slowly. 'Remember, these men come of a race who can fight. Their case is desperate, and more than all, their honour will forbid them to yield to Chinamen; already in affairs of outposts your Mongols have found this out.'

'I admit all that you put forward,' said Orloff; 'still, I must rout them. In the Crimea the English won at least one battle without the aid of their officers, but the day when bull-headed courage and cold steel could win battles is long past. The rabble in our front, brave as they doubtless are, will never get close enough to cross bayonets with my Mongols. Badly armed, worse led, and too short of ammunition to be really dangerous under any circumstances, I will sweep them away like flies. Their very heroism will help me to annihilate them.'

'*Pardieu!* if what you say is a fact, they are in a bad case; but,' added Zenski, 'are you sure of all this?'

'That most of it is true, you should know yourself,' retorted Orloff. 'As to their leadership, a spy just returned from their camp reports that even now the various commandants are squabbling as to who shall assume the chief command.'

'Then, at what hour may I inform Commissioner Wang that you will expect him to share in the honour of victory?' asked the Count maliciously.

'He is jackal enough to discover that without your aid,' retorted Orloff.

'You are irritated with our Celestial compatriot, my friend.'

'I am more than irritated,' muttered Orloff.

'The pair of you always remind me of that charming infant legend entitled "The Monkey and the Nuts,"' murmured Zenski, watching a smoke-ring float towards the roof of the tent.

'By heaven, you're about right!' exclaimed Orloff, a dark flush showing through his sun-tanned skin. 'But this is the last nut I will pull out of the fire for the yellow hound!'

As he spoke Orloff rose, and stood in the tent-entrance. Zenski had placed the position before him in a manner which he could not gainsay. In point of fact, he had himself already realized it, and late events all combined to strengthen his long-wakened suspicions. Now he understood that others were also aware of the Chinaman's designs, and, filled with a fierce sense of shame by the thought that his contemptible position was known to outsiders as well as to himself, Orloff became imbued with a savage desire to choke out the life of the barbarian who dared thus to make a cat's-paw of him.

Watching, Zenski could see his companion's hands clench with passion. Satisfied with the effect produced, the Count went on smoking. Personally, he rather admired Wang, and in effect had long admitted to himself that, were he in the Chinaman's position, he would have acted exactly as he was doing. To make use of other people had always been the Count's motto, and so, as a brother diplomatist, he cordially endorsed Commissioner Wang's methods. As, however, these methods, admirable as they might be, regarded from the Chinaman's standpoint, were opposed to the Count's own designs, the old Russian was now prepared to render them inoperative, even if this demanded the absolute extinction of Wang. In face of what had happened since Heather Cameron's appearance at Charleville, Zenski fully recognised that, for the safety of his own future plans, either she or the Chinese Commissioner must be removed. Personally, he would sooner have got rid of Heather at once, and Wang at a later stage of the game; but, knowing Orloff, he despaired of accomplishing the first part of his designs, and so to-night his real object was to induce Orloff to sweep Wang out of his path diplomatically.

When at last Orloff turned, his face was set, and the cold look in his eyes appeared to Zenski full of promise.

Seating himself beside the stretcher, the General said quietly :

'What do you think this Chinaman means to do ?'

'Make use of you till such time as he thinks he can do without you, *mon ami*, and then remove you,' replied Zenski frankly.

'But how ?' asked Orloff, unmoved by the other's statement. 'My officers are devoted to me, even the Mongols recognise that I have a use ; jackals don't turn on their feeder.'

'You are blind, Philip !' retorted Zenski, a trifle contemptuously ; 'had you followed my advice given in Spero's cabinet the night you landed, Wang's designs could have been easily met, and when the time came, you could have hoisted him with his own petard. As it is, you have given the game into his hands—for what ?'

'Well, for what ?' asked Orloff coldly.

'For a woman !' retorted Zenski, with a gesture of disdain.

'No, for an angel.'

'Bah ! why trouble to classify her ?' growled Zenski. 'You have ruined yourself by bringing her here, and if you fall, a worse fate awaits her than the embrace of the Kalmuck from whose arms you took her to be a curse to all of us.'

' Zenski, what do you mean?' demanded Orloff, in a voice, low, but full of concentrated passion.

'What I say,' replied the Russian. 'This woman, by inducing you to save your prisoners, and to punish those barbarities which these Mongols regard as sacred privileges, has alienated their respect and devotion from you. Her beauty—for I admit she is beautiful, Philip—has caused these very officers you trust to cast longing eyes on their General's leman.'

' Liar !' thundered Orloff, stretching out his arms.

' As they call her,' Zenski went on. 'Don't be a fool, man ! can't you understand these men well enough yet to see how they must interpret the position?'

' My God, you're right, Zenski !' groaned Orloff. ' Go on.'

' Quick to see how the wind blows, Wang has made capital of all these things. His agents have sown disaffection among the men ; he himself has begun to tamper with the officers, and already not only your position, but the possession of the woman for whose sake you have risked everything, has been offered to another.'

' The hound !' growled Orloff through his teeth ; ' I could forgive everything but this last.'

' I was wrong in that,' interrupted Zenski ; ' he has not offered Miss Cameron to anyone.'

' Then what did you mean by a worse fate than the one I saved her from?' demanded Orloff, his mind full of dread apprehension.

'He intends to keep her for himself.'

When he asked the question, Orloff knew what the answer would be; yet now that it had come he sat silent. There is an anger which is too deep for words; such a one possessed the man who sat facing Count Zenski.

'Who told you all this?' Orloff asked after awhile, and his voice was strangely expressionless.

'Some of these facts I have gathered in various ways; but Redski, a man you can afford to trust, has confirmed all I have told you,' replied Zenski.

'It is too late to do anything now,' muttered Orloff. 'Should I happen to fall to-morrow, and'—he went on bitterly—'one of my own men may see that I do——'

'No,' interrupted Zenski, 'you are safe from them as yet. *Pardieu!* you are still too useful, *mon Général.*'

'That being so,' exclaimed Orloff coldly, 'after I have beaten the enemy, I will attend to his Highness Commissioner Wang.'

'He will want your individual attention,' retorted Zenski, adding, in the low, earnest tones of a friend, 'Philip, as one who has some claim on you, let me implore you, for your own, for her sake'—he omitted to add principally for his own sake—'send Heather Cameron into the enemy's lines. While she remains with you danger must also remain. With her away, you can regain your lost position in a day. And when the time comes, we can attend to Monsieur Wang.'

'No!' replied Orloff, in a tone which forbade further

argument. He had sacrificed honour, trampled his better nature in the dust, and filled his birthplace with misery and blood, to regain her; and now, even though her presence threatened his own destruction, he dared not let her go. Face to face with the awful products of his infamy, and now reaping in the treachery of his followers the dread results of a sowing such as his must be, he clung to this one woman, content to risk the possibility of her wrecking his dream of ambition so that she saved him from himself.

Recognising the folly of further discussion, Zenski rose, and, shrugging his shoulders, walked to the entrance. Calling the orderly who held his horse, he mounted, and saying, 'Good-night, Philip; I will return in the morning in time to congratulate you,' he rode slowly through the lines in the direction of Charleville.

Left alone, for he had early dismissed his staff in consequence of the Count's visit, Orloff threw himself on his stretcher. For the morrow's result he had few fears. In everything save the personal courage and dash of his men, he held overwhelming advantages, and, as he had said to Zenski, he had no intention of allowing the Australians to cross bayonets with his troops. Not that the Mongols were cowards, but simply because there was no necessity for the risk of pitting them against a foe fighting alike with the courage of inheritance, pride of nationality, and despair.

It was his course of action after the battle which troubled the Mongol General.

Each day he became less inclined to continue this gruesome leadership, which, in proportion to its success, increased in infamy. Now that he realized the fact that he was surrounded by traitors only waiting a favourable opportunity to wrest even this ignoble pre-eminence from him, Orloff's mind was divided between a desire to pour out vengeance on his false comrades, and a powerful and hourly-growing longing to cast himself free from the whole honourless mercenary crew who fought under the Dragon banner.

To-night this last impulse, fed by the thoughts of the woman he loved, struggled so strongly for the mastery that the Mongols narrowly escaped having no leader for the impending battle. But military instinct, and the natural repulsion of a soldier to deserting his post in the face of an enemy, fought for them; and so when General Leroy fell asleep, he had determined to stand to his colours, leaving the question of his future action to be decided when the victory was won.

CHAPTER XVIII.

AT THE OUTPOSTS.

ABOUT the time that Count Zenski left General Leroy's tent, Ted Johnson, now a Major, having finished the circuit of his outposts, dismounted, and, unbuckling one rein to give his horse every available inch of foraging room, sat down with his back against the wheel of a gun-carriage. Opening his cartridge-pouch, the Major brought out a pipe and stick of tobacco, and soon, with the briar between his teeth, became absorbed in that occupation, dear to an honest smoker, aptly termed ' cutting a fill.'

Since the day he carved his way out of Fort Mallarraway, Ted Johnson had seen much of life and not a little of death, with the result that the easy-going manager had now developed into one of those self-reliant, dare-devil guerilla leaders of which the Australian Bushman is the ideal prototype.

Once through the cordon which surrounded the Fort, Johnson had discovered the loss of Heather and his old master. Loyal to the core, he now refused to desert his friends, even though to attempt their recovery promised nothing but his own destruction.

In face of the surroundings, the whole decision was a matter of seconds.

' Go on, Ryan,' he said to his second in command ; ' I've forgotten something ;' and, wheeling his horse, he galloped back.

How he intended to accomplish his task, splendid Bushman though he was, Ted hardly knew. However, that question was settled for him by the appearance of Hatten's party, followed by a cloud of yelling Kalmucks. As the situation had now become impracticable even in his eyes, Ted wheeled about, and, in company with the last of Fort Mallarraway defenders, struck South. Aided by picked horses in splendid condition, the remnant of Hatten's Ringers soon out-distanced the pursuing cavalry, and after a march lit by suns of fire, and dogged alike by the Kalmuck horse and the demons of thirst, their Bush-craft saved them.

About Heather and her father there was no room for even the slightest hope, and, despite his love, even Hatten had to admit that to attempt to solve it by remaining in the North was worse than madness. But while both men now recognised that Ted's first impulse must have ended in useless suicide, Hatten, during that desperate retreat, thought only of revenge. Ted, in common with every man who opposed the Mongols, was filled with the same spirit, but with him, as with many another, there was something beyond. His mate, on the other hand, hugged this one passion to his heart, and sought to live only because life was necessary to feed it.

Not one of Ryan's party ever rejoined Hatten, and

so the few ill-armed, stern-eyed men, fighting every foot of ground with a heroism which made their backward march historic, knew all were dead, and swore that all should be avenged.

During their retreat South, the gaps made in Hatten's Ringers by Mongol bullets and the manifold dangers of such a march were not only filled, but his strength increased every day ; and on this nucleus a stout-hearted, irregular force, formidable in numbers, and splendid in physique and courage, rapidly formed. Powerless to provide them with orthodox weapons, their leader fell back on his original inspiration, and armed them—or, rather, told them to arm themselves—with shear-blade lances. At the head of these natural soldiers, Hatten and Johnson eventually reached the Roma-Brisbane railway, to find that on its southern side a force was concentrating to take the field against the Mongols. Leaving their men in camp, the two leaders pushed on to Brisbane—Hatten to make every effort to get a supply of carbines and ammunition, and Ted to help his chief, and look after his lady love and her mother.

After parting with Johnson at Cloncurry, Edith and Mrs. Enson had reached Brisbane without adventure. There, however, the news of the invasion soon reached them, and the days which followed were to Edith heavy with almost hopeless longing; for, much as she desired news from the North, she yet felt for its coming a dread before unknown in her joyous existence. The possibility of Johnson's death awoke in her the certainty that she had never prized his devotion as she should have done, and with this

24

realization, the tender desire which had glowed in her heart when saying farewell at Cloncurry became a living, ever-increasing flame. With bitter self-reproach, she now recalled the many acts by which she had made light of his love, and, stricken with self-condemnation, she most illogically held herself to blame for not having stayed behind with Heather, and shared the fate which she felt certain had befallen both her lover and her friend. This quixotic desire was, however, in no wise held by her mother. That estimable woman, being at a considerable distance from the Mongols, assured her daughter that their friends were in God's hands, and consequently quite safe ; and then, after the manner of certain Christians who cheerfully cast all the responsibility of their fellows on the Almighty, Mrs. Enson, somewhat inconsistently, began to wonder whatever would become of herself if Brisbane were bombarded. In her heart, the old lady really nursed a grievance so tremendous that there was little room in that organ for speculation as to how the coming of the Mongols would affect her friends.

The invasion of these barbarians ' had put the times out of joint,' so far as she was personally concerned, not so much by their actual coming, as by the time of it. Their precipitancy had not only interfered with her daughter's marriage ; it had, if nothing worse, put back indefinitely her affair with the Count, and at her time of life this was more than a disappointment : it was a calamity.

Of the Count himself nothing was known in Brisbane, but much was surmised ; some few still held to Mrs. Enson's view—namely, that he was, if alive, fighting gallantly for his dear adopted land. But the vast majority spoke of the leviathan railway director in connection with lynch law, and tar and feathers.

A telegram at last set Edith's fears at rest so far as her lover was concerned, and, soon after, Johnson's arrival in Brisbane put the two women in possession of the dread story of the past weeks. Clouded as it was by the realization of her fears with regard to Heather and Cameron, Johnson's arrival brought back new life to Edith, and as the careworn soldier caught her in his arms, she realized as she had never done before what manner of man this was who loved her.

The times had changed the light-hearted Bushman into the resolute, masterful leader, still as loyal and true, but now a lover after a woman's own heart—one to look up to and obey, not because he would ever ask obedience, but for the reason that his personality would ever suggest it. For long these two talked on of much that was sad and much that was tender; then, as Johnson rose to go, the woman spoke out in Edith.

'When are you going to get your new uniform, Ted ?' said she.

'They've got to find us arms before we bother them about that, old woman !' laughed Ted; and then he kissed her, and went in search of Hatten.

When, after a useless search for arms, the two men again left Brisbane, Hatten had been gazetted Colonel commanding his own irregulars, and Johnson Major in the same force.

At first an attempt was made by certain members of Parliament to give these two appointments to infantry officers, neither of whom could ride, and whose only known qualifications as military leaders were that they could command two or three hundred votes apiece. Realizing, however, the gravity of the crisis, and warned that such an attempt would cause a mutiny, McLoskie put his foot down on the job, and placed their natural chiefs at the head of the Ringers.

For the past fortnight Johnson had scarcely been out of his saddle.

With the first strain, the Australian commissariat service naturally had gone to pieces, and the question of how to feed the men concentrating on the border grew less easy of solution with the arrival of each column. Absolute disbandment, or a reversion to cannibalism, based on the theory of the survival of the fittest, were the alternatives which stared the authorities in the face when Hatten and his Ringers rode into the camp.

The northern districts of New South Wales had sent a squadron splendidly horsed and respectably armed; but these, with a few companies of Queensland Mounted Rifles, represented all the cavalry the allied forces could muster, or, rather, all they could provide with arms. Consequently, superior as these men individually were, they were totally unable to offer a serious resistance to the overwhelming masses of Mongol horse who now scoured the country, cutting off convoys, and attacking isolated parties of Australians who were on the march to join their main body.

Being nearly all 'out-back' men, the Ringers possessed revolvers and rifles of their own, and now that they were further armed with Dick's Australian lances, their value as scouts, or in any operations against cavalry, was considerable.

Brought up in the saddle, inured to danger, and schooled to quickness of eye and hand on cutting-out camps and in branding yards, and accustomed as they had become, while overlanding with cattle or looking for fresh country away on the Western plains, to do with little water and less food, the men who followed Hatten were more than a match for the Kalmucks in Bush-craft, and their equals in skill and endurance. To them the task of providing supplies and guarding convoys was entrusted, and so, both at the camp and during the march on Charleville, the guerilla horse hung like a protecting cloud on the flanks and front of the Australian army.

To-night a portion of them, under Major Johnson, formed part of the advance guard, with orders to feel and keep in touch with the enemy, and Ted had just made a round of his outposts, and was now waiting the arrival of his friend Colonel Dick Hatten.

Thoughts of the woman he loved naturally came to the soldier as he watched the smoke-rings float lazily into the hot, breathless air of the summer night. Ring followed ring in almost unbroken succession, and as he noted their upward flight, the possibility rose before him that he, too, might be as one of them

ere another sunset; and then what of Edith? But
the man was no dreamer, and, besides, he had grown
so used to Death, had met him face to face so often,
that he had ceased to regard his horrent front as men
less accustomed to such company do. He had a part
to play, and, though her voice was a sob when she
said it, his promised wife had told him she would
sooner mourn a hero than not have known one.
Still, to-night, with the enemy in front, and faint
echoes of the morrow's battle even now ringing out
from the rifles of the opposing scouts, Ted felt that he
would have given much just to hold the girl in his
arms once more, just to hear the benediction of her
love murmured into his ears—so soon to be deafened
with the riot of trampling hoofs and sharp-tongued
rifles.

So he sat until the close atmosphere grew chill,
and that nameless shudder passed through the air
which only comes when the night is dying. Then
the sound of horses' hoofs, followed by a challenge,
broke the quiet, and a man rode up beside him, and,
dismounting, threw his reins to an orderly.

Rising, Johnson said :

' Well, what have they decided on ?'

Walking out of earshot of the trooper, Dick Hatten
replied bitterly :

' To throw away our one chance.'

' How ?'

' By fighting Leroy.'

' It's risky, I admit ; but, hang it all, Dick ! we
can't run away from them.'

' We may have to,' retorted Hatten.   ' You ought

to know better than to talk such clap-trap. This absurd British cheek sickens me; here we are without discipline, short of arms and ammunition, practically leaderless, and miles from our base.'

'Where the deuce is it, any way?' grinned Ted.

Ignoring the interruption, Hatten continued:

'And we are asked to face a picked army, that we, at any rate, know can fight, splendidly armed and disciplined, led by European officers, and in absolute touch with an impregnable base.'

'Remember, if reports don't lie, these Chinkies are not quite a happy family themselves.'

'They do lie!' retorted Hatten. 'All this information is a trap, I'll swear, and we'll find it out to-morrow; but the chuckle-heads over yonder have swallowed all the humbug Leroy has kindly seen them supplied with.'

'Was the decision unanimous?' asked Johnson.

'Yes, the only one that was. I tried to point out the advantages of retiring, and working our raw levies into condition while we were getting the enemy away from his permanent supplies, but my suggestion was scouted as unworthy of our high traditions. They were only Chinamen, and so must be attacked, or our prestige would be gone for ever.'

'Then you do think it's a mistake?' said Johnson doubtfully.

'It's a crime!'

'Well, we must only do our best,' replied Ted, who in his heart felt all an Australian's scorn for a China-man, despite the lessons he had learned. 'Who is to lead us?'

' God only knows !'

' What ?' exclaimed his companion, now thoroughly alarmed.   ' Hasn't that been settled ?'

' Well, no.   You see, they weren't unanimous on that point,' sneered Hatten.

' You are joking, man.'

' It's all such a farce, you could hardly blame me if I were,' replied the Colonel wearily.

' But surely to heaven something has been decided upon ?'

' Certainly, Ted—a sort of go-as-you-please tournament.   You remember all the fuss there was as to which colony should provide the commander for the Indian contingent ?'

' Yes.'

' To-night we have had a repetition of it.   As you know, the commandants of the New South Wales and Victorian forces could not leave their colonies.   Well, their seconds in command refused to play second fiddle to Colonel Don, our man.'

' What d——d rot !   He's senior officer in his own colony.'

' Any way, the other beggars were backed up by their Ministers for War.   They're both soft-goods men, and reckon that neither of their colonies can afford to miss what they term a magnificent advertisement.'

' Hang it all! they don't look on it in the same light as a cricketing-tour or a boat-race, do they ?' gasped Johnson.

' No—as a second Soudan contingent, only localized ; and as they still cling to the idea that Leroy and his men are merely improved market-garden chows, each man is simply beside himself to command our army —save the mark! Such little matters as shortness of cartridges and want of discipline are too trivial to consider. You see, according to these sucking warriors, we're going to end it all in half an hour, and, to help us, the Chinkies, who at their best can only fight behind earthworks, have come out into the open just for us to mow them down, don't you know.'

'I can't understand that move myself,' muttered Johnson. 'Surely you'll admit we're too good for them man to man!'

'A lot too good,' admitted Hatten. 'And that's what troubles me. You may be sure Leroy knows all about us, or he would never have risked it. The beggar never means to let us get close enough to do any harm, and reckons the prestige it will give him more than worth the risk.'

'By God! some of us will reach the yellow dogs all the same,' growled Johnson. 'But go on; how did it end?'

'It all resolved itself, as usual with our politicians and soldiers, into a question of stars and titles. Each Minister felt that a possible P.C. hung to his decision, each officer that a baronetcy and C.B. would probably reward the General of the victorious army. So no one would give way, and to-morrow the troops of each colony will be led by their own commanders acting in unison with each other.'

'What! three Generals? God help Leroy!' laughed Johnson.

' God help us ! you mean,' muttered Hatten, as an orderly rode up with some despatches for his companion.

' I'll be back in half an hour, Colonel,' said Johnson, walking towards his horse. ' Will you be here ?'

' Yes,' replied Hatten, as his brother officer cantered away.

Like his friend, Dick had entered upon a new *rôle* during the last few months, but with him it had made little apparent difference. He had always been accustomed to a life of adventure and more or less personal risk, and when the time came, it found the man ready to step into his new position without effort.

A soldier's life such as he was called on to follow absolutely realized his aspirations. For while he had a natural aversion from the professional killer of men, classing him as a butcher without even that individual's excuse of necessity, he fully realized the nobility of fighting for his native land.

Beloved by the men he had gathered round him, he in return treated them as comrades, who, having tacitly acknowledged him as their leader, were prepared, while calling him friend, to obey him with unquestioning promptness.

Wrapped up as he was, not only in the fortunes of his country, but also in those of his men, the apparently inevitable disasters of the morrow filled him with a feeling akin to despair, and still he was powerless. To speak his thoughts openly would only be to fan the already waking spark of discontent into flame, and Dick was too good a soldier to do that, least of all with the enemy in front.

With him this question of to-morrow overshadowed all else. For Heather, the woman he so madly loved but a few weeks ago, he still felt a tender regret; nor did the desire to take revenge on her murderers even for a moment forsake him; but in this connection a strange thing had happened, for now the desire to kill had in great part taken the place of that love for which he had so long pleaded but never won.

Still brooding on the folly that promised ruin for them all, Hatten remained unconscious of the travail in the east, where now amid waves of blood the sun rose slowly above the radiant horizon. Then above the mutterings of the men a sharp rattle of musketry rang out, as if to salute the waking day, and, shaking off his gloom, Hatten walked to his horse, and, mounting, galloped to the front.

CHAPTER XIX.

THE BATTLE.

On the summit of a slight rise a group of cavalry officers stood looking through their glasses out over the level lands which stretched towards Charleville.

As Hatten neared the foot of this vantage-ground the roll of musketry grew more sustained. Pulling up on the crown of the hillock, the Colonel of the Ringers could see puffs of smoke bursting from some vineyards which occupied the farther distance, and nearer could detect through his glasses Major Johnson's column standing under cover of a belt of timber.

Beyond the vineyards the Mongol skirmishers could be easily made out through his field-glasses, but so far the total absence of smoke above their lines pointed to the conclusion that they were not returning the fire of the Queensland Mounted Infantry. Another thing which struck Dick as not only strange but ominous was that their advance seemed wholly unchecked by the Queenslanders' volleys. Inferior as the men's weapons were, Hatten felt certain that the enemy were now within range, and knowing that every one of the skirmishers was a crack shot, their inability to make any visible impression on the enemy was the more unaccountable.

The solution of both enigmas was simple. Realizing its probable effect on raw troops, Leroy had decided to use not only smokeless but noiseless powder in this first real battle, while the failure of the Mounted Infantry to stay the advance of the opposing skirmishers, even when within easy range of their rifles, was due to the fact that the bullet-proof uniforms of the Mongols were quite equal to resisting the penetrating power of these obsolete weapons at anything beyond point-blank range.

Firm in their determination to attack Leroy, the Australian commanders had set their forces in motion at daybreak, and now their unwieldy columns began to pour round the base of the hill from which Hatten was watching what looked like a similar movement on the part of the Mongol General.

Numerically the national army mustered between thirty and forty thousand men, but of these the great majority were totally without discipline and miserably armed, while the enemy they were now being drawn up to oppose consisted of fully forty thousand magnificently armed and trained regulars, supported by a horde of fierce guerillas.

'For hearths and homes!' That one appeal, which has never failed to arouse a people not wholly enslaved by luxury or oppression, had waked Australia at last.

When the summons came, the farmer left his wheat to the birds of heaven. The tradesman cast aside his life of sordid bargaining, and girded on that manhood which even the tricks of commerce had been powerless to take away. The clerk forgot his cigarettes, and the Bushman thanked God that he had a horse left fit to carry him to the border.

So from the far western plains and the heat-cursed inland towns the Southerners poured, disorganized, ill armed, and full of that turbulent spirit which deems that to obey is the watchword of a slave, but also ready after their own fashion to fight for, and if need be die with, their brothers of the North.

In that strange host unionist and free labourer, squatter and shearer, marched side by side, for despite the conscience-wakened distrust of capital, and the craven promptings of a few of their own self-constituted leaders, the unionists as a body came out of the ordeal scathless. They had wives and children, fathers and mothers, whom they loved every whit as well as did their masters, and Australia was as dear to them as to the men to whom it had proved a more generous mother. Though New South Wales, Victoria, and Queensland were naturally most largely represented, the other two colonies had sons among the ranks of the national army, men who had travelled thousands of miles by rail to strike a blow for their native land.

Taught from their birth to look on Chinamen as inferior beings, creatures to be tolerated chiefly because they grew vegetables, and so saved their customers the trouble, human footballs on which the youthful larrikin might with safety practise those mighty kicks, later to win him place and fame as an exponent of the national game, the Australians advanced upon the Mongols not only without fear, but with positive contempt.

Had the enemy been Russians, the question of their own want of discipline and arms would doubt- less have been treated with a proper measure of con- sideration; but now, because their opponents were only Chinamen, both officers and men wrapped them- selves in a mantle of fatuous self-confidence, as little borne out by logic as the head-covering manœuvre of the danger-threatened ostrich.

Hatten, and a few of the Queenslanders who had already come in contact with the Mongols, grasped to a greater or less extent the gravity of the situation, but their voices were drowned in the clamour of men who refused to regard the Chinamen from any other than a Little Bourke Street standpoint.

The three commanders, with their respective staffs, had taken up a position on the rise occupied by Hatten, and as it soon became palpable even to them that Leroy did not mean to wait to be attacked, they now decided to draw their forces up in line of battle.

Taking his orders from Major-General Don, the Queensland Commandant, Hatten formed his brigade under the cover of the rise. Having intelligent men to deal with, all able to ride, and nearly all quick to grasp a common-sense command, Hatten had little trouble in carrying out his chief's instructions. Nor, beyond a certain unsteadiness, which seems inseparable from militia, could much fault be found with the manner in which a couple of the Queensland regi- ments, the artillery, and the New South Wales cavalry took up their respective positions.

The disposition of the raw levies was, however, quite another matter. An attempt had been made to classify these into regiments, and in some cases, where a considerable number of the members had already served, a fair measure of utility had been arrived at.

Major-General Don now suggested that the most efficient of these should be placed in fighting line, and that the rest should be held in reserve, urging that their want of discipline would be almost certain to cause confusion during any movements made under fire. This, however, failed to fall in with the ideas of his colleagues, most of whose men would thus be debarred from sharing in the repulse of the first onslaught of the enemy.

While the dispute was at its height, Hatten drew his General's attention to the fact that the skirmishers were falling back on their supports.

The enemy had suddenly pushed forward a battery of machine-guns, and even as the Mounted Infantry poured out of the vineyards, the leaves were cut from the stems as if struck by a hurricane of hail.

' These beggars seem to know what they're about,' muttered Don, a trifle uneasily. Then, recognising that a misunderstanding now might prove even more fatal than his colleagues' proposition, he gave in, and, calling Hatten, whispered, ' For God's sake, Colonel, try and help them to get these poor devils decently dressed !'

' They're not butchered yet, sir !' retorted Hatten.

' Never mind ; they soon will be, if these devils handle all their batteries like that one,' growled Don, upon whom the truth was beginning to dawn with unpleasant distinctness.

The task of forming an undisciplined mob into any semblance of military order is herculean enough on a peaceful parade, even when entrusted to efficient officers. Now, with the men under the influence of an overwhelming excitement, and with their officers in many cases more ignorant than themselves, the attempt promised to be hopeless.

But for a happy thought of Sir Peter McLoskie's, it would doubtless have been. That astute politician, while for diplomatic reasons silent on the subject, had long recognised the utter incapacity of the average Australian volunteer officer. Fortunately, in his hour of peril he had turned to the one sheet-anchor of the existing military system, and wired to Sir Robert Blake :

' Send me every drill-instructor procurable, drunk or sober.'

Afraid to cause jealousy by interfering, and, indeed, hardly capable of doing much good with infantry if he did, Hatten remarked to the officer commanding the brigade :

' Why don't you make those lazy ' non-coms ' do this pottering work ? It's what they're paid for.'

' Bai Jove! you're right,' gasped the Colonel thankfully.

And so the ' non-coms,' as is their wont, untied one more knot in the Australian military service.

Riding down the line to join his brigade, Hatten's mind reverted to the account of that army of the ' beggars ' which occurs in Dutch history. Every

description of uniform was represented here, from the
gold and blue of the staff, to the moleskin pants,
Crimean shirt and 'soft felt' of the digger and Bushman.   And, alas for the men who handled them here!
every class of weapon found a place—save only those
adapted for modern war.   Of the thirty thousand men
who stood waiting with sublime, or, rather, childish,
confidence the onset of the foe, not more than one-
third were from a military standpoint armed at all;
the rest waited the Mongols with weapons originally
bought, and only fit, for the annihilation of crows
and ducks.   Glancing at the men themselves, the
Colonel was struck by their sturdy bearing and
admirable physique.   So it always is; the best and
bravest are the victims the God of War demands, and
to the end will get.

In the bright, restless eyes the light of battle had
already begun to burn.   Last night many a tear for
the dear ones in lonely huts and flower-scented
cottages had trickled all unchecked down sun-tanned
cheeks, and many a beardless lip had quivered with a
not ignoble emotion; but now the night, with its
tender whisperings, was dead, and the war-warm sun
lit up the pathway alike of glory and revenge.

Hatten could almost have laughed aloud to see
such self-deceit, and yet it was so pitiful that he
dropped his head and rode on in moody silence.

Falling back on the Ringers, under Major Johnson,
the Mounted Infantry quickly re-formed, and, under
cover of the fire from a battery of field artillery, they
now advanced to again occupy the vineyards. Moving
forward in loose formation, they had almost reached

their former position, when a biting fire cut into their ranks. Reeling back, they again answered their commanders' call, but again the automatic rifles of the Mongol light infantry poured forth a very tempest of bullets, and, breaking, they fell back in confusion.

From their position on the hill, the commanding officers of the national army could see their skirmishers falling back all along the line. Limbering up, the battery which was attached to the Mounted Infantry now attempted to retire, but, in crossing a water-way, one of the guns jammed, and, seizing the chance, a regiment of Kalmucks charged.

Determined to protect the gun, and bending over their quaint lances with the fierce satisfaction of men who know that now they must meet hand-to-hand, the Ringers rode at the enemy. There was a thunder of opposing hoofs, a glitter of steel, and the hoarse cadence of a yell, and then a wild thrusting home of lance-heads and hacking of sword-blades, and the men who lay under the vines were avenged. Man to man, the white race had once more triumphed, and the Kalmucks were a broken, flying mass.

Still, there was no time to delay; already fresh bodies of horse were gathering, and the machine-guns began to re-open fire almost before their own men were behind them; so, still covering the battery, Johnson gave the order to retire.

From his vantage-ground, Hatten could see the whole of the Mongol advance. The scene was so suggestive of a panorama he had somewhere witnessed, that for a moment he could not realize that the level stretches, broken here and there by clumps of timber, the fields of grain fresh-stored, the bright green vine-yards, the puffs of white smoke, the glitter of arms, and the hurried movements of horse, foot, and artillery, were not all parts of some giant battle-picture.

Leroy, in his plan of attack, had followed as closely as possible the lines laid down in the Chinese manual of war. Moving behind clouds of skirmishers, his main fighting line somewhat resembled a bow, the flanks being thrown forward to overlap those of the Australian army. On either side rode masses of cavalry, supporting the Maxims, while other batteries of quick-firing field and machine guns showed in the Mongols' centre.

Surrounded by his staff, the General directed the advance in person. The self-constituted criminal of last night was gone, and in his stead rode the leader of the Mongols.

With an armed host in front, all his fighting instincts rose, and amid the opening rattle of the enemy's musketry, Philip Orloff vanished for a time. Perfect in discipline, and armed with weapons capable of discharging two hundred rounds per minute, the Mongols now swept on with a confidence that was ominous for the ill-armed militia who lay in their front.

Already men were falling in the Australian lines, and shells, hurtling through the hot morning air, began to fill all the upper world with their shrill, implacable cries.

Someone has said that most men are by nature cowards. Be that as it may, the ordeal of fire-discipline is a terrible one even for veteran troops, and to the men now undergoing it for the first time the tension became every moment more insupportable.

A shudder went through the lines as the iron hail swept over and among the close-packed ranks. Still they answered volley with volley, save that their discharges, while making all the sound, produced little, if any, effect, for the pride of race was still strong enough in these green levies to make them stand like sheep and be slaughtered, rather than run from Chinamen.

Practically without artillery, for his few obsolete Nordenfeldts and muzzle-loading siege-guns were useless in the face of Leroy's modern weapons, and wretchedly weak in properly-equipped cavalry, Don now realized that his position was a desperate one.

The battle was hardly begun, and already he was powerless; for the enemy, totally unchecked by his fire, were now within two thousand yards, and pouring showers of death-dealing missiles into his ranks with momentarily-increasing precision.

Turning to his two colleagues, he said :

' It's madness to wait here and be slaughtered ; the men won't hold together for another quarter of an hour. We are overmatched. I suggest that we retire before the inevitable rout sets in. Hatten can cover our retreat.'

But it was too bitter a pill to swallow—at least, just yet. No, they could not consent. Retreat from Chinamen ? Never !

' Then, damn it, we must advance !' growled Don ; ' raw troops must not be kept standing still under a fire like this.'

While the General was speaking, Johnson, supported on either side by a trooper, rode up the rise.
As he passed Hatten, the wounded man gasped :

' It's warm work, old mate !'

Silently Dick grasped his chum's limp hand ; then,
as he disappeared behind the cover of the hill, the
Colonel turned to his commander, and exclaimed in
hard, set tones :

' I've a couple of thousand men, General, sitting
doing nothing ; give the order, and I'll steady these
yellow devils !'

' No, Hatten,' answered Don ; ' they are too good
to be butchered ; I have other work for you.'

Still the leaden storm swept on.

' Hand-to-hand is our only chance, if we can get
near enough,' muttered the General, as, taking
matters into his own hands, he gave the order for a
general advance.

As the command ran down the lines, cheer after
cheer rose through the smoke-clouds, and, putting
himself at the head of his centre, Don showed the
way.   But now want of discipline and want of proper
handling alike began to tell their tale.   As the
regiments moved off, their order grew more and more
broken, until at last a wild, breathless mob, without
either purpose or cohesion, rushed on to inevitable
destruction.

While they had stood shoulder to shoulder, each
man gained a certain confidence from his neighbour,
but now the spell was broken ; they were individual
atoms, their physical contact gone, and consequently
their moral touch shattered.

Bringing all his artillery to bear, Leroy plied the advancing Australians with shot and shell. Then, as they still came on, he opened on them with both rifles and machine-guns. Meanwhile, aided by their Maxims and overwhelming force of cavalry, Dromeroff and Redski had respectively turned the flanks of the national army. Surrounded by a cordon of fire, the Australian centre wavered. Brave as each man in it probably was, it was still, as a whole, nothing better than a mob ; and now that a check was given to the onward impetus of the *élan*, the inevitable reaction set in, and, despite all Don's efforts, panic began to possess the practically leaderless levies, and they wavered beneath the carnage. As the shattered infantry fell back, the Kalmuck cavalry again charged the whole front, determined to change the slaughter into a massacre.

Dick Hatten's opportunity had come. For the last hour his brigade had waited for something to do, and now the time for cavalry to charge home and sacrifice themselves had arrived.

Putting himself at the head of his squadrons, Hatten pointed to the enemy ; then, sitting down in his saddle, he rode straight at the advancing brigades.

On the left, the New South Wales cavalry had charged again and again into the vast masses of hostile horse, in vain, though heroic, attempts to cover the broken infantry. But, mowed down by the machine-batteries, they now, almost to a man, lay dead on the hoof-trampled ground. On the right, too, all was practically over, and, flanked and ill supported, the Queensland Mounted Infantry and a battery of artillery were first decimated from safe range, and then worn down by repeated and over-powering charges of cavalry.

Only an hour had passed since the outposts had begun to fall back, but already ammunition was running short, and Major-General Don and his colleagues were vainly attempting to rally an army, individually as brave as any who ever rushed on to victory, but which for want of arms, ammunition, and discipline was now little better than a panic-stricken horde, outflanked and broken alike on either wing and in the centre.

Putting himself at the head of two regiments of regular militia, Don made desperate efforts to re-form his centre under cover of Hatten's charge, and, despite a raking flanking fire, the Australians again began to rally.

Placing all the guns he could command on his flanks, the General succeeded in checking Dromeroff and Redski, but only at fearful cost; for, drawing off their cavalry, the Mongol commanders now began an artillery duel, in which their superior ordnance swept away both the Australian gunners and supports with terrible precision.

Knowing that the success of his charge could alone avert an absolute butchery, Hatten rode on with a grim resolve to break the advancing lines, even if the attempt demanded the sacrifice of himself and his brigade.

Marshalling his squadrons as they came on, their Colonel hurled them full on the Kalmuck regiments, who, with lance-heads glittering in the sun and sword-

blades whirled above their wild, hair-shrouded faces,
galloped over the dead and the dying. Gathering
impetus with every stride, the horses of the Ringers
now shook the death-garnished plain with fierce,
impatient hoofs. On right and left the dull booming
of the field-guns, the shrill cries of the Maxims, and
that dread mingling of sound which rises from all
battle-fields, filled the smoke-shrouded atmosphere
with dread thunderings.

Sitting down on Io as he had sat at Randwick when
one fence only lay between him and victory, Hatten
waved his sabre above his head, and, striking aside a
Kalmuck lance, dashed into the advancing line. Rough
and ready, but handling their horses like centaurs, the
Bushmen followed their leader.

Skyward rose a dense cloud of dust, through which
the red flashes of the revolvers shone like innumerable
fireflies, and out of this dim panoply rang shrill cries,
fierce curses, and all the twin echoes of triumph and
despair. In that wild melée horse and horseman sank
to meet the awful fate which lay in the plunging
chargers' iron-shod hoofs, and lance-heads that were
a moment before kissed by the watching sun now
bore upon their dripping blades hot baptisms of
blood.

For a little, locked in each other's ranks, the hostile
squadrons fought like very demons, but once again
the white man at his best, and hand-to-hand with the
Asiatic, triumphed over odds, and the Kalmuck horse
wavered, then broke into pieces before the men who,
fighting for hearths and homes, rode in the wake of
the gamest horseman in the North.

Correcting his formation as his men raced forward
on the heels of the disordered enemy, Hatten rushed
on the guns. For a moment the gunners stood irreso-
lute, then opened fire, though their own troopers were
between them and the enemy.

Shielded by this human buffer, the Ringers were
almost on the batteries before their fire began to take
its full effect. With a shout, the guerillas went at
them, and, bursting through the line of guns, they
rode down the infantry despite their death-dealing
rifles, only to find themselves surrounded by the
reserve cavalry. They did all that men may do ;
they proved that cavalry is yet good for something
better than skulking on the outskirts of modern
battles, and although half their number lay dead or
wounded within the narrow radius of their gallant
ride, they showed, as the Prussians showed at Mars-
la-Tour, that it is not so easy to annihilate cavalry
even with breech-loaders. Sounding the recall, Dick
Hatten led what remained of his brigade back over
the ground and through the foes just riven asunder.

Again lance-heads and sword-blades met, and men
went down, and some rode on dead in their saddles ;
but the enemy's lines were broken, and the fierce
horsemen of the North burst through them as strong
men tear weak bonds apart. Meantime, General Don,
taking advantage of the check to the enemy's centre,
had almost completed the re-formation of a part of his
command. But now, just when a prospect of retreat
opened, the ammunition for the artillery gave out.
Moving up their machine-guns, Dromeroff and Redski
began to pour a simultaneous and terrific fire on both

flanks, and, unable any longer to bear the strain, the Australian infantry broke and fled.

Realizing that all was over, Hatten, who had just burst free from the hostile lines, now extended the remnant of his brigade as a cover for the fugitives, and so, less than two hours from when they advanced, the national army fled from the field of battle, leaving their baggage and artillery in the hands of the enemy, and with nothing between them and destruction except half a brigade of worn-out Ringers, men whose strength lay in the fact that they were well led by officers who understood them, and that their natural dash had not been cramped by artificial conditions alike unsuited to their temperaments and surroundings.

CHAPTER XX.

SAUVE QUI PEUT!

FROM the hill lately occupied by the chief of the
national army, General Leroy now directed the
pursuit. With the exception of the cavalry who had
borne the brunt of Hatten's charge, and the columns
which had turned the Australian flanks, the Mongols
had suffered little loss, for their General had strictly
adhered to his original plan, and his infantry had
practically never come face to face with the enemy.

The Australians, on the other hand, had suffered
heavily. Almost from the first shot they had been
exposed to his long-range artillery and rifle fire,
and during their gallant but futile advance they had
been swept away in files before the discharges of his
machine-guns and automatic rifles. With their fight-
ing-line broken, all hope of re-formation was at an
end, for the panic-stricken centre had become inex-
tricably mixed up with the reserves, and now the
whole of the national army, with the exception of
the remnants of the Mounted Infantry and Hatten's
brigade, were merely a disorganized mob.

Aided by the splendid heroism of his cavalry and

Mounted Infantry, Don, who, now that the day was lost, was tacitly left with a free hand, might yet have turned the rout into a retreat but for the incapacity of some of his officers. Never safe when out of earshot of their drill-instructors, these men now provided a grim object-lesson of the future by making the confusion worse confounded.

'Each man for himself!' was the motto which became every moment more in evidence, as, realizing the utter inability of their leaders and the alarming nearness of the enemy's fire, the whole of the infantry melted away in search of more than doubtful safety. Rallying all the horsemen still left, Hatten continued to show a front to the Mongols, and, weakened as his brigade was, they still by repeated charges checked the hostile advance.

At last, extricating himself from the mass of fugitives, General Don rode up to the Colonel of the Ringers. Covered with battle-dust, the latter saluted his chief with mournful respect, for however much his folly in underrating the foe had cost, Hatten felt a soldier's admiration for the gallant attempt at reparation made by his commander.

'We can do nothing with these,' exclaimed Don, pointing after the flying infantry. 'Their utter dispersion is their best chance.'

'But, sir,' retorted Hatten stoutly, 'I must cover the poor devils while I have a man.'

'At their present rate of extension it will be impossible,' replied Don, adding bitterly, 'Not that I blame them. My one duty is to save my best men, not to allow them to be annihilated.'

'Then what can I do?'

'Retire, and save your men for another day. This one is lost beyond all hope of being retrieved.'

During the time Hatten had been holding the enemy in check, the flying infantry had again reached the position from which they had advanced to the attack. There the horses on which most of them had ridden during the forward march were picketed.

In the distance the Colonel could now see a blurred picture of stampeding horses, from which body after body of fugitives began to detach themselves, and as he watched them scatter over the plains, he had to admit that his chief was right, little as he relished leaving the field in the hands of the Mongols. Once more he looked towards the enemy, now massing as if determined to annihilate his feeble squadrons by sheer force of numbers. Then, as the batteries belched forth from their new position a dread salute, Dick Hatten at last gave the word, and, followed by all that were left of his brigade, galloped from the field.

With the retreat of the Ringers all semblance of offensive opposition to the Mongol advance practically ceased. Still, while realizing that the further sacrifice of life was not only suicidal but useless, Hatten, in withdrawing his brigade, was careful to show a firm front to the hordes of Kalmuck horse who now began to hang on the outskirts of the routed army.

Awed by the determined face maintained by the Ringers and the fragments of the Mounted Infantry and Southern Cavalry, the Kalmucks as a whole devoted themselves to the pursuit of the scattered bodies of men who now rode with mad haste from the field. Sabre - cut and lance - thrust had already accounted for the unfortunate wretches who had failed to secure mounts, and now the fierce nomads, fired with insatiable lust for blood, raced in the wake of the men who, lying on their horses' necks, sought to shun the keen spear-thrusts of their pursuers. Recognising the cohesion still maintained by Hatten's troopers, Redski, to whom Leroy had entrusted the direction of the pursuit, directed the full force of a personal attack on them; for, however little his men might relish the attempt, the Russian was determined not to let so dangerous a nucleus escape.

Afraid to 'burst' his already overworked horses, Hatten made no special effort to escape the Kalmucks who now thundered in his rear; keeping just enough speed up to induce the best mounted of their squadrons to outpace the others, Dick held on his course until he reached the top of a low, sloping rise. Then, suddenly halting, he wheeled about and charged down the incline straight into the foremost squadron.

Already cowed by the Ringers' desperate heroism, the savage irregulars reeled before their onslaught, awe-compelling in its stern purpose, and girded with additional force through the falling ground. Vainly Redski, both with sabre and curses, strove to hold his command together; he was swept away by his own men, who now in their wild dismay crashed into and through the squadrons they had left behind in their onward rush.

Riding down the disordered enemy, Hatten now wheeled to the right-about, and, safe from immediate pursuit, soon placed some ranges between himself and the Mongols.

Calling a halt, Dick, at General Don's request, provided him with an escort, and after arranging for an immediate attempt at remobilization, the old officer rode away towards the telegraph-line.

Appointing a rendezvous, Hatten now split up the remainder of his command, ordering each squadron to make for the place of meeting by different routes.

Sitting on his horse, he told his men what he thought of them in a few manly words, and then, waiting until they had all disappeared in the timber, he rode away in company with about twenty troopers.

For the present all attempt to check the Mongol advance was worse than foolish, and by thus dividing his men Dick made the work of pursuit more complicated, and that of obtaining supplies less difficult. Further, he hoped that each body of Ringers would be able to pick up stragglers to augment the new force to be raised for the defence of the capital. With this object, General Don had already started to get in touch with the telegraph - lines, and Hatten had arranged with his commander to push on by forced marches to Toowoomba, gathering all the men available *en route*. Here Don was to meet him, and together they were to attempt a new system—not certainly of attack, but of stubborn resistance.

Riding hard, and by tracks only known to one or two of his troopers, Hatten's party, though only actually travelling about forty miles, put at least sixty between themselves and the Kalmucks before nightfall. During the march no one said much. Few men care to talk of their failures, least of all when they are fresh upon them; fewer still can cast aside the memory of a lost illusion without painful effort. So these battle-smirched troopers rode on mostly in grim silence, slowly digesting the disagreeable fact that even Chinamen, armed with machine-guns and automatic rifles, are more than a match for Australians without either.

At a water-hole surrounded by acacias they camped for a few hours. Safe from immediate danger, saddles were pulled off, and sweat-stained backs cooled with water dipped out of the hole with their hats. Then, hobbling the horses with their stirrup-leathers, they let them go, keeping one picketed in case of accidents. Treating with Bushman-like indifference the legend that acacia-roots are poisonous, the men supped on a drink apiece, and then, lighting their pipes, stretched themselves on the grass. Under the soothing influence of the weed they began to drawl out their experiences and opinions with a strange mixture of shrewdness and simplicity, now and again relieved by quaint touches of dry, unconscious humour.

For a time Hatten took part in the discussion, for he always was careful to keep the fact in evidence that he was their comrade as well as their leader. Then, remarking that he would go and turn the horses, he strolled towards the head of the gully for a quiet 'think.'

At the result of the battle he was in no way surprised, bitterly as his pride resented the Mongol thrashing. As to the future, Dick realized that everything depended on the rallying powers of his

26

countrymen. Not only armies, but also arms and
ammunition, must now be evolved from local resources,
if the enemy were to be seriously resisted. The battle
just lost had proved that the raw material was forth-
coming. As to the question of arms and powder,
Hatten, remembering the American example, took
heart of grace, and at last, summing up the situation,
he actually found himself considerably more hopeful
than he had been before the action began. Absolute
as the rout was, it had cleared away many foolish
illusions, and exposed weaknesses which might now
be repaired; for defeat often teaches more valuable
lessons than victory.   The question as to whether
the leaders would profit by the past had certainly to
be faced, but this gave Dick little uneasiness, for he
already reckoned that the men themselves would see
that a complete system of reconstruction was carried
out in the ranks of their officers. Still, for all his
hopefulness, Dick Hatten had never felt more personal wretchedness. For the soldier there were still
vast possibilities, but for the man all seemed over.
But a few weeks ago the woman he loved had been
done to death amid surroundings the thought of
which made his hands clench with impotent rage and
despair, and now the chum of years—the single-
hearted, gallant comrade who had raced beside him
on far-off plains at the tail of piker and outlaw, and
fought at his right hand against the Kalmuck hordes
—was gone out of his life as well. For, riding back
from his last desperate effort to check the Mongol
advance, Hatten had sought in vain for Ted Johnson.
He had seen him led to where, under cover of the

hill, the medical staff had rigged up a field-hospital, but on his return the ambulance had disappeared. Among the dead and dying, over whom a flanking fire was already playing, Dick failed to recognise his mate, and at last, as a matter of duty, he had to abandon his search. Since then nothing had been heard or seen of the wounded man, and, knowing the barbarous customs of the victors, Hatten held no hope of ever seeing his friend again.

For a little he stood gazing down the gully on the resting forms of his troopers and the ungainly lurches of the hobbled horses, his heart full of a dull, implacable desire to kill. Then arose the thought of the winsome girl waiting in Brisbane for the lover who could never come to gladden her vigil more, and lifting his hand, the Colonel of the Ringers drew the back of it across his eyes half impatiently as he walked to the water-hole.

CHAPTER XXI.

WHILE Leroy, surrounded by orderlies and accompanied by Dromeroff and other staff-officers, was watching the pursuit of the Australians, a cloud of dust, rising from the direction of Charleville, caught the sharp eyes of a Kalmuck colonel.

Turning his head at the officer's exclamation, Leroy saw lance-blades glittering above the heads of the horsemen, and, with a gesture of contempt, remarked: 'Doubtless, gentlemen, his Highness Commissioner Wang.'

Presently the leading files of the escort reached the foot of the rise, and then the group of officers could see that the General was right, for the open carriage which now dashed up the slope contained Count Zenski and Commissioner Wang, the latter magnificent in his costume of a military mandarin.

Riding forward, the staff saluted; but appearing not to notice the arrival, Leroy continued to view the operations through his glasses.

The General was making a rapid mental calculation; he felt that about him glowed all the prestige of a splendid victory, and that the contrast between himself and this effeminate Chinaman could never be more strongly marked in the eyes of the men around than now. All the surroundings urged on his long-cherished desire to, by one bold stroke, reign alone. Insensibly his hand fell on the stock of his revolver, and he half wheeled his horse just in time to see Dromeroff salute his colleague with marked deference. For a moment he hesitated, and as he did Zenski shot a glance full of warning into his face. Dropping his hand to his side, Leroy decided to wait for a more convenient season, and riding forward, he received the Chinaman's congratulations with an impassive politeness which equalled that of the Commissioner himself.

Leaving his carriage, Wang, with an Asiatic official's inherent love of cruelty, walked down the slope to where the ground presented all the dread character-istics of a shambles. Here the ambulance had been stationed, and here one of the militia regiments had made a desperate stand in attempting to defend the wounded. Exposed to a raking flanking fire, the loss had been terrific before those gallant fellows melted away, and now their bodies, horribly distorted and mutilated with the Maxim explosive bullets, lay literally in heaps on the dark, clotted ground. As the Commissioner stood watching with critical interest the agonized features of a poor wretch who had been stabbed as he lay by some of the pursuing cavalry, he was joined by Dromeroff.

'*Pardieu!*' these gentlemen are worth watching,' muttered Zenski to Leroy. And resting his hand on the General's horse's mane, he moved after the Chinaman.

'Our artillery has been most effective, *mon Colonel*,' remarked Wang in French, glancing over the gruesome heap. Then noticing a leg quiver which stuck out from under another man's body, the Chinaman gave it a contemptuous kick, saying: 'One devil is still alive; run your sword through this dead *gaillard* and you will reach him.'

'Pardon, your Highness,' began Dromeroff haughtily, when a sudden upheaval made both men step back.

Rising out of the blood-soaked bodies, a figure with hair and moustache matted, and face streaked with the grime of battle, staggered towards the pair. Through his open shirt a bandage, covered with darkcaked fluid, showed in relief against the skin; but despite his wound and the long agony of his late position, his face exhibited more of anger than of weakness.

Making straight for Commissioner Wang, the apparition shouted: 'Murder me, would you, you d—— Chinaman!' as he spoke shooting his left fist straight into the astonished Celestial's face.

Before the well-directed blow Wang fell like a log; but as he did so half a dozen swords were out of their scabbards and pointed at the assailant, who stood looking with grim satisfaction at the prostrate Chinaman.

'Ted Johnson!' Zenski had gasped as he heard the Australian's voice, and in an instant Leroy recognised the name as that of Heather's friend.

'Kill him!' hissed Wang from the ground, and

with one accord the sabres flashed upwards; but they never fell, for a voice no man among them had the hardihood to disobey thundered out:

. ' Hold!'

As the swords dropped, Leroy added to one of his staff:

'Take the prisoner to Charleville; I hold you answerable for his safety.' Then, with marked politeness: 'Gentlemen, escort his Highness to his carriage; his life is too valuable to be risked among such scenes.'

No sign on the impassive face told what Wang really thought as he thanked his colleague for his consideration. But Zenski felt that now more than ever one of these two men must kill the other.

Not anxious to court recognition, at any rate for the present, Zenski had turned away after his exclamation. At first foreseeing fresh complications, he regretted having made it; but now Johnson's presence at Charleville suggested such possibilities to the Count that he blessed the impulse that had unwittingly saved Ted's life.

In the man who had stood beside Wang Johnson naturally failed to recognise the clean-shaven rival of the Randwick Winter Meeting; nor did Dromeroff dream of connecting the Commissioner's assailant with the station manager with whose *fiancée* he had flirted in the saloon of the *Barcoo*. To Johnson the whole affair was like a dream, for though he could understand their actions, the conversation of his captors, being in French, was wholly unintelligible.

Just as the surgeon had bound up his wound, the

position got too hot for the ambulance corps, and almost immediately after Johnson found himself half buried under the bodies of the men who were falling around him.   How long he had lain insensible under this ghastly cover he did not know.

When he regained consciousness he heard voices near him, and then Wang's kick woke him up thoroughly.   From under the arm of the corpse which lay above him Ted now caught sight of his assailant, and from the Chinaman's gestures and expression he guessed at the substance of his words to Dromeroff.

Determined not to wait to be stuck like a pig, Ted made a supreme effort to get free, and to his surprise found that his strength had returned—at any rate, sufficiently for his purpose.

Once up, he went straight for his man, fully expecting to be cut down, but determined to get one good left-hander in first.   Then someone called his name, and someone else saved his life ; and now Ted found himself in the centre of a troop of Kalmucks riding straight for Charleville.

CHAPTER XXII.

AN ALTERNATIVE.

LED by Dromeroff, the Mongol columns resumed their march on Brisbane the day after the battle. Had the defeat been less than a rout, the Commander-in-Chief would have been the last man to leave his army. As it was, however, he as a soldier realized that the enemy was past all possibility of immediate resistance, and so, as a matter both of duty and inclination, he returned to Charleville.

Bringing all his skill to bear on the matters of its defences, Major Hoffman had converted the Bush town into a formidable fortress, and here, at the headquarters of Leroy, Major Johnson was now being examined by the General, in the presence of Wang, Hoffman, and such staff-officers as happened to be in the town.

To Heather Leroy had pledged himself to save the Australian; still, under the circumstances, he realized that the present function was unavoidable, for while his colleague retained his position he was bound, as a matter of example and discipline, to respect it.

Determined to give no hint that might be used

against his countrymen, Johnson stolidly refused to
answer every question which in any way bore on the
national portion of defence.

At first the purity of Leroy's English filled Johnson with a suspicion that his examiner was one of
his own race; but when he observed that his questioner spoke with equal ease in other languages, Ted
remembered having heard of the Russians' skill as
linguists, and so thought no more about it. In
common with most educated Chinamen, Wang could
both understand and speak English; and now, veil-
ing his personal grudge under the plea of the general
safety, he expressed his opinion that the prisoner,
being useless as a means of gaining information,
must be shot, to prevent the possibility of his carrying any away in the event of his escape. Still
treating his colleague with all respect, Leroy retorted that, as the military head, he considered the
Australian more valuable alive than dead—at any
rate, for the present—adding that he would probably
find means to make him speak.

While gratified by the grim possibilities contained
in the General's last words, Wang still urged his
immediate execution; but, rising, Leroy remarked,
'I will be answerable alike for his safety and punishment,' and, as a sign that the examination was at
an end, ordered the guard to remove the prisoner.

While Johnson was under examination, Count
Zenski had taken the opportunity of calling on
Heather Cameron. After careful weighing, the old
diplomat had decided to try and utilize Johnson as
a means of disposing of the chief obstacle to his

present plans and future hopes; and so, with this
end in view, he now approached the woman of whom
he wished to rid himself.

The room in which the Count found himself was
more than semi-Eastern in its rich, almost barbaric,
hangings and grotesquely-carved belongings; but the
suggestion of heaviness was removed by the masses
of flowers which rose, above green under-growths of
cunningly-set shrubs, from the polished surface of a
floor littered here and there with delicately-woven mats.

Here, guarded by men of Leroy's own regiment,
and waited on by women of her own race, Heather
had lived since her arrival in Charleville. Determined to do honour to the woman he loved, Leroy
had taxed all his resources in providing a regal
temple for his idol; but, striking as all this magnificence was, Heather had accepted it without comment,
and now lived among it without ever noting that it
existed. The mind only takes heed of the surroundings when graver issues are vanishing from the
mental vision. In cases such as Heather's, the
contemplation of brain-created pictures leaves scant
room for the recognition of mere externals.

The woman who rose to receive the Count showed
little evidence in face or form of the sorrow which
now was always her companion. Constitutionally
perfect, her body still refused to reproduce the agony
of its mental part; and so, as Zenski bowed over the
cool, firm hand, he feared, because he saw no physical
evidence to the contrary, that Heather was learning
to become content.

Deeply as she resented the old Russian's treachery,

Heather received him with calm politeness; for, being really anxious to see her out of reach of Orloff, the Count had taken the trouble to throw himself in her way lately, and gradually he had brought the girl to believe that, despite his betrayal of her country, he really wished for her escape.

This she now ardently desired; for the more she realized her love for Orloff, the more abhorrent became the logical sequence of this passion. Death or escape were the two alternatives which now hourly presented themselves before her; not because she had any fear that Orloff would ever by actual deed take from her the position of a free agent, but because she had realized unwittingly the great truth, so little reckoned with by human beings, that love is paramount when backed up by the inexorable law of natural affinity.

Ignorant of the fundamental principle, she knew that this deathless desire was mightier than all the resisting powers of her being, and that sooner or later it must hurry her into a union which under other circumstances would be a consummation holy in its natural fitness, but which in the light of late events could only cover her with a mantle of self-contempt and shame so black that she must lose herself for ever in its folds.

Self-destruction was abhorrent to her strong sense of duty, and utterly opposed to the clear, simple faith which adverse storms had only beat against to strengthen; so in her extremity she turned to the prospect of escape as the one means given by her Creator for salvation from herself.

Zenski she had brought herself to look on as the

instrument; and so, now that he had come, she frankly let him see that his presence was in a certain sense welcome.

In the conversation which followed, the old diplomat soon discovered that Heather, despite his first impression, was quite as eager to go as even he could wish. Once only doubt of her sincerity crept back into his suspicious mind. Absolutely unselfish, and at all times holding it as part of her duty to sacrifice herself for others, Heather suddenly asked the Count if he thought she was justified in leaving a post where, through her influence, she was able to save, or at least alleviate the lot of many of her countrymen who fell into the hands of the Mongols. The question, though addressed to Zenski, was really one put to herself; but, taking it in its literal sense, the Russian inwardly placed it to the credit of woman's duplicity. Outwardly, however, his manner was one of respectful admiration, as he explained that General Leroy held her in such esteem that he felt sure the result of her influence would be paramount with him after her departure; while, on the other hand, did she remain, he pointed out as delicately as possible the terrible complications which might arise, only to culminate in worse than death for her, and the handing over of the Mongols to a leader whose lust for blood was now hardly held in check by their present commander.

Knowing how much truth lay behind her companion's reasoning, Heather soon accepted it, and when Zenski made his adieus, it was with the understanding that she was to do all in her power to induce

Leroy to let her go, and failing this, that Zenski was to attempt to bring about her escape with Johnson into the Australian lines.

As the Count passed the building where Johnson's examination had taken place, Leroy came out.

' Where away, *mon Général?*' queried Zenski.

' Where you will,' replied the other.

' Then come and have one cigar with me,' suggested the Count, slipping his arm into that of his companion.

As they walked towards Zenski's quarters, neither man spoke. Leroy was busy thinking out the question of his prisoner's escape, which, autocrat as he was, could only be safely effected by the exercise of considerable finesse on his part. The Count was also troubled about an escape, but more so still with regard to how best to handle the man who walked beside him. Once in his room, Zenski gave orders that he was not to be disturbed; then he settled his friend in a chair, only a trifle less comfortable than his own, and pushed a cigar-box towards him. A thorough believer in the thawing influence of tobacco, the Count sat back and said never a word, and so silence reigned between these two until the ash on Leroy's cigar was half an inch long, and Zenski had counted at least fifty perfect rings float upwards from under the grizzled cover of his own moustache. Watching his companion keenly, the old Russian judged that the weed had done its work, and that Leroy was prepared to be in some sort confidential. This being the case, he decided to save him the embarrassment of breaking the long silence, and so he asked, with a show of considerable interest :

'What have you decided to do with Monsieur Johnson ?'

'Send him back into the Australian lines,' replied Leroy.

'But how, *mon ami?* In the first place, where are their lines ? For the present, at least, they have no existence. Then what of Commissioner Wang? Will it be politic by one act both to balk his revenge and to give him such a lever ? Doubtless Major Johnson knows nothing that can harm us ; still, he is an enemy, and his surrender to his friends may be made much of by a man such as your colleague.'

'I have realized all you say,' replied Leroy impatiently, 'and personally I would hold him as a hostage—at any rate, for the present. But I have promised that he shall be removed from all danger of Wang's vengeance at once, and, at all risks, I must keep my word in this matter.'

'Bah ! what can Wang do, after all ?'

'Nothing while I am here, but you forget I go North to-morrow, and during my absence many things may happen.'

While his companion was speaking, the same thought struck Zenski ; he felt that, if he were prepared to risk it, many things might be accomplished during the week that must elapse before the General's inspection was over. But even as the vague possibility flashed through his mind, its almost certain annihilation rose before him. Determined to avoid all self-deceit, no matter how alluring, he now remarked :

'Then, shall I have the honour of watching over Miss Cameron and her friend during your absence ?'

'Miss Cameron goes with me,' Leroy answered coldly. 'Not that I doubt your friendship, Zenski,' he added, misjudging the look on the other's face; 'and in proof of it, I want you to help me in getting Johnson away; perhaps it can be best managed while I am up North.'

Taking advantage of his companion's mood, Zenski now, with diplomatic skill, again attempted to point out the madness of his present relations with Heather Cameron. He showed that Leroy's personal knowledge of her purity was not enough, and that, in point of fact, he was condemning her to an equivocal position for the sake of his own selfish passion. To the men who surrounded him, his action could bear but one interpretation; and, as Zenski further pointed out, both Leroy's past treatment of her and his present intention of taking her with him pointed to a relationship between them alike dishonouring to her and ruinous regarded as an example for the men he was trying to wean from their habits of rapine and lust. Urged on alike by self-interest and a certain quaint personal fondness for his one-time protégé, the Count played in turn on all the strings of human passion in his attempts to win Orloff back to the shrine of ambition. At last, because of his love for the woman, Philip wavered. Trained to note and seize every chance in a battle such as this, Zenski suddenly placed an alternative before him. Leaning forward, he looked into his companion's eyes, and said:

'If you love this woman, you must either make her your wife or give her her liberty.'

In suggesting that Philip should marry Heather, Zenski knew he was safe. Though, even if he did do so, it would have suited the Russian better than the existing state of things. In Orloff's eyes, however, the suggestion gained a peculiar significance from the fact of its contradiction to Zenski's long-expressed opinion that Heather's absence was the only sure guarantee for future safety and success. Now that the Count was willing that she should remain under conditions which even he had to admit were not only reasonable, but absolutely essential to the preservation of her good name, Leroy discussed the question calmly, and at last yielded so far as to promise to place the position before Heather during his journey North.

'You have decided well, Philip,' said Zenski, 'and if you hold to your determination, you may yet make me a convert to this most unreasonable deity called Love.'

'For the sake of it I can do much. God knows I have already done more than He may forgive,' retorted Leroy; 'but in this matter of letting her go I can only put my will against all the desire of my being.'

'Be guided by her in this matter,' retorted Zenski.

Then, warned by the sudden despair which began to show itself in Orloff's eyes, he dropped the subject, more than content with having moved the man sufficiently to bring it there.

If Heather was to be taken North, Zenski at once decided that it would be best for Johnson to go also. It seemed to him that Ted would be a constant spur to the girl's inclination; and, further, that if by some happy chance Orloff did bring himself to let her go,

27

the presence of Johnson would all the more readily suggest some practical means of setting her free.

Even if Orloff, as was most probable, refused to sanction her escape, Zenski felt that with Johnson at hand he might himself devise a means, away from the strict espionage of Charleville, for getting both of them off without even Leroy's knowledge.

With this part of his scheme the Count had little trouble, for Leroy admitted, almost without comment, all he put forward in its favour. The fact that Johnson would be safer with the General than if left in Charleville was undoubted, and, as Zenski said, the facilities both for getting him away quietly and letting it appear that he had suffered due punishment for his crime would be all greatly increased by removing him up North.

With the decision as to Johnson's destination settled, conversation began to flag, and now Leroy wished of all things to be alone, so, tossing his cigar-butt into the fireplace, he rose. Satisfied with his night's work, Zenski made no effort to detain his visitor, for he, too, desired for the next hour or so no better companionship than his own.

Nodding his head, Leroy passed out into the hall, and as the door closed on him, Zenski lit a fresh cigar, and, watching the white ash lengthen, he lazily wondered for what strange reasons men make mistresses of creatures created for, and possessing all the attributes of, slaves.

'Faithful slaves once in a way, perhaps,' murmured the Count, as a compliment to Heather; 'but, *mon Dieu!* slaves for all that.'

CHAPTER XXIII.

ON BOARD THE 'HI LUNG.'

LEAVING Charleville the day after his conversation with Count Zenski, the Mongol leader travelled direct to Point Parker, which for the time became his head-quarters. Here, in the Mitylene Palace, both Heather and Johnson were now located.

The firm of Spero, Aloysius and Co. still ruled the commercial world of Point Parker, now, however, by reason of the risks attending both the export and import trade, shrunk to less than half its former importance. For all that, the Levantine firm still did an immense business as army contractors for all sorts of warlike supplies, and though both Spero and Bourouskie had sunk for ever below the political horizon, they still in their natural sphere as commercial hucksters reaped a rich harvest.

Naturally anxious to retain the favour of the Commander-in-Chief, Spero had at once placed his house at his disposal. For Heather's sake the offer was accepted, and, placing Zenski in charge, the General had for the past few days been inspecting the various columns left to hold the conquered North.

Leroy's desire to throw up the command of the Mongols, which had approached perilously close to a resolve before the battle of Charleville, had since his victory grown less keen, as, after his conversation with Zenski, he had begun to realize more clearly than ever the impracticability of his present position with Heather. The day of his arrival at Point Parker he had fulfilled his promise to the Count, and from the lips of the woman he loved had heard his sentence, and, bitterest stab of all, she had admitted her love, while sadly insisting on its impossibility as regarded any union with him.

Without this woman, for whom he had sinned so much, the thought of inaction became intolerable; and so when at last he promised to let her go, he stepped from the presence of Love again into the arms of Ambition. Not because he loved this wanton mistress, Ambition—he hated her; but because all things were as nothing now, and the harsh music of her voice rang out in unison with his proud despair.

From Heather, Zenski had heard of Leroy's decision, and in the General's present actions he recognised a return to his old allegiance; still, as a wise man, he said nothing.

Determined, so soon as he had fulfilled his promise to Heather, to carry on aggressive operations on a larger scale than ever, Leroy now began the work of concentrating every man who could be spared from the North at Charleville. Daily fresh reinforcements were expected from China, and with part of them the Mongol commander now intended to seriously attack

Brisbane from the sea, thus placing the capital between two fires. The absence of English men-of-war held out every prospect of success, not only for such an expedition, but for similar attacks later on all the Australian capitals; and recognising that nothing was to be gained, and perhaps much lost by delay, Leroy determined to lose no more time in carrying his plans to their logical conclusion.

Aware that in leaving his present base he must be prepared to subject his commissariat train to an acute strain, the Commander-in-Chief further busied himself in arranging for the forwarding to Charleville of a constant supply of warlike stores and provisions. Beyond the Warrego he was prepared to march through a country stripped of all vestige of vegetable and animal life; but holding, as he did, the immense food-supplies of the North at his disposal, this prospect troubled him not at all. A week after his arrival in Point Parker everything was in train for the combined attack, and now the time had arrived when he must carry out his promise and part with Heather, or break his word and carry her back a prisoner to Charleville. Since that interview in which Heather had wrung from him her liberty, Leroy had not again approached her. Strong as he knew himself to be, he yet dared not risk the all-powerful desire which he knew must arise in her presence, and so on his return he made all the arrangements for her departure without ever even mentioning her name.

His plan for her escape was simple enough, for the reason that no man about him dared question his commands.

Personally he would have wished to send her to
some country safe from his Mongol hordes, but
Heather thought otherwise, and, in obedience to her
entreaties, she was to be landed near Sydney. Ted
Johnson was really responsible for her determination
in favour of the Southern capital, as he had told her
during the journey North that Edith and Mrs. Enson
were to go South in the event of Brisbane being
threatened. The *Hi Lung*, an obsolete turret cruiser,
now propelled by electricity, happened to be lying at
Point Parker on Leroy's arrival, and as her captain
was a man devoted to him, he decided to entrust the
two fugitives to his care.

Now that he had decided to devote himself to
ambition, the question of how his colleague would
regard the escape of Johnson (if he ever heard about
it) did not trouble Leroy one whit. Man to man, he
recognised that he was more than a match for the
Chinaman, and with Zenski at his back, and un-
trammelled by the presence of Heather, he felt that
the future, if lost for Philip Orloff, was still pregnant
with possibilities for General Leroy. But now, when
everything was ready for Heather's departure, the
strong man's heart rebelled, and, in opposition to all
his instincts as a soldier, he made a compromise with
the rebel instead of crushing it. He suddenly determined to visit the defences on Thursday Island before
going South, and at the last moment announced to
Zenski his intention of going so far in the *Hi Lung*.
Recognising the possible failure of all his plans in
this determination, the Count still felt powerless to
oppose it in any way, for Leroy was not a man to be

turned from his purpose by any argument such as he could bring to bear. So, inwardly cursing the folly of his leader, the old Russian had to silently accept the assurance that he would return by Jansen's yacht.

In the state-room of the *Hi Lung* Heather parted from the old diplomat with a feeling so near akin to regret that she was conscious of a vague feeling of self-condemnation. His whole life, so far as she had known it, had been a lie unsoftened by one cloud of remorse, and still, now that she was parting from him for ever, sorrow rather than righteous contempt and loathing filled her eyes with tears. There was a bond between these two—strong and pure where it issued from the noble, unselfish woman's heart, weak and corroded by self-interest where it clung to the sin-cased organ of the old man. They both after their own fashion regarded Philip Orloff more than any other human being. Bending over Heather's hand, Count Zenski listened to her words of farewell, and then, lifting the long white fingers to his lips, he kissed them with a gesture in which reluctance at having to part was mingled with a certain suspicion of self-shame. As he walked to the landing-stage, Johnson met him, but the effect of the scene below had already gone, and, nodding, he said with a sneer :

' *Bon voyage, mon ami!* Present my compliments to Madame Enson, and express my regrets that her trousseau should grow old-fashioned.'

'I'll see you to the devil first, you infernal cad !' retorted Johnson wrathfully.

'Till then adieu, *mon brave!*' replied Zenski, looking back from the steps with a cynical grin.

Now, so far as his movements were concerned, a perfectly free agent, Ted stayed on deck watching Point Parker sink swiftly into the embrace of the waves. Soon it was gone, and as he stood looking towards the place where it had been, the night began to steal softly out of the East.

To the practical Bushman the events of the last few days had in them more of the unreality of dreams than aught of solid fact, and even now Ted had to rouse himself every now and then to realize that he was thoroughly awake. Personally, he had every reason to congratulate himself, and to thank Heaven that Heather, instead of finding a horrible death, had chanced on so considerate a captor as the Mongol leader. How this had all come about, and who this man really was, were alike mysteries to Johnson. At Orloff's request, Heather had not disclosed his real personality, and so Ted had to be content with the information that he was a man she had first met when travelling on the Continent.

For all that, Johnson had vague suspicions as to Leroy's identity, and the more he thought them out the less he was satisfied. Still less was he at rest as to his chum's chances with Heather should they ever meet again. In the few talks they had had, Hatten's name never failed for a place on the girl's lips; but while she never grew weary of speaking of his courage and loyal friendship, even Ted could see that love was as far from her thoughts as ever.

Now with the deepening shadows came other fancies so warm and full of tender imaginings that all else stepped back into the night; and, looking out on the silver streak that coiled and glittered amid the gloom astern, Ted realized that he was homeward bound, and so fell a-thinking of dark eyes set in skin of snow, and coils of blue-black hair where blood-red roses seemed to nestle lovingly.

Beneath his feet who dreamt of Love's sweet comedy, the tragedy of passion occupied the stage.

In the state-room Heather Cameron sat, clothed in a robe of scarlet, and crowned with a coronal of golden coils. From the dead whiteness of her face her eyes looked down with infinite pity on the man who knelt at her feet. The dress she wore was one that he had given; the jewels which lay beside her were the gems he had showered upon her, but which she had never worn. Just now she had asked him to take them back, and at this most natural request his strength had forsaken him, and now on his knees before her he exclaimed, with all the bitterness of a last despair:

'I will not let you go!'

Softly, as one that soothes a child, she bade the man remember his promise; and then, as he made no sign, but still knelt there, looking with hungry longings into her eyes, she spoke in a whisper, as one who recalls a holy memory, of the days when first he sought to read Love's book to her. But still he made no answer.

And now a silence fell on both; for, with the memory of the past around her, how could she taunt this man with all the sin and shame with which he had built a wall, over the bloody sides of which even Love dare not climb?

Rising, Orloff moved towards the door; then, turning, he walked up and down the narrow cabin, and, watching him, Heather's heart went out towards him with a great—ay, a nigh irresistible—longing. That he would let her go she still did not doubt. The thought that filled her with dismay was the letting him go back to the renegade's work—the traitor's hopeless goal.

'Philip,' she said—and he started eagerly at the name—'you say you love me, and I know you do. For the sake of your love, will you do something for me?'

'I will do anything but let you go.'

'I must go,' she answered simply. 'But will you go, too?'

'With you?' he asked strangely.

'That is impossible,' she answered sadly. 'But will you, for my sake, leave this life of murder and dishonour?'

'No!' he interrupted sullenly. Then, again standing before her, he implored her not to leave him to himself. 'See what your influence has done already,' he urged. 'If you will stay with me, I pledge myself that nothing you ask will be refused; that for your sweet sake I will change the face of Asiatic war.' And so, by every promise which one so powerful as he might make, he entreated this woman who loved him to remain.

Then, in his despair, he grew unworthy of even his fallen being.

'But be my wife, and you will be a queen! Life and death shall be yours to give or take!' he exclaimed. 'For you I will conquer both Australian and Mongol, and together we will found a new race of kings. Only be mine, and I will march beside the heroes of old, owning obedience to none but you!'

Silently she let him talk on; but, as he drew picture upon picture of future glory, all having her image in the foreground, the knowledge of how he had wrapped his very heart about her filled her with a vague gladness and a very present fear.

At last he ended, and then her fears took shape; for, sitting beside her, he told her calmly, and with the set face of one who hates himself, but yet has no power to change his resolution, that, even though he broke his word, now that he was face to face with the prospect of her loss, he dared not let her leave him.

There are times when we know a man speaks truth, even though it may be when he is telling us of his resolve to break a former promise. So Heather now realized that Orloff had in his last words uttered a determination not to be shaken.

Back to the Mongol camp she was resolved not to go under any possible conditions, and still his deathless desire for her had something in it which awoke a responsive chord. She knew that, in spite of all, she not only did not hate, but that she loved this renegade; and now, rising above all her natural horror of his present life, came the thought that love such as this might help her to redeem him. Under any circumstances, she recognised that she must not go back with him to a life where such a work must be well-nigh hopeless. On the other hand, did he forsake it for her, she would be doing her country incalculable service; and if he was ready for such a sacrifice, surely it would not be in vain.

'Philip,' she said again, but not with all the entreaty of the past, 'will you let me go?'

'No!' he answered. 'Call me liar, coward, what you will, I will not!'

'Then,' she exclaimed, 'will you leave ambition and power behind, and come with me?'

At first he looked at her as one who has not heard aright; but when she repeated it, he laid his hand on her shoulder, and answered in the deep, tremorless voice of a man who has won back his manhood:

'Heather, I will go with you to the end of the earth!'

Then she laid her hand in his as a token that she was content; and so, putting all the past aside, she took up without more ado the task of working out this man's salvation.

CHAPTER XXIV.

IN THE DEPTHS OF THE SEA.

NIGHT now shrouded the waters of the Gulf, and the clouds spread out their heavy mantles between the stars and the sea. Sobbing in endless discontent, the waves broke across the prow of the *Hi Lung* as she raced on through the darkness, but their sullen beats against her iron sides woke no answering echoes in the heart of the man who now strode up and down the deck.

Philip Orloff was filled with the ecstasy of a victory such as never was won by the sword on sea or land. The woman he loved was to be his for evermore— well, if not for evermore, until that time when one or other of them had to solve death's mysteries. But to- night he had little thought save for life—life with her. Then came the thought: Where in all the world could he hope to find a resting-place? Not certainly among the haunts of civilization, for now the East would execrate his name even as the West had done.

But what need he care for all their impotent hate? Heather was now his; and surely in the vast Pacific

he could yet find some spot where he could rest forgotten, and forgetting all else but her.

Then he began to wonder what Zenski would think,
and, for the sake of the friendship he held for the old
Russian, he determined to send him a warning of his
intention from Thursday Island. For the others what
did it matter? Half of them were already traitors,
the remainder soldiers of fortune. Looking ahead,
he saw the Mongol army divided and its strength
shattered by internal discontent, and the vision filled
him with grim satisfaction, for, excepting a few men
like Redski, he cared nothing for what became of the
rest. Accustomed to regard himself as the head and
front of the invasion, Orloff failed to realize that
another might arise to take his place, one perhaps
who, now the master-mind had left a scheme, might
work out the details as successfully as he himself
could have done.

Dismissing the past, he began to work out his
future plans. Johnson had to be disposed of, and
now that he began to meet it face to face, the question
of his own disappearance grew less easy of solution.

Leaning against one of the turrets, Orloff fell into
so deep a train of thought that he failed to hear
Johnson approach him; but as the Australian laid his
hand on his shoulder, a sharp call from the bridge
made him look up. From the darkness innumerable
eyes seemed to glower upon him. Then in a moment
he realized what it meant. ' The Chinese fleet !' he
exclaimed; and the voice of the captain answered
back from the bridge, as he signalled to the engine-
room to go astern :

'The lubbers will be into us! Close the water-tight compartments!'

On the starboard bow a dark mass showed not a ship's length away, and now from her deck hurried words of command floated across the narrow space. But Orloff waited no longer; the thought of Heather's peril rose before him, and, rushing to the companion-way, he dashed into her state-room just as the iron doors of the bulk-heads shut with a dull crash.

Left to himself, Johnson ran towards the bows of the *Hi Lung* in obedience to one of those sudden impulses which so often change the course of human lives. As he reached them, the cutwater of the advancing ship crashed into the plates of the Chinese cruiser, and for a little the two vessels lay the one embedded in the other.

Above the cracking of spars and grinding of steel on steel, Ted thought he heard English voices; still, this might mean nothing, for in a service such as the Chinese their presence was likely enough. Like a flash the thought went through his brain, 'Shall I chance it, or go down where I am?' Already he could feel the *Hi Lung* heeling over, and see the bows of the ship that had rammed her drawing clear. A second more, and the alternative would be gone for ever; so, scrambling up on the shattered bulwarks, he leaped for life or death on to the bows of the unknown ship just as a blaze of light lit up the sea in which the *Hi Lung* was slowly turning bottom upwards. Un-noticed by the sailors, who were now using every effort to keep their own ship afloat, Johnson rose to his feet just in time to see the last of the Chinese man-of-war.

Top-heavy, like all her class, and, in view of taking
in supplies at Thursday Island, almost without ballast,
the *Hi Lung*, once she listed, had no chance of righting. Still, as became a daughter of the sea, she went
with stately dignity to where the good ships lie on
beds of sand, and shelves of rock, and depths unknown
save to the dead. On every side strange vessels
floated on seas of flame, while from the one which all
unwittingly had done this deed a flood of light fell on
the dying ship.

Johnson could see her captain standing on the
bridge, and round him a group of officers; but keenly
as he looked, he could see no sign of either Heather
or Leroy.

Why the men before him made no effort to save
themselves struck him as strange, but no reason
came—at least, not then; for now the *Hi Lung* gave
a weary lurch, and as the crew, mad with fear and
despair, began to leap from her sides and stern, she
suddenly rolled over and shot prow first into the
depths below, her propellers reflecting back the rays
of the search-lights as they drove her downwards to
her grave.

When, realizing that a collision must take place,
Orloff rushed into Heather's state-room, it was with
the idea of bringing her on deck; the closing of the
bulkheads, however, not only prevented his doing
this, but practically made prisoners of them both.
Taking the girl in his arms, he rushed to one of the
doors, but even as he struck with impotent rage at its
iron panels the collision took place, and sent both
himself and his burden against the side of the cabin.

Pulling himself together, he staggered to the divan and laid his senseless companion tenderly upon it; as he did so, he began to realize that the ship was not only not righting, but that the list became more acute each second. Yes, there was no doubt of it; now he had to hold Heather to prevent her from slipping off the divan. The *Hi Lung* was going over, and they were trapped like rats, and, like them, must drown. God! if Heather would only awake, only speak to him once! In another minute it would be too late! Down in that fearsome prison he felt the dying ship's last gasp, and, catching the girl in his arms, he kissed her white, beautiful face, holding her as though in defiance of death itself. Then a shiver ran through the cabin as the propellers rose out of the water, and then he and she lay together on what but a moment ago had been the ceiling. No lamp now burned to show him his position, but as the minutes passed, and death did not come, awful possibilities began to fill his brain.

A gruesome theory put forward after the sinking of the *Victoria* flashed into his mind. Here, as there, the bulkheads had been closed; the vessel had gone down bottom upwards, but, unlike the English ship, there were no boilers in this one to burst, and so provide a merciful escape for any wretches imprisoned in the air-tight compartments. Alone with his own fearful imaginings, for Heather still lay wrapt in merciful unconsciousness, Orloff crushed back the demons of despair, and, as he sank to his grave, began to calculate how long he and his companion had to live. At best his reckoning was a rough one, but so far as he could judge, seven hours at least, perhaps as much

more, still remained for them. For an instant a
desire to kill himself, and so leave more air for
Heather, came to him, but he put it away. Such
sacrifice could only add horror to the final scene;
better that she should die in his arms than live a few
short hours to die at last alone.

Now the moment that he dreaded, yet of all things
desired, came, and Heather recovered consciousness.

Holding her closely to him, he told her the dread
story of their imprisonment in the depths of the sea;
and when she understood she found his lips, and
kissed him, and told him she was well content, as
death must come, to meet it here with him.

So in this strange sepulchre these two, who had
spent all their lives apart, sat waiting death together,
and the woman, partly because she had lived her life
'in the shadow of the grave,' but chiefly for the reason
that she of all things wished to take this man with
her when the hour came, refused to waste with him
the minutes in sorrowing for the shortness of their
reunion, seeking rather to induce him to prepare to
go with her on that last long journey whose starting-
post was so close ahead.

*   *   *   *   *

Philip Orloff and Heather were dying. The air of
the state-room where they lay entombed had of necessity gradually heightened in temperature, and was
now saturated with aqueous vapour. For some time
Orloff had been possessed of a species of delirium, and
the narrow cabin rang now with hoarse words of command, now with bitter exclamations of shame and
despair.

Before him the scene at Charleville, where he stood beside the bed of the murdered sisters, rose continually ; nor could he blot from his eyes the look of the old man he had saved from the knout on the earthworks. Visions limned in blood and framed with pain floated around him, and even Heather's voice had now no power to save him from himself.

But now, as the oxygen disappeared and the noxious effects of the carbonic acid became more potent, the dying man's fancies took other shapes. All was forgotten, save that past when Love and he first met : Heather was again to him the child full of tender possibilities, and he the lover who was to make them blossom into glorious realities.

Lying in his arms, the girl caught his words from the very borders of the Silent Land. Past power of speech, and so close to death's deep sleep that all things earthly had grown indistinct, she, too, had bridged the intervening years, and now spent the short moments that remained of life in treading once again the gladsome meads of early youth.

So side by side they died down in the depths of the sea. The plants of that cold land where sun is not will clamber over their sepulchre, and strange monsters swim in stupid wonderment round their tomb; but, oblivious alike to the wash of the waves that beat against their prison-house and the restless winds that waft the good ships overhead, these two will lie at rest till the sea gives up her dead.

THE END.

BILLING AND SONS, PRINTERS, GUILDFORD.

G., C. & Co.

STIRRUP JINGLES

FROM THE BUSH AND THE TURF.

BY

KENNETH MACKAY.

EXTRACTS FROM REVIEWS.

'. . . . A volume of verse from the pen of the well-known cross-country rider, Captain Mackay. The work is aptly dedicated to the memory of the late poet-horseman, A. L. Gordon, whose footsteps the author evidently follows. The opening number gives a spirited description of Tattersall's Grand National Steeplechase, and the writer has to be complimented on the racy and graphic style in which the story is told. The bush sketches which follow give ample evidence that the author has not wooed the muse in vain, and he may be regarded as the poet-horseman of the colonies.'—*Sydney Morning Herald* (Sporting Columns).

'It is not too much to say, after reading Mr. Mackay's rhymes of bush and turf, that we have one who gives promise of being called a "poet rider." Mr. Mackay is well known upon the turf as a good unprofessional rider, and when he chooses riding as his theme he has a right to a fair hearing. But it is not upon this claim alone that Mr. Mackay is entitled to an audience. He has the real poetic touch as well. His verses are just what they profess to be—bits of music and incident born of the life which they seek to portray. . . . The bush rhymes in the book are as good, if not better than the racing bits. . . . They are well-builded, and have a warm and quick fancy which is Mr. Mackay's chief characteristic.'—*Sydney Morning Herald.*

'Mr. Mackay . . . is known upon the turf as an amateur horseman of great ability ; and as such his verses should command, as they deserve to, notice from every sporting man. . . . Even the most casual observer will note that their author claims the possession of a poetic touch only too rarely found in beginners. . . . Anyone taking an interest in the turf, and more especially those who love the rattle of the rails, will find something highly interesting on almost every page of Mr. Mackay's maiden attempt at singing what he himself loves so well ; and should he meet with sufficient encouragement to justify him continuing in his new line, "Stirrup Jingles" will always deserve a place in every racing man's library, and its author grow into a worthy substitute of "poor Gordon." '—*Sydney Daily Telegraph* (Sporting Columns).

'Mr. Mackay's verses betray the feeling of a poet and no mean power of expression. He is able to paint in words what he feels. . . . It is Australian life that is depicted. The framework of the picture is local. It can be mistaken for nothing but Australian. Mr. Mackay writes of what he knows ; he has opened his eyes and recorded what he saw, finding that around him were materials for poetic treatment. . . . His bush sketches are manly and full of go and of the hardy natural life of the cattle, camp, and stock-yard. . . . Mr. Mackay shows to advantage also as a painter of natural beauty : only a poet could have written "Meanderings in an Austral Arcade." We have had much pleasure in perusing the work, and hope that this collection is not the last we shall get from Mr. Mackay's pen.'—*Maitland Mercury.*

'There is undoubtedly a very true ring of poetry pervading the whole—the poetry of thought if not of rhyme. We do not therefore hesitate to predict for the writer that he will yet attain a place, and a good one too, amongst our lyric and descriptive Southern poets. . . . The lines upon "Hypatia" are very beautiful, and with an easy fall that would imply the true poetic gift of thought and metre fully harmonized. We have forborne to quote from Mr. Mackay's little book, but we do not hesitate to recommend it to our readers, and heartily wish for the author the success he deserves.'—*Sydney Quarterly Magazine.*

'Mr. Kenneth Mackay . . . has just issued a little book entitled "Stirrup Jingles," which, as its name would indicate, deals with such themes as Gordon loved to sing. The book is, in fact, dedicated to Gordon's memory in some good verses . . . and off the author canters in a lengthy and racy description of a Randwick meet somewhat in the "Dagonet" vein, and follows this piece with a number of fiery, dashing, strong-pulsed "Bush Sketches," " Yarns by Old Stagers," . . . and a number of short pieces. . . . Mr. Mackay shows in his little book quite enough talent to go a lone hand.'—*The Bulletin.*

'Mr. Mackay has an easy, natural style of versification which makes some of his poems very pleasant reading. He is deserving of credit for his laudable endeavour to make his verses as far as possible representative of Australian life and scenery—an effort which has been attended with considerable success on his part. . . . The poet who is to succeed in securing the title of a representative Australian poet must be he through whose spirit the genius of Australian scenery and national life is distilled into pure verse, uninfluenced by the style or mannerisms of the old-world poets, or those who owe their inspiration to such sources.'—*Freeman's Journal* (Sydney).

'These "Jingles from the Bush and the Turf," by Mr. Kenneth Mackay, dedicated to Adam Lindsay Gordon, and perfumed with the aroma of his poetic fervour, are sufficient evidence that young Australia is not lacking in that imaginative gift without which average human life is but a sordid round of plodding toil. . . . Mr. Mackay has listened to the singing of a greater than Gordon—to that same spirit of the Bush which inspired the earlier poets, and which has alike influenced their dreamings ; . . . and Nature has woven her spell about him, developing his perceptive faculties and showing him that hidden beauty of wilderness and gully, that underlying poetry of civilized life to which the conventional glance is blind. . . . We want more such writers as Mr. Mackay to infuse poetry into a sordid social atmosphere, and to point out the beauty, truth and nobility that lie about our path unnoticed by the busy crowd.'—*Sunday News.*

OUT BACK.

THIRD EDITION.

BY

KENNETH MACKAY.

SOME PRESS NOTICES.

'A welcome reproduction . . . is "Out Back," a novel by the deservedly popular Australian writer, Mr. Kenneth Mackay. . . . Certain episodes of early Australian life . . . are narrated with remarkable spirit and graphic *verve*. "Out Back" forms a brilliant pendant to "Stirrup Jingles," an admirable work, which gave its author popularity.'—*Daily Telegraph*.

'"Out Back" is a stirring and sensational story. The scene is laid in the back blocks, and the various aspects of bush and station life are described with much truth and reality. . . . We should be sorry to lose such a thrilling incident as the robbery of the gold escort, which is one of the best things in the book. . . . The account of the ride by Sergeant Caban and his prisoner through the blazing forest, and the terrible fate that befalls the chief villain, is among the most powerful scenes in the book. . . . "Out Back" is a vigorous and readable production, in which there is scarcely a dull page.'—*Australasian*.

'"Out Back" is a story of Australasian life, which has already reached a third edition and acquired a well-merited popularity. The story is powerful, original, and possessed of an exciting plot, which develops on sound lines. Mr. Mackay is favourably known as a writer, and his happy descriptions of life in the bush, of the romance and adventure which may characterize it, and the racy, if profane (and therefore, we fear, characteristic), types of humanity to be found there, will add to his reputation here as at home. . . . Certainly Mr. Mackay s one of the most gifted of a clever band of writers who are making a fine literary reputation for Australia.'—*Leeds Mercury*.

'The story is full of life and incident, illustrative to a large degree of the characters and customs and haunts and daring of the bushranger and his confederates, white and native, in the not very remote times when these undesirable products and adjuncts of the earlier settlement were so troublesome. The story will interest home readers quite as much as those of the Antipodes.'—*Liverpool Daily Post.*

'"Out Back" is a good, straightforward tale. . . . Mr. Mackay knows his Australia, which is more than can be said of every Australian novelist.'—*Sydney Morning Herald.*

'The reader of "Out Back," who looks for local colour and evidence of an intimate acquaintance with squatting and up-country incident of the older days, will not be disappointed in these pages.'—*Sydney Mail.*

'In "Out Back" Kenneth Mackay shows his knowledge of the true inwardness of Australia and the inhabitants thereof, and his work throughout shows that he has seen or lived—bushranging excepted—and become letter-perfect in the scenery of which he writes. . . . Kenneth Mackay is a word-artist in the best sense of the word.'—*Sydney Bulletin.*

'"Out Back" is full of incident, and gives an excellent description of social life in the "back blocks" during the bushranging period in the Australian Colonies. . . . The character of Captain Scarlett, the bushranger, is very well drawn, and the interest of the story is kept up to the close.'—*New Zealand Herald.*

'"Out Back" is a book which argues extensive and intimate knowledge of station life, if, indeed, additional proof were needed in view of the author's contributions to Australian poetical literature.'—*Freeman's Journal* (Sydney).

'"Out Back" is a story of the Australian bush, and is full of vigour from start to finish. . . . It is as interesting and exciting a story of adventure as one could wish for, even at Christmas-time.'—*Poole and Bournemouth Herald.*

'"Out Back" has plenty of incident, and maintains the reader's interest to the close.'—*Glasgow Herald.*

'"Out Back" is a spirited tale of life and adventure, having a good plot, with love-making, bushranging . . . and many interesting pictures of native Australian customs and characters.'—*Scotsman.*